SCORCHED

Book Four in the Surrender Series

By
Melody Anne

SCORCHED
Book Four in the Surrender Series

Copyright © 2013 Melody Anne

ISBN-13: 978-0615894669
ISBN-10: 0615894666

Cover Art by Edward
Edited by Alison
Interior Design by Adam

www.melodyanne.com

Email: info@melodyanne.com

 /MelodyAnneAuthor @AuthMelodyAnne

First Edition
Printed in the U.SA

DEDICATION

This is dedicated to my grandma Janet. Your memory will be with me forever, and I will cherish the time I had with you. I lost you way too soon, but you will remain in my heart forever!

OTHER BOOKS BY MELODY ANNE

Billionaire Bachelors:
*The Billionaire Wins the Game
*The Billionaire's Dance
*The Billionaire Falls - Amazon
*The Billionaire's Marriage Proposal
*Blackmailing the Billionaire
*Run Away Heiress
*The Billionaire's Final Stand
*Unexpected Treasure
*Hidden Treasure
*Holiday Treasure

Baby for the Billionaire:
*The Tycoon's Revenge
*The Tycoon's Vacation
*The Tycoon's Proposal
*The Tycoon's Secret
*The Lost Tycoon

Surrender:
*Surrender - Book One
*Submit - Book Two
*Seduced - Book Three
*Scorched - Book Four

Forbidden Series:
*Bound -Book One
*Broken - Book Two
*Betrayed - Book Three
*Burned - Book Four

Unexpected Heroes:
*Her Unexpected Hero
*Who I am With You - Novella
*Her Hometown Hero
*Following Her - Novella
*Her Forever Hero - February 23rd 2016

*Safe in His Arms - Novella - Baby, It's Cold Outside Anthology

NOTE FROM THE AUTHOR

Thank you to all of you who have stuck with me through this series and my other series, as well. What a joy it is to hear from you and to see your response to my books. What started out as a pastime for me has turned into a great and unstoppable passion.

I love writing. I love coming up with characters and putting them in seemingly unimaginable situations. This is the greatest job on earth. Thank you to all my fans for your words of encouragement and for your loyalty.

Thank you to all my new friends in the author community. It's a close group, since we share a lot of the same experiences, both highs and lows. I love being able to spend time with you, and to share ideas. After my fantastic weekend in South Carolina with the fabulous Ruth Cardello, Kathleen Brooks, and Cali MacKay, I couldn't wait to get home and start writing again. There's something about hanging around amazingly talented women that kick-starts the creative process.

Thank you to my amazing team — Jeff and Patsy Winchester, Ray White, and Kathiey Dame — who do so much behind the scenes to allow me to sit down comfortably and write to my heart's desire.

I owe a huge thank-you, as always, to my family, whom I love more than life itself. My daughter left for college at the end of September, and my heart broke a little bit, but it also expanded because she's having so much fun and is really thriving there. It's hard to let go, but she will always be my baby girl. I have my son at home for only another two years before he's off into the world. Family is what life is all about.

I hope you all have a wonderful holiday season this year.

Melody Anne

PROLOGUE

"THIS TRADITION OF not seeing the bride before the wedding is ridiculous. I think it would be so much wiser if we just met up for one hour to help...ease our...nerves," Rafe said with a seductive purr.

"Mmm, sounds good to me. Now if I could just get away from my mother for *two* seconds, I would think about taking you up on that offer, Mr. Palazzo," Ari replied with a giggle.

"I can pull the fire alarm," Rafe suggested.

His tone implied that he was 100 percent serious about doing just that. The strange part was that Ari was actually considering it.

"I think our parents would disown us," she said.

"I can live with that."

"I love you, Rafe," she told him, overcome with emotion as she cradled the phone to her ear, wanting so badly to touch him, feel him there next to her. She'd only been apart from him for one night, but today was her wedding day — the day she would become his wife.

She wanted to throw out all tradition and simply be in his arms. Their years apart now seemed like such a waste, though she knew that the time had helped them grow and mature.

"You are the center of my world, Ari," he replied.

It meant more to her to hear him say that than a simple *I love you*. To be the center of a person like Rafe's world was indeed a compliment.

"After the wedding is over, I have a very special surprise for you," she whispered as she glanced over at the bathroom door to make sure it was still tightly shut.

The breath rushed audibly from his mouth. "What is that?"

Oh, the excitement she felt at so easily arousing her fiancé.

"For starters, what I'm wearing beneath this wedding dress wouldn't even cover a Barbie doll," she replied.

"You're going to give me a heart attack before I'm able to say my vows," he whispered, strain in his voice.

"I wouldn't want to do that. I couldn't do a striptease for you then, and… Oh, I shouldn't give it all away," she taunted him.

"That's it! The alarm is getting pulled right now."

Ari didn't want to argue. She wouldn't mind getting rid of her pre-wedding jitters by spending an hour in his arms. Heck, she'd take fifteen minutes.

Sandra knocked. "Ari, I can hear you on the phone," she said through the door. "That's cheating, young lady," her mother added with a smile in her voice.

"We've been busted, Rafe. I guess you will just have to wait until tonight to see my bright red negligée."

"We'll see about waiting that long. I may not be able to stand it — just like I can't wait to say my vows with you."

"Becoming Mrs. Palazzo can't come soon enough for me."

They hung up and Ari reluctantly left the bathroom so the huge team who had been hired to make her perfect could continue to prep her. Soon, she would be Mrs. Rafe Palazzo. The minutes would creep by, but at least the end was in sight.

CHAPTER ONE

PERFECT TIMING.

Damned makeup. Damned mirror. Damned nausea.

Up until this point she hadn't felt even the slightest indisposition, but here it was, the day of her brother's wedding, and she was suddenly overcome with morning sickness. In the middle of the freaking afternoon. She dropped the mascara, reached down to feel her stomach, and groaned heavily.

"Please, just let me get through the ceremony. Then we can tell the family all about you. We don't need to make your presence known by my throwing up all over your uncle Rafe's polished new shoes," Rachel said aloud.

She had to smile. She hadn't wanted be a mother yet, but that didn't change the fact that it was going to happen. It seemed that she'd gotten past most of the fear and was now moving on to acceptance. Amazingly enough, she was beginning to love this little creation she'd made by accident.

It hadn't taken her as long as she'd thought. Only three and a half months. Now, she couldn't picture her life without this child.

"I promise to buy you a pony if you just allow me to get through the wedding with no problems," she offered with a chuckle.

Didn't all children want their very own pony? Well, she'd find out very soon whether the bribe worked.

"Maybe our child wants his presence to be known to the world. After all, he *is* the future king of Corythia and shouldn't be hidden, even while still in the womb."

Rachel froze as she peered into the mirror and discovered Ian, or *King Adriane*, standing just inside the door to her room.

Of course. The day was just getting better and better.

It was more than obvious that this man wasn't going to simply disappear. Why make it easy for her and her unborn child? She should have known he wouldn't have the patience to wait for a better time to seek her out.

It was all about *his* schedule and what was convenient to *him*. This was one of the reasons she had refused to answer his calls — he was too damn impatient. She didn't know what she wanted to do yet; she didn't have any answers for him, so there was no point in them talking just yet.

"You weren't invited here, Ian," she said in her haughtiest tone. She quickly regained her composure after the initial shock of seeing him.

"I didn't ask for your permission, Rachel. You've been avoiding me for too long now. Don't you realize how rude that is?" he asked with irritation as he prowled about the room, coming closer to where she was sitting.

"I would say that you're the one being rude. I didn't invite you to any wedding, much less my brother's. And I certainly didn't allow you into the room I'm dressing in."

"You've apparently been coddled too long, because your manners are appalling."

Rachel gasped at his audacity and lack of self-awareness. If her stomach hadn't been rolling, she'd have shot to her feet to confront him more forcefully. The man needed to be taught a lesson on how to treat a lady. He was no knight in shining armor, and certainly no Prince Charming — or *King* Charming in his case.

"Yes, you are right, Ian Graziani, or I guess I should say Adriane, since even your name was a lie. I have been very well taken care of my entire life because I have parents who adore me as I adore them. This is my brother and my best friend's wedding, and I don't have time to fight with you today. Leave now, and I will talk to you next week."

Rachel's choice of words and abrupt dismissal lit a fire inside him that went shooting through his eyes. Well, tough, she thought. They were having a child together, one *she* was carrying, and as long as he continued treating her like a servant, he'd have to get used to her attitude. She didn't submit well — not well at all.

"I've been trying to be reasonable with you, Rachel, but you insist on acting like a spoiled brat. I tire of this game you are playing." He stood directly behind her, lifted his hand and placed it on her shoulder as if he had a right to do so.

He didn't.

Now it was Rachel's eyes that were blazing. How dare he! Twisting around, she threw his hand off her shoulder.

"Look, Ian. I really don't want to say something that can't be taken back. It's more than apparent that you don't have the same consideration toward me. Before this goes any further, I suggest you do as I've requested and make yourself scarce," she said between clenched teeth.

"I was invited here, Rachel — by your brother," he told her smugly.

"Why in the world would he invite *you*?"

"We are friends. I told you this already. It seems you don't listen when I speak. Rafe and I have done business together for many years."

"You didn't tell him about the baby, did you?" She hated the hint of worry in her tone.

Adriane paused. He looked at her, his head slightly tilted as if assessing her mood along with her words. She didn't like feeling as if she were under a microscope — and that's exactly how she was feeling as his gaze seared her.

"No. I thought you should be the one to do it. But you obviously have a difficult time communicating with your family," he replied.

"I do not!" Did this man have a death wish?

"Then why haven't you said anything yet?"

"That is none of your business." Because she was afraid of their reaction. Their good little girl had screwed up. Literally. Why else wouldn't she have told them?

"The fact that you carry my heir makes it very much my business."

"Doesn't the baby have to be a boy to be your heir?"

Puzzled, he looked at her for a few moments before he responded. "Of course it's a boy."

"You don't know that. There's a fifty percent chance that I carry a girl. If *he* is in fact a *she*, will you go away and leave us alone?"

Rachel didn't like the pang that thought caused. No, she wasn't in love with Adriane. How could she be after spending only a week with the man? But she did want her child to know his or her father, even if the man wasn't completely active in the baby's life. Rachel just didn't want to deal with him at this moment. Eventually, though, the two of them would have to come to an understanding.

"Throughout our country's long history, the first child of every king of Corythia has been a boy. It is invariable in the royal line."

MELODY ANNE

"Well, maybe this time the little girl swimmer was the fastest out of the bunch," she countered.

"In that case, she *is* still a princess of Corythia."

Rachel thawed just the tiniest bit — he'd said those words with a hint of a smile. So he probably wouldn't reject the child if it turned out to be a girl, after all. That was a point in his favor. Still, even if he wasn't a complete ass, her anger with him was through the roof.

"But that is a moot point, Rachel, since you will produce a son for me. Our second child can be a daughter," he said matter-of-factly.

Rachel gaped at him and waited for her voice to return. Was he kidding?

"You say I'm the one who is spoiled. Have you looked in a mirror, lately, Adriane? A second child? There won't be one. I'm hardly ecstatic about being stuck with you because of the first. Don't get me wrong — I will love my baby with everything I have. It's the fact that *you* are involved that displeases me."

There. Maybe that would get through his thick skull.

"When we are married, you will learn to be more respectful. I have no doubt about it," he told her with an indulgent glance.

"I've already told you that I won't be marrying you, Adriane. The sooner you accept that, the better off we'll all be," she replied, trying desperately to hold on to her temper. It wouldn't do her body any good to raise her blood pressure.

"I think you will make a mighty fine first wife," he said with a smirk.

Rachel forgot all about her blood pressure as she saw spots start forming before her eyes.

"*First* wife?" she roared.

Adriane actually had the nerve to laugh. Never before had she felt such a desire to bloody anyone, but she was close to finding a sharp object and impaling him. The makeup table had a few promising weapons.

"I'm just kidding, Rachel. You will be my only wife," he said with a laugh as he held up his hands in surrender.

"You'd best find a more willing partner, Adriane. I won't marry you — not for all the gold in the vaults hidden beneath your dungeons — not for all the jewels in your kingdom. I don't know how many times I need to say that until it sinks in," she snapped.

"Well, then, although we appear to be at an impasse, one way or the other you *will* marry me, Rachel," he said with a confident grin, not fazed in the least by her rejection of him.

Rachel's temper heated up to molten levels. She leaped to her feet to confront him at her full height — a less than intimidating five foot four.

It was the wrong move. The room suddenly started to spin and black spots began to interfere with her vision. She was about to pass out and there was absolutely nothing she could do to stop it.

"Rachel!" Adriane called out, but her name sounded as if it were coming through a long black tunnel.

Adriane caught her just before she slammed against the floor.

CHAPTER TWO

I T STARTED OUT in slow motion. Adriane stood in horror as Rachel's eyes rolled back and she drooped forward.

He sprang into action, catching her before she hit the ground. What a fool he'd been. Why had he pushed her so hard? She'd always been so tough, and he'd thought she could handle it. But he'd been wrong, and guilt consumed him.

Laying her down carefully on the couch in her room, he snatched up his phone. "Nico, have the car readied now," he commanded before hanging up and rushing to Rachel's temporary desk.

He was going to take her to his private villa, where his personal physician was waiting, and had been since Adriane found out Rachel carried his child. But Adriane couldn't whisk her away without leaving a note for her family, so he paused long enough to find a pen and paper.

Almost frantic, he scrawled a few words:

To Rachel's family,

I have taken Rachel to see my personal physician. After he clears her for travel, we will leave for Corythia, where I will be able to care for her and my child. Though Rachel is hesitant about the upcoming nuptials, I will notify you of my plans for the wedding when they are final. You are welcome to join us, but I must inform you that I will not change my mind on this matter. She carries the heir to the throne of Corythia, and she will be my wife. Rachel will be well taken care of as the royal consort.

King Adriano of Corythia

Tossing the note onto her dressing table, Adriane carefully lifted Rachel into his arms and made his way from her room, using the back staircase. Nothing was going to stop him at this point and he'd rather not have to bother with a confrontation.

Rachel needed medical care — which, in Adriane's opinion, only *his* physician was qualified to give. After all, she carried royalty, and she deserved only the best. He didn't have time to deal with somebody trying to play the hero. He knew there would be hell to pay when she woke and found they were on their way to Corythia, but he'd face that problem when he had to.

His luck held, and he made it through the resort without any interference. Nico was waiting for him out back, and he shifted Rachel to his trusted adviser while he climbed into the car, then carefully held out his arms to take her back.

Adriane cradled Rachel as Nico rushed to the villa. When Rachel began stirring about five minutes into the drive, Adriane breathed a sigh of relief. She blinked up at him when she realized she was in his arms.

It took a few moments for her to recognize that they were in a car.

"Where am I?" she asked, her brow wrinkled as she tried to look around, but the night surrounded them and there wasn't much light from the moon.

"We're heading to my villa, where my physician can have a look at you," he said as he stroked her hair and tried to give her a reassuring smile.

"You took me from the resort?" Her voice came back stronger than ever. She began to struggle against his hold, so he had no choice but to release her.

She pulled back from him, scooting as far away as the seat would allow.

"Of course I took you from there. You passed out in front of me. My doctor must examine you and make sure that both you and the baby are healthy," he said calmly.

"I demand that you turn this car around right now, Adriane," she snapped, looking at her door as if contemplating opening it.

Adriane snaked out his arm and pulled her back to him. He wasn't about to take any chances.

"If you behave and let the doctor look at you, then we will discuss your return," he said, crossing his fingers. He knew that nothing but his doctor saying she was unfit to travel would stop him from taking her home.

"I have a wedding to attend," she said, spacing out the words in an attempt to remain as calm as he was.

"I left them a note. They will understand. Your health comes first."

When it was obvious he wasn't going to change his mind, she glared at him, but sat back and waited for the car ride to end. It did about ten minutes later.

Adriane rushed from the car when she threw her door open and dashed out. She looked around as if searching for an escape route. She wouldn't find it. The villa was on a lake and far from other houses.

When she knew there was little choice but to accompany him inside, she followed him up the stairs and inside, where his doctor was anxiously pacing.

"Hello, Ms. Palazzo. It's a pleasure to meet you. If you would please come and sit over here, I can make sure you are in good health," the doctor said.

Rachel sent Adriane one more withering glare before she followed the doctor to a chair and had a seat. "I'm fine. I just haven't eaten much the last few days, because my stomach has been too upset. I need to get this ridiculous exam over with so I can return to the resort for my brother's wedding." She wasn't happy about taking her anger out on the doctor, but still, he was loyal to Adriane, so she overcame her sense of guilt.

"She fainted while we were at the resort. It took her about five minutes to wake. I want to have everything tested," Adriane told the doctor.

"Of course, Sire," Dr. Ricord said. He slipped a cuff on her arm and, having taken her blood pressure, listened to her heart rate at the same time.

Several minutes passed as he also checked her breathing and temperature, plus other matters of significance, while asking the occasional question. How was she sleeping? How much was she eating? Did certain foods trigger her nausea?

She answered each one, growing more frustrated as time passed. Rafe and Ari were supposed to be getting married in about half an hour. She was barely going to make it in time.

"She's breathing well, and her color is only slightly flushed," the doctor told Adriane as he jotted down notes about Rachel's condition.

"I'm right here. You can speak to me," she said, a bit ashamed when the doctor flinched slightly, but still royally annoyed to be spoken about as if she weren't in the room.

"I apologize, Ms. Palazzo." He bowed and scooted back.

"What does the fainting mean?" Adriane asked.

The doctor turned his attention back to Rachel and perused his notes to form the best answer to the question.

Adriane looked on at the scene. His physician wouldn't argue with his king, no matter what, but also he had to treat his patient with respect. No, only Rachel would argue with him — in fact, continually fight him, Adriane thought — and she wasn't afraid to push or defy him each step of the way. This might be one of the reasons he couldn't seem to stop thinking about her.

What did that say about him?

"I think the fainting was just low iron, Rachel. You need to try to eat more whenever you are feeling well enough to take in food. You also need to rest more. The swelling in your feet demonstrates, of course, that your body is holding water. There is nothing damaging or life-threatening to you or to the baby right now, but your blood pressure is slightly high. Remember that you're carrying another life within you now, and some mothers have it easier than others. You have to give your body time to adjust. Other than that, you should be fine," Dr. Ricord assured her.

"Thank you. I'm sorry for snapping," she said. Damn him for being so kind to her!

"I understand," he said with a pat on her hand. Then he packed up his tools and left her alone in the room.

"Take me back to the resort now!" she demanded.

Adriane smiled at her, and she was surprised he was suddenly so accommodating. When he walked to the door and held it open, she followed him.

They got into the car and Nico began driving. All the upheaval and tension of the last hour and a half got to Rachel and she leaned her head back, telling herself she would close her eyes for only a moment.

Soon, she'd be back at the resort and the wedding could start. She didn't think they would begin without her. She thought for a minute of calling them and letting them know she was on her way, but she didn't even have her purse, let alone her cell phone.

Rachel involuntarily fell asleep against the seat. It was a huge mistake, she would later find.

*****

As they arrived at his jet, Adriane thanked the heavens for Rachel's slumber. When she woke up, she wasn't going to be happy with him, but at least he didn't have to deal yet with the fight that was sure to come. Being careful not to wake her, he lifted her into his arms and climbed aboard, letting his staff know not to make a sound.

He took his seat, still holding her cradled in his arms. If they could just get into the air…

"Sir, we've been cleared for takeoff," his pilot's voice came over the speaker, making Adriane tense. The one person he'd forgot to tell not to make a sound. Rachel stirred, but didn't open her eyes.

As the jet lifted into the air, Rachel became more restless in his arms. And the reality of his situation was hitting him with full force.

He was going to be a father.

It was both exhilarating and terrifying.

Now he just had to convince Rachel that she was his — and only his. They would wed no matter how much she fought him, no matter what he had to do to get her to walk down that aisle.

Convincing her of this fact would be stimulating and a challenge. The woman made him feel emotions he'd never experienced before. She made him feel like a man, not just a royal with specific and often tiresome duties.

Yes, he liked her fight, liked that she couldn't simply be placed into a box. And he had to admit that he was looking forward to their inevitable altercations.

He also liked to win, and with a prize as valuable as the heir to his country, this was one battle he wouldn't back down from.

Still, the journey the two of them would take was well worth traveling.

His hand brushed her hair from her forehead as he looked into her sleeping face. She was a true beauty, a real gem. He would never allow her to escape.

CHAPTER THREE

RACHEL WAS WARM and cozy. As she drifted up from the deep lake of sleep, she struggled to hold on to its blissfulness.

But, no. Something jostled her, and she knew that no matter how badly she wanted and needed to stay asleep, it was over. Stretching her arms, she hit solid muscle. What?

Her eyes finally creaked open and she tried to focus in the harsh light. When the blurriness faded, she locked eyes with Adriane and instantly stiffened. What was she doing sitting on his lap, leaning into him?

"You're just fine, Rachel. You simply had a little nap," he said, stroking her back.

Rachel tried to focus on Adriane. Where was she? Why was she with him? As she woke up all the way, the night came back with the violence of a slamming door and she pulled away, nearly falling on her butt in her haste to jump out of Adriane's arms.

"What's going on, Adriane?" She looked around the roomy jet in puzzlement.

"You were just having a little dream, darling," he said. It was obvious she hadn't quite figured out where she was yet. She'd be a whole lot more upset when that happened.

"I'm not your darling," she said, and sat down on the chair across from him.

"Oh, Rachel, you most certainly are," Adriane said.

A shiver passed through her. If only she weren't so attracted to him — hating him was so difficult. But did she want to hate the father of her child? No. Of course not. She just wanted to find a happy medium, be able to breathe normally in his presence, and then work out what she was going to do next.

"We were in the car," she said, confused as she again looked around. Adriane could see she was starting to get her bearings. This wasn't going to end well.

As she looked around the jet, they suddenly hit a pocket of turbulence, and that's when she noticed the vibration. She looked toward the curtained windows and her eyes widened. This wasn't a normal room. The curved walls, the small window openings, the confined space…

"Are we on a plane?" she asked with an exasperated gasp.

"You need to remember what the doctor told you back at the villa. You have to keep your blood pressure down, and fighting with me will surely raise it," he said in a quiet, calming tone.

"I am trying *really* hard right now not to freak out, Adriane, but I swear by all that's holy that if you've kidnapped me, my blood pressure is going to go straight through my head and explode," she said, gritting her teeth.

"I'm taking you home for a little while. I have to take care of you." Adriane prayed that the remark didn't send her into another faint.

"The doctor said I need to not get stressed or overexert myself, so I'm trying really, *really* hard not to yell right now, but all I want to do at the moment is reach out and strangle you," she said, fire returning to her eyes.

"I just want to make sure that all is well with you and our child. It's important that I look after you. I won't bring up our wedding until you're feeling better," he said, offering his idea of a compromise.

"I will be just fine looking after myself," she told him.

"Please try to understand. My country is in upheaval right now with the death of my father, and my brother making a play for the throne. I must return home — it is my duty — but I can't leave you behind if your health and that of my child are not at one hundred percent. You are my duty, too," he said. He couldn't back down from this and leave her behind. She was too important.

"I am nobody's duty, Adriane. I demand that you turn this plane around this second." She looked toward the cockpit and considered pounding on the thick doors and informing the pilots that their king had kidnapped her. Yeah, right. That would do a lot of good.

In their eyes, as in the eyes of everyone who worked for him, Adriane could do no wrong. She didn't see that she had a whole lot of choices right now.

Why had she let her exhaustion overwhelm her? If she'd only stayed awake, she wouldn't be in this mess. Yes, Adriane was stronger than she was, but surely she could outrun him — even tired and pregnant.

OK, she didn't know if she could, but she would have made a valiant effort.

Her eyes still narrow, Rachel looked from him to all points of exit on the jet. Adriane watched her under his eyelids just in case she tried to do something foolish, but he tried to portray a man at ease. He felt relief enough that she wasn't screaming, that she didn't seem to be getting overly upset. Maybe she would compromise with him. As well she might; he was doing her an amazing favor by bending at all. He'd prefer to march her straight to the altar, but she certainly wasn't making things easy for him even just to talk to her. He was already working on a new strategy.

For now, however, it would suffice to have her under his roof, where he could ensure her health and know her whereabouts. Where he could force her to communicate.

"Your country's problems are not my concern, Adriane," she said. At the hurt that flickered briefly in his eyes, Rachel felt a pang of remorse. She shouldn't, though. The man had taken her against her will, and she had a lot of other grievances against him. If his feelings were hurt, that should be just too bad, because he'd been nothing but a bully since returning to her life. And yet…and yet she didn't like to hurt anyone intentionally, and it was obvious that her words had done just that.

"I would like for them to be your concern, since they will be the concern of our baby," he said after a long pause.

"I get that our child will be a part of your life. I can see that you aren't going to accept anything less than being an active father, but that doesn't mean the two of us have to be friends, or even have to deal with each other at all. Many children grow up happy when their parents aren't together."

"That's just not how it's done in Corythia, Rachel. You carry the heir. He needs to be raised to know and love his land," Adriane insisted.

"Would you stop saying 'he'?" she growled. "That is driving me crazy!"

Adriane's eyes grew round, and then a grin split his face as he lifted his hand and brushed back her hair.

"I love that you have such spirit, Rachel. It's unbelievably sexy," he said, wanting so badly to reach over and take her lips. If he hadn't feared that she might bite him, he would have done just that. Hell, it might have been worth it, anyway.

"Don't try to distract me, Adriane. I'm angry with you," she said, but he watched as her breathing quickened.

He enjoyed seeing that he still affected her as much as she affected him. But he also knew that she'd rather eat dirt than admit that to him.

"I like distracting you," he murmured, his hand sliding down her face and then caressing her shoulder and arm as he sat down next to her.

"Adriane…" she warned.

"Yes?"

"Stop touching me. You're making my blood pressure spike again."

Adriane immediately withdrew his hand, though it was exceedingly difficult for him to do so. After the doctor had examined her again, he would be doing a lot more touching, in a lot more-intimate places.

"I will back off if you stop fighting me long enough to come and see our child's birthright. Don't you want to see his — I mean, the baby's land?"

Rachel was furious, but as she had to keep her blood pressure down, and as they were already on the jet, she really didn't have a lot of choices at the moment. Once they landed… Well, that was a different story.

"Am I free to leave the minute I want?" she asked, looking him in the eye so she could detect if he was being anything but honest.

"Rachel…" he began.

"I swear, I'll call in the U.S. military, Adriane," she threatened.

"Not if you can't get to a phone," he countered with a small grin.

"Oh, I have ways," she warned him. She also had a family that would move heaven and earth to get to her. She wasn't concerned about her rescue. She might have little choice but to play his game, but he'd discover soon enough that it was a game he would lose.

"We will discuss your departure later if you still feel like leaving," he said.

Rachel knew exactly what he was doing. He was trying to pacify her with vague promises. OK, she would let him believe it was working. If he thought she'd surrendered to his will, it would be so much easier to make her escape. Still, she couldn't help but make one more snarky comment, damning her plan as soon as she'd formed it.

"I'm not going to fight you any further right now, because I'm smart enough to listen to what the doctor has said. But don't think it means that you're off the hook, Adriane. When I get the all clear from the doctor, we're going to have one hell of a battle. That's a promise."

Then, before he could answer, she stood up and moved to the back of the jet. She had no doubt that there was a bed aboard, and she was going to find it. All the fighting had drained what little energy she had left, and since she was stuck here, she was going to at least try to catch up on her sleep.

He tried to talk to her, but she just hummed as she walked away, finding a room and closing the door behind her. She was sure the king of Corythia didn't appreciate her less-than-respectful treatment of him, but the poor sap would just have to get used to it.

Adriane found himself wanting to chase after her to teach her a few lessons on royal behavior. Her health was the only thing stopping him from doing just that.

As soon as she was better, though...

That thought made him smile as he kicked back on the sofa. Yes, they would certainly battle when she was back in full health, and Adriane was a fine warrior.

CHAPTER FOUR

RAFE PACED THE small room while he waited for his family. It was supposed to be his wedding day, the day Ari would become his wife, the day he'd have her for all time. He didn't deserve this day — but, miraculously, Ari had said yes, and she was going to be his.

Though not today.

Instead, his tuxedo was rumpled, his tie cast aside, the top buttons of his shirt undone, and fury rolled off him in waves. How dare Adriane take Rachel! The man would pay for this betrayal.

"She'll be fine, Rafe."

His heart calmed at the gentle sound of Ari's voice, and at her sweet touch as she wrapped her arms around him from behind and smoothed her hands up his stomach, resting them on his chest.

"I'm sorry our day has been ruined, Ari," he said softly as he turned, pulling her closer to cradle her head against his chest.

"It's not ruined — just postponed. I could marry you wearing cutoff shorts and a tank top in a grungy courthouse in front of a hung-over justice of the peace. It's not the wedding that matters, Rafe. It's having you as my husband for eternity," she said as she lifted her head and looked deep into his eyes. "Or at least the next eighty years."

"I'm so grateful you saw through the bad, Ari, so happy that you have forgiven me. I love you beyond the limits of speech, and I *will* have you as my wife. Thank you for putting the needs of Rachel above everything else. Most brides wouldn't be so accommodating," he said as he leaned down and ran his lips across hers in a brief kiss.

"Rachel is one of my best friends, and she would do the same for me. I could never have a wedding without her being there, even a courthouse wedding. I honestly don't care where we marry as long as the people we love are with us. Let's make sure she is well, and then we will become husband and wife."

Rafe ran his fingers through her silky hair, his eyes trying to convey to her all the emotions bottled up inside him. How he loved this woman.

"Son?"

Rafe turned to find his mother and father standing by the door, their eyes dimmed with worry, and everything was brought back into focus. Being in Ari's arms soothed him, but right now, he didn't need to be soothed, he needed to find answers, and seeing the strain on his family members' faces prompted him to find those answers fast.

"I'm sorry, Dad, for springing this on you. We had no idea what was going on until Ari and Lia came to check on Rachel and found her gone. Here's the note that was left by Adriane. I've done business with him for years, and he recently ascended the throne after his father passed. I was unaware that he'd ever met Rachel," Rafe said with disgust, and he handed the note over to his parents.

After a brief pause, his father looked up, almost shell-shocked.

"Why...what...I don't understand," Martin said, the note hanging limply from his fingers.

"I don't either, Dad," Rafe said, helplessly. It wasn't like him not to have the answers. He was always the one on top of every situation. To be put in this position of weakness now infuriated him all over again.

"Let me try to explain," Ari said, releasing Rafe and leading the group to a sitting area. She felt slightly awkward telling Rafe's family what was going on with Rachel, but since Lia wasn't back yet, she had to shoulder the burden.

"Please do, darling," Rosabella said as she sat down.

"Rachel met Adriane, knowing him only as Ian, about three months ago while she was in Florida. They...uh...clicked," Ari said cautiously.

"Clicked?" Rosabella asked.

"I don't think you really want details," Ari said, completely mortified and instantly blushing crimson.

"No, cara. I think that would be a little too much for me," Rosabella agreed.

"They got along really well, and they spent the week together. Then Rachel left and started her job in Italy, thinking she was never going to see him again. Well, it turned out that Adriane had discovered a...um... well, a...broken condom," Ari choked out, the red on her cheeks turning an even deeper hue.

Rafe scowled at her and she just shrugged. It wasn't her fault that she was talking about condoms. If he had a problem with it, then he *really* needed to take it up with his sister. Ari was just the messenger, and she was filling them in on the essential facts with as little detail as possible.

"Yes, well, it turned out that the man who she thought was Ian was actually Prince Adriano, who now is King Adriano, though he goes by Adriane Graziani when in the States. That he has so many names is a whole other matter," she said with a faint smile before continuing. "When he discovered the...um...unfortunate accident, he didn't want to take a chance that a child might be created and he wouldn't know about it. He apparently had Rachel watched. After she went to the doctor and had a positive pregnancy test, he showed up on her doorstep," Ari said, speaking as quickly as possible to get through all the information that she had.

"He had my sister followed!" Rafe roared.

"Seriously? That's what you're focused on?" Ari asked. Of all the information she'd just given, she'd have thought he'd be a bit more upset with some of the other details.

"He should have come to me the minute he knew she was my sister," Rafe bellowed.

"I hate to break this to you, Rafe, but Rachel is twenty-six, not a five-year-old toddler. She's an adult and can therefore make grown-up decisions. She doesn't need your permission to date," Ari reminded him, feeling affronted for her friend.

Rafe shot an indignant look Ari's way, but when she didn't back down, he sat back and kept silent so she could continue. Ari rubbed his arm, trying to ease his temper, and yet to let him know that she disagreed with the way he treated his sisters — like adolescents.

"So, Adriane told Rachel she was carrying his heir and that they must wed at once. As you all know Rachel, you can imagine how well that went over," Ari said with a chuckle.

"You're laughing?" Rafe asked incredulously.

"I'm just picturing the poor man's face when he got a hint of Rachel's temper," Ari replied with a slight trembling in her voice as she struggled to suppress her mirth.

"I wish he had gotten the full force of her knuckles," Rafe muttered.

23

Ari ignored his comment. "She pretty much told him to shove it. I guess he didn't appreciate that, because here we are now. I don't think Rachel's in any danger. She can certainly hold her own against Adriane, or King Adriano, but still, I'm sure we'd all like to talk to her, make certain she's fine," Ari said, trying to defuse the bomb waiting to go off in Rafe's head.

"Of course we're going to see her. Adriane can't just come in here and abduct my sister. And this isn't like Rachel not to talk to me." Rafe stood up and started pacing again, too restless to continue sitting.

"Remember that she *is* pregnant, Rafe. Her emotions are all scattered right now, and she may not be making decisions she normally would make. Perhaps she has decided it best to try to get along with Adriane, try to make a go of things for the sake of the baby," Ari told him.

"Why would you think this?" Rafe asked.

"Because from our discussions before, I know she really liked this guy. Yes, she was ticked that he had come back demanding marriage, but if you'd seen the look in her eyes when she talked about him, you'd realize there is more to their story than a weeklong affair. I wouldn't be surprised if we do end up going to a wedding."

Rafe was silent, taking in all that Ari was saying to him. Everything inside him shouted that this was wrong — he had to rescue Rachel right now.

"My little girl is going to have a baby." They all turned to see the look of wonder on Rosabella's face.

"Mom?"

"I know everyone is worried. I am, too. But, have any of you stopped to really think about this? Rachel, my youngest child, is going to be a mother. I'm going to be a grandmother. This may not have been how I wanted it to happen, but I can't help but be filled with joy," Rosabella said as a tear slipped from her eye.

"Oh, my. I'm going to be a grandpa," Martin said.

They were all silent as they thought about the new baby. They'd been so focused on the shock of Rachel's apparent abduction that, until Rosabella's reverent words, none of them had paused to think about the blessing of a new family member in their lives.

"I haven't had time to think about that," Rafe admitted, his own tone far more tranquil as he considered his sister's pregnancy anew. It wasn't just an unwanted pregnancy as he'd been thinking of it, but his sister was actually carrying a child inside her. That would make him an uncle.

"Yeah, it's pretty amazing," Ari said, her gaze connecting with Rafe's. The two of them hadn't discussed children, but she wanted a dozen of them. Well, maybe not quite that many, but she certainly wanted a couple of kids tearing around their house.

The thought of a little boy with Rafe's beautiful eyes staring back at her made her heart leap. She would enjoy carrying his child even if she were sick every day of her pregnancy.

"Yes, I want a lot of babies with you," Rafe said as if he could read her mind. Ari's heart was filled to overflowing, though she hadn't imagined she could feel any happier than she had that very morning.

"Nothing would please me more, Rafe," she said, smiling at him as he crossed the room and sat back down next to her, pulling her tightly against his chest.

"Sorry I keep snapping. It's not at you, I promise. It's just that I have always felt the need to protect my sisters, even when they don't need or want protecting. I hate that Rachel is going through this alone, or that she feels that she is alone in her decisions, and I hate that I can't be there to take care of her."

"She knows how much you love her, Rafe, and that is what will help her to get through it. She's frightened, but if you stand by her side, accept that she made a mistake, not dwell on it, and be her big brother, not another parent, she will trust you and lean on you. She'll gladly let you help take care of her," Ari said, hoping he would get it.

Rafe paused for several moments as he absorbed her words, let them sink in.

"How did I make it through life without you, Ari? How do you put up with me? I shouldn't question you, because then you might come to your senses and walk away from me again, but I am just so surprised that I not only found you, but also managed to hold on to you," he said, his lips turned up in a crooked smile.

"We both have our faults, but I think that, overall, we make each other better people. I love you," she said in answer. "And in our case, love was enough to conquer all that stood in its path."

"I wish Rachel had just trusted me," Rafe said.

"If you want your sister to trust you the next time, then you have to be understanding and not berate her for something she already feels terrible about."

"I wouldn't do that!" he insisted.

Ari just lifted an eyebrow, and waited.

"OK, I might have given a small lecture," he admitted.

Ari knew she wouldn't get him to confess much more than that. She gave him a hug and was glad that he was at least willing to listen to her.

They would be able to help Rachel, but if he went in there in all his furious glory, it would only make the situation worse.

"Let's try and get ahold of Rachel before we just jet over there. Maybe she wants to be with Adriane," Ari said. She knew she should try to be the voice of reason.

"I need to see her, Ari. What if she tells me that she's fine while we're on the phone, but that's because a sword is being held to her throat? I need for her to tell me in person that she is where she wants to be," Rafe insisted.

"A sword, Rafe? Such melodrama! Adriane is a modern European king, you know, and he does have the civilized world to answer to. I do understand your feelings, however, and I'm sure Rachel is very glad to have such a loyal big brother, but I really think you ought to give this a little bit of time."

Rafe held her close as he struggled with what he wanted to do and with what Ari was asking of him. He couldn't just sit idly by — it went against everything he stood for.

"Ari..." he said, forcing down the man inside who wanted to come out, the man who would just do whatever he wanted to do.

"All I'm asking is that you give her a little time — a week. That's not much, is it?"

He froze in her arms. He couldn't do this. No way. If he went against Ari, though, he feared she would think he hadn't changed at all.

To go or not to go. That was the decision he needed to make quickly.

CHAPTER FIVE

"STOP SQUIRMING," SHANE said as he walked into a private room, setting Lia down on her feet. She glared at him and quickly backed away. He followed, placing his arm around her and pulling her to him.

Lia twisted to escape his grasp, not appreciating his boldness, and *really* not liking her body's reaction to being close to him. How was she supposed to get over her feelings toward him when he didn't give her room to breathe?

"I leave in two hours. We have to talk," he whispered in her ear, causing her body to shiver — and she hated him for making her betray herself.

"We've done all the talking I'm willing to do for now, so you can just scurry on out of here," she said, tugging against his hold.

"I can never seem to find the right words to say to you," Shane said. He set her free, but he refused to back too far away.

He had to go soon and didn't know when he'd get back. But he couldn't leave with Lia upset with him; his mind wouldn't be with his team, and he needed to be there with them, not half there and half here with Lia.

"Try *goodbye*, Shane. I have been a fool to love you so much. How can I love a man who I don't even know?" she asked, hurt heavy in her voice as she gazed up at him.

"Lia, I was going to tell you all that I could, but there never seemed to be the right time," he told her, running his hands through his hair in frustration.

Life was so much easier when he didn't have to think about what he could and couldn't talk about. He wanted to make a relationship with her work, but how could he when all he was allowed to share with her was a small piece of himself?

"That seems to be something you say to me all the time, Shane. *I was going to tell you this or that. I wanted to, but I couldn't.* This is the theme of our relationship. I open my heart to you, trust you, and then you betray me. I can't keep doing this. You're just about out the door — heck, out of the country — and there is no way that I'm even close to letting this go. You're going to have to give me some time, some *real* time to think about what I want to do. All I know right now is that I feel betrayed, and even worse, I feel that I can't trust you, that I don't know you. I thought I did, but then I keep finding out more secrets you've kept from me."

The anguish in her voice ripped through him.

"I don't know how to make this better," he said, inching back toward her.

"Don't touch me, Shane. I mean it. Yes, you can make me melt at your touch, but is that what you really want? Do you want a piece of my body when it will only make me hate you afterward? Because I will despise you for making me want you. I will forever block you out, just like you've been blocking me," she warned him as she retreated.

"Damn it! I don't know what you want!" His frustration was clear, as was the agony running through him.

"Just go, Shane. Go and give me time. You've betrayed me, and that doesn't disappear in a day or even a week."

"You didn't give me a chance to earn your trust," he said.

"Yes, I did, Shane. We had five days on that island. You shared your past with me. I didn't turn from you, I didn't treat you any differently. When we were there, you could have told me everything, trusted me with your life. Then, after we got back, you had ample opportunity to tell me. No. I find out a couple days before you leave. And not only that, I find out that my brother once again knows so much more about you. I understand your not telling me before we were a couple, but it just isn't OK for you to keep shutting me out now, making me feel less than my own brother.

I have loved you for so long that I can't remember a time I haven't. You keep proving to me over and over again that you don't feel the same. It's crushing," she said, fighting the closing of her throat as she wrestled to turn off her emotions.

"I will make this up to you. I will prove to you that you can trust me, that I will never keep anything from you again," he vowed.

"It may be too late, Shane. I just don't know," she sighed, feeling more drained than she could ever remember feeling before.

She wanted nothing more than to rush into his arms, but she couldn't do that. She couldn't keep letting him hurt her so badly.

Maybe they just weren't meant to be. As much as she loved him, she couldn't change him, couldn't erase the past, and couldn't undo what had already been done. That meant she might have to let him go forever. He would take a piece of her, but at least if they parted now, there would still be something of herself left to rebuild from. If she stayed with him, she might just fade away.

"I will prove to you that we are meant to be, Lia. I swear to that."

Shane stepped forward and leaned down, his lips capturing hers in a sweet kiss that made her eyelids droop.

When she opened her eyes again, she was standing alone in the room, longing coursing through her body as a deep loneliness filled her. Was that really it? It was what she wanted, wasn't it?

As she walked into the quiet hallway in search of Ari, Lia just didn't know anymore. This was all too much for her to deal with.

Trying to keep her head high, she took a breath before opening the door to the room that held Ari and Rafe. Even if she hadn't known which one it was, she couldn't miss her brother's loud and frustrated voice coming through the thick wood.

At least she didn't need to explain what had happened with her and Shane. Rafe had to deal with a very missing Rachel. Lia wasn't worried about her little sister. She was concerned about her, of course, but she saw the light that entered Rachel's eyes when she spoke of Ian, or Adriane, or Adriano — whatever the heck the man's name was — so she knew Rachel would be fine. This was just another journey that Rachel seemed destined to take with the man who had caused her to do something so against her cautious nature.

The thought was almost enough to make her smile. Time did heal all wounds, right? She'd soon find out. OK, *soon* might be the wrong word.

CHAPTER SIX

SOMETIME IN THE late afternoon, the plane landed and an extremely exhausted Rachel was transferred to a vehicle. There was no fight in her as she was tucked in the back seat with Adriane at her side.

Ian, the man she'd grown feelings for, the man who had been so carefree when she'd met him on the beach, was long gone. Now, she was having a child with a king, Adriane, or Adriano of Corythia. She'd wanted to do some living and she certainly had done just that — but not in the way she'd planned.

The medicine the doctor had given her did its magic and she fell asleep again, drifting against Adriane's chest as he cradled her securely. She could hear Adriane speaking, but his words came to her faint and distorted as she gave in to the medicine and rested.

"Sire, is this a wise choice?"

Adriane turned to Nico, a question in his eyes. His adviser resumed speaking.

"I don't wish to speak out of turn, but she was raised in America at least half the year, and attended college in an American university. She doesn't understand our culture or what would be expected of her as our queen. You have a list of potential brides who are supposed to start arriving here — a list that has been approved by the council."

Adriane knew that his adviser was simply doing his job, counseling him in matters of state, but he still didn't appreciate the man's words.

"As Ms. Palazzo carries my child, none of that matters. Would you have me deny my heir?" Adriane asked with a deadly calm.

"Of course not, Sire. But do we know for certain that the child she carries is yours? You haven't been with her for months," Nico reminded him.

"Yes, Nico, I am very aware of that fact, and I won't allow a statement like that to be made again," Adriane warned. Nico backed off immediately, and he handed Adriane a folder containing documents for him to go through and sign.

Adriane's country was in a fragile state at this moment and he really didn't have time to cater to Rachel, but because she was carrying his child, he also couldn't afford not to. What he was doing was less than ethical, but in his mind, it didn't matter. His biggest concern was getting her to see reason, having her accept that as she was carrying the heir to the Corythian throne, the only way for them to move forward was for her to remain with him as his wife.

Her brother would be a problem. Adriane had known Rafe for some years now, and he knew he wasn't a man to back down. As king, Adriane surely didn't want a major diplomatic disaster, but he'd do what he had to do. And Rafe would have to admit that he'd behave in the same way if it were his child a woman carried.

It was time to speak to the man he considered a friend and occasional business associate. If Rafe could just see reason, maybe they could avoid an international scandal.

Both he and Nico were lost in thought as the car moved through his country. It was a beautiful land, one that he'd always been proud to belong to. The hills were lush with foliage, and the fields were abundant with crops.

Their country's main source of income was tourism. The island offered several large, exclusive resorts that catered to the rich and famous, giving them a private place in paradise to escape from the media and from fans and stalkers. These visitors were free to walk the islands with no one bothering them or taking pictures.

They also spent a good deal of their money at Adriane's casino, his pride and joy. He'd fought a lengthy battle with his father to build it, and he had finally won the argument five years before. It had brought much wealth to Corythia.

The villages all prospered with seasonal fishing, and they offered quaint restaurants and authentic souvenirs. Though Adriane's country wasn't large, it was hardly the smallest in the area.

The country and its wonders would be around long after his death, long enough that his line could rule for centuries to come.

Though Adriane hadn't wanted to be king, his brother had left him no choice. Still, his initial reluctance to ascend the throne didn't mean he wouldn't fulfill his duties to the fullest. The people were a good people and he would never show them disrespect by leading them with a heart that wasn't true.

Adriane smiled as the car passed an orchard. It was good to be home, even if not all was going as planned in his life.

Nico wasn't happy, but his adviser would get over it. Nico had learned long ago that Adriane would listen when it was truly needed, but he was a man and now a king who didn't lean on others, didn't let himself get strong-armed into positions he wasn't comfortable with.

His council had butted heads with him on more than one occasion — and they'd lost.

Their car reached the dock and Adriane scooped Rachel into his arms before striding to the awaiting boat.

There were only two ways to get where he planned to take Rachel. By boat or chopper. Tonight, he preferred going by boat.

This was where he parted company with Nico for now. The man had a lot to get done over the next few days, and Adriane had a plan. As he smiled down at Rachel's softly lit face, he knew there would be hell to pay when she awoke.

It would be well worth it.

CHAPTER SEVEN

DESPERATELY TRYING TO calm herself, Rachel walked back and forth the huge room for the thousandth time, or at least what felt like it.

When she woke up a few hours before, she'd forgotten for a few moments where she was and had simply luxuriated in the comfortable bed, and in the fact that her too constant companion, nausea, was taking a leave of absence.

Then it had all come back to her, and anger had quickly taken over.

Trapped.

She was trapped in a gilded cage that was disguised as a large room, and there was nothing, absolutely nothing, she could do about it. Pounding on the doors, issuing threats, begging. None of it had worked. The men and women who had brought in food and drink either didn't speak English or Italian, or just pretended they didn't; no one would talk to her.

They simply smiled, offered her items, and then quickly scurried away. When she'd made an attempt to get past the guards — yes, actual guards — they had gently but firmly shut the twelve-foot-tall doors after mumbling something in French.

It was decided. She would have to murder Adriane.

Yes, she'd either be executed or spend the rest of her days in prison, but it would be well worth it. The man needed to be murdered. He was begging for it.

Furious with Adriane for bringing her here and then leaving her alone all day, Rachel looked around for possible weapons. But when she stopped and took a moment to think about her murderous intentions, she sagged against the couch.

Of course she wasn't going to kill him. But throwing a glass at his head — that was a real possibility. He deserved to be hit. King or no king.

Rushing over to the closed and locked doors, Rachel raised her voice, yelling as loudly as possible. "I swear by all that's holy, if you don't get your worthless, kidnapping, traitorous king into this room right now, I'll break every priceless item in here! And I'll start by smashing one of these vases over the head of the first person who comes in to try to calm me down!"

"The guards tend to frown upon visitors who threaten their king. As a matter of fact, they like to throw said 'threateners' into the dungeons for some much-needed attitude adjustments."

With a gasp of shock and outrage combined, Rachel spun to her left to find Adriane standing in the middle of the room, looking far too smug and pleased with himself.

Chest heaving, she took a menacing step in his direction, her eyes darting to one of the crystal vases nearest to her.

"I would advise against that, Rachel," he said with a twinkle in his eyes, as if he were enjoying her tantrum.

"Then you'd best talk fast, Adriane. If you don't set me free this instant, I will carry out my promise and this room will look like a tornado has swept through it."

"You are spectacular in anger, do you realize that?" he gasped as he met her halfway, then stopped, standing only a foot from her trembling body.

Why didn't he just say, "You're pretty when you're mad?" His statement was bad enough, but she was angered further by the attraction she felt toward this man, a man who had taken her basic rights away. How pathetic. All she should have felt was contempt and outrage, not even the barest inkling of lust. But with his dark eyes crinkled at the corners, and his smooth shirt molded to his perfect chest, she was having a difficult time not appreciating his beauty.

Those midnight eyes were trained on her right then, and the heat pouring from them was enough to singe her skin.

Leaning her head toward the floor, Rachel inhaled, trying to get her temper and her hormones under control before she spoke again. To continue yelling at him obviously wasn't going to do her any good, so it would be best if she tried another tactic. Maybe she could make him see reason.

Through gritted teeth, she began: "You bring me to your country and then I wake up and am left in this room for hours! Your loyal servants have tried to force-feed me all afternoon, but no one will speak to me, let me near a phone, or give me any answers. I'm getting more and more irritated by the minute, and according to your doctor, that's a bad thing, so you need to back the hell off."

Darn. Though she'd tried controlling her temper, she wasn't doing very well. Yet if she didn't get to a phone soon, her fury was going to spike another few notches.

"I do apologize for not being here when you woke from your nap. I had some matters of state to attend to. They've all been taken care of, so for the rest of the night, you have my undivided attention," he said, as if that were something she wanted.

Rachel's mouth hung open.

"Are you expecting my gratitude because you are granting me — a measly peasant — your undivided attention? Are you *kidding* me, Adriane?" she snapped.

His carefree expression evaporated; his lips thinned and his dark eyes narrowed. King Adriane obviously didn't like to be mocked or spoken back to. Well, too damn bad!

"You would be wise to try to hold your tongue instead of just letting any asinine statement pop from your beautiful lips." He tried to look down at her with a sneer, but he had to fight the smile that was twisting his mouth in the wrong direction.

"That's it!" Rachel shot over to grab the vase. It was going straight for his head.

"I don't think so, Rachel." Adriane easily caught her and held her hands trapped against his chest as he pulled her to him.

She leaned her head back so her glare would hit his eyes dead-on.

"I've had enough, Adriane. I mean it," she warned him, almost hyperventilating. She chose to believe it was from her temper alone and had nothing whatsoever to do with being pressed up snugly against his hard body.

"Oh, Rachel. You haven't had nearly enough of me. I don't think either of us can possibly get enough of each other," he said, his tone silky smooth as he lowered his head, bringing his mouth just a centimeter away from hers.

"Don't you dare kiss me, Adriane. Believe me, you will regret it," she said, struggling against him.

To her surprise, he released her, and Rachel stumbled backward before regaining her footing. She looked at him suspiciously before she searched the room with her eyes and spotted a door that was cracked open — the secret door he must have snuck through.

"I wouldn't try it. I'm not letting you leave."

The foot that was lifting to make a run for it dropped as she looked at him. "You can't keep me prisoner, Adriane. I have family and friends who won't stop until they see me safely home."

"I've already spoken with your brother. We came to an…understanding," he said with a slight wince.

"What do you mean?" she asked. Surely Rafe wouldn't allow this to happen.

"We have a week to work out our differences before he storms the island with the United States military," he said with a chuckle.

"What? He's not coming to get me for an entire week?" Rachel gasped, feeling utterly betrayed.

"Don't get me wrong, Rachel. It wasn't easy to convince him that you were being well taken care of. He had to speak to my doctor, adviser and prime minister. It helped that both Ari and your sister felt we should try to work this out. I think I quite like them."

"Those traitors," Rachel gasped, and she now looked for a phone.

When she managed to speak to her family, they were all in serious trouble. How dare they leave her with this pompous jerk of a man?

"I don't believe you," she said. It couldn't be true.

"It really doesn't matter. If you are still opposed to our marriage in one week, then it looks as if Corythia is going to war," he stated matter-of-factly.

Rachel stared at him in horror before her eyes narrowed again. There was no way the country would go to war. Yes, there could be an international incident, but Corythia was small and this matter wouldn't cause a war. If it did, they'd be wiped out instantly. Adriane wasn't that stupid.

"I am not an uneducated woman, Adriane, and I don't appreciate you treating me as such. If you want a war, I sure as hell will give you one," she promised with fire shooting from her eyes.

"I'm up for the challenge," he said boldly, taking another step closer.

A little over three months ago, she hadn't wanted to crawl from this man's bed. Now, he had changed into a person she didn't know and certainly didn't like. He was arrogant and unfathomable, and he was holding her captive.

Why then was her stomach knotted with a strange desire? She should want to bash him over the head with any blunt object that came to hand and flee his presence; to feel even the remotest form of passion for him was just bizarre.

Still, she was stuck here for the time being, with no idea precisely where she was. Did she continue to fight him, or did she try to win back her freedom another way? She needed to think. Obviously she was all on her own.

That was a depressing thought.

"How do you think this can work, Adriane?" she asked. Maybe he'd see reason.

"I want it to work; therefore it will," he stated firmly. He spoke as if his words were law. Of course, here in Corythia, what he said probably *was* law.

"I was raised in both Italy and America so you're not my king. I'm sorry, but I don't allow dictators to tell me what to do. I make my own decisions. I certainly won't marry a man because he demands it or tells me that's the way it's going to be. You will release me, and then, and only then, will I consider what I will do next. Right now, you aren't gaining any points with me in the father department. I won't be jerked around just because I'm your living incubator. Do you understand me?"

Her breathing was heavy as she finished speaking. She'd wanted so badly to keep calm, but the more he looked down his arrogant straight nose at her, the more upset she became. He wasn't listening to what she was saying.

Sure, he was letting her speak, but he certainly wasn't paying attention. He thought he was too important to listen to the peasant, obviously.

"Oh, Rachel, I am so grateful that if I am to have a child before I am ready to have one, it is with you. I will never tire of your temper; nor will I ever grow bored with you. Everyone all around me agrees with everything I say. I need your dose of reality in my world," he said with a smile.

Rachel's face heated as he chuckled while bending down to pick up a glass. Then he began to fill it with bourbon as if he didn't have a care in the world. He was seriously going to turn his attention from her while she was steaming mad, and laugh at her on top of it?

That was it. Rachel reached for the vase and threw it before she could convince herself it wasn't the best idea. Right before it hit him, Adriane looked up, shocked.

Take that! Rachel thought before turning on her heels and running full speed toward the open door.

CHAPTER EIGHT

I T WAS A good thing he'd been trained in the military practically from the time he could walk. Adriane dodged the vase at the last second, and it crashed into the wall behind him. Then he just stood, stunned, as Rachel sprinted away toward the door.

He knew that running too hard couldn't be good for her at this point, but she was incredibly fit and a bit of exercise wasn't going to damage the baby. The blood pressure, on the other hand, he had to worry about. Maybe he should let her go for a while, cool down.

She wouldn't be able to escape his castle. It was well guarded. Even if she did manage to get outside the walls, she would be sadly disappointed when she discovered where they were.

He decided to sit back and wait for her return. After contemplating the shattered crystal, he chose a seat that faced the door through which she'd have to return. He didn't want her launching another item at his head without any warning.

Taking his double shot of bourbon, he sat and waited. It wouldn't take long.

No more than ten minutes had passed when Rachel came back through the door, her eyes blazing as she stalked closer.

His body pulsed back to life as he saw her chest heaving beneath her shirt and color splashing across her cheeks. She caused his blood to turn to lava, bubbling hot and flowing thickly through his veins.

Rachel was beautiful, and it would be no hardship for him to lead her — hell, drag her — to the altar. It would be his great pleasure, in fact. He'd not been happy when he first learned he'd have to wed because of an unplanned child, but since then, he'd grown more than used to the idea.

He was actually looking forward to it. That meant he'd get her in his bed. Every night.

There would never be a need for other women to entertain him — not as long as he had Rachel by his side every day, and beneath his blankets after the sun went down.

A smile curved his lips at the thought. He could just imagine her reaction if she knew his countrymen didn't frown upon mistresses — they even thought it healthy for the king to have a voracious sexual appetite. And he did.

The queen was to produce heirs and stand by the king's side, or rather two paces back. She wasn't expected to like or enjoy sex. Ah, but his queen certainly enjoyed sex. She would never bore him, just as he would never bore her, or grow tired of their play.

The thought of her beneath him again had his body hardening to a painful degree. He hoped he had her beneath him very soon — tonight if he could manage it.

"Did you have a nice stroll?" he asked, knowing he was pushing his luck with her, but unable to stop himself. Her fire was too bright for him to ever try to dim it. All he could think was that temper of hers would lead to some amazing makeup sex.

"I am going to remain calm and I'm going to refrain from throwing another priceless artifact at your head. *However*, you are going to show me a phone. You *will* let me leave."

She was trying hard to act as if she had it all under control, but she was far from calm. It was too bad he couldn't push her further. He didn't mind her flying at him. He'd take her, claws and all.

"What's so wrong with being here with me? Our week together in Florida was…intense. If you would simply stop fighting me, we could get…better acquainted again," he said, his eyes flashing with a desire he made no attempt to hide.

Rachel stared at him, trying to figure out whether the man had lost his mind. Did he seriously think she was going to simply walk on over and make his fantasies come true? "Really, Adriane? You are either the dumbest man alive, or you have one hell of a false image of yourself.

This may come as quite the shock to you, but you *are* resistible," she said scathingly.

"Ouch," he replied, a grin spreading over his face.

"Wait. You're King Adriano," she said in a sugary voice, dragging out the *o* in the name that he rarely used. "I should, of course, fall to your feet and strip off all of my clothes, and then thank you repeatedly for the honor of being chosen to please you."

His eyebrows rose and his grin grew even wider. "Well, if you insist."

"Ugh, you are unbelievable. You take me from my home, leave me for hours on end trapped in this ridiculous castle, and then actually expect me to roll over for you. Sorry to disappoint, but it's not happening. Not in this century," she said as she resumed pacing so he couldn't see the blush overtaking her features.

Sadly, the thought of him throwing her across his bed wasn't quite as abhorrent as she wanted him to believe.

She blamed the pregnancy hormones. That had to be it, because she certainly didn't want this man, didn't want to lie beneath him, not after he'd deceived her, stalked her, and kidnapped her. Her body just needed a little bit of time to be as angry with him as her mind was. Then the desire would die down.

"Nothing inside you is burning up with the need for my touch?"

Rachel jumped as Adriane's words whispered across her neck. She hadn't even heard him move, and the shiver that passed through her at his nearness was too noticeable for him to have missed it. Yet though her body was burning, she'd make sure her words were just as scorching.

Turning and looking up into his dark eyes, she smiled, doing her best to put him in his place by humoring him.

"Been there. Done that. It was forgettable. There's no need to go down that road again," she mocked, quickly scooting away before her body fully betrayed her and she swayed toward the hard comfort of his chest.

"You know what they say about liars, Rachel?" he said, stalking closer.

"I don't know, Adriane, but since you are such an expert in that subject, I'm sure you can inform me," she said with shrug.

"No woman has ever entertained me like you. Being in your presence is quite pleasurable."

"Get over it, Adriane. Our fling is over and done with, kaput. I have moved on. Maybe you should try doing the same," she said as she reached the double doors. She thought of going through them this time, thinking maybe it would be a better route, but what good would it do?

She wouldn't be able to get out of the castle. Even if she somehow managed to, where was she going to go?

"You see, Rachel, that's where you are *very* wrong. We aren't even close to being over, you and I. This child may not have been planned, but not once have I felt regret over your pregnancy. I very much look forward to making you my bride. I look forward even more to our nights. The two of us together will continue making magic."

"You just aren't thinking. It was an affair, Adriane. A stupid, foolish affair. It doesn't mean we should be locked together for the rest of our lives," she told him. She was worn down, exhausted. She had to get away from this man before she did something else that was foolish. Where he was concerned, it seemed to be a regular occurrence.

"It may have started as an affair, Rachel, but now we *are* locked to each other forever. This child you carry," he said as he reached out and ran his fingers across the planes of her still-flat stomach, "is very much wanted. It also helps that I want you. It will make our marriage very... pleasant."

"This just keeps going in circles, Adriane. Why don't you be the bigger man and let me go while there's still a chance of our getting along, of our being able to communicate for the sake of our child?" she pleaded with him.

He looked at her for several moments, and for just the briefest of seconds, Rachel thought she might have finally gotten through to him. Then he opened his mouth.

"It's a good thing you already think of me as an ogre, Rachel, because you are requesting the one thing I am unable to give you. I think that if I were the meek sort of man you speak of, one who would so easily let you go, you would grow bored quickly. I may rouse your wrath, but I also make you burn with need. I make you scream in the bedroom, and I can quench those fires that are so easily lit within you. I'll give you some time to cool off, and then we will have dinner together," he said, backing up a few feet.

She finally had some space from him, but his words were making her head spin. Yes, she wanted him — and she hated herself for that weakness. And hell would freeze over before she admitted any of it.

"I'm tired, Adriane. I wish to bathe and sleep, so kindly leave my room," she huffed.

"This isn't your room. I have something much more special planned for you," he said, and he held out his arm.

"I won't be sleeping in *your* room," she insisted, her hormones now securely encased in armor.

"I wouldn't think of asking you to do that until after the wedding," he said, his arm still held out.

"Just show me where I'm sleeping," she said, no fight left. She was hungry, dirty, and tired, and she felt as if she hadn't had a nap at all. Her eyelids felt like weights, and she was afraid that if she continued her confrontation with Adriane, he would eventually start making sense. She couldn't allow that to happen.

Ignoring his arm, she stepped past him and opened the door, waiting for him to join her. A smile hid beneath her pursed lips when he glared. Adriane didn't seem to like having a lady hold the door open for him. Hey, if she'd known he was so easily agitated, she would have started tormenting him long before.

Taking the door from her grip, he held out his hand, indicating she should step through before him, even though it was customary for the king's wife or future wife to walk behind him. See, he was being very generous to her — even breaking royal protocol.

Sighing, she did as he wanted, fearing a standoff that could take hours. After all, she was just too tired for their battle of wills to continue. As she entered the hallway she'd run through not long before, she looked around, thinking that she could do this. Once alone, bathed, fed and rested, she would come up with a plan of escape. If Adriane really thought she was going to bend to his will, then he had chosen the wrong woman to mess with.

Freedom was just a few hours away. That thought carried her through the seemingly endless halls of his castle.

When entering the room he had prepared for her, she gasped, unable to hide her reaction. Turning to look at his face, she knew she'd given him the reaction he wanted, and she closed her mouth, narrowed her eyes and walked inside.

"Enjoy your room, my beautiful fiancée," he said before shutting the doors behind her.

Rachel gazed at a room that looked like living quarters for a concubine, with a large maharaja-style four-poster canopy bed in the center, draped elegantly with colorful jewel-toned fabrics, enclosing the mattress for privacy.

Everything in the room screamed sensuality and eroticism, with low lighting, Asian-inspired lanterns and candles smelling of musk, and with pillows and benches strategically placed to make a woman think of sex — sex in many different places and in varying positions. And, of course, there were mirrors, mirrors everywhere. Nothing that lovers did here would likely go unseen or unsavored.

Walking over to a draped table, Rachel grinned at the overflowing bowl of fruit; she picked up a bundle of grapes and ate a couple. From the tastefulness of the décor of the other room she'd been in, Rachel had a pretty good idea that this was Adriane's idea of a joke.

He wanted to resume their affair, take her back to his bed, so he was sending her a message, loud and clear, that she was now in his harem. Her brow furrowing, she remembered him making a comment about multiple wives.

Like hell she would ever allow that!

Why was she even thinking of that comment? It didn't matter, as she wasn't going to sleep with him ever again and she certainly wasn't going to marry him. Not even if his harem room had done its trick and she was feeling the pressure build in her core.

"You just need to eat, rest and plan. If you can make it through to-night, you are one step closer to escape," she reminded herself as she walked to the bathroom.

Stepping through the doors, she actually laughed, surprising herself.

Of course, this is my bathing room, she thought, taking in the marble room with a pool-sized bathtub that was level with the floor; steps led down into the water. Steam rose from the filled bath, and the scent of roses drifted to her nose. The room was lit only by the flickering of hundreds of candles.

Though this was what he wanted her to do, she couldn't resist stripping and walking slowly down the steps, then sinking to her chin in the tub, grateful it wasn't too hot to bathe safely, without fear of harming her unborn baby.

This was what she'd needed. Pure heaven, she thought as she closed her eyes and forced herself to relax and not think about her predicament.

Tomorrow would be soon enough to deal with King Adriane once again. She had no idea how many times she would be thinking this same thought over the next few weeks.

CHAPTER NINE

"I'M NOT COMFORTABLE with this, Ari," Rafe said, and he paused in his pacing. He took off his jacket and tossed it over a chair, then began undoing the buttons on the front of his shirt.

Ari's stomach fluttered as his beautifully tanned chest became more exposed to view. Oh, how she wished they'd been able to wed that day. She so much wanted to have this man as her husband, know that he would always be hers.

"Are you paying attention?" he asked, agitation clear in his tone.

"Oh, yes, darling…I am," she purred, her attention mainly on her rising need for him to join her in bed.

She was wearing far too many clothes, and she'd have to remedy that situation sooner rather than later.

Rafe deciphered her tone, and he turned to look fully at her as he opened his shirt, showing his rippling abs.

Her face must have been a mask of passion, of smoldering desire, because his frown evaporated. Rafe licked his lips and began walking toward her, undoing his cuff links and letting the costly gold clatter to the floor to roll off somewhere unknown.

Then his shirt was gone, and Ari could think of nothing better to do than run her fingers along his hard flesh.

Rafe sat on the bed and kicked his shoes off before lying down on his side and snaking out his arms to pull her up against him, his lips brushing over hers before he pulled back, making her whimper her disapproval.

"I'm trying to be serious, woman, and you are making it virtually impossible to have a conversation with your 'take me now' expression following me around," he said, and then kissed her nose.

"Ah, I see. You want to talk?" she asked while her fingernails trailed seductively up and down his naked back, slipping inside the waistband of his pants to squeeze the taut flesh of his buttocks. He had one fine ass.

"I'm forgetting all about the topic of conversation," he said, leaning in to kiss her again, another soft, light kiss that made her want him desperately, but again he pulled back, fire igniting in his eyes, though his movements were controlled.

"I think a little forgetting is just fine with me," she said, pushing her hips against his, reveling in the feel of his arousal.

"If I didn't know better, I would think you were deliberately trying to sidetrack me," he said with a small chuckle.

"Now, why ever would I do that?" she asked.

"Because you know that I want to find a certain king and hang him by his toes," Rafe said, bending down and kissing along her jaw, his tongue heating her skin.

"Mmm, forget about Adriane. Think about me," she whispered, laying her head back to allow better access.

"I can't believe I agreed to give him a week! How did I let you talk me into that?" he asked, his tone hardening for just a second.

Ari simply moved her hands down further, squeezing his flesh as she rubbed up against him.

"You trust your fiancée. That's not a bad thing, Rafe. I've spoken to Rachel a lot lately, and she isn't as over Adriane as she wants us all to believe. There's a spark between them. After their week together three months ago, she hasn't been the same. Let's give him another week to rekindle the fire. If she still wants to be rescued at the end of that time, then you have my full approval to go in there with guns blazing."

"So, now I need your approval?" he asked, quickly spinning them so he had her trapped beneath him. "I don't think I like the sound of that, Ms. Harlow," he said menacingly.

"Then what are you going to do about it, Mr. Palazzo?" she teased, twisting beneath him in a feigned attempt at escape.

"I have ways of inflicting my own torture," he warned her. He stretched her arms above her head, pinning them in place with one hand, and rolled slightly off her so he could trail his other hand down her body.

"Mmm, I think I like this torture," she murmured, as his hand slid inside her shirt and traveled up her ribs, skimming the side of her breasts.

"Really? You enjoy this?" His fingers moved gingerly back down and made a circle on her stomach, causing her to squirm beneath him.

"No. I don't enjoy that. I would enjoy it if you finished traveling back upward, though," she said, her body catching fire as his fingers traced over her skin. Her nipples were pointed, pushing against the restraints of her bra, needing his fingers or mouth to tease them, to give her some relief from the ache that was building up unbearably.

"I don't know. You're supposed to obey me, remember?"

"There will be no obeying, Mr. Palazzo," she warned as she pushed her hips against him, sending her heat to scorching levels.

"Well, then, I don't think I can relieve this tension building inside you," he taunted her; his head came down and he kissed her throat, swirling his hot tongue across her flesh.

"The payback will be merciless, Rafe," she gasped as he pushed his own hips against hers, his solid manhood pressing into her thigh. "I want you pressed against a much hotter place," she said, her body beginning to shake.

"I don't know..." he said, then took the top button of her shirt into his teeth and tugged, ripping the white circle off and spitting it out.

"Rafe..." she warned, done with the game. Now, she just wanted sweet relief.

"Yes, Ari?" he asked as he reached her next button and quickly tore it away, opening her shirt so he could see her chest straining toward him.

"Lick my nipple," she begged, not even caring that she was giving in to him.

The next button came off and then the rest, her shirt parting for him, her chest barely contained in the lacy bra she'd bought just for the push-up effect. It was obviously worth the extravagant price, because his eyes darkened as he gazed down at her.

Without another word, he bent and ran his tongue along the upper edge of the bra, wetting her skin, but still not giving her sensitive peaks the relief they so desperately needed.

Then his tongue ran just under the lace, coming so near her peak that she cried out when he retreated. She wondered if a body could actually shut down from frustration. When the tables were turned, it would be her delight to repay him in kind, even if she also caused herself pleasurable pain in the process.

After what felt like an eternity, he released her wrists, and her fingers tingled slightly as blood flowed through her hand again. He reached down, unclasped her bra, and gazed at her breasts.

"So unbelievably beautiful," he sighed before filling his hands with them, and running his thumbs across the peaked tips.

"Not half as stunning as you," Ari said as she moved her arms, threading her hands into his hair and tugging him down, demanding his lips on her nipples.

His mouth engulfed one hardened peak and sucked it into the heat of his mouth, making her cry out as she arched into him. She was desperate to lie with him without clothes, without barriers.

"I could play with your body day and night, Ari. You turn me on even more now than the first day I met you, and I didn't think that was possible. Every time I touch you, it feels like the first time. Every chance I get to sink inside you, it feels like coming home. I always want you, and discovering new ways to make you quiver in need is my new mission," Rafe said before sitting up and removing the rest of her clothes.

He shed his own clothing, standing at the side of the bed in all his magnificence, his erection standing proudly, making her mouth water with the desire to taste him.

"Wait," he said as he suddenly turned, making her moan in frustration.

"I'm done with games," she warned him. "Get back here and fill me!"

Rafe turned with a shocked smile on his face. "I love this new, demanding woman," he said before turning back and walking to the closet. Ari groaned as she threw herself back against the bed, thinking she might just have to take care of her ache herself if he didn't hurry.

What a sadly unappealing thought. No one, including herself, could give her body the relief that Rafe could. His touch was better than magic.

He came back, holding something in his hand, and sporting an almost shy smile on his face. It was enough to tamp down her sexual frustration.

"This was supposed to be a wedding gift, and I should wait, but I want to see you wear it," Rafe said, sitting next to her on the bed as he reached out a hand and helped her sit up.

Ari was a little self-conscious sitting there in the buff with him now that they weren't touching, but when she tried to grab the blanket, he stopped her.

"No. Don't cover yourself. Perfection like yours needs to be on display," he said, leaning over and kissing her again, reigniting the fires in a single heartbeat.

"Then, cover me with you," Ari said, forgetting all about the box he was holding.

"In one minute," he promised as he opened the box. Ari's eye filled with tears as she looked at the stunning necklace placed on midnight-blue velvet.

"I found this in a shop in Italy when we were apart. I walked past the window and there it sat, and several minutes later, I was still rooted to the spot. I had a vision of you wearing this necklace and nothing else, with your beautiful hair spilling across my pillow while the gems gleamed on your porcelain skin," he said as he took the sapphire-and-diamond necklace from the box.

"I...it's...oh, Rafe, so beautiful," she gasped, barely able to speak.

"When I heard the story behind the necklace, I knew I had to get it," he said as he drew her against him so he could see behind her neck. Ari lifted her hair as he clasped the necklace and then ran his hands down her shoulders.

"Tell me," she requested as she leaned back against the pillow, no longer self-conscious as his gaze traced every inch of her.

"It was a necklace passed down in a royal family of Italy, dating back to the early fifteenth century. A prince passed the necklace down to his son to give to his bride on their wedding night, as had been done for generation upon generation. Most of the royal weddings were arranged marriages between royal families, marriages of advantage, not of love. This one was no different, except the prince knew his bride. A few years before they were to be wed, he'd been out riding and his horse was spooked by a snake, throwing him down a ravine. The princess was out walking and saw it happen. She rushed quickly to the mountain to see if she could help, though she feared it was hopeless. This same cliff had taken many lives."

"She saw him below, and heard the cry for help, but she could also hear that his voice was weak. So, risking her own life, she scaled down the cliff, and reached him, tearing pieces of material from her dress to stop the blood from escaping his wounded and broken leg. There was no way for her to carry him from the spot, and she feared attempting to climb back up the cliff, as her journey down had been dangerous enough. She knew her maid would search for her, though, so she held his head in her lap, calling out every hour or so, hoping someone would come to their rescue."

"Is this true?" Ari gasped as she hung on his words.

"Yes; now listen," he said before kissing her nose. "The prince was in horrific pain, but the sound of her voice gave him something else to focus on. They spoke the entire night, and he fell deeply in love with her without knowing his father had plans already in place for their union. When the morning light came, search parties found both of them, safely pulling them from the ravine. They were only fourteen at the time, but that was nearly marrying age back then."

"That's horrible," Ari said, shocked at even thinking of a fourteen-year-old marrying.

"It was the way things were back then. It was a different time. They weren't scheduled to wed for three years, though. Over the next three years, they spent much time together, falling even more deeply in love. The day of their wedding, the prince held the necklace in his hand, anticipating placing it on her neck and finally making love to his bride. It wasn't often that royalty married for love, and he felt truly blessed that he would get to have it all."

"Oh, this is special," Ari sighed, running her fingers along the necklace.

"So they wed, and he was even more in love than ever."

"Is there more?" Ari asked, almost afraid to know. She didn't want her necklace marred.

"The rest of the story doesn't matter," he hedged.

"Now, I must know," she insisted.

"She grew pregnant almost immediately, and their marriage was happy even when war broke out within their country. The prince went to defend his land, and she was so afraid he wouldn't return, but he did the night she went into labor. He was filled with joy to be there for the birth of their first child."

Rafe turned for a moment, and Ari's stomach tightened, knowing she didn't want to hear the rest. Let the story just end on a happy note, she prayed silently.

"She didn't live through the birth, but a healthy baby girl was born. The prince was devastated by the loss of his wife, and at first refused to even hold his child, blaming the baby for taking his beautiful wife. Then his daughter cried out, and as he looked down at his wife, at her flawless skin, a slight smile on her lips, he knew he would love their daughter as much as he would always love his wife."

"Breaking the tradition of passing the necklace down to the oldest son of the family, the prince gave their daughter the necklace when she reached the age of fourteen, the same age he'd met her mother. He told her the story of their love, though he was now remarried and had sons. He told her to pass it down to her oldest daughter and never to forget the story of their love, never to let his princess die. She would live forever through this token of his love for her. The owner of the antique jewelry store received the necklace from the last heir, along with the story, which was written down. The final woman in the line had not married, had not produced a daughter to pass the necklace down to. The only stipulation she'd given the woman I purchased the necklace from was that it go only to someone truly in love. It must be a wedding gift, and the story must live on, she told me."

Tears streamed down Ari's cheeks as she touched the precious gift around her neck. She felt connected to the princess who'd died far too young. Nothing would ever compare to this present.

Yes, there had been tragedy connected with the necklace, but there had also been great love. The love is what she would focus on — what she needed to focus on.

Her relationship with Rafe was similar. There had been heartbreak and pain, but also pleasure and love. The love — the passion — the comfort she felt in Rafe's arms was what was important. If she thought back to the pain, her heart would tear open.

As she looked in her lover's eyes, she pulled him close. "Now, where were we?" she whispered.

"Mmm, I think right about here," Rafe said. His fingers drifted across the priceless necklace around her beautiful neck and then he slowly sank into her body. As he brought her to completion, he watched the glimmer in her eyes outshine the sparkle in the necklace.

CHAPTER TEN

NO MORE STRESS, she thought with a sigh.

Rachel drifted in and out of sleep in the scented bath. In this luxurious prison, she could almost forget she was being held against her will.

Yes, this tub could take her to another world, a place where tyrants didn't exist and she wasn't facing the toughest of choices. While she soaked her tired body, Adriane became nothing more than an inconsequential figment of her imagination.

After some time, she reluctantly climbed from the tub and stood for a few moments in the room-sized shower, rinsing the bath oils from her skin. She'd almost forgotten what it felt like to be spoiled, and being here was a clear reminder that it was OK to take care of herself — to pamper herself emotionally and physically.

Since she was trapped in Adriane's castle, she might as well take full advantage of what he had to offer. That didn't mean, however, that she wasn't going to seek her freedom. No. She'd just let him think she was being compliant, as much as her temper would allow her to pretend.

As she wrapped herself in the satin robe, a rumble sounded from her stomach, reminding her she hadn't eaten in hours. Her nausea was gone and she was ready to do what the doctor told her — eat her fill. A nice meal and then a full night's rest and she would be back to herself, ready to take on Adriane, and ready to find her way from this hideaway.

As she opened the door to her room, a divine aroma accosted her nose, unleashing more vicious growling from her stomach. At least Adriane wasn't planning on making her seek out his dining room in the vast castle. She might never find her way back to her room if she left it tonight.

In the morning, when she was ready to escape, she didn't care if she couldn't find it. She had no intention of sleeping in this bedroom for more than a single night. Whatever Adriane's plans were, he'd just have to learn to adjust his expectations.

"I was wondering if you'd gotten lost in the bathroom."

Rachel froze for a moment, then turned in the direction of his voice. Her hand reached up, automatically gripping the lapels of her robe, ensuring that the front stayed closed. She should have known he wouldn't just go away and leave her in peace.

That would be too kind of him. Too un-self-centered.

"You aren't welcome in here, Adriane," she said when her voice returned. Looking down her nose at him, she stiffly approached the set table in the corner of the room, doing her best to freeze him out.

It didn't help that at just the sound of his voice her body heated. She was also very aware that she had nothing on beneath the thin fabric of her robe, and it wouldn't take him long to see how easily he affected her.

She crossed her arms against her chest and sent him a withering stare, daring him to argue with her. Of course, he wasn't able to resist the challenge. She would do better to freeze him out, not challenge him — even unconsciously.

"I'm welcome in every room of my castle, Rachel. Why don't we put aside our differences for the night and enjoy the meal my chef has prepared?"

Oh, the arrogance in his tone, the expectation that she would just roll over and do as he commanded without thought. He truly didn't know her if he expected easy compliance.

"I don't care if this is your home, or at least your castle. You forced me to be here, so for this night, at least, this room is mine. I get to choose who I want to join me in it," she informed him, wanting desperately to unfold her arms, sit and lift her fork. The food looked exquisite and her stomach's incessant protesting would become apparent to Adriane soon enough with its ever-growing volume.

"I wish to have a nice meal with my fiancée. *Deal with it*, as you Americans like to say." He sat down and lifted his wine glass, taking a sip as if they were having a normal meal and discussing mundane subjects. The lout even leaned back and crossed his ankle over his knee as if he didn't have a care in the world.

"You're either incredibly dense or unbelievably arrogant. From what I know about you, I would say both. I told you earlier that I'm done being with you tonight. Do you have so little pride that you always show up where you are so obviously unwanted?"

"Let's eat. We need for you to have your energy for later…activities," he said with a wicked smile.

She had no doubt what activities he had planned. Wanting to refuse anything he suggested, even at the expense of going hungry, Rachel shook her head. Then she thought of the child she carried. It wasn't just herself she would be denying. Still, if he were any kind of gentleman, he would leave and let her have the rest of the night to herself.

That wasn't going to happen, so why even attempt to kick him out again? With luck, if she just ate the meal and remained firm in her denial, he'd leave.

Sure, sure. But she could dream.

"If you expect me to eat in your company, the least you can do it offer me some fresh clothes," she said, proud of her haughty tone.

In answer, his eyes took a leisurely stroll from her neck to her feet and back up again, and he spent far too much time on her neckline before he met her furious gaze. "You look just fine to me," he finally said, and heat flowed between the two of them.

Spinning around to break the connection, Rachel paced the large room. It was obvious she wasn't going to get rid of him, more than obvious he wasn't going to be a gentleman and get her something decent to wear, which meant she was eating a meal with the cad in too short a robe.

It would be so easy to fall back into his arms, and that was the worst thing she could do. Even in his arrogance, though, he had a way of drawing her toward him — making her desire run rampant.

It had to be the baby.

She'd read that during pregnancy, a woman's body went through all sorts of bizarre hormonal ups and downs. Obviously that was happening to her, because if she were in her right mind, she wouldn't feel the slightest emotion for him except utter disdain.

When she turned back to face him, he'd risen from his chair, but his gaze hadn't left her as he waited at the table for her to rejoin him. With a defeated sigh, she walked stiffly over to him, then took the seat he was holding.

"I love this color on you. The blue brings out your eyes," he whispered, his mouth grazing her ear as he spoke.

Unable to hide her body's betrayal at his nearness and the warmth of his mouth, Rachel chose to say nothing. He would just call her on her lie if she denied wanting him again. The thin material wasn't hiding a single thing from his view and she couldn't keep her arms crossed forever.

Fine. Let him look, because that's all he was going to get to do.

After a moment, Adriane circled the table and sat down. He waited until she picked up her fork, then he joined her in eating. With her stomach in knots of indecision, Rachel was at first barely able to get much of the meal down, even with her hunger nearly at supernova levels.

Her anger had at least squelched any remnants of desire. Refusing to look up and meet his gaze again, she speared a moist piece of meat, taking a bite and nearly sighing as the flavor hit her taste buds. The tender morsel fell apart in her mouth and slid effortlessly down her throat, answering the distress signals her stomach had been sending in droves.

"I have decided you're simply playing hard to get," he said with a careless shrug, instantly making her blood boil. She had to remind herself not to allow him to get a reaction from her. "From my experience, there are some women who enjoy being chased, who like keeping their man dangling on the end of a rope. It's OK. I'll give you your excitement, play along with your little game, since that seems to be what excites you so much."

Rachel nearly choked on the vegetables she'd just swallowed. She lifted her head and stared at him, her mouth agape. Did he honestly believe the crap he was spouting, or was he trying to push her buttons?

She didn't know and tried not to care. Either way, she was close to flinging some steaming-hot potato gnocchi at his smug face. So much for her good meal.

Before she made one more decision she might regret, she closed her eyes and took a long, deep breath, then counted to ten in her head.

"I will make this more than clear for you, Adriane, since you are obviously a little bit slow on the uptake," she began, proud she wasn't screaming, though it was only because she was talking between her teeth. "I do *not* want to be here, do *not* want to marry you, and will *not* be falling back into your bed. This isn't a game, and I'm not saying this because I'm bored or because I want you chasing after me. I will gain my freedom, and if you're really lucky, I may eventually allow you to see my child. As long as this baby lies within the safety of my womb, he or *she* is *mine* and *only mine*," she finished, her breathing coming out in short huffs as her fury rose to unhealthy levels.

"From what I can see, Rachel, you are quite the little liar," he said, a smirk tilting his lips up as he directed his gaze to her heaving chest.

"How dare you be so crass!" she snapped, rising from the table and storming across the room, getting as far from him as she could.

Adrenaline flooded her, because he was right — her body was betraying her. Yes, in these moments, she despised him, thinking he was about as classless as a sewer rat, but she also remembered that week with him, remembered how he'd brought her to the peak of pleasure over and over again.

She could hate him all she wanted, but that didn't take away her body's craving for more of what only he could give her. Still, even if she did desire him, it didn't mean she would do something so foolish as to cave in to her hormonal demands.

It wasn't worth the disgust she would feel for herself afterward.

"I tell it as it is, and I am really losing patience with your game of hot and cold. Fire burns in your eyes, yet you continue to fight me. Don't forget that you are on my island now, Rachel. Here, I am king and I can take what I want," he said as he also stood and took determined steps in her direction. There were rules he had to follow, even if he was the king, but he wouldn't think about that right now — not in his anger.

Her fury intensified as she watched the small flex of his jaw. How dare he be angry with her! He was the one throwing out nonsensical statements and then expecting her to drop to her knees before him.

Wasn't going to happen.

"You're not *my* king, Adriane. You seem to keep forgetting that. I am an American and an Italian. I don't follow you, or owe you my respect. Only a man who treats his woman with love and kindness deserves my loyalty. The only thing you will earn from me is pity for the emptiness your life is bound to be filled with, considering you have to force your subjects to honor you," she told him, wanting to anger him to the point he would storm from the room.

As his face tensed and his dark eyes narrowed to dangerous slits, Rachel wondered whether she had pushed him too far. How well did she really know this man? She couldn't be sure he wouldn't send her to the dungeon to be tortured. Was that still done nowadays? If it was, she didn't want to be the one to find out.

"If you simply succumbed into the obvious lust between us, I would have a pleasant night, but then there would be nothing to look forward to. However, Rachel, be very careful when you push me. I have my limits, and you seem to have a way of reaching them in record time."

"If you don't like what I have to say, you know where the door is. Please, be my guest, and feel free to use it. Maybe you can find another room in this giant castle where you are far more welcome," she replied, not afraid of him or his little speech.

"Maybe I should do that. Would it bother you, Rachel? Would the thought of me in the arms of another woman make you jealous?"

His taunt hit its mark. Rage flew through her. She shouldn't care — she should be relieved if he chose someone else, but the vision of him lying entwined with another woman as her own belly grew larger with his baby made her want to puke.

That angered her even more.

She closed the gap between them and lifted her hand, intent on striking him, so mad that she wasn't even thinking of the consequences.

He effortlessly grasped her wrist in his large hand, his hold strong but not punishing.

"We are going to go up in flames when we come together," he promised as he held her gaze captive and then looked pointedly toward the bed. He was breathing heavily.

"We are not having sex again, Adriane!"

A smile softened the tenseness in his jaw, and his eyes captured hers again and refused to release them. "That's where you're wrong, my future queen. We will be having sex — plenty of it. And I'm not a patient man, so be warned."

A shudder traveled down Rachel's spine at the pure hunger his statement caused, a hunger that had nothing to do with the rapidly cooling meal she'd abandoned.

Then, as if he hadn't just been stalking her with his words and eyes, he smiled, his anger seeming to evaporate as quickly as it had appeared. He released her and took a step back. She took in several deep breaths.

This was just another reason to curse the man.

Yes, he tempted her, made her think of the nights she'd spent with him, but she also knew that to do that again would be a mistake — a mistake she wouldn't be able to take back.

If Rachel slept with him now, he'd assume he'd won, and he'd never let her get away from him. No. It would be much better for her to resist him, to irritate him, even. Then, if she did it right, he wouldn't be able to get rid of her fast enough.

There was a good plan. Tick the man off so badly that he purged her from his life.

As Rachel looked up into his eyes, a wide grin split her face, making Adriane look back with suspicion.

"What's going on in that mind of yours now?" he asked.

"I was just thinking it was truly time for the games to begin," she said, enjoying the worry in his eyes. "Batter up!" Laughter spilled from her. And with that, she took her seat.

CHAPTER ELEVEN

"IT'S TIME FOR bed, Rachel."

Oh, my, can he speak, Rachel thought.

He'd uttered just a few simple words, and she was ready to melt into a puddle at his feet. She wouldn't do it, though. She had her pride and she was determined to keep it. Heck, what else did she have at the moment, now that her basic freedoms had been taken away?

But still, his voice was a killer.

"Yes, Adriane, I agree," she said, sending him a seductive glance, enjoying the leaping flames in his coal-black eyes. "So you should probably leave now," she finished.

Her little pause — her game — was worth it: she watched his face turn to stone.

Slowly, he rose from the chair, not taking his eyes off hers. Even if she were capable of moving, which at that moment she wasn't, she was trembling too intensely to try to escape his prowling.

"Why fight the inevitable? We both know what's going to happen. You may be telling me no with your words, but your body is certainly saying yes," he whispered as he reached her side and circled his arms around her, pulling her up against him.

A shudder passed through her as she tilted her head to look into his eyes. "Obviously, you've never taken a self-defense class, Adriane. No means *no*," she told him, proud of herself for not yielding to his embrace.

"Mmm, maybe we'll have to go to one of those together." He bent down and ran his lips across hers in a seductive caress. "There's more than one way to seduce a woman, Rachel," he said, his tone filled with promise.

The satin material of her robe caressed her aching nipples, and heat pooled in her core. It would be so easy to succumb, so easy to let him lead her to the bed right behind them. He'd set the scene well, and she felt herself falling for his charms.

The man was…powerful.

His hands smoothed along her back, catching the end of the short robe on his way up her rounded backside, forcing a whimper from her throat before she was able to stop it. She was already pregnant. What was the worst that could happen if she spent a night in his arms?

Maybe it was just meant to be. Maybe this was the way their night was supposed to end.

As he leaned down and his mouth took hers, Rachel couldn't seem to pull back, couldn't seem to convince her muscles to react. She was melting, and it was even better than she remembered.

His hands stroked her barely covered skin while his mouth devoured hers, dancing along her lips before plunging inside and conquering her tongue.

Only Adriane had ever inspired this pure ecstasy that coursed through her. Why did women ever need drugs? All they needed was a man like Adriane to fly higher than they'd ever been before. When he moved his head down and sucked on the skin of her neck, she was turned on, tuned in, and dropping fast.

She knew she should be saying no, but she couldn't bring her voice to work.

Need.

Pure, unadulterated, hungry need boiled within, and the worst part was that the guilt was dissolving, leaving her as surely as his touch was filling her.

As he pushed his hips against her and she felt the evidence of his desire, she whimpered again, knowing how good his arousal felt inside of her. *Just one night*, she begged her conscience, *one night to feel this pleasure again.*

As his fingers skimmed up her sides, then slid slowly down her neck and entered the gap in her robe, her breasts seemed to grow even fuller, and she arched toward him, wanting their weight cupped in his palms.

"You are more perfect now than you were a few months ago," he whispered, need dripping from each word. "And you were perfect then."

She was so hot, so wet where she ached to have him most. He was good, the ultimate seducer.

When his fingers found her bare nipples, her body jerked against his. He squeezed the sensitive flesh with just the right amount of pressure, and her knees went weak as she leaned back, wanting his mouth to follow his skillful hands.

Dropping to his knees before her, he untied the sash and held her robe open. "I have big plans for you tonight, Rachel," he promised before leaning forward and running his hot tongue along her stomach.

As much as she was turned to mush, the action seemed to wake her up. As she looked at the top of his dark head while he kissed the place where their baby lay safely, reality rushed to the forefront.

Who was she and why was she allowing this to happen?

This man had gotten her pregnant, then had her followed, then kidnapped her right before her brother and best friend's wedding. She'd repeatedly told him she wouldn't make love to him, wouldn't sleep with him again, and then at the slightest of touches, she was falling all over herself to climb into his bed.

No!

With a strength she didn't know she possessed, Rachel lifted her foot and pushed him back, catching him off guard. He fell backward, landing hard on his delectable ass. Then she stepped back, grabbing her robe and closing it, tying the sash with a vicious tug in a double knot that was sure to stay together.

"Rachel?" he asked, looking more perplexed than angry.

"No, Adriane. No. No. No. I told you this wasn't happening, and I meant it!"

"I don't understand," he said as he slowly rose to his feet. "You weren't acting so put out fifteen seconds ago."

Trembling with unfulfilled desire and a new rage, Rachel stared back at him, her features set, her determination high.

"That was a moment of weakness that won't happen again. Unless you're OK with rape, this night is officially over. Now get out of my room!" she said as she made her way to the door and wrenched it open, turning to look pointedly at him while she waited to see what he would do.

"What do you want? You have already received a marriage proposal from me, so what is it you're seeking by holding out? It's obvious that you want me, so I just don't understand the point of your coyness."

Rachel stared at him with bafflement. She'd repeatedly told him no.

"You have seen only what you want to see, Adriane, not what is right in front of you. I won't deny that I desire you; that would be *point*less. However, I have been very straightforward with you when I've said repeatedly that I won't join you in your bed. I want my freedom and I want you to get the hell out of my room!"

"Oh, Rachel, you will change your mind. All you're doing is putting off the inevitable. And, no, I'm not into rape, so I guess this will be continued tomorrow," he said, moving toward her and the open door.

When he reached it, she breathed out, thinking he would just walk on through and she would finally be left in peace. She should have known he wouldn't make it that easy for her. Stopping, so she was forced backward into the doorjamb, he loomed above her.

"Here's something to think about when you're aching all night," he said before dipping his head and taking her lips.

By the time he released her mouth, Rachel was breathless; she hung on to the doorway to keep herself upright.

"Goodnight, my sweet Rachel. This will be continued," he said, and then slipped outside the doors, leaving her to watch his retreat.

When she was able to move again, she stepped back into the room, closing the doors behind her. She made her way over to the bed and flopped down on it, her body in an agony of frustration and her lips still tingling from his touch.

Two hours later, sleep still eluded her.

"Damned man!" she thundered aloud as she pounded against her pillow, trying to make it more comfortable.

Yeah, it's the pillow's fault, she thought sardonically. The sooner she got away from this castle, the better.

CHAPTER TWELVE

STANDING ON THE beach, looking out at the serene ocean, Adriane should have felt peace, should have felt at rest. Yes, his brother's bid for power was causing great turmoil in the kingdom, but still, he was home — he was where he belonged.

But, no. He didn't feel peace. One stubborn woman was causing a massive amount of strife right within his body. She was stringing him out to dry with insomnia and aching frustration that he just didn't need right then.

Until Rachel, he hadn't realized how easily things had always come for him. When he grew up as a prince of Corythia, he had lacked for nothing. Then, when it had been established that he was the future king, there had been many challenges thrown his way, but the people of his kingdom had been willing to do anything for him. His "subjects" wanted him to be pleased.

Rachel certainly wasn't worried about his pleasure.

A mordant smile crossed his face. Just the opposite, in fact.

He couldn't remember a time his body had burned so badly. At this rate, he might have a problem producing future heirs for his kingdom. It was a good thing Rachel was already pregnant.

Sipping his coffee, he looked out into the vast waters, searching for the tranquility that was eluding him. When a sound reached his ears, he turned and found the source of his disquiet strolling from the castle grounds, her eyes narrowed to slits as she approached him.

He waited.

"Where have you brought me?" she demanded. No polite preliminaries; no pleasantries. That would have been too normal for the two of them.

"Good morning, Rachel. I hope you slept well," he replied.

"No, Adriane, it's not a good morning. I asked you a question," she snarled, her hands on her hips as she looked up at him.

To judge from the dark circles beneath her eyes, Rachel had slept as poorly as he had. That should have given him a measure of satisfaction, but instead, he was filled with worry. She couldn't afford not to get proper rest. He was beginning to regret his temper the night before.

Why was he unable to abide by the doctor's request that nothing be done to agitate her? Somehow, whenever they were around each other, he just lost his head.

Sighing, he turned toward her. "I've brought you to my sanctuary. This is where the royal family comes when they are in hiding, when they need to attend private meetings with no fear of interruption. Very few people know of this location," he answered her.

"I thought we were in Corythia," she said as she stood by his side, looking out at the vast ocean before them.

"We are. It's just a small island off the coast of the main island," he said. It wasn't as if she would know where they were, even if she did manage to get to a phone — she'd left *her* cell phone with GPS built in at the resort. He still had six days to convince her that marrying him was the right thing to do.

Adriane had no doubt that Rafe would be able to locate him. It might take the man a little while to do it, but her brother wasn't one to give up. This bought him some time, but Adriane knew Corythia couldn't afford the diplomatic and consequently the financial fallout if Rachel didn't come around to his way of thinking. His nation's life's blood, tourism, could take a devastating hit if he weren't careful.

If Rachel still refused him after their week was up, he would have no choice but to let her go. There was no need for her to know that, though. He needed her to stay, needed her to be there with him to raise the child she carried. His child.

Luckily, the thought of being married to her didn't repulse him. Not at all. He was beginning to picture a life with her, a life quite to his liking. The two of them created sparks together that he couldn't ever see going away. She was a challenge, but even in their short time together, he found that he not only desired her, but also liked her.

Duty, his need to do the right thing, was beginning to turn into a pleasure for him, even with her constant battle against him. Maybe because of it.

And that helped him focus on his efforts to keep her.

"No wonder you have been so confident. All the while I have been making my plans of escape, you knew there was no chance that I'd get off this island on my own," she said, now sounding defeated.

Her sudden change from outrage to despair — that was something he definitely didn't like. Adriane turned toward her and noticed her lack of color. She didn't look well. All traces of his frustration and anger evaporated as he looked into her eyes.

"Rachel, let's get you back inside," he said gently, and he placed a hand beneath her elbow.

"I don't want your help," she bit out, wrenching her arm from his as she spun around.

Adriane was going to let her go back on her own, but then he saw the trembling in her legs, and he held out his arms just in time to catch her as her eyes rolled back and she fell against him.

Lifting her, he raced back up to the castle and called for the doctor to meet him in her room.

This time, she wasn't out nearly as long as before. The doctor examined her, and found she still wasn't eating enough, her body was working too hard, and she wasn't getting enough rest.

"Am I making it worse by keeping her here?" Adriane asked, hoping the answer was no.

"Honestly, Sire, I don't know. She's having a difficult pregnancy, and she had these problems before you brought her to Corythia. I think she needs to have constant supervision until she gets stronger. If you think she will get that back home, then maybe it would be best for her to go there."

Adriane stood outside her door and thought about that. No. His Rachel was stubborn and didn't like to ask for help. She wouldn't seek it out, leaving her and his child in danger. This situation might cause her a little more stress, but at least he could ensure she was taken care of while she was in his sight.

"Thank you. No. She won't take care of herself. She is much better off here, with you to keep an eye on her," Adriane said before dismissing his physician.

He paced up and down the hallway as he waited to go and see her. It wouldn't do him or her any good if he went in there barking at her. He needed to make sure he had himself fully under control before he spoke with her.

After looking at her door, he turned and resumed his pacing. This might take a while.

CHAPTER THIRTEEN

RACHEL PACED, TOO, once she began feeling better. The crackers and warm tea had done amazing things for her body, giving her back energy and taking away all traces of morning sickness. She still didn't feel at a hundred percent, but it would do.

Good enough for the next confrontation with Adriane. She knew it was coming.

As if on cue, the man stepped into the room, once again not bothering to knock. *Why should he?* the arrogant ass was no doubt thinking, if he was thinking at all. It was *his* castle and he felt he had rights to every room in the place. But if she was stuck here for a few days with him, he was going to have to learn that wasn't the case. She valued her privacy.

"This fighting is not doing your body any good. Can we please come to a reasonable solution, Rachel?" he asked, his voice low, as if he were doing something foreign. She was sure he wasn't used to asking for anything.

He'd be learning how to do so as long as he was in her presence.

"The solution is for you to accept the fact that I'm not marrying you — certainly not just because I'm pregnant with your baby," she told him.

"That's not a solution, Rachel. I've told you that I can't abandon my child," he said as he sat down on her bed.

Not good at all. Having him there was calling up all sorts of wrong images in Rachel's head. She cursed at herself for feeling any desire for him. Why did she have to go through this every time he came close to her?

As she stared at him in his harem-inspired room, he looked more like a king than ever before. How had there ever been a time she'd thought him just a simple man? Even in Florida, he'd exhibited a grace no regular man could possess.

That's why she'd been so attracted to him. Now, however, it was a thorn for her to deal with. OK, so she was drawn toward the wrong sort of man — obviously — but that was something she was determined to fix about herself.

"Look, Adriane, I'm not princess material. I'm just a woman — a woman who has lived a good life, with great parents. I don't want to be responsible for a kingdom. I don't want people to watch me beneath a microscope. If I feel like wearing workout clothes, eating ice cream all day, and not putting on makeup, then I want to do that. I don't want to be all over the media, to have to think about every decision I make, to be worried that I may embarrass your country. I just want to be me," Rachel said as she sank down beside him on the bed. Maybe she could make him see reason.

"It's too late for that, Rachel. And you don't have to worry. You won't be a princess," he assured her.

"I wouldn't?" she asked, now confused. She thought that by marrying him, she would automatically become royalty, not that she knew much about it.

"No. You will be queen."

Her stomach dropped.

"Yeah, that doesn't help," she said, her lips turning up the slightest bit. "If that was your attempt at humor, you need to practice a little more."

Adriane's gut clenched at her smile. She was so unbelievably beautiful. She also had strength, and that would make her a fine queen. Now, it was his job to convince her of such.

"You need not worry about royal protocol. We have teachers here who will guide you, instruct you in everything you need to know. In addition to the usual ceremonial duties, the queen normally does a lot of charity work and assures the people they are cared for. My mother is waiting to meet you, anxious to see whom I have chosen as my bride. She wasn't from our country, either, and she looks forward to having an American daughter-in-law. I think the two of you will become very close."

Rachel hadn't even thought about his mother. A new fear filled her. She wasn't cut out for any of this.

"Wouldn't she remain queen even after you are married?"

"No. That isn't how it works. She is the queen mother, and doing the duties you will perform until our wedding takes place."

"Isn't she upset about this? About having to give up her crown?"

"Not at all. She's ready for the next generation to come in. Besides, you won't replace her; you'll assist her in projects she's already started. However, she will get a little more freedom, be able to take more vacations and also be able to take some time to grieve the loss of her husband. She may even take some days to go without makeup," he added with a grin.

His joke fell flat. She was in full panic mode now. It was obvious he didn't want to let her go, but Rachel couldn't do this, couldn't be a queen. It was too much.

"Adriane, there is another solution; I know there is."

"There's not, Rachel. Being with me won't be the hardship you think it is. I will take very good care of you," he assured her.

"Look, no one knows about me yet, well, no one except your adviser and doctor. I won't go to the media. Not a soul will know. Why don't you just find a proper bride who will be more than happy to give you all kinds of heirs for your kingdom, and let me go and live in peace?"

Adriane looked at her for several heartbeats without saying a word. Then he stood and began pacing in front of her. Maybe he was considering it.

"Do you think so poorly of me that you believe I would be able to do something like that? What kind of man can walk away from his child? Even if I weren't the king, I wouldn't let you leave, Rachel."

He stepped back over to the bed, stood in front of her before kneeling down. Lifting both his hands, he first placed them on her hips and then used them to cover her stomach. "This is my baby, too. Yes, you carry him, but he is mine, and I will be there for your pregnancy, his birth, and then for the rest of his life."

The intensity of his expression left her unsure what to do or say next. The feel of his hands cradling her stomach made tears spring to her eyes.

She was in trouble. Serious trouble.

"You can't force me to the altar, Adriane. I won't walk down it willingly and I won't agree to wed you. When the priest asks whether anyone protests, it will be me raising my hand. Won't that cause more of a scandal for you?"

Adriane smiled as he continued to caress her stomach, then leaned forward and pressed a kiss on her belly. "I'm not worried. You will agree. It's already been arranged."

With that, he stood, and he looked down at her with such confidence, she felt her own convictions waver. Was he going to get his way, no matter what she wanted?

"You can't take away my free will!" She stood as she began pacing the room. Obviously, reason hadn't worked with him, either. The man was an impenetrable wall.

He caught her quickly and held her close, his hands moving down her back, stroking her tight muscles, and though he was the one causing her turmoil, he was also the one comforting her. It made no sense.

"This will happen. No matter where you run to, I will find you and bring you back. No matter how much you deny this, it's the right thing. Our child deserves a mother *and* a father. It's a bonus that we are so compatible, because it will make the long nights we have together very enjoyable."

He leaned down and kissed her, as if sealing their fates.

Maybe he was right. Maybe she would fall at his feet. She wasn't sure about anything anymore.

CHAPTER FOURTEEN

SHOTS RANG OUT from every direction, deafening and deadly. The enemy was determined to leave no survivors.

Shane Grayson was just as determined to disappoint them.

"Stay down!" he shouted at his men.

The radicals were firing from the side, not very organized in their strategy but still managing to make it damn hard for Shane's group to reach its target. Worry wasn't at the forefront of the soldiers' minds yet, but they were cautious, always cautious when dealing with extremists like this who had nothing to lose.

"I'm going in for the hostage. Cover me," Shane said, before getting ready to storm the warehouse.

"I'm coming with you," River insisted.

Shane knew there would be no arguing with his teammate, so he simply nodded.

"We've got your back. Let's fry these assholes," Paul said.

Shane took off with River on his flank, staying behind anything they could as they approached the target. Men were hanging from the windows of the large warehouse, and his men easily picked them off as he and River moved forward.

"To your left," River said and Shane spun around, firing his automatic, taking out two men with their weapons aimed.

"I don't think they're too happy with our arrival," Shane said.

The two men made it to the building, both of them talking quietly through their mouthpieces, looking about for the next enemy band lying in wait.

"Yeah, and they're going to be really pissed soon, when they no longer have a leader," River said.

Yes, the situation was intense, but they'd been through worse. Every mission had the possibility of going bad in so many ways. The worst would happen if they grew too confident, let their guard down.

They went silent as they searched the building, peering down and through the aisles of merchandise, and hoping like hell that they reached the hostage while she was still in one piece. The extremists were trying to free their leader and had announced that the girl, a diplomat's daughter, would be killed that day if their demands weren't met.

Shane's team was there to effect her release without giving the enemy a damn thing.

Shane and River made it to the back of the building, where they had good reason to believe that the young girl was being held. They stayed hidden behind a pile of industrial crates while they discussed their next maneuver.

"Shit!" Shane exclaimed when he saw about ten men all packing weapons with the girl tied to a chair in the corner — behind them, and looking terrified.

"You go right. I'll distract them," River said. Shane nodded, and River got into position, popping up and shooting the man up on a catwalk overlooking the warehouse floor.

The men in the back of the room erupted as they began firing their weapons toward River and the crates he was using as protection. River kept moving, staying under cover as he shot. Soon, the radicals were running around, not paying attention where they were firing, and one of them killed one of his own men.

Good; let them take each other out, Shane thought.

Rushing forward, he kept behind a wall as he aimed and began picking them off, one by one, careful not to hit the sobbing girl. A round from one of the enemy guns hit the wall two feet above her head, making Shane's heart race. She was in a dangerous position right now, and he needed to get to her.

"River, you need to get them to chase you so I can extract her," he said into his mic.

River showed himself, and the remaining four men tried to surround him, leaving the girl unattended.

Shane bolted toward her, slicing through the ropes holding her to the chair, then grabbing her without saying a word, flinging her over his shoulder and rushing toward safety.

The men turned just as he reached the wall, and a bullet shattered the wood just above his head. Sweat broke out on his brow. That was too damn close. But wasn't it always?

"Please let me go," the girl sobbed as she pounded against his back.

"We're the good guys. Just trying to get you out of here alive," Shane said, not taking any more time than that to explain. If she resisted, he'd have no choice but to knock her out. It was either that or let her be killed.

Hell, they could still all be killed. That was a part of their job.

River, after taking out the last four men, joined Shane as he and the girl were making their way back to the front of the warehouse. There, more of the enemy group was still exchanging gunfire with the rescue team.

Now the difficult part was going to be getting through the enemy and back to his men. It would have been much easier without carrying a girl over his shoulder — even a small one.

"I'll cover you; make a run to the men," River said.

Shane took a deep breath, alerted his men through his coms that he was coming, then took off, saying a quick prayer that he made it with no bullet holes in him or the girl.

He felt the heat of the gunfire as he wove his way back to the men, knowing River would cover his back. When he reached the men, he said a silent but fervent thank-you to them and to the powers above, then left the girl with his men as he got into position to help cover River.

Once River returned to their unit, they could get the hell out of there and have a cold beer to celebrate their success. Nothing had ever sounded so great.

"We've got you," Shane said into his mouthpiece.

River popped up, and began the treacherous journey through the front parking lot, diving behind whatever he could find to take cover as he wove toward them. This mission had turned out to be easier than others, making Shane a happy man.

Of course, he knew not to think that until they completely were in the clear. It was just bad luck.

"Easy as usual…" River said as he turned the corner and began to kneel down with his team while they got into formation for their exit. That's when their smooth mission went from easy to instant hell.

Before River could finish his sentence, blood spattered from his mouth as a bullet went through the back of his head.

"No!" Shane screamed, jumping up and firing in the direction the bullet had come from, wiping out the shooter, who had just rounded the corner of the warehouse.

"Shit! Where did he come from?" Doug yelled as he jumped up to look around, shooting down another man running from the same direction.

"We need to go now!" Shane yelled, gathering the girl.

But it was too late.

River was dead.

Their mission had just failed in all their eyes, even if they did get the girl to safety. They'd let down one of their own and Shane took the full burden on his own shoulders. It was his team — his mission to keep that team safe.

The men grabbed their fallen brother, who lay at their feet, his eyes empty. Doug threw him over his shoulder and they made their escape to the booming sound of gunfire. Three of their guys covered their backs, returning fire as they exited the industrial area.

Once they were all out of the danger zone, it was a solemn journey back out of the field as they carted the girl away. Yes, they'd completed their objective, but they'd lost one of their own.

There was no victory for them today.

CHAPTER FIFTEEN

"**Y**OU DID WHAT?"

Adriane stood frozen as his mother berated him, making him feel like a child once again, a child who had just been caught undoing the straps on the guards' horses for the third time. It had been amusing to watch the men fall off their steeds in front of the king when they'd been so determined to look and act worthy of guarding the royal family.

His mother, Queen Octavia, hadn't been amused back then.

And she wasn't too thrilled with him now, though he didn't understand exactly why.

"I told her we would be wed — that there was no other way," he said again. Maybe his mother had misunderstood him. Surely she could understand and support his refusal to let Rachel go. After all, Rachel carried the royal heir, his mother's first grandchild.

"Oh, son. Where exactly did I go wrong in raising you?" she asked, shaking her head in disapproval and bafflement.

"I don't understand why you are upset. Rachel cannot leave. Surely you can see that," he said, raising his voice just the slightest in his frustration.

The withering look his mother sent him calmed him immediately.

He was speaking disrespectfully not only to his mother, but also to Corythia's queen. "I'm sorry," he said softly.

"Hmm, if you are talking to *me* this way, I shudder to think how you have been speaking to poor Rachel. No wonder she is less than enthusiastic about your proposal," his mother told him.

"Do you think that I should let her leave?" he asked, with his fingernails biting into his palms.

"I think you should try courting her instead of giving her orders," Octavia replied.

"I am doing that!"

"Really? From what you have told me, you have kidnapped her, demanded she marry you, and not even allowed her to speak to her family."

"I have just let her know that there's no other choice."

"There's always a choice, Adriane. This isn't the old days; things need to be done a bit more diplomatically now. Yes, I understand that you don't want your child to grow up elsewhere. I agree with you on that. What I disagree with you about is the way you are going about it. If you want this woman to stay loyal to you, you will have to give her a reason to be so."

Adrian turned and looked at his mother. What was she trying to tell him? He was lost. Was his courting not up to snuff? If not, what exactly did she mean by the word? He'd never had to woo a woman before; they just naturally wanted to be with him. Of course they did; he had been a prince of Corythia, and since age seventeen, the future king. Now that he was king, there was a line of women who would be more than willing to be his wife.

A line of women that didn't include the one who carried his child.

It was exasperating!

"How did you and my father come together?" Adriane had never cared to ask such a question before now.

"Now, that is a good question." She sat back with a soft smile on her face. "I'm surprised that I haven't told you this before. Your father was visiting the United States to get advice on improving Corythia's economy, and he was a featured guest at a glittering fundraiser. I and a number of other American actors and actresses were there, and when I met him, his dark eyes, his stature, and his strong personality swept me off my feet." Octavia stopped for a minute or two, and sighed. "Yes, a very strong personality. He did the barbaric thing that you've done: he kidnapped me. Not smart."

"But you married him, Mother."

"Yes, I did. But his actions almost turned me completely against him, attracted to him as I was. I let him know in no uncertain terms that I wasn't an object, a treasure he could add to his collection. When he calmed down and actually courted me, I fell in love almost instantly. The story is longer, of course, but the bottom line is that he didn't win my heart until he showed me he had one of his own. Once he did that, I didn't leave his side."

"Why do women need this? I don't understand. I will provide well for her, give her a life most women would envy. Why isn't that good enough?"

"Because women should be cherished, son. A good woman at your side will complete you, make you the ruler you are meant to be. She will be strong when the rest of the world has abandoned you. She will know you better than anyone else. She will embrace you when the weighted decisions of this country hang heavy upon your shoulders. You need to cherish her, love her, and give her a reason to hold you tight even through the strongest of storms."

"How do I do that?" Adriane could figure out his country's problems, but he didn't know how to open his heart to Rachel. Hell, he didn't feel a need to.

"How did you win Rachel's affections in the first place? You must have done something right if she carries your child."

Adriane stood silent for a moment as he thought back to his time on the beach. "I didn't do anything different from what I normally do. She was swimming. I thought she was drowning and I 'rescued' her, though when she stopped laughing at my valiant attempt to save her life, which irked me just a bit, there was an obvious connection. I invited her for dinner. She didn't leave for a week."

"What did you do that made her want to stay with you for the week?"

Why all these questions? He didn't want to think about the past. It was time to move forward, think of their future. But he knew his mother wouldn't stop interrogating him until he gave her something.

"We just got along well. I spoke to her more than any other woman I've taken for the night. I wasn't expecting to be with her all week. It was just that one day melted into the next." Adriane threw up his arms.

"Then be that man again — the man who made her choose to stick around for a while," she said, as if speaking to a young child.

"I don't know how to do that. At that point in our relationship, we were both just looking for a good time; neither of us was worried about the future. Now, I need to persuade her to marry me willingly," he said. "Besides, if she would fall back into bed with me, maybe I could persuade her more easily," he mumbled under his breath, grateful when his mother didn't hear.

Everything had been easier, though, so much easier. When they'd spent their week together in Florida, they hadn't fought. That must have been because they'd been in bed half the time.

"You will have to give her something, Adriane, or she won't stay, no matter what threats you issue."

"What do I give her? What will make her stay?"

Why did his mother need to talk in riddles? This was important. She needed to guide him, not sidetrack him with silly talk of love. This wasn't about love — this was about a child the two of them had created together, a child who deserved a mother *and* father in his life. A child he desperately wanted.

"That, my son, you will have to figure out on your own. And, I fear, until you do, you won't ever earn her heart. You will never truly hold her. Yes, you can refuse to let her go, but at the first opportunity, she will be gone, taking your child with her. It is a privilege to hold a woman's heart, and you had better figure out how to take care of it properly, or it's never going to be yours, no matter how much you demand it of her."

Women. His mother couldn't be right. There were other, better ways to make a marriage work besides this love so many spoke of. He and Rachel had laughed together, spent passionate nights together, gotten along swimmingly. Love was simply an emotion that people professed to feel in order to get something from someone else. He'd never been in love. He never would be. They had something far better than love — they had companionship.

Many couples married with less in common. If Rachel would just open her eyes, she would see that they would be good for each other. They would never be miserable, not with the attraction burning so strong between the two of them.

Women were to be appreciated. He could understand that. They were pleasurable to hold in your arms, pleasurable to sink deep inside, and they filled an ache that had to be met, but this sugary, hearts-and-flowers emotion, love, that so many spoke about was nothing more than a myth, a meaningless fantasy.

His mother meant well. She believed what she said. But she didn't understand his relationship with Rachel. The two of them had passion — which was so much greater than mere words of love.

Their marriage would work and it would be excellent. He would show Rachel and his mother. Love didn't need to be in the equation.

However, maybe he could change his approach just the slightest. If Rachel believed she had a choice, then she might possibly soften toward him.

It was worth a shot. Everything else so far had failed.

"Thank you for your time, Mother. I appreciate it," he said as he sat down next to her and kissed her cheek.

"I just hope that it wasn't wasted, that you will listen to me," she said, but there was doubt in her eyes.

"Of course I will listen to you," he replied. And he had listened.

He'd learned that he needed to be a lot more savvy in the way he spoke to Rachel. She had to be playing some sort of game. And she was sure to lose.

She hid from their passion together, pushed him away, but he wouldn't give up. The prize was too valuable.

His child.

And, of course, Rachel in his bed again.

CHAPTER SIXTEEN

RACHEL POKED HER head through the doorway, peeked around the corner and made sure the path was clear. Today was the day. She was getting off this damn island if it was the last thing she did.

After creeping down the endless hall, she peered around the next corner, and breathed a sigh of relief when she saw no one about.

Adriane must be supremely confident if he'd taken away his security detail. She wasn't so foolish as to believe the guards were no longer there, but he was getting lax.

Since she'd heard the helicopter fly out an hour ago, she knew he had left the island. All she had to do was get ahold of her brother, Rafe, and she was home free. He'd trace the call and have a rescue party here quicker than Adriane could blink.

That would teach the king he wasn't lord and master over all.

Rachel checked inside a few doors but had no luck finding a phone. Did this castle lack a single connection to the outside world? This was ridiculous.

Finally, she entered a large parlor with a writing desk in it. There had to be a phone there! It wasn't possible that Adriane would have no communication with the rest of the world. He might be king of Corythia, but he was also a businessman with properties all over the world. He would need to stay in touch with them.

With an ear cocked for the sound of anyone approaching, Rachel slunk to the desk and smiled when she saw the large black telephone.

Bingo!

She picked it up and nearly shook with happiness at hearing a dial tone. Freedom was within her grasp. When she heard ringing, showing she'd made a connection, she was so grateful that her knees started shaking. She quickly plopped down on her butt in case anyone happened to look in the door.

"Operator," the voice on the other end of the line said.

"Hello?" she whispered. *Operator? Who was this?*

"How can I help you, Ms. Palazzo?"

Who was this and how did they know who she was?

Rachel's stomach sank to her toes. Of course escape wouldn't be this easy.

Adriane wasn't worried about her wandering about the castle because she was on a stinking island with no chance of escape, and he had an operator monitoring his phone calls.

Still, she wasn't going to give up that easily.

"I would like to place a phone call to the United States, please," she said, raising her voice to a normal tone, trying to make sure she sounded calm and sure, as if she weren't doing something against the king's wishes.

"I'm sorry, Ms. Palazzo, but any outgoing calls are not authorized at this time. Is there something else I can help you with?"

No! That was all she wanted. Sighing in disgust, Rachel slammed the phone down. Why bother being quiet now? Though frustrated, she was undeterred. If she had to swim off this damn island, she was going to do it. If she drowned in the process, then King Adriane would just have to live with his guilt. Not much consolation, but still…

Standing up, she faced the door, then stopped in her tracks at the sight of a man standing there with a lifted eyebrow.

"Is there something you need, Ms. Palazzo?" he asked with a slight accent, but in perfect English.

Though she knew she was doing nothing wrong, the man made her feel as if she were.

"I need to get ahold of my brother," she said, firming up her voice as she stared him down. "It's important."

He gazed at her a moment before giving his head the slightest shake.

"I apologize, but that's something we cannot do right now." His voice was customer-service friendly, but unyielding at the same time.

"You do realize that my basic rights are being violated by your refusal to let me make a phone call. Heck, even prisoners are allowed their one call," she snapped, no longer even pretending to be friendly.

If these people were going to keep her trapped here, pretend not to speak English or Italian when it suited them, and refuse her basic liberties when speaking in words she could understand, she wasn't going to dance to the tune they were playing. She was going to throw a giant-sized fit.

As she watched the man look down his nose at her, Rachel realized he might not want her to be here. He probably didn't think she was good enough to serve as his queen. What if she could turn him to her side? Maybe he would help her to escape so a proper queen could be found for his country.

Her attitude changed, and she put a bright smile on her face. His gaze narrowed suspiciously.

"What's your name again?" Rachel asked, seeming to recall him from the States. He had to be one of Adriane's right-hand guys.

"I am Nico," he said, his expression not changing.

"Well, Nico, maybe you can offer your assistance," she said, batting her eyes.

From his unaltered expression, she didn't think her pathetic attempt at flirting was doing her any good.

"Of course, Ms. Palazzo. I am willing to assist you with anything I *can*," he said, though his suspicious expression was telling her otherwise.

She had to try, though.

"I need to speak to my brother so he can return me to the States. We both know I'm not the right fit to be queen of Corythia. Wouldn't it be better for everyone involved if I just disappeared? Adriane could then find a proper woman of royal or at least noble birth to be his wife and the queen of this exquisitely beautiful country."

OK, so she might be laying it on a bit thick, but she was desperate.

"It is King Adriane's baby you are pregnant with, is it not?" he asked, looking pointedly down at her stomach.

"Does it really matter? Many, many children have been born out of wedlock to royalty. They and their mothers don't join the family. So we can all just pretend I never existed. Everyone can get on with their lives." Rachel spoke in pleading tones, growing a little more desperate at the hardening in his eyes.

"Why do you want to leave?" This time there was no expression on his face, not a clue of what he was thinking.

"Because I won't marry a man simply because I carry his child. I only spent one week with Adriane, knowing him then only as Ian, a beach bum who was romantic and made my world spin. Corny, no? That certainly isn't enough of a reason for us to wed."

He seemed thoughtful as he looked at her. Had she made him understand?

She continued to work on him. "You must know, Nico, that it's not right for him to hold me captive here. I have a family back home. All you have to do is let me make one little bitty phone call. Just turn your back while I get through to my brother. Adriane need never find out."

Nico's lips tilted almost imperceptibly as he stared at her.

"I like your determination, Ms. Palazzo. I think perhaps that I may have misjudged you. Most Americans I have encountered aren't as... resourceful as you. But still, I can't go against my king. That would be profoundly disloyal, even treacherous. I will say that I believe you will make a fine queen," he said, dashing the last of her hopes.

He was doing his job, so there was no use in getting angry with the man. But someone here had to be willing to help her. She had never found a group of employees to be completely happy in their jobs.

"I will see myself out," she said, and she walked past him to the door. There was no point in continuing the conversation.

"I do apologize, Ms. Palazzo," he offered as she passed him.

Rachel paused for a moment before continuing on. She wasn't going to say anything more. She certainly wasn't going to thank him. He hadn't helped her.

With her head tilted up, and more determined than ever, Rachel retreated, for now, back to her room. This wasn't over — not by a long shot.

CHAPTER SEVENTEEN

NOT AGAIN! YET another night in which sleep played the merciless tease. If this didn't stop soon, she was going to make herself sick — far sicker than just a mere fainting spell and slightly high blood pressure.

And yet, while sitting on the balcony, Rachel was at least able to enjoy the pleasant breeze as the sun rose in the sky. If she hadn't been there against her will, she would think it an ideal place to be. The sea was so gloriously fresh that it was almost clear, making her desperately eager for a swim. The food was amazing, and the accommodations beyond luxurious.

This could be a resort.

There was just one minor problem: she'd been abducted, and that tended to color her mood. She wasn't so relaxed that she'd forgotten the reason she was here.

She hadn't seen Adriane since the morning before, but she knew he was back. If she were able to fly the dang helicopter, she would have been hot-wiring it and making her escape. But, no, she knew how to fly only as a passenger, and she had no interest in ending up on the bottom of this beautiful sea.

This morning, when she'd looked in the mirror, she'd noticed the tiniest hint of a bump on her stomach, not enough that she looked pregnant, but enough that it was all becoming more and more real. Each time she experienced morning sickness, or felt dizzy, each time she looked in the mirror and found minor changes in her body — it all added up to the fact that she was going to be a mother.

In about five and a half months she would have a baby.

At this moment, it would be so nice to sit down and talk to her mother, ask her how she'd felt the first time she'd noticed a change in her body. Had she been afraid or overjoyed? Had she run to the toilet and thrown up or lay back and rejoiced? What had gone through her head and heart?

Of course, her mother had been happily married to a man who loved her completely and utterly. Rachel was sure that made a world of difference, softened the fears that went along with the condition.

Maybe if she played nice, Adriane would allow her to call her mom. Rachel wouldn't burden her with the knowledge of her abduction. She just wanted to hear her mother's warm voice.

Adriane had to understand that much.

If he didn't, he was an even crueler man than she took him for.

"I hope you slept well."

There was the man of the hour, or maybe of the nine months. Rachel didn't turn to acknowledge him as he stood behind her. But just knowing he was there was causing her stomach to stir in ways that weren't making her happy.

"No. As a matter of fact, I didn't sleep well. If I'd been in my own bed, I'm sure I would have had a great night's sleep," she said.

"If you'd been in my bed, you would have been well pleased and then would still be sleeping," he countered.

The most infuriating part of his statement was that it was most likely correct. Not that she would admit to that. His ego was bloated enough without her puffing it up further.

Silence stretched on for several moments before he sat next to her.

"The doctor is here. He brought a device so we can see our child."

Rachel perked up at the thought. She should have had an ultrasound already, but she'd been too busy with denial to do it. Seeing the baby residing in her stomach, knowing he or she was healthy, would cheer her immensely in these less than encouraging circumstances.

"You had ultrasound equipment brought in?"

"Of course. We need to make sure the baby is healthy, and there isn't a medical facility on this island," he said matter-of-factly. Even though she'd grown up with amazing wealth, the excesses wealthy people were prone to always amused her. So much for her dreams of living like a normal person — but she'd given up on that for quite a while now.

She was thankful for her mother's influence. Thankful she had made sure Rachel, Rafe and Lia knew money wasn't something to take for granted. Yes, they'd had nice things, but they'd also lived humbly, at least when in Italy.

No, Rafe hadn't lived that way since adulthood, but he'd been taught those principles, too, like his sisters. Rachel had been jealous of Rafe a time or two, envious that he could do whatever he wanted whenever he wanted to do it. Now, she understood more why her mother had instilled her values in her children.

Too bad Rafe hadn't listened more. But at least his love for Ari proved that his obscene wealth hadn't totally destroyed his character.

"Are you ready, Rachel?" he asked softly, laying a hand on her shoulder.

If only he actually cared whether *she* was all right. But she knew his concern was only for the child she carried. She was glad he cared about the baby, but she didn't think it was possible to go through with a relationship with him when she knew she was simply an incubator for his little one.

Would he simply discard her after the baby was born? Ignore her completely? It seemed very likely to her. Still, she wanted the ultrasound, and as she was stuck here for now, it looked as though she was going to see her first pictures of the baby with him at her side.

Without saying anything more, Rachel stood, pushing away his hand. She could get up on her own. His eyes sharpened just a bit, but he didn't say anything about her rejection of him.

He should be well used to it by now.

Her bladder was full, which was apparently a good thing for the ultrasound, but not as wonderful for her as she walked beside him from her room and into the hallway. They made their way in silence through the maze of hallways until he stopped and opened a door on the far side of the castle.

"I know you are upset with me, but this day is special. Try not to let what's been happening between us ruin that for you," Adriane said as the two of them stepped inside a room that had been turned into a mini-clinic.

"I won't let you affect how I feel, period," Rachel said as she looked around.

His team of doctors had brought in a medical bed and an ultrasound imaging machine, along with other equipment that she had no clue about. Was he planning on never letting her leave this opulent hide-away?

It seemed to be set up for delivery. A chill went down her spine — she might be trapped here forever. The princess — no, dammit, the queen — in the tower.

One of the nurses led Rachel to a partitioned-off area where she changed into one of the unflattering gowns all patients wore. As she slipped the soft cotton around her, she worried that eventually she'd not even care. She thought for a moment about letting her ass hang out the back and walking out, giving Adriane a good view. She could title her memoirs "I Mooned the King"!

Then she thought better of it.

She couldn't deny that she had feelings for Adriane. Not love, but certainly feelings. She desired him, but she was sure that was par for the course with his women. He'd been an excellent lover, and though she'd tried to forget, it was impossible not to remember his hands and mouth caressing her body — and his impressive manhood sinking within her. Showing him her ass might push him, and she didn't think she'd be able to say no if he put forth a serious effort to seduce her.

Nope. Much better off leaving the gown nice and closed.

A tremor washed through her as she stepped from the partition and approached the table, where Adriane was waiting to help her up. She didn't refuse him this time, not wanting to teeter over the other side of the table and let everyone in the room get a good gander at her tush.

This was all so confusing. Once again she blamed it on pregnancy hormones. That had to be the only explanation, because suddenly she had to stop herself from laughing at her own lame jokes.

"Just lie back and relax. We'll have an image of your baby in just a few moments," the nurse said as she lifted Rachel's robe and applied a cold gel to her belly. Any thoughts of laughter evaporated just as fast as they'd appeared.

When the woman pressed the small wand to her stomach, Rachel was afraid she was going to embarrass herself and lose bladder control right there in front of everyone, but as the screen flashed on, Rachel forgot all about her discomfort and gazed at the monitor in fascination while she waited to see the first image of her baby.

When the doctor's brow furrowed and he leaned down to start whispering with the ultrasound technician, turning the screen away and pointing at it, Rachel felt her pulse escalate.

Adriane turned his full attention to them and she felt like an outsider as she heard them speak urgently — in French again! Why did they keep doing that!

Rachel hadn't wanted to be pregnant, had been devastated when she found out she was going to be a single mother and that her best-laid plans for her future had to be altered. But over the last couple of months, she'd had time to come to terms with her condition, and now she felt an unbelievable urge to protect her child, to ensure it had a healthy arrival into this world.

From the looks on the medical staff's faces, something wasn't right. Her throat closed up on her as she tried to ask what was wrong. She needed to speak to them, but she couldn't get any sound out.

Adriane looked up and must have noticed her distress because he bent down to her. "Are you all right?"

Finally her voice came back to her. "What's wrong with my baby?"

Adriane grabbed her hand and squeezed with a look both of wonder and of shock on his face. He turned back to the monitor while he tried to figure out how to say the words.

In Rachel's panic, she gripped his hand tightly and leaned on him for comfort, though he had been the one to cause so much of her stress lately. It didn't matter at this moment. Right now, all that mattered was that their baby be OK. Just for now, they needed to present a united front.

"Sorry about worrying you, Ms. Palazzo. I didn't want to say anything until I was sure," the doctor said, speaking in English again as he turned and looked at her with a reassuring smile.

That didn't drive away her worries.

"It seems you are carrying twins."

Adriane's face broke out into a huge grin, and he looked down at her with such pride and…love in his expression that it took her breath away. Rachel had to remind herself it was love for the babies she carried, not for her.

Still, she was floored.

Twins.

Not one baby but two rested within her womb.

What was she going to do now?

CHAPTER EIGHTEEN

RIFLE SHOTS SOUNDED in the quiet cemetery. Seven rifles, fired in three volleys.

It was supposed to be for honor.

It was supposed to signify respect.

Yes, it did that, but saluting one who had fallen while serving his country didn't take away the pain of losing him.

River Delzado was gone forever. He would never serve with his team again.

Shane hung his head. An endless silence surrounded him before taps began playing. Then, the only sound that could be heard above the bugle was the quiet sobs of River's wife and young daughter.

Time didn't matter. Though he had stood amongst his team, listening to the minister speak of what a good and honorable man River had been, Shane heard none of it — heard nothing but the pounding of his own heart.

He'd lost men before, men who'd been his friends. But River was different. He was a true friend, and he was now gone. There would be no more nights on the field together, nights of playing cards, laughing over something River's daughter had done, of River pestering him to settle down.

His brother-in-arms would never be there again.

They all knew that the risks were high when they were on a mission. They all knew they or their comrades could die. They were trained for this. But none of that helped. No amount of training could really prepare them for the worst.

Shane didn't know whether he could continue to do this.

It was just one more loss in a million other losses. The difference now was that Shane had people he truly cared about at home.

Lia.

He'd hurt her so much in the last few years. And he'd never wanted to hurt her, which was why he'd felt justified in keeping this part of his life separate from her.

But still, he'd managed to lose her trust, to make her heart ache. The two of them — they were something he'd never intended to happen. But now it seemed that he couldn't live without her.

She might seem tough to the world, as if she had it all together, but Shane knew the insecurities she dealt with. Yes, she'd grown up in a loving family, but somehow Lia had been the one to get forgotten about most.

She'd been the middle child. Her younger sister got a lot of attention because she was the baby; her older brother got a lot of attention just because of who he was. Then there was Lia. She had been painfully shy for years.

He'd never known that — never knew she had been afraid to talk to people, afraid to make friends, not until many years later when she'd confided in him. It had been difficult for her to make changes, but when she'd decided to break free of her shell, she'd done so with a vengeance.

Despite the solemnity of this occasion, the thought almost made Shane smile.

Almost — but not quite.

Shane's eyes moved back toward River's casket as he and his men placed their hands on the flag covering it, and all other thoughts disappeared.

His friend was about to be laid to eternal rest. Yes, it could happen to any one of them at any time. But why River?

His widow was handed the traditionally folded flag, and to the slow, measured music from the bugler, his wooden casket was lowered into the ground. *Day is done, gone the sun.*

For the first time since he was a small child, Shane felt a stinging sensation in his eyes. Surprised, he blinked away the emotion, then stood at full attention to honor his friend and colleague.

People began clearing out from the cemetery, their moods as gloomy as the overcast sky. Many sobbed quietly as they held on to one another.

Shane stood tall, watching as the staff began disassembling the protective tents they'd put up in case the sky decided to pour down its own sorrow.

His men stood wordless by his side and behind him, none of them leaving until he began to walk away. They were close, and they'd been lucky, until now, not to lose one of the team.

"Grayson!"

Shane turned to see his commander approaching. The man was only about fifteen years older than Shane, but he'd seen a lot in his years in the military, more than Shane ever cared to see. There was a hardness to the man's voice and tone that bespoke authority and grim experience.

The men followed him, always with no questions asked.

"Yes, sir?" Irritated at the quietness of his own voice, Shane stood even taller and squared his shoulders more fully. It wasn't OK for him to show weakness in front of his commander — even weakness caused by the loss of a teammate.

"Your team did well. The girl has been safely returned to her family, and the diplomat is extremely pleased. I know you're all having a difficult time with this loss. I am truly sorry. River was a good man."

"Thank you, sir. We'll feel better if we can just get back to work," Shane said, desperate to go into battle, to shoot something or someone. He needed to vent his rage, his frustration and the feeling of free-falling that had been running through him for too long now.

"That's a negative, Grayson. Your team is on leave as of right now. No one is cleared for duty until the doc gives his OK."

Shane's gaze narrowed just the slightest, and his commander narrowed his own in turn, making Shane back down immediately. Never once had he shown disrespect to a superior.

"Sir, I don't think that's necessary. We know the risks we take in the field. We know it could be any one of us at any time. This call-in was supposed to last a month," Shane said, keeping his tone neutral. He was skirting the line here.

"Well, the call has been suspended, Grayson — for all of you. You're to see the doc next week. Follow me over here. I want to speak to you privately for a moment," he said, and Shane walked away from his men. He stood at attention and waited. "Grayson, I've thought of you as more than a soldier for a lot of years now. I respect you. Like you. I don't say that to a lot of men. May I be frank with you?"

Shane couldn't imagine what the man wanted to say. "Of course, sir."

"You've been finished with this life for a long time, Shane," he said, using his first name for the first time that Shane could ever recall. "You do know that if you decide to retire, you do so with honor. You have a life outside of the military, which is something a lot of us can't say. Maybe it's time you embrace that, get out of this before it destroys you the way it does so many."

The commander didn't give him time to respond before turning and walking away, leaving Shane standing there unsure of what had just happened. His commander was right: he was finished with military life — he just didn't know how to make the final break.

Slowly, Shane walked back over to his men, who had waited for him, and he looked each of them in the eyes before he gave an attempt at a smile.

"You all heard the commander; you're dismissed," Shane said. Each man clapped him on the shoulder before taking his leave. They didn't ask what the commander had spoken to him about. They knew he didn't want to talk and they respected him for it. They most likely felt the same way.

Rage and sorrow tore at his heart as Shane cast a long last glance at the open grave. The casket had been lowered, River laid to rest.

He'd been so young, had so much life ahead of him.

Now, he had a widow and a child left behind with only memories.

Lifting a loose clump of dirt in his hand, Shane watched as it sifted through his fingers before he tossed it on top of the casket, looking so final as it sat six feet below the surface of the earth.

"Goodbye, River."

Shane clenched his jaw and turned away. It was time to go home — time to decide the rest of his life. He couldn't do that without speaking to Lia.

She was his life.

All the rest of it was meaningless if she weren't with him.

It was time to claim his bride.

CHAPTER NINETEEN

"IT'S BEEN A week. I know we were all for allowing Rachel time to figure this relationship out with Adriane, but I'm starting to worry. If she truly wants to be there, wants to work things out with this guy, then why hasn't she called anyone?"

Ari and Rosabella watched Lia walk slowly about the room while voicing her alarm. All three of them were uneasy with their role in this matter. Each one of them had spoken to Rafe, had talked him into giving Adriane a week to win Rachel's heart.

"I agree, darling. I think it's time we go and see her," Rosabella said, a worried frown settling between her eyebrows.

"I just hope she doesn't hate us for talking Rafe out of flying in and bringing her back," Ari said. "What if things have been really bad for her?"

The women fell silent as they thought for a moment about Rachel and her circumstances.

"So what do we do now?" Lia seemed so lost, so downtrodden, which was the opposite of how the normally confident woman always appeared.

"We go over there. If her entire family descends on the palace and she's being held against her will, then he either hands her over or we begin a war."

Both Lia and Ari looked at Rosabella with their mouths agape. She was such a small woman, always quiet and respectful. They'd never imagined something like the word *war* would come from her mouth.

"I'm with you, Mom," Lia said, a small grin making an appearance on her face.

"Where did this fire come from?" Ari asked, unable to help herself.

"I usually have no reason to get riled up, Ari darling. But, when I can't speak to my child, I will willingly go into battle. I wasn't always just a mother. Did you know I once served in a volunteer organization that traveled the world doing service work and teaching young women self-defense? We went to many countries and the places I saw opened my eyes to the tragedies people encounter. It was why I was so insistent with your father that you children be taught humility. Just because we were always blessed with money didn't mean that's how the rest of the world is. Too many wealthy children have no idea of how many kids go to sleep at night with a hungry belly."

"I didn't know that, Mom," Lia said as she looked through new eyes at the woman who'd raised her. For her mother to leave the comfort of her home for an extended period of time to help others was impressive. Lia felt selfish as she sat with her mom and waited for her to continue.

"Yes. My family was well off and I thought I would go with this group and save lives while also seeing the world. I was humbled pretty quickly. It wasn't all glory, all sitting ensconced in a nice, safe hotel room. We stayed in the impoverished areas with these families, lived in the conditions they lived in, learned why and how they were there. Sometimes, it was as simple as they'd been born into it, and sometimes it was because life had just been hard, but no one chooses to sleep in the streets. They do it because they have nowhere else to go. I will never judge the world again in the way I did when I was a young teen."

"Where did you go?" Ari asked, mesmerized by this new information.

"My favorite place was America. That was a culture shock for me back then. Before that time, all I'd known was our small village. Your grandparents had a beautiful garden that we ate from all summer long, that we appreciated and we used it all. In America, I was shocked by the abundance of everything, but shocked more by how so many still went without in the midst of plenty."

"Were you safe?"

"Oh, yes. We never were alone and learned where we could and couldn't go. It was a time of learning for me and I grew much stronger, but I was always safe. By the time I left the group, a full year had passed. I was almost sad to see that time end. I grew stronger, more independent, and learned to never take my own life and its privileges for granted again. I also learned to fight for what I wanted and what I believed in."

"I'm so proud of you, Mom. Why didn't you suggest that Rachel, Rafe or I do something like this?"

"The world is different now. Yes, there are some great programs to expand the horizons of young people, but with the wealth that your father had accumulated, we worried someone might try to kidnap you for ransom. That's why we volunteered through local programs instead," Rosabella said.

"I guess I understand that," Lia said, though her mother's tale had showed her how much she'd missed.

"Remember that summer we all built a home with Habitat for Humanity. Shane fell off the roof while he was showing off in front of the girls who were there," Rosabella said with a laugh.

"Yeah, Shane is always showing off *or taking off*," Lia muttered.

"I think you are too hard on Shane. He's a good man, Lia."

"He's lied to me over and over again. I never even knew he was a part of the military," Lia defended herself.

"Don't hold it against Shane that he cares about others' safety," Rosabella told her.

"You knew?" Lia asked. Was she the last to know everything?

"Of course I knew, darling, but it wasn't my information to give out. Shane keeps his secrets because it's his way of protecting himself. You need to understand that and forgive him for not always sharing. The life he led before meeting Rafe wasn't a pleasant one."

"I know. I met his mother," Lia said, feeling a little shame at what he'd gone through. She'd been so mad at him, but if she'd grown up the way he had, wouldn't she be leery of showing vulnerability to others? Maybe she'd judged him too harshly.

"The first time he met our family, he had quite a chip on his shoulder; his anger at everyone and everything was really weighing him down. He and your brother had become close friends before they ever entered college, but Shane was still very suspicious of strangers' motives. When he came to our home and saw the kind of money Rafe had grown up with, he became even more suspicious. He automatically assumed that your father and I wouldn't want Rafe associating with him. He was wrong. I loved him from that first day. It took him a while to let us in, but when he did, we learned what a truly big heart he had. He wants to share it, Lia. He's just afraid that his gift of love will be thrown back in his face. After all, it *has* been, many times, and by people who should love him more than any other."

Lia felt like squirming beneath her mother's knowing gaze. Is that what she'd done? Had she thrown Shane's gift away? But he'd lied to her, she tried to reason.

Hadn't she protected herself, too, quickly judging him so she could be the first to run when the relationship didn't work out? This was a man she'd wanted for so long she couldn't remember a time of not yearning for his touch. Yet at the first sign of rejection, or of seeing him threatening to pull away from her, she'd rushed to pull away first.

She had a lot to think about.

"I'm afraid," she admitted, not knowing what to do now.

"If you aren't scared, then you probably don't have true feelings for him, Lia. You are a passionate girl, and that will carry over into every aspect of your life. Just don't be so afraid that you pass up a good thing. Nothing truly worth having comes to us easily."

Lia thought over her mother's words as the three women had afternoon tea and waited to hear from Rafe. Soon, they would go see Rachel and one worry would be alleviated. Then Lia needed to focus on how she felt about Shane and what she was going to do about their relationship.

The afternoon passed, and still no answers came to Lia. This wasn't easy — not easy at all. But if it were easy, would she want it? She'd always been up for a challenge, always wanted what she was told she couldn't have. Was that her problem? Now that Shane wanted her, was she losing interest?

She ruled that out with a definite no.

She could never lose interest in him.

That left her with the challenge of trying to figure out what her next move would be. As of now, she still didn't know.

CHAPTER TWENTY

RACHEL HAD BEEN a little sad to leave the safe haven of Adriane's castle on his private island. She'd hated the place at first, felt trapped and left with no choices, but then the castle had grown on her. She'd enjoyed the peacefulness there.

It didn't make up for the fact that Adriane hadn't given her any choice but to stay in his country, but she would enjoy showing the island to her children one day when they were old enough to visit.

"What do you think of Corythia?" Adriane asked quietly, then continued speaking before she could answer. "It is quite beautiful. I'm still hopeful you will fall in love with my country and won't be in a hurry to leave."

Rachel looked at Adriane across the table and didn't know what to say. Yes, Corythia was beautiful, and she was enjoying the small café he'd brought her to, their table sitting on an open deck overlooking the ocean. But this wasn't her home, and it never would be.

Add to that the fact that she was still in shock after learning a few days ago that she was going to have not one but two babies, and in less than six months — she couldn't seem to process anything at the moment. Even Adriane's words were taking longer to filter through her head.

Still strongly against the idea of marrying a man for the sake of children, she was confused beyond that point. Should she try to get to know Adriane?

They were both going to be parents whether they were ready or not.

If she left Corythia now, she would know virtually nothing about him. Yes, he'd been wrong in taking her from her home, but he hadn't done so out of malice; he'd acted out of loyalty to the child — or children — she carried in her womb.

If he'd been monstrous toward her, then she'd have her answer. But he hadn't been. He'd pushed her, and tried demanding marriage and talking her into having sex again, but he hadn't actually forced her to do anything besides stay in his castle.

It was time to get to know him. That wouldn't happen if she were focused only on escape.

"I'm not going to marry you, Adriane, but I have decided to spend one month with you — not in a sexual way," she hastened to add when he began to smile. "I believe it's important for me to know the father of my children. When the time comes, I will be leaving, though, either with your blessing or under fire from your guards. I will not be held against my will any longer."

Rachel didn't take her eyes from Adriane; she wanted to watch his reaction. She was hoping she would be able to trust him at some point. There was no way she'd allow her children to spend time with him if she feared she wouldn't get them back.

"I can agree to a month," he said, and from the expression on his face, she had no idea whether he was speaking the truth or not.

Only time would tell.

"So you will stop with all this insistence on marriage?" she asked, needing his promise.

Adriane grimaced, but he didn't turn away from her.

"I will stop speaking of it," he said.

That wasn't a good enough answer.

"Look, Adriane, on the jet you said you would back off on the marriage thing, but you haven't honored that promise. If you want me to trust you, then you have to give me a reason to do so. You have to keep your word."

She looked him dead in the eyes as she spoke, letting him know she was serious and wasn't going to back down.

After a long pause, he nodded. It wasn't agreement, but it was the best he was going to give her right now. Because she didn't want to fight, she decided to let this one thing go. The next time he brought the subject of marriage up, she'd light into him.

She enjoyed their meal, and they spoke about safe topics through the main course. For the first time since the two of them had met again after

Florida, they'd agreed to a cease-fire, and Rachel felt a smidgeon of hope that the two of them could become friends.

"Did you always know you were going to be king?" she asked as their dessert was placed before them, an elaborate chocolate torte.

"No. My older brother was supposed to take the reins of the king-dom, but he left when we were teenagers. My father was heartbroken. There was never any question that I would step up, though it wasn't something I wanted."

"What if you had said no?"

Adriane looked at her with surprise, as if such a concept was com-pletely foreign to him. "That was never going to happen."

He didn't elaborate.

"Would the country fall apart? What happens if no one wants to be king?" It was something she'd never really thought about before.

What if Adriane had no more children and the babies she carried didn't want to ascend to the throne?

"Corythia has always been ruled by the direct descendants of my family line. Each father has passed the crown to the eldest son, unless something happened to that child; then it went down to the next-eldest son. If there is a male heir, which there always has been, then the oldest living son takes the crown. If there were nothing but female heirs, the crown would be passed to the next line of male heirs, such as an uncle or the closest in line of the male cousins. That has never happened here. There has always been a male heir."

"That's sexist," Rachel said.

"There's a reason behind this, Rachel. The king is supposed to be able to lead his troops into battle," he said, as if that were a perfectly acceptable reason.

"A woman could just as easily lead the troops," Rachel interjected.

Adriane sighed as if speaking to a small child, and he looked at her indulgently. "The women are to be protected," he said, then with a glint in his eye, added, "so that they can tend the home front, prepare the meals and serve their husbands."

Rachel looked at him and couldn't tell if he was kidding or not. The gleam in his eye seemed to say he was trying to rile her, but she was worried.

"My children will not be raised thinking that women are the weaker sex, Adriane. I think men should cherish and protect their women, love them, but also give them respect. The way you are talking are the ways of our ancestors. Women can now protect their husbands, too. Today, there isn't anything a man can do that a woman can't."

"I disagree. There are many tasks that are more suited to a man than a woman. But don't fret, there are also many tasks that are more suited to a woman than a man," he said, obviously trying to rile her now.

"Do I dare ask which tasks are suited to which sex?"

"Well, men are the hunters, the ones to bring home the food and keep the home safe. Women keep the home fires burning, so to speak, having the home ready for her warrior when he returns home with provisions."

Rachel's mouth dropped open as she looked at this modern king, wearing his hand-tailored black Armani suit and silk tie. Had he really just said that?

"Did we just lose two hundred years? Am I missing something?" she finally asked.

"I am pushing you a bit, Rachel. I'm sorry, I can't help myself. The fire that lights in your eyes is too irresistible. However, I don't like all this modernization the world is so into these days."

"You don't like phones?" she asked with open sarcasm, not even close to forgiving him.

"That's not what I'm speaking of. I don't like the fact that women are now sent off to war, only to return in a flag-draped casket. I think it's wrong that a man so easily walks away from his children to leave the woman to struggle, tearing up her hands while she tries to earn the barest pittance so her young ones won't starve. It is wrong that the men of today don't take care of their families. That is our duty, our responsibility. What is so wrong with believing that a woman should be looked after?"

His words were wrong, in thinking women lesser than men, but she could see that his heart was in the right place. He thought it a man's responsibility to take care of his woman. She couldn't fault him for that — she even respected him a little for it. However, he would have to learn that women could do whatever it took to survive. And not only that, they could make a great life for themselves without the aid of a man if they so chose.

"I don't see that we are going to come to an agreement on this subject. I was taught from a young age that I could do anything I wanted. Yes, there are tasks more suited to the male or female sex, but not what you're speaking of. There were many things I tried just because I had watched my brother or sister try them first and I wanted to be just like both of them. I went through a phase where I refused to wear a dress because it slowed me down. I have slid into home base in the rain, covering myself from head to foot in mud, I have pitched my own tent, and

I've even taken a class to learn how to change a tire and handle basic auto mechanics. Women are capable, Adriane. It's their choice which direction they want to take their lives in."

"You do amaze me, Rachel. I know your family, know how you grew up. You are not what I would expect you to be," he said as he reached across the table and took her hand, lifting it to his mouth and kissing her knuckles before laying their entwined fingers down on the table.

Before Rachel could respond, there was a racket inside the restaurant, and suddenly the doors that separated them from the rest of the diners flew open and slammed against the wall. The two guards on duty while they were out had their guns drawn; they spoke in rapid French, yelling at the intruder to stand down.

Adriane jumped from his seat, immediately thrusting Rachel behind his back as he yelled to the waiter, who ran over and grabbed hold of Rachel, pulling her away from the scene, toward what she assumed was an emergency exit.

"I'm getting my sister right now!"

Rachel froze at the sound of Rafe's voice, nearly tripping as the waiter continued tugging on her.

"Rafe?" Rachel called, shocked to see her brother burst through the doors in a rage.

His eyes connected with her, and he rushed forward.

"Fire!" one of the guards cried.

CHAPTER TWENTY-ONE

"NO!" RACHEL SCREAMED as she struggled furiously to get free of the waiter. "Don't touch my brother!"

Before the guard was able to shoot, Adriane called out an order and his men turned toward him in confusion. The waiter who held Rachel lost his grip in his surprise. She couldn't tell what Adriane had said, but it was enough that it allowed Rafe to get onto the deck and rush forward.

He reached her, and the waiter placed himself between her and Rafe — a stupid move on his part. Without pausing, Rafe lifted his fist, dropping the waiter with one solid punch to the jaw, and then he pulled Rachel against him in an embrace that was warm and full of relief.

"I'm sorry I didn't come sooner. Ari thought you would want the time to get to know Adriane better. I disagreed, but she insisted. So did Lia and our mother. *Women!*" Rachel gave him a severe but affectionate look, and he continued. "Oh, sorry, Rachel. Anyway, then, when I was unable to get through to you, I panicked, thinking I'd made the wrong decision. It took some major connections of mine to help me find out where you were today, but I got here as quickly as I could. Have you been harmed?"

The world saw her brother as a heartless business tycoon. She knew the truth. He was a good man, one who loved his family more than anything else in his life. He had been an ass when it came to his personal relationships, but being with Ari had changed him. He was back to the brother she'd always loved and respected.

"I'm fine, Rafe. I promise. I came out to this nice little café without being dragged. I'm glad you love me enough to risk your life to rescue me, and a few days ago I would have run away with you in a heartbeat, but Adriane and I are talking now. He's a fool to think he can demand marriage, but if I can get the chance to know him a little more for the sake of my baby, then I think I owe that to…him or her, and to myself." She was afraid to mention that there were actually two babies, fearing that her brother would pass out.

"You can tell me the truth, Rachel. I'm not afraid of Adriane or his guards. If you want to leave and you're worried about what will happen, you don't need to be," he said, looking carefully at her expression in case she might be sending him a secret signal.

"I promise I'm doing fine now, Rafe. I wouldn't lie to you. I need to stay for just a little longer, but when the time comes for me to leave, if Adriane gives me any trouble at all, I will contact you — well, I will if I can get through on the freaking phone line," she said, looking past her brother to where Adriane was glaring daggers at Rafe, obviously not happy about this intrusion. He was most likely worried that Rachel would try to leave now.

Soon. But not now.

"I need to be certain. I'm not going anywhere until all of us speak," Rafe said, turning his head to meet and return Adriane's glare.

"You could have gotten yourself killed, Rafe. You should know better than to burst in the way you did," Adriane said as he approached.

"And you should know better than to kidnap my sister and then not allow her to contact me," Rafe snapped, keeping his arm protectively around Rachel.

Adriane noticed the gesture and he didn't seem to like it.

"Why don't we head back to the palace, where we can speak privately?" Adriane suggested.

Rafe looked as if he wanted to refuse, but Rachel threw him an encouraging smile and he nodded his head.

"Good," Adriane said, and he turned and walked stiffly toward the open doors, where his uneasy guardsmen stood by.

The waiter Rafe had knocked out was now rising to his feet and looking none too pleased. Divining that he might be happy to stab her brother with a steak knife, Rachel positioned herself between the two of them without her brother's knowledge.

Adriane had a short conversation with one of his men and then the guards followed them out, watching Rafe as if he could be a snake about to strike.

They all left the restaurant and made their way to the vehicles parked out front.

The drive to the palace was silent and tense, and when they arrived and walked inside, they moved through the palace with distinct uneasiness.

Once Adriane had led Rafe and Rachel inside his sitting room, he headed immediately to the liquor cabinet, dismissing his guards so the three could be alone. Rachel had no doubt the men were pressed up against the door, waiting for any aggression on Rafe's part.

"Your week is up, Adriane. I've come for my sister." Rafe walked up beside him and took a glass without bothering to ask. He also ignored what Rachel had just said to him at the café. Pouring himself a large glass of whiskey, he then moved over to the couch and sat down as if not worried in the least about the way the confrontation would end.

"Your sister and I will wed," Adriane said, speaking calmly as he sat across from Rafe.

Rachel was irritated as she watched the two men puff up their chests. Shouldn't she be the one speaking? What she would say, though, was a bit of a problem, for after wanting nothing more than to leave for the past week, she was now confused by her desire to stay. She'd probably start off by expressing her disgust for the ludicrous display of testosterone in front of her.

Before she could say anything, Rafe jumped in again. "She hasn't agreed to marry you. Rachel wouldn't do that without talking to her family first."

"Did you bother to ask your family's permission before proposing to your bride?" Adriane countered.

"They all love Ari."

"That's not the point. Rachel is an adult who can make her own decisions. She doesn't need your blessing in order to be married."

"Well, she sure as hell needs to agree, and not be forced to marry you!" Rafe thundered.

"She carries my children," Adriane thundered back.

Rafe sank back at Adriane's words before he turned his head in Rachel's direction.

"Children?" he asked.

"I'm having twins," she admitted, as a smile turned up the corners of her lips and she fought back tears. Finally, she was telling Rafe something firsthand. Well, sort of, since Adriane had been the one to blurt out the word *children*. She was glad that her brother was sitting down.

Rafe was stunned speechless, something she'd never seen before. It was almost enough to make her giggle — almost, but not quite. Not with the amount of tension in the room.

"Are you happy, Rach?"

Was she happy? No. There was too much pressure weighing down on her right now. But she was glad to be carrying her twins. She felt protective, felt like a mother. She was looking forward to meeting them. By then, she would have a clear plan of what she wanted to do.

"I'm not unhappy, Rafe. I already love these tiny babies growing inside me."

"I think you need to just come home with me. You need your family right now," he advised her.

Rachel saw Adriane tense at those words. It was obvious he wasn't going to allow that to happen without one hell of a fight. Would the battle be worth it? Rafe could get hurt or even killed trying to protect her. Then, she would never forgive the father of her children.

"I will come home soon, Rafe. I promise you. I want to spend time with mother, and I need my sister and best friend. Oh, my gosh!" she exclaimed as her eyes widened.

"What?" he asked, tensing with concern.

"I have been so wrapped up in myself this week, I haven't even thought of poor Ari and the wedding. Adriane told me the wedding was put off because of this situation. I'm so incredibly sorry, Rafe. That shouldn't have happened. How is she doing? Are you both OK?" she asked as she stepped up to him.

"We are both fine. I want to make her my bride as soon as possible, but she won't go through with it without you. That's just another reason for you to come home with me," he said.

"Oh, Rafe." Talk about feeling torn.

As if Adriane understood her indecision, he popped in with a proposal.

"We will hold the wedding here. It would be my honor to host it in the royal cathedral."

Both Rafe and Rachel turned toward Adriane, who was looking quite pleased with himself for finding an adequate solution to the problem.

"Your family can all be guests here at the palace," Adriane continued. "Then Rachel can also visit with her mother. I am quite certain our mothers will get along remarkably well. They will probably drive the staff crazy," he said with a fond smile. It was obvious his mother had a special place in his heart. That was something that was certainly in his favor.

"Having the wedding here would be too much trouble for everyone here," Rachel said, but she really liked the idea. She would have those she loved here, and at the same time, she'd have even more time with Adriane. It would help her discover whether she could comfortably leave her children with him for holidays or summer breaks. After all, if he wanted to be a dad, she would be in the wrong to deny him those rights, as painful as not having her children around during those times would be.

"Of course we can. I am the king and can do as I wish," he said with a wink.

"Could we, Rafe?" Rachel asked, turning to her brother, her eyes lit with excitement at the thought. It would be quite romantic, in her opinion, to see a wedding on the palace grounds.

"I would have to talk to Ari," he said hesitantly, annoyed that he was being backed into a corner.

"Oh, you don't have to wait. I'll call her right now," she said, but her eyes narrowed as she turned to Adriane. "I can call her, right?" she asked with a clear threat in her tone.

"Of course. Be my guest," he said as he gestured grandly toward an antique writing desk.

Rachel marched over to the phone and picked it up, dialing the number and expecting to get the operator. When the call went straight through, she sent another withering glare Adriane's way. Did the man have a timer set for when the calls could go through and when they couldn't?

That would be another discussion the two of them would have.

Ari was thrilled at the idea of a royal palace wedding, and the two girls laughed as they reconnected. Then Ari insisted on talking to Rafe so she could get the transportation arranged.

By the time Rafe got off the phone, it was obvious that he was going to do what Ari and Rachel wanted.

"It looks like we will have our wedding here. How quickly can it be arranged?" he asked.

"As soon as your family arrives, the women can speak to the palace coordinator. It could be arranged in less than a week if you'd like," Adriane said, relaxed now in complete satisfaction because he'd managed to get what he wanted.

"Good. We'll come back to the discussion of my sister leaving when this is all over."

"I look forward to it," Adriane said.

Challenge issued — challenge accepted.

CHAPTER TWENTY-TWO

"IF SEX COULD be bottled, labeled and sold, Shane's picture would be the image on the glass." Lia was watching him emerge from the ocean and fling back his head, his dark strands gleaming as the droplets of cool ocean water soared toward the sky.

That was just the beginning. With his shorts hanging low on his hips, showing that appealing line of hair disappearing beneath the dark blue fabric, and water trickling to areas her fingers had stroked before — hell, more than her fingers — she was quickly becoming a puddle of lust.

He had to be doing it on purpose.

Damn the man.

"You just took the words from my mouth," Ari said as she fanned her face, though when Lia looked over at her in surprise, she had to smile because Ari's eyes were nowhere near Shane. They were glued to Rafe, who was currently riding a wave on a surfboard.

"Yuck. Quit drooling over my brother," Lia teased.

"Not gonna happen," Ari said with a grin as she managed to tug her gaze back to her friend. "This place is pure heaven. No wonder you're in no hurry to leave, Rachel."

"I didn't say that," Rachel replied. "I just said that I'm going to get to know Adriane. It's the responsible thing to do." Her gaze took in the king of Corythia as he ran down the beach and dived smoothly into the water, his back muscles flexing. "But the view isn't half bad," she admitted with a frustrated sigh.

"Why don't you just get it over with and screw his brains out?" Lia asked with a giggle before she picked up her coconut cocktail and leaned back, taking a long sip.

"Because that's not what this is about," Rachel said, though she didn't even sound convincing to herself.

The last few days, Adriane had upped the ante, so to speak. He'd been charming, and sweet, and his mother was amazing. Rachel was very grateful her family had arrived. Her resolve was wavering, and nothing good could come from her joining Adriane in his giant bed. A lot of pleasure — but nothing good.

That didn't even make sense to her, so she decided not to analyze it.

The women were all silent as their eyes once again strayed to their men, whether they claimed them or not.

Lia hadn't said a word to Shane since he'd arrived a few hours before. She could see the stress behind his eyes, but before she'd worked up the courage to ask him about it, he'd given her a cocky smile, leaned down and kissed her hard, then run off.

Now, he was prancing in front of her on the beach, half naked, and he didn't seem to have a care in the world. She must have imagined the haunted look. The man obviously didn't have a soul, so what could possibly be haunting him, anyway?

The guards, ever present wherever King Adriane might be, were a bit of a distraction, and they had to be overheated in their full gear, but Lia brushed it off. She was sitting at the beach on a wonderful day and she wasn't going to let anything ruin this.

Lia didn't know how long the silence among the three females stretched on, but she was rudely interrupted by a soft towel smacking her in the face.

"What the hell?" she muttered as she grabbed the white towel and turned to see who'd been so rude.

"I just thought you'd want to wipe the drool from your face. You're overheating like a dog in some serious need of water. Do you want us to carry you out to the water to cool you down?" Rachel asked with a laugh.

"I was *not* drooling!" Lia said, but she couldn't help but join in the laughter. Maybe she had been salivating just a little. Once you'd slept with a man as appealing as Shane, it was impossible not to picture lying beneath him when he was bouncing around in front of her with nothing on but a pair of low-riding shorts.

Was it terrible of her to wish for a sneaker wave to pull those shorts right off him?

Maybe. But she didn't even care. His ass was solid and fine, and she wouldn't mind another glimpse. Maybe she should just give in to what her body wanted and have one more hot night with him.

No!

If she didn't have feelings for the man, then that might have been possible, but as it was, she felt far too much for her sexy ex and she still hadn't come up with any answers. Sleeping with him before she did would just break her heart all the more when he ended up leaving her again. If she decided she could handle that kind of fallout, then they'd stay in bed for a week together.

Maybe she should come to the decision that she could handle it.

"It's just very humid here," Lia finally said, knowing the two girls weren't going to believe her for a minute.

"That's OK, Lia. Your brother gets me all hot and bothered to the point that I can't even breathe when he looks like he does now. I can't believe we're going to be married in just a few more days," she said, her eyes following Rafe as he fell from the board, splashing into the water.

"Seriously, I know you're in love and all, but it's a bit disturbing to hear my brother talked about that way," Rachel said, grimacing. "Don't get me wrong. I don't mind him being looked at like a sex object. I mean, how many guys do the same with our gender? It's just being forced to picture *my own brother* as a sex object that I object to. I don't want to hear about him and sex in the same sentence. I've avoided all magazine articles about him for that very reason."

"Mmm, your king is a close second," Ari said as she looked over to where Rafe and Adriane were paddling out side by side.

They weren't smiling.

Both men were still at odds, but it had to get better eventually. Neither of them would cry uncle, so it was a macho-man contest now to see who could ride the biggest wave for the longest amount of time.

"I hope they both face-plant," Rachel muttered as the men lifted up on their boards and began riding the wave toward the beach.

"Me too," Lia said just for the heck of it.

"You two are terrible," Ari said, but her eyes never strayed from Rafe.

"You're just sickeningly in love," Rachel grumbled.

"You could be too, Rachel. That man's eyes stray to you about every five seconds, which is why he just belly-flopped. It's kind of amusing, actually. Look at the guards. They don't like this one bit. They keep edging closer and closer to the water," Ari said with a giggle.

Just then a wave came up and soaked one of the guard's pristine black shoes and the bottom of his trousers, making the man jump back. Ari was impressed that his face never showed his discomfort. As he stood there, he had to be miserable with the heat and now soaked oxfords. He should have just taken them off, but she knew he wouldn't.

"So you're not even considering going for it with the king?" Ari asked. "Come on. You were practically panting like a dog in heat when you talked about your weeklong affair. The man wants to marry you. Why not just give it a chance?"

"No. It would never work out. We're too different. Besides, if I married him, I'd be queen. It's not something I've really processed, but I do know that I don't even have my own life figured out, let alone know how to rule a country."

"It's probably not that bad. Don't you just wave a lot for the cameras? How hard could it be?" Ari asked.

"From what I've learned, there's a lot more than smiling and cutting ribbons," Rachel replied. "You're on charity boards, and you help organize fundraisers. People come to you and expect answers. I wouldn't know what to say or what to do. What if I did something that ended up leaving the people of Corythia scandalized forever? What if I embarrassed my children as they got older?" When Ari and Lia laughed, Rachel said, "OK, I'll most likely do that anyway, but I hope not on camera in front of the entire world. Anyway, no. I can't marry him. Besides, I won't marry for anything less than love. I've always felt that way."

"Isn't it possible that you will fall in love?" Lia asked, her eyes drooping a little as she spoke the words.

"Yes. I could fall in love, could give my heart to this man. That's the biggest problem of all. He has told me he won't fall in love. It's about duty and honor and the heir to the throne. None of it's about me," Rachel replied. Her voice was thick with melancholy.

"Aww, Rachel. He'd be a fool not to fall in love with you," Ari said, and she wrapped her arm around her friend's shoulder, giving her a reassuring squeeze.

"Well, you are agreeing to stay here and get to know him. That says something," Lia reminded her.

"Yes, that says that I want to know the father of my children. I don't want to tell them that I had a seven-day affair and then never saw him again. We have great parents, Lia. I think Adriane and I can be great parents, too. We just have to get past the bickering. He's agreed to quit talking about marriage, at least for now, but he seems to slip a little too often."

"I can't imagine that he's a man who's easily swayed. Maybe he's just trying to appease you for now. We could always sneak you out of here at a moment's notice. All you have to do is ask," said Lia.

"I know. You have no idea how much I appreciate that," Rachel replied. "I love you both so much."

"Well, Mom will be here in a couple of days and I dare the king to tell *her* no. If you want to leave, nothing in this universe will stop her from bringing you home," Lia said.

"True. I may just have to keep her here until I'm ready to go. She's quite protective," Rachel said. She felt better just sitting there with her sister and friend and knowing her mom would be there soon. There was so much she needed to talk to all of them about.

"Yes, but be prepared for the lecture of a lifetime for not telling her about the pregnancy sooner. She was devastated to find out secondhand that you were carrying her first grandchild," Lia warned.

"I feel so bad about that — like a terrible daughter. I should have trusted Mom."

"She is pretty excited about it, even if she had hoped you'd be married to a wonderful man and settled down first. When she finds out you're having twins, she's going to be over the moon. I want to be there when you tell her. It's taken every ounce of control I have not to spill the beans over the phone," Lia said.

"Thanks for waiting, sis. I want to see her reaction. I do have to admit that I was grateful to miss the initial reaction, though. She must have turned white as a ghost."

"That about describes it," Ari said.

"I am really sorry about the wedding, Ari."

"You have apologized ten thousand times now for something that was beyond your control. Please stop, because you're making me feel bad about it. Everything worked out perfectly anyway. Now, I get to marry in a royal cathedral, just like a princess," Ari said.

"Everything happens for a reason. This will be the best wedding day ever," Rachel promised.

"I have no doubt about it."

Just then, all three men stepped from the water, walking up the beach together.

All conversation stopped as the girls watched the show almost in slow motion: water dripping down toned stomachs, hair practically sparkling in the hot sun, and strides, long and muscled, as the men made their way on the sand.

It was a calendar photo shoot come to life, and it was one hell of a picture. The three girls stared, their breathing becoming a bit more shallow as the oxygen seemed to be sucked from the air.

"Do you ladies mind sharing?" Rafe asked as they reached them.

Ari forgot to speak as she looked at Rafe, relaxed, tanned and sexy as hell. *Oh, this man is about to declare to the world and God that he's mine forever,* she thought, dancing with glee inside.

"Of course not," she replied, wanting nothing more than for him to join her on her chaise longue. She could forget there was anyone else on the beach as long as she was looking into the rich purple-blue eyes of her lover.

"You look good enough to eat," Rafe said as he sat down at her feet, lifting her legs up and placing them in his lap.

"I was thinking the same thing about you," she said, leaning forward for a kiss. She just couldn't resist tasting his mouth.

"Why don't I take you back to the palace so we can get cleaned up?" he asked, and her stomach clenched.

"Yes, I really should get out of this sun," she agreed, leaping from the chair and bounding forward with Rafe right on her heels.

"Go for a walk with me, Lia," Shane suggested while he grabbed a crystal glass full of ice-cold water from a table and guzzled it before sitting down on her chair.

"I'm fine right here," she told him, knowing that if she went anywhere with him, talking would be the last thing on her mind.

"Yes, you are," he replied with a deep rumble in his voice as he scanned her from head to toe, making her feel as if she'd just been thoroughly loved without the happy ending.

"Shane..." she began, still not knowing what she was going to say.

"These two need to be alone," Adriane said as he held out a hand to Rachel.

Lia was horrified when her sister took his offered fingers and then walked away without another word to Lia.

Then it was just the two of them — she and Shane, all alone — because the guards followed Adriane, and this was his private beach.

"Alone at last and we didn't even have to go anywhere," Shane said as he leaned forward.

"I don't want to do this, Shane," Lia said, holding out her hand.

"Oh, yes, you do, baby. Just as much as I do," he countered.

Closing the small distance between them, he kissed her the way she'd been imagining him doing all day.

Her will went from strong to gone in a heartbeat as his tongue slipped across her closed mouth.

What was one more mistake? she thought as she caved in to her body's demands.

CHAPTER TWENTY-THREE

"I HAVE NEVER WANTED so badly to pound someone into a bloody pulp!"

Ari walked beside Rafe as they strolled down the beach, watching as the sun slowly lowered, and its beautiful rays cast colors on the calm ocean water. She smiled as he ranted about Adriane and what a terrible man he was.

"He just thinks he can do whatever he wants — take her away and not suffer any consequences from it!"

Now it was time for her to speak. She'd been waiting. "And you have never done anything like that?" Her voice was quiet as she waited for her words to sink in.

"I wouldn't..." he began to say as he stopped and turned toward her. She simply raised an eyebrow in response.

"Why are you with me?" he asked as he saw his past actions in a new and thoroughly unpleasant light which left him amazed to see her still standing before him.

"Is that an honest question? Do you want the real answer?"

He looked at her, his mind spinning while the muscles in his jaw tensed in apprehension of what she might say.

"Yes," he finally said, taking her hand and leading her to a small hill looking over the picturesque beach.

"I'm with you because you saw the errors of your ways. I'm with you because before you, I was merely going through the motions of life, doing what I was supposed to be doing, being the perfect daughter, the honor student, the person I thought everyone wanted me to be. And then I met you." She stopped for a minute. "You certainly weren't part of what I was supposed to be doing. You terrified me, Rafe. You were a monster in my eyes."

Rafe winced as she spoke, until she lifted her hand and caressed his cheek.

"I was afraid of you, but not for long. Then, something changed. I was angry that you were forcing me into the situation you did, but the bottom line is that I wouldn't have stayed had I not also felt some excitement about it. Yes, I was mad, and, yes, there were times I wanted to throttle you, but you also made me feel things I never imagined feeling. You may have been a barbarian in your methods, but — I am almost ashamed to admit this — you stirred excitement in me that I had never felt before."

"The entire time?" he asked, as if completely awed.

"Yes," she admitted. "When you pushed me to do those things in the bedroom, I thought I would be filled with terror and maybe even disgust, but I was aroused. When you tied me to that toy, that circular apparatus, my entire body was turned on. I was afraid of you for all of two seconds. I've been turned on by you since the moment we met. Yes, you were a very sexy monster. I didn't want to be only your plaything, only someone you thought you owned; I wanted your love, too. But the way you make me feel has never changed. I feel desired, and sexy, and the sex …well, it's out of this world." Ari's face flushed.

"Out of this world, huh?" he asked, his eyes darkening as the sun sank, and its tangerine hue started to evaporate into the gentle wind.

"Oh, Rafe, the sex is indescribable!" she said as his hand trailed up her leg and slid beneath the hem of her shorts, making her breath rush from her mouth.

"So my sweet little Ari likes a bit of excitement in the bedroom?" he pushed.

"Oh, yes," she gasped as his fingers reached the edge of her panties. Thank goodness for loose shorts. Ari leaned back to give him easier access.

"I have been so afraid of chasing you away that I've been a complete gentleman for the last few weeks. I figured that was what you wanted."

"I love the man you are, Rafe. I can't wait to be your wife. I do like my control-freak lover, too, though," she said shyly. Would he think less of her for admitting this?

"Oh, Ari. You have made me one very, very a happy man," he said as he removed his hand, making her whimper in frustration before he grabbed her by the waist and hoisted her onto his lap.

"Then show me how happy you are," she demanded, grabbing his head and pulling him closer so she could taste the sweetness of his lips.

"Are you trying to take control, my darling Ari?" he asked as he grabbed her arms and tugged them behind her back, holding them together with one hand.

"Would I try to do that?" she asked, pushing her hips against his, glorying at the friction as her tingling core met his arousal.

"I think you might. What should I do about that?"

The excitement in his voice made her blood heat as it all rushed to one very sensitive area of her body. This was a game she'd missed playing with him — it was a game she could play well. A game of who would be in charge. It was also a game they both got to win.

"What do you think you can do about it?" she mocked him, leaning back, exulting in the power she felt flowing through his grip as he held her tightly.

"You're about to find out," he growled before reaching his other hand up and tugging on her loose hair, pulling her face toward his.

His lips grazed her mouth, his tongue tracing the edges of her lips, but he didn't connect their mouths fully. He tugged again, making her head fall back as he kissed her jaw, then he ran his lips down the sensitive column of her throat until he met her shoulder, where his teeth nipped her skin just enough to leave the slightest sting.

Before she could say anything, his tongue swept out, soothing the area and making her forget to admonish him. She tried to lift her hands to his shoulders, but his hold on her arms didn't allow it.

She tried to pull away, but to no avail. Instead, her struggles made her core rub vigorously against the solid proof of his desire.

He drew back, his eyes dark and molten in the shadows cast by the last moments of light before night quickly stole over the land.

Releasing her wrists, he shifted her off his lap, then stood up, helping her to her feet, and pulled her to his side. He gave her a seductive smile before grabbing her by the waist and throwing her over his shoulder — showing her he was still the one in control.

Shocked, Ari grabbed his back as he headed up a trail, his movements making her body bounce. "What are you doing?"

"For what I have planned for you, we need total privacy," he said, not pausing in his stride as they neared the palace.

"And I can't walk?" she asked as they entered the palace grounds and passed a guard. Ari was more than a little mortified at being seen like this by Adriane's men.

"No. You are my captive," he said as his hand caressed her bare thigh. "Good evening."

Ari turned her head as they passed another guard protecting the back door of the palace.

"Evening," Rafe replied as he walked past the man. Ari refused to look. Why wasn't anyone asking whether everything was OK? This seemed a bit off.

The two wound their way through the palace. When they arrived at their suite, Rafe strode through the door and didn't quit moving until he reached their "sleeping" quarters. There he released her with a slight bounce onto their massive bed.

"Rafe, that was a bit awkward," she scolded him, crossing her arms and sending quite a glare his way.

His eyes were on fire; he stepped forward without saying a word. His excitement ignited her own desire, though she wasn't going to admit that to him — not after he'd hauled her though the palace like a caveman, and done it in front of witnesses.

"Good," he finally said, and he grabbed the bottom of her shirt and quickly pulled it from her.

"I don't think I'm in the mood anymore," she told him, her slightly breathy statement undercutting her words.

"Liar," he said as he unclasped her bra, freeing her heavy breasts, her hardened nipples proof that he was right.

Still, she had to make a point, didn't she? He'd embarrassed her.

She scooted away, and he grinned as he pulled his shirt off, then stripped off his pants and briefs, freeing his manhood, which stood proud and ready. Her core was in meltdown mode, more than ready for his penetration.

"I think I will make you go unsatisfied," she gasped, and made an effort to retreat as he dropped to the bed and began prowling after her.

"Not going to happen, Ari," he warned, grabbing her legs and pulling her toward him, his body covering hers, his erection pressing against her shorts, causing a moan to escape her throat.

Yeah, he was right. There was no way she would be able to resist him.

Moving quickly, he slid to the side of the bed and stripped the last barrier of her clothing away before once more covering her body with his.

"I can't believe how much I always want you," he said. She knew how he felt.

His lips finally captured hers in a kiss worth receiving, his mouth thoroughly devouring her as his tongue plunged inside, sweeping across the contours of her mouth.

More.

She needed... wanted...had to have...more.

She grabbed him, holding his head securely against her as he seized her mouth, owned it.

Sliding his arousal against her slick folds, but not entering her, Rafe tormented her, making her burn hotter and hotter as his hand slid down her side, grabbed her leg and pulled it up, his hips rocking against hers, his hand clasping her bare behind.

Rafe released her mouth and Ari grumbled. Then he moved away from her, and Ari cried out. *No!* She needed him inside her.

Before she could give voice to her complaints, he rose from the bed and grabbed her feet, pulling her toward him.

Without a word, he lifted her so she was standing flush against him, and his hands circled around her waist before he bent and began sucking on her neck. OK, this was almost as good as the kiss.

His hands caressed her back as his mouth trailed across her shoulder, then moved to the top of her breasts.

"Oh, Rafe, more," she cried out.

His tongue swept across her breasts, circled her nipples and wet the peaks before quickly retreating. It was too fast. She wanted more attention bestowed on her sensitive nipples, not just a quick flicking of his tongue.

Before she could complain, he turned her in his arms, his chest pressing against her back as he placed his hands on her stomach and began raising them upward until his palms cupped her breasts, his fingers grabbing the nipples and pinching them in the most pleasurable ways.

Ari groaned and pushed her backside against his arousal, loving the way he felt in the soft cushion of her derrière.

Rafe suddenly brought his hand around to her back and pushed her forward, making her fall against the bed with her buttocks in the air; his hands moved quickly to grip her hips. Spreading her legs wide open with his knees, he had Ari completely exposed to him.

"Rafe?" she asked, her voice unsure.

"Trust me," he said as the thick head of his arousal rubbed down the line of her cheeks before sliding into her wet core.

Her excitement reached a peak as he sheathed himself deep inside her, his arousal stretching her swollen folds.

With a hard thrust, he sank fully inside, his hips pressed against the curve of her backside, his hands gripping her flesh, holding her firmly in place.

"Oh, my, Ari, you feel so damn good," he growled as he pulled backward before slamming forward hard, hitting her rounded behind with a slap of his hips, making her pleasure build quickly and her core begin to pulse.

He pulled back again, and thrust forward so forcefully that her chest slid along the bed, but his hands held her hips tightly in place as he rocked her rhythmically.

Ari soon felt herself fall over the edge of pleasure, and it didn't take him long to join her. Rafe groaned as his body shook, his hands tightening on her as he convulsed inside her heat.

When his body relaxed, he released his hold on her, and Ari had no doubt his passion would leave its mark on her flesh. That thought only made her excitement and passion begin to build again.

Only with Rafe had she ever felt so possessed. He could do it anytime he wanted. She hoped he would.

"I lose control with you, Ari. I've never experienced that with any other woman," Rafe said as she turned and looked at him. She couldn't tell if he was apologizing or just stating a fact.

"I wouldn't have it any other way," she said, lifting her hand to caress his cheek.

"Mmm," he said, a slight grin lifting the corner of his mouth.

Without warning, he swept her up into his arms as he moved toward their bathroom, not stopping until he reached the shower.

With a turn of the knob, he started the strong jet and stepped inside with her, gently setting her down and facing her toward the water, where the spray began flowing over her still-sensitive skin.

When he moved her so the spray hit her nipples, she cried out and tried to move. Rafe held her in place, and Ari's body began to shake.

"We have all night, baby," he whispered in her ear before his hand moved down her stomach and he found her swollen womanhood.

All night turned out to last until the sun began rising in the sky. Ari fell asleep a very satisfied woman, with Rafe wrapped around her.

Mmm, she would be extremely happy to have her controlling lover at night, and her sweet fiancé during the day. It was the best of both worlds. Of all possible worlds.

If it could last forever, that wouldn't be long enough.

CHAPTER TWENTY-FOUR

Would you please accompany me on a date tonight?
Adriane.

RACHEL LOOKED AT the note with suspicion. What was this new game? Was he actually attempting to court her? That made no sense. Was he asking because now there were witnesses around and he was afraid that one wrong move would send her away from the island on the next available boat or chopper?

Did it matter?

No. Not really. She was determined to get to know this man as much as she could for the sake of her unborn children. If it took going out on a date with him to accomplish her goals, then that is what she needed to do.

"Tell the king I would be pleased to accompany him," she told the servant who was standing by awkwardly while awaiting Rachel's response.

The girl beamed a smile her way before telling Rachel the time to be ready and then giving a small curtsy and scuttling away to inform her king that his message had received a positive response.

Rachel supposed she'd been a little harsh with the palace staff, but what else should they expect when she was held against her will? Of course she would be testy.

Upon finishing her bath a couple of hours later, Rachel stepped into her room, then stopped at the sight before her. Hanging on a rack that must have been brought in while she'd been soaking in the deep tub was an incredible red gown.

Walking to it, she smiled as her hand ran along the silky fabric, which was dotted with shining crystals. The skirt was full, and the dress looked like a perfect fit.

Since she'd been brought here without anything formal of her own, she hadn't even thought about what she would wear, but Adriane had apparently taken care of that matter.

She could be bratty and refuse to wear the lovely gown, but deep down she wanted to put it on, so she relented. Carefully taking the gown off the hanger, she slipped on a pair of her fancy undergarments, then stepped into the dress, sliding the side zipper up before turning to look in the mirror.

It was stunning, and it made her feel like...royalty, actually.

The gown's top dipped low in front, hugging her chest and waist before flaring at her hips, hiding the small bump that was forming on her lower stomach and accenting her femininity and sex appeal. She stepped into the crystal-covered heels with delicate straps that completed the outfit.

She was starting to really look forward to her night out.

"This is not a date — just a night to get to know Adriane better," she said aloud to her reflection in the mirror.

She would have to remind herself of that often if she hoped to keep her heart untouched. It would be too easy to be swept off her feet in her condition. Stupid hormones.

After applying a fresh coat of lip gloss, Rachel was ready when she heard a knock on her door. She turned just in time to see Adriane step through her doorway, and it took a moment for her to catch her breath.

Standing before her in a hand-tailored tuxedo and holding a single rose in his hand, Adriane was drop-dead gorgeous. It didn't hurt that he was looking at her with unalloyed pleasure.

She'd have to fight to remember that they would never be more than friends.

"You are exquisite," he whispered as he approached, the rose dangling in his fingers.

"Thank you, Adriane. You look very debonair," she replied, the intensity of his expression making her cast her eyes shyly downward.

"But something is missing," he said, and her head snapped back up.

As she looked quizzingly at him, he pulled a small box from his pocket, making Rachel take a step back. He hadn't spoken of marriage all week. She really hoped he wasn't about to start again — especially with a ring. It would kill her chances of going out tonight, and she was very much looking forward to it.

When she didn't make a move to take the box, Adriane opened it and held it out. Inside were a breathtaking pair of ruby and diamond earrings, the gems sparkling in the light of the room as he moved the box toward her.

"These will match your gown to perfection," he said as he took her hand tenderly and turned it palm up, placing the small box in the center before releasing her fingers.

Rachel clutched the box carefully, afraid of dropping it. Never before had she received such a lovely gift. Yes, she'd received her share of amazing presents, but never such an expensive — and beautiful — piece of jewelry.

"I can't take these, Adriane," she said. It wouldn't be right, even if she really did want to wear them.

"Of course you can," he countered as he slowly turned her around, leading her to the large mirror of her vanity.

He reached into the box, which she was still holding in her hand, pulled out one of the earrings and handed it to her. "Put them on. I want to see how they look."

She should refuse again, but she couldn't seem to stop herself. She removed the simple gold hoops from her ears and replaced them with the earrings he'd just presented her with.

Adriane was right: they matched the dress as if they had been made just for it. Indeed, they probably had. Turning her head, she couldn't stop her smile as the light sparked off the jewels decorating her small ears and danced in the mirror.

"They are stunning, and I'll wear them tonight, but I won't keep them." She thought that was a fitting compromise, the right thing to do.

"I told you, they are yours. This will complete the outfit," he said as he placed his hands around her neck. Then she felt the cool touch of metal at her throat as he closed a clasp. Looking in the mirror, she was awed by the matching necklace he'd just put on her.

"Oh, Ian," she gasped, reverting to the name she'd called him during their brief affair. "This is simply beautiful. We can argue later about it," she said as her fingers ran along the jewels in the necklace.

The set had to have cost a fortune. This wasn't a gift you gave to a friend, and since she didn't plan to be anything more than that with him, she couldn't rightfully keep it. But, hey, she'd feel like a superstar tonight.

"My lady," he said as he held out his arm. Slipping her arm into his was easy as he led her from the room and straight out of the palace, where a limo awaited them.

Climbing inside, Rachel accepted a glass of sparkling water, then sat back and waited for their night to begin. She had to remind herself again that this was just a night out with a friend when his leg brushed against hers, sending shivers down her spine.

If she hadn't slept with him before, she wouldn't know what she was missing now. Of course, if she hadn't slept with him before, she wouldn't *be* here now. The only reason he was entertaining her was because she carried his children. Otherwise, he wouldn't have anything to do with her. She was just a girl from the States, not someone worthy of being his queen. It would do her well to remember that.

But still, they spent a pleasant evening at a nice restaurant, then watched the opening night of a new musical, one with exquisite costumes and sublime vocal talent, and a full orchestra. The music was touching on many levels, and though she couldn't understand the words, she could fully understand the mood they were conveying. The cast was thrilled when Adriane went backstage and congratulated them on an enjoyable show.

What a pleasure it was for Rachel to see firsthand how much his people adored him. The performers treated him with absolute hero worship, and their manner toward her was very flattering, as well. They must figure that anyone worthy of sharing the company of their king was someone they wanted to know.

If only they knew how wrong they were.

Still, she didn't feel out of place. Adriane kept her at his side, included her in the conversations, and made her feel special. She wished he weren't quite so good at that. This was the charming man she'd fallen fast for in Florida, the man who had made her laugh during the day, and cry out in pleasure during the night.

This was the man she'd had a hard time walking away from.

She just hoped it wasn't so difficult this time, because she knew they weren't right for each other.

He was a king, for goodness sake, not just an average man she could marry and spend the rest of her life with. Even if she wanted to marry him, it would never be just the two of them. He would always be owned by his people, and so would she. That wasn't a responsibility she wanted.

Did that make her a bad person?

Maybe. But it wasn't something she cared to analyze too closely.

One thing she was discovering about Adriane, however, was that he was made to be a king. He was confident with his title, the people loved him, and he would rule this country fairly. She felt pride in knowing him — even if it was for a short time.

"That was pretty fascinating to watch," Rachel said as they walked from backstage, making their way from the theater.

"Yes, it was an entertaining performance," he agreed.

"No. That's not what I meant. You are good with your people, Adriane. It's obvious that you care about them."

Adriane stopped and turned to face her. "I do love my people, Rachel. This kingdom has done well through the years when others have faltered. The reason it's done so well is, quite honestly, because of the people. They work hard even in the worst of times. They are dedicated to Corythia, and they are good to my family. There isn't anything in my power I won't do for them."

"Then they are very lucky to have you," she said, meaning it.

"And I them."

Together they resumed their walk, the doors opening to a virtual mob scene out front. "I'm sorry, Rachel. Word must have leaked out that we were here." He pulled her closer and his guards and a group of police moved in, blocking the people from overwhelming them.

"They're just excited to see you," she said, in a bit of awe as cameras flashed and people called out to their king, asking who Rachel was and whether Adriane could answer questions.

He smiled at the people, spoke a few words in French to tell the crowd he'd like to escort his companion home, and then moved forward, toward the limo.

Out of the corner of her eye, Rachel noticed a commotion, and she turned her head in time to see a small child being knocked to the ground. The people around him were so focused on the king that they didn't notice that the boy was about to get trampled.

Before she was able to pull from Adriane's grasp and rush over to the child, Adriane let her go and took a few quick steps, surging into the crowd, much to the dismay of his guards. He scooped up the boy, who couldn't have been more than six or seven years old, and pulled him from the crowd, then returned to Rachel.

The boy had bruised his cheek in the fall, and there was a tear on his face as he leaned his head against Adriane's shoulder.

"Oh, sweetie, you must have been so scared," Rachel said, extending her hand and gently running her finger down his cheek. When he looked back at her blankly, she realized he would have no idea what she was saying.

"Mon Roi," he whispered as he raised his eyes and looked worshipfully at Adriane.

"What did he say?" Rachel asked, continuing to smile at the boy's little face.

"*My king*," Adriane replied, then spoke to the boy. "Où est ta mère?" *Where is your mother?*

"Elle est dans la foule. Nous sommes venus ici aujourd'hui pour voir notre roi, mais il y a tellement de gens ici que je me suis perdu," he answered in a frightened voice.

"What did he say?" Rachel again asked, determined to start learning French. Otherwise, her children would learn and then talk behind her back. That wasn't going to happen.

"He is here with his mother. The two of them got separated as the crowd grew," Adriane told her.

The guard approached with the boy's mother, and Adriane started to hand him over when the boy clutched his neck and said, "Je vous aime, Sire." *I love you, Sire.*

Rachel had picked up enough of the language to know those words. Her eyes welled up with tears as Adriane whispered in the boy's ear, something that made him laugh in delight while he went back to his mother.

The woman bowed to Adriane before the guards escorted both her and her son to safety. Adriane waved one last time to the crowd and then helped Rachel into the car.

As she sat across from him on the quiet ride back to the palace, looking at him in a new light, Rachel was filled with a sense of fear.

Whether she wanted to fall in love with this man or not, she might have no choice. The more she learned about him, the harder it would be to keep her heart guarded.

She'd seen both the good side and the bad side of Adriane. The good was starting to outweigh the bad — outweigh it in a huge way.

Rachel was in trouble.

Her heart might indeed get shattered as she continued on this quest to know the man who had fathered her children.

Still, it was a quest she had to continue, no matter the consequences. She owed that much to her unborn babies.

CHAPTER TWENTY-FIVE

STANDING IN FRONT of the flashy club, Lia began to think that maybe this wasn't such a good idea. She'd had to get out of the palace, though. She'd run into Shane too many times, and her need for him seemed only to escalate. It was best to just slip away for the evening.

Maybe she could dance. Definitely, she would drink.

Tonight was about nothing but pleasure, no matter what it took for her to achieve that goal.

The setting for her revels was a beautiful piece of land on the sea surrounding Corythia. Children were laughing as they ran along the boardwalk, parents on their heels. It was getting late, and the night crowd was starting to take over, while the families were enjoying their last moments of fun before heading home.

It sent a pang through Lia. She was finding that she'd much rather be a part of one of the families getting ready to come home, versus the single girl heading inside a bar.

Shaking off that thought, she opened the door and tried to enjoy the blast of music that instantly washed over her.

This was what she wanted — to dance and drink and to forget all about Shane for one single night. There was no place better to do just that than in a room full of rowdy people looking for a good time. Then why was she hesitating at the bar's entrance? Why hadn't she stepped through the doors yet?

It was always a little frightening to go to an unfamiliar place, but Adriane had assured her that crime was low in Corythia and that the locals raved about this particular club, so Lia felt a bit safer. She'd gotten a ride to town from one of Adriane's drivers, who had given her his number. When she was ready to return, all she had to do was pick up the phone.

There was no risk in escaping for the night. So she needed to shake off this feeling of unease and just enjoy herself like the single woman she was.

If any of the men thought she was there for more than dancing, then they'd be sorely out of luck. Her desire to be with other men had been zip since Shane, and her attempts at dating had been pathetic, to say the least. The only pleasure she was looking for was the kind of warmth a bottle of Jack Daniel's gave and some heavy-duty dancing. She wasn't going home with one of the locals of Corythia.

It seemed Shane had ruined her for any other man. Maybe she should just get over the misunderstandings. She was, actually. Now, it was just fear. Fear that she would hand over her heart fully, only to have that horrible phone call saying he'd never be home again — that she'd lost him forever.

Finally pushing herself to get over this very different anxiety, she stepped inside the club, forcing a smile to her lips. Smoke filled the air, and she could see people laughing, but their laughter could barely be heard over the loud bass of the music. Bodies tangled wildly in front of her on the dance floor. Yes, this was exactly what she'd needed. The smile would soon become real.

This would pull her from the mood she'd been in for the past several months; this would relieve the ache in her body from going so long without fulfillment. Nothing cured sexual frustration like what she had in mind. Plus, it would help her ego if one or two men gave her a bit of attention. Yes, that made her a slight tease, but she wasn't feeling at all good about herself at the moment. She needed something to lift her spirits.

The worst part of the continued ache in her body was knowing that she was the cause.

All it would take would be a single word and she could be crying out in ecstasy as Shane took her to the edges of the universe and beyond. The man knew how to bring her pleasure, and only her own stupid pride and stubbornness was preventing her from taking advantage of it.

Pushing those thoughts to the furthest recesses of her mind, Lia looked around the crowded room, then began to make her way toward the bar. First order of business was a drink — anything would do. Something to take the edge off her sexual appetite. That was all she was looking for.

As the crowd parted, she froze. She would recognize those broad strong shoulders and that dark hair anywhere.

It was Shane, and he wasn't alone.

Instant jealousy jolted her heart awake at the sight of a sleek, scantily dressed brunette hanging all over his arm, her breasts brushing his shoulder and back, her top revealing more than it was hiding.

So what? She shouldn't care if he was enjoying himself with some trashy woman who was obviously looking to get laid. Lia had told him it was never going to happen again with her, so of course he'd move on. He was young and gorgeous, and he had his entire life in front of him.

What did she expect? That he'd pine over her forever?

Well, kind of.

That was ridiculous.

And so was this. She'd come out to get a break, to turn her thoughts away from Shane, and instead she had to watch him being pawed.

Getting ready to turn, she noticed the expression on his face.

A surge of joy calmed her ever-pounding, erratic heart. He wasn't on a date. He was clearly trying to enjoy a drink and instead getting some very unwanted attention. Lia watched as he tried to pry the woman's fingers from his thigh — without any success.

It reminded her of the old days. The days she'd been in love with him, and he'd still looked at her like a little sister.

Well, those days were obviously long past, but she couldn't stop herself from moving through the wall-to-wall crowd of people. She'd decided to ride to his rescue.

She even managed to convince herself that she was doing it as a favor for a friend, not because she wanted to stake a claim on her territory, a territory she had no right to.

"Hi, babe. Did you order my drink yet?" Lia asked as she pushed herself in beside Shane and sent him a wink.

He gazed back at her in shock at finding her there, shock that quickly turned to relief as he figured out what she was doing.

"Sorry, I haven't had a chance yet," he said, his arm snaking around her waist and pulling her close, leaving her no choice but to hoist one leg over his as she half sat on him.

Oh, my, her body heated up fast. She was expecting to save him, but she wasn't expecting such close contact while doing so. It felt entirely too good to pull back, however. Plus, she rationalized, that would be sending a clear message to the annoying brunette, whose smile had disappeared as soon as Lia showed up.

The entire game would be defeated if she didn't play along. And that was just no fun.

"Well, you know what I like," she said, then glanced up with a start, as if just noticing the other woman.

Lia looked the woman in the eye and then raised her eyebrow as she pointedly turned her glance on the hand the woman was pressing down on Shane's free thigh.

"He's taken, sweetie," the brunette growled. "Why don't you run along?" She squeezed just a bit more closely against Shane's side. Her breasts were so squished on his shoulder that Lia was getting far more of a view than she cared to see.

"Sorry, doll, but he's been taken for a long time. If you don't remove your hand from my boyfriend's thigh, I'm going to have to get mean — and you won't like me very much then." Lia spoke with just enough menace to get her point across.

Shane's head whipped back and forth between the two women as if he didn't know what to do. Typical male.

The girl lifted her hand, grabbed the back of Shane's neck and brought her painted red lips to his, kissing him hard and fast. "When you get sick of her, I'll be over there," she said, then released him and sauntered off.

Lia felt a real urge to chase after the skank, but Shane's arm tightened around her as if he knew where her thoughts were going.

"Thanks for the rescue. I've been around some persistent females, but damn," he said before giving forth an involuntary chuckle.

Lia's gaze was drawn to the perfection of his lips, and as he caressed her lower back and the crowd pushed her even closer to him, she was forgetting why it was a bad idea for the two of them to make love again.

The reason had to be stupid.

"No problem. You've saved me enough times," she said.

The bartender stepped over to them, breaking the spell Shane had her under, and Lia ordered a Long Island Iced Tea. She'd need the extra kick the drink would give her.

Neither of them said another word as her drink was mixed and set before her. Shane paid the man, giving him a healthy tip and encouraging him to come back when their glasses got low, then waited as Lia took a few long swallows.

She knew she should try to put some distance between her and Shane, but as the crowd surged, the music pulsed, and the drink warmed her blood, she decided that distance was vastly overrated.

Somehow she ended up fully on his lap, with his arm around her waist, his mouth within inches of her own.

She could blame it on the alcohol, blame it on the club — but the reality was that she wanted him, wanted him more than any other man in the universe. More than anything, period. She loved him, and no matter how much she fought it, she was always going to love him.

So why not have one more night together? Soon he'd be gone again, leaving her and going to parts unknown. Wouldn't she regret it more if she didn't have this memory of them together? What if the next mission ensured he never returned?

Surely it was better to have a piece of him than nothing at all.

When he leaned forward with the clear intention of kissing her, Lia didn't hesitate. She met him halfway, groaning in celebration as their mouths joined together.

Yes, this was where she wanted to be. This was where she should have been all night. Who needed alcohol when she could get drunk from his touch?

Shane pulled back. "Do you want to leave, Lia? The choice is yours." His lips grazed her ear as he spoke so she would be sure to hear him above the noise.

Lia paused for only a second. Could she do this and still stay strong?

Did it matter?

No. No, it didn't.

"Yes, Shane."

She didn't have to say anything else. Shane threw another tip on the bar, lifted her from his lap and set her quickly on her feet. Taking her hand, he parted the crowd with the sheer size of his masculine frame, and they exited the club.

CHAPTER TWENTY-SIX

S HANE KNEW HE shouldn't do this, knew she was feeling vulnerable and might regret her decision later, but he wanted her so badly. He wanted it all, but he'd take what he could get.

He also knew she cared about him. Yes, they'd both messed up, but he had come to claim her again, and he wasn't leaving without doing just that. The only problem was that he wanted all of her — forever.

And he was going to make that happen.

First, though, they had to appease this hunger. Neither of them could think straight otherwise. He would show her, in the one way he was sure of, how much he loved and desired her.

They didn't have any trouble in the bedroom and that was a step in the right direction.

Walking from the club, he moved swiftly down the street. His hotel was only two blocks away, and he was damn glad he hadn't taken Adriane's offer to stay in the palace.

Shane liked his own space, his privacy. Sure, the palace was luxurious, but this hotel was damn nice, too, and it was a hell of a lot closer right now than the palace was.

As his body throbbed, he adjusted his stride. It would be a miracle if the two of them made it back to his room in one piece.

It had just been too long since he'd sunk inside her body. He hoped and prayed she didn't change her mind, that the cool night air didn't somehow wake her up and let her think she was making a mistake.

When the two of them came together, it was never a mistake.

He reached the hotel, her hand gripped tightly in his, and he didn't pause as he swept through the front doors and headed straight to the bank of elevators.

Lia's step never faltered beside his.

When the elevator doors opened in invitation, they allowed the car to swallow them up and he delighted when the doors closed with just the two of them inside. Privacy was now theirs and Shane couldn't wait any longer.

Pushing her up against the wall, he bent down, his mouth devouring hers, wordlessly pouring out his intentions. Lia clutched his shoulder; she moaned even as she was thrusting her tongue inside his mouth.

His knees nearly shaking from pure need, he slid his hands to her backside, holding her tightly in his palms and squeezing her rounded flesh. She responded by pressing up more tightly against him, encouraging him to continue his conquest.

Shane swept his hands down her thighs, and was exceedingly grateful for the high hem on her shorts. With the barest of efforts he lifted her, pulling her legs around his waist as he pushed his solid erection against her. Too many bloody clothes in the way.

"I want you so damn bad," he groaned, lifting his head so he could trail his mouth down her throat.

"Mmm, you make me crazy with just your touch," she admitted as she ground her hips against the ever impressive bulge in his pants.

The elevator chimed, and the doors swept open. No one was in the hallway, thank heavens. Particularly since Shane didn't want to set Lia down.

"Hold on," he told her as he strode down the hall with her clinging to him.

Pulling the key card from his back pocket, he unlocked his door, pushing it open before sliding inside the room and slamming the door shut with his foot. He pressed her back against the still-rattling door.

"Please, Shane," she cried as her hips pressed into his. "Take me."

"I plan to," he replied, then captured her mouth again with his.

Lia cried out as his hands ran up her sides, then grasped her breasts and squeezed. Her breathing was rapid, her lips urgent, but soft. Her hands tangled in his hair, gripping him tightly, guiding him where she wanted him.

This was perfect — it was right — it was everything and more.

Shane was losing control too quickly. He had to rein it in. They hadn't been together in a long time, and he wanted this night to be something she wouldn't soon forget. He had to make her see that they were much better together than they were apart.

With a herculean effort, Shane ended the kiss, then pulled away from the door and moved over to his bed, where he gently set her down.

Lia reached for him, whimpering when he didn't immediately fall on top of her. But he was resolute. Even if he died pleasing her, expired from holding his own fulfillment back, she would remember this night because he was going to make her ecstasy stretch out endlessly.

Kneeling at the foot of the bed, he pulled off her shoes, then kissed the soles of her feet, rubbing his tongue along the arch of her foot. She stopped struggling and moaned at his soft caress.

His hands rose slowly up her calves, massaging the firm muscles in her legs and making his tongue follow the path he was laying with his fingers. She quivered as his fingers moved higher, stroking the sensitive skin of her thighs while his tongue swirled around the underside of her knees.

Twisting beneath him, she wanted more.

His fingers slipped beneath the hem of her shorts, rising, slipping inside her tiny panties and plunging into her wet core.

"Shane!" she screamed.

He stroked her a few times, then pulled out. She began to protest, but she felt his hands at the clasp of her shorts, releasing the fabric, slipping inside the waistband and pulling them down.

Shane couldn't get enough of Lia's flesh. His mouth trailed kisses back down her thighs, and he tasted her sweet skin.

She writhed beneath him, calling his name and begging him for more — more of what, she didn't even know, but the pleasurable sensation he awoke within her was turning her inside out.

Tossing her shorts aside, he began kissing her ankles, laving her heated flesh with his tongue, moving upward slowly, then sliding across her thighs until he reached the source of her heat. His tongue ran along the edges of her panties, her taste coming through the fabric and making him gasp in passion.

"You are perfect, Lia, absolutely perfect," he moaned, overcome.

"Shane, please," she cried, her voice urgent with need.

"I'll please you, Lia. I'll please you until the sun is rising in the sky, and then we will sleep in each other's arms. When you wake, it will be to feel of my body surging inside of yours again. We won't leave this bed for days, weeks, months. All I want to do is please you," he said, and was surprised by how much he meant it.

She groaned as she reached for him. He obeyed her silent commands, sliding up her body, taking the hem of her shirt and lifting it, exposing her lacy bra to his view. Having discarded the shirt, he unhooked the clasp on the front of her bra, with a sharp inhale at the sight of her beautiful breasts. It had been so long.

Caressing her curves, he used his hands and mouth to prolong her pleasure, making her cry out, over and over again until she was shaking, and a single tear slid down her cheek.

"Please, I need to feel you inside me." As she begged, she tried to look into his very soul.

"Yes, right now," he agreed.

Shane tore off his clothes, wanting nothing more than to ravish her and end the ache that was now a constant in his body.

But instead, he lay on top of her, reveling in the feel of the thick head of his erection rubbing along her slick folds, until finally he pushed forward, and slowly, inch by beautiful inch, he sank inside her heat.

Lia gripped his flexed behind, wrapped her legs tightly around his waist, then rocked her hips against him. "Fast, Shane. I'm so close," she begged.

His heart nearly stopped at the urgency in her voice, at the raw need pouring from her. He'd brought her to this point — he'd made her beg.

His heart thundered in his chest as he began thrusting fiercely, quickly driving in and out of her lush body. Yes, they both needed this release, they both needed to fall over the edge into paradise, and then... then, he'd start all over again.

He would love her so much, so long, so hard, she wouldn't have the energy to fight him ever again. She wouldn't even have the energy to move from beneath him.

With compulsion and need propelling him on, Shane drove inside her, his pleasure building, her screams of desire pushing him over.

Whimpering, moaning, crying out in an intense sequence, Lia dug her fingernails into his flesh as her body tightened around him. Shane was a goner. He let go, spilling inside her, his body pulsing with the force of his release.

It was several minutes before either of them could move.

Finally, Shane shifted, turning to his side, and then he quickly pulled her on top of him. No escape.

She didn't fight him, and soon he found himself relaxing, caressing her back with a languid hand, loving the feel of her head against his chest.

"Shane?" Her voice was quiet, almost timid.

Worry filled him. This wasn't how Lia spoke.

"What is it, babe?" he asked, praying she didn't ask to leave. He didn't think he could let her go — not now.

"Is it time for round two?" she asked, a quiet laugh escaping against his chest.

His heart filled with joy.

He really did love this woman.

"Let's go take a shower. Then we can get started with rounds two, three and four," he said before softly biting her shoulder.

Lia giggled as he sat up, pulling her with him.

He kept his promise.

Neither of them got any sleep that night.

CHAPTER TWENTY-SEVEN

A S LIA'S BRAIN struggled toward consciousness, the first thing it noticed was the big smile on her face. What a night! Hell, what a great two nights! Lia stretched her arms and legs before turning over and deciding she didn't want to be awake yet.

The bed was too warm and inviting, and there was nothing on this earth that could pull her from it. Well, nothing except for the fact that her bladder was screaming at her.

She could just ignore it. That was the right thing to do.

Lying there for another five minutes, she angrily reopened her eyes. Nope. Ignoring it wasn't going to happen, and now she was so irritated with her body that she'd never be able to get back to sleep again.

Dang it.

As she stumbled from the bed, the last two days came flooding back to her. Lia made quick use of the bathroom, then staggered back to the bedroom and flopped down on the bed.

Her entire body was sore — in a very good way — and she had barely taken the time to eat. The rumble in her stomach attested to that fact.

Shane.

Oh, Shane. He hadn't given her a moment to regret her impulsive decision to sleep with him again, and, man, had they slept together. In fact, why was it called "sleeping together" when it was anything but that? They'd made love again and again and again.

She waited for the guilt to hit, the regrets.

The sour emotions didn't come. It had just been too good between them.

Not once had they brought up any of the past issues plaguing them. What good would it do? The two of them coming together was like putting a flame to explosives.

Still, it couldn't continue, could it? The more she was with him, the more she *wanted* to be with him. Because Shane was her first love, she could hardly just put him on a shelf and forget about him each time he had to leave.

She'd been trying to do exactly that for the past couple of years and it hadn't gotten her anywhere but achingly lonely.

So she had a big decision to make. Did she continue giving herself to him, continue pleasing her body and ignoring her heart? It was a reality she didn't want to face.

She didn't know how long she sat there, but soon the smell of freshly brewed coffee and something doughy and delicious snuck through the cracked bedroom door.

Lia's rumbling stomach ensured she wasn't going to avoid whatever smell was enticing her so.

She needed fuel!

Getting up and heading again to the bathroom, she decided on the world's fastest shower, turning the spray on scalding hot so she could wake up fully. Then, she found a large cotton robe and threw it around her, tying the sash as she walked to the door.

She sauntered from the bedroom and down the short hall, turning the corner, and then she stopped in her tracks.

Oh, my, my, my. If she hadn't been awake at this point, the sight of Shane in nothing but a low-slung pair of boxers and a hot plate in his hand would have had her on high alert.

Turning, his eyes caught hers, and a slow, sexy smile crept over his features as he set down the plate and stalked toward her.

"Good morning, beautiful. I hope you slept well," he said as he reached her, wrapped his arms around her back and leaned down to crush his lips to hers.

Lia stopped in her tracks temporarily, then circled his neck with her hands and captured his tongue, playing a mating game where they both came out winners.

When he let go of her after too short a time, Lia groaned her disapproval. That hadn't been her plan when she'd walked out to find him looking so unbelievably dashing, but plans do change. Hell, she could easily learn to go with the flow, just as long as his hands and lips were connected with some part of her body.

"I have to feed you, woman, before you wither away. Be good and sit down, because having you standing this close is making me want to throw away this nice meal I prepared and instead haul you back to the bedroom."

Lia's forehead wrinkled as she considered her options. Her body was actually growing weak from lack of nourishment, but she could most certainly survive on orgasms alone if they were with Shane. If not, she'd at least die a very happy woman.

"No." Shane said as if he could read her thoughts. With that, he turned back to the counter, where their plates were sitting beneath covers.

"Wait a minute. You didn't prepare this," she said with a smile as he slid the plate over to her and she scooped up a heaping fork of potatoes and eggs.

"I certainly did," he exclaimed, sitting next to her and diving into his own plate.

"Really? On what stove?" she asked, pointedly looking around.

With a big grin, he leaned over and gave her a fleeting kiss before admitting his white lie. "Well, I did dial room service," he said with a chuckle.

"Well, that's good enough for me," she said, and continued eating the fluffy eggs.

She was grateful he'd thought of getting them anything, because if it weren't for him, she'd probably forget to eat altogether. It seemed that Shane was quite the caretaker. That was just one more thing to check off on the list of good qualities he possessed. This would all be so much easier if he were a monster, or if she just wasn't attracted to him. Being with Shane again had opened up her appetite in one hell of a voracious way, and now she didn't know how to turn off the need.

Not that she was too keen on turning anything off at the moment.

"Eat more, and quit looking at me like I'm the dessert," Shane said, with a look of a special hunger that belied his words.

"Mmm, you will make a mighty fine dessert?" she said with a wink, scooping up another bite of her food, groaning as the flavors burst on her tongue.

"Oh, no, *you're* the dessert," he said, looking up and capturing her full attention with his deep dark eyes.

"I'm full," she said, letting her fork clatter to the plate, only half her meal finished. The growling in her stomach was long forgotten. After making love once more, she could always find the strength, somehow, to seek out food again.

Cold eggs were just fine with her.

Shane looked as if he were going to protest, but when she untied the sash at her waist and parted the soft fabric, she knew she'd won.

Pushing his plate away without another word, he stood from the table and quickly circled around to where she stood. Picking her up in his arms, he kissed her hungrily while he walked through the hotel room, apparently knowing the way by heart, since his gaze never left hers.

Oh, yes, dessert was splendid.

CHAPTER TWENTY-EIGHT

"I THOUGHT *YOU* MIGHT be the one to skip out on my wedding this time."

A guilty blush stole across Lia's face, and Ari was ready to pounce. It was the day of her wedding and butterflies were practicing ballroom dancing in her stomach, but she knew this was right, and there were no regrets, zero, or thoughts of running. Her feet were happily warm.

Still, she really did want to know where her bridesmaid had been the last few days. She refused to walk down the aisle until Lia spilled all.

"Cat got your tongue? Come on, Lia. We're not stepping outside these beautiful doors until you tell me exactly where you've been. I'm dying here with curiosity!" Ari said, her hands on her hips, not looking nearly as ferocious as she wanted to look, because she was wearing a big, poufy wedding dress with miles and miles of satin flowing off her.

"This is your day, Ari. Let's keep the focus on you," Lia said as she walked into the bathroom and began changing into her crimson bridesmaid dress.

"A closed door isn't going to stop us, Lia. Spill now, or we get Rafe to interrogate you," Rachel said as she pounded her fist against the heavy wood.

"Go away. I'm changing," Lia insisted, her voice penetrating loud and clear.

"Not a chance," Ari said. "You disappear for three days. It just so happens that no one has seen a lick of Shane in three days, either. From what you told us last, the two of you were kaput, so you had better give us the details."

"Seriously, you two are a pain in my ass," Lia grumbled, pulling the door open with a scowl.

"Yes, we are, and we're extremely proud of it. Now, if you don't want to make Ari late for her second attempt at a wedding, then I'd suggest you start speaking," Rachel said. She and Ari stood on either side of the dressing room table while Lia began applying her makeup.

"Fine. You two should both work for the FBI. You'd catch all the criminals and get every last secret from them," Lia replied with a heavy sigh, looking them both in the eyes for a moment via the mirror.

"Yeah, that's our next job application," Ari said with a giggle. "Sorry, my nerves are just fried," she explained as she attempted to stifle her laughter.

"Is everything OK in there?"

The three girls turned toward the suite door, holding their breath, but the knob didn't move.

"We're fine, Rafe. Don't worry. No one is running away or being kidnapped this time," Rachel called.

"Well, we're waiting…" he said with a clearly heard sigh of anxiousness. "It's bad enough that my best man just stumbled in."

His voice faded away while he most likely resumed pacing.

"All right, Lia, you have to spill fast because I don't think he's going to wait a heck of a lot longer," Ari said, her own eyes a bit anxious as she glanced toward the door.

"Yes, I was with Shane. I saw him at the bar and sparks flew and the next thing I knew, we were still in bed together three days later," Lia said, and began putting on her mascara.

"That's *it*? You have hot, steamy, hopefully long-lasting sex for three solid days and those are all the details you're going to give us?" Rachel asked. "It's a mistake to irritate me, sister dearest."

"That's all the time we have for now. Ari is ready and Rafe will bust down this door if we don't get her out there to him ASAP!"

"Fine, but at least tell us what this all means. Are the two of you a couple again?" Ari asked as she stepped back and Rachel assisted her with her veil.

Lia sighed as she finished her makeup, stood up, and turned toward them with nothing but confusion showing on her face.

"I don't know what it means. I'm scared," she admitted, her voice catching.

"Oh, sweetie, please, please don't cry or I'll join you." Ari rushed over awkwardly in her overwhelming dress to throw her arms around Lia and bring her as close as the layers of fabric would allow.

"Then quit questioning me, because I'm on the brink," Lia said with a watery laugh.

"OK, we'll wait until the reception, and then you are absolutely talking to us," Rachel conceded.

"Deal," Lia promised, and then the three women moved slowly to the door.

Rachel opened it a crack and peeked out. "Go to the cathedral, Rafe. We're coming out," she said with a chuckle. She waited a heartbeat before turning to Ari. "It's time."

Ari smiled as she walked through the door and out into the hallway. This was it. She was finally going to become Mrs. Rafe Palazzo.

Excitement carried her through the hallway and out the front door. Stepping outside, she smiled at the sight of the carriage parked at the curb.

"Oh, Ari, this is so romantic," Rachel sighed as the groomsmen stood on either side of the old-fashioned door and waited for the bride to approach.

"Yes. I'm glad we're getting married here. I have to admit that I feel like a princess," she said before facing Rachel. "It's quite unreal to think that you could actually be one if you just say yes to Adriane."

"No, Ari, she would be a queen," Lia said, lifting an eyebrow at Rachel as if her sister were crazy for not accepting.

"Yeah, that thought isn't at all appealing," Rachel had to say, fear obvious in her voice.

"It can't be that bad to be a queen in such a beautiful country," Ari remarked, then the women quieted as they neared the carriage.

"Let me help you," the well-dressed man said, taking Ari's hand and helping her inside. The luxurious and surprisingly roomy interior, with its soft white velvet and its gold plating, had hundreds of years of wedding stories to tell.

"This is amazing, Ari," Rachel gasped.

"I know. I will have to thank Adriane for allowing this," she said. Ari had to value the man, even if he had been a fool. Would someone unromantic allow this wedding to happen? She had some hope that her friend and soon-to-be sister-in-law would find real love with him.

"Yes, even a dictator can do a kind thing now and then," Rachel grumbled, but she sat back and gazed at the carriage's furnishings with awe.

As the horses drew the carriage down the cobblestone streets of Corythia, the three women were surprised but waved and smiled when people cheered as they passed, though the villagers had no idea who Ari was. But since the three were traveling in the royal carriage, the people assumed she was somebody important.

"Imagine if this were you," Lia said to Rachel.

"It won't be," Rachel said, her voice hushed.

Ari could imagine the fear she was feeling. She herself would lose some of her anonymity just being married to Rafe, a man so regularly in the media. But if Rachel married Adriane, she would be an actual queen. There would be no more days of leaving the house on a whim, or being grumpy in the mall. Everything she did would be carefully scrutinized. The thought sent a chill down Ari's spine. It was so overwhelming to imagine.

"If you love him, then nothing else matters," Lia said, as if she could read Ari's thoughts, and Rachel's fear.

"Sometimes love just isn't enough," Rachel reminded her sister.

"Do you love him?" she asked, both the girls focusing on Rachel.

"I just want to know him — want to find out if he's a person I want influencing my children," Rachel said, avoiding the question.

"You don't have a lot of choice in that matter, Rachel. The babies are already brewing," Lia reminded her.

"I know, but if he's a monster, how could I let him be in their lives?"

"Is he?" Ari asked.

Rachel sat back as she looked out the window, pausing for several long moments. "No. His actions are sometimes reprehensible, but he's not a monster. He just doesn't like to lose."

"That sounds like you," Lia commented.

"Yeah, well, I wouldn't talk if I were you," Rachel remarked, looking pointedly at her sister.

"I'm not stubborn — I'm just always right," Lia informed her with a wink and a smile.

The tension evaporated and the three women laughed.

They arrived at the royal cathedral, the steps lined with people, guards keeping a clear path from the carriage to the door. The people of Corythia were wondering who was important enough to get married in the royal cathedral, and, speculating among themselves, they waited for the women to emerge.

They would be disappointed to learn she wasn't a princess who had traveled from afar to marry in their land. Too bad.

"It's time, and you are breathtaking," Rachel said, all her attention turning to Ari.

"Thank you. Yes, it's time," Ari replied with a nervous grin as she took the hand of the man ready to help her from the carriage. "I can't wait to be Rafe's wife."

Looking only ahead, Ari made her way to the huge doors, then stood impatiently as Rachel and Lia stepped ahead of her and began the long, stately walk down the aisle.

When they were finally in view of the altar, Ari's breath left her in a trembling sigh. Shane was there beside his best friend, looking devastating. But Ari's eyes were only on one man — the man she would stay beside for the rest of all time.

Ari's steps faltered as Rafe mouthed *I love you* to her when she was still several feet away.

With her eyes filled with happy tears, she quickened her step, breaking time with the wedding march. She was unwilling to wait any longer to hold his hand in this sacred moment, to look deep into his eyes and take him as hers forever.

"I love you, too," she whispered as he lifted his arm and caressed her cheek.

Forgetting about what she was supposed to do, Ari lifted her arms and placed them around his neck, leaning against him as she lifted her head. He quickly accommodated her, and bent down, taking her lips in a soft kiss that had her knees trembling.

The priest cleared his throat and the audience laughed softly, as Ari reluctantly pulled back and a blush stole over her cheeks. She turned to look at the man who would preside over the wedding, without an inkling of remorse for having tasted Rafe's sweet kiss a little too soon.

"Now that the kiss is out of the way, we can begin," the man said in a beautiful accent and with a sparkle in his eyes. "We are gathered here today..."

The ceremony flashed by in a blur, both Ari and Rafe repeating vows as they promised to love, honor and obey each other. She didn't miss the mischievous grin on Rafe's face as she repeated the word *obey*. She was sure he'd specifically asked the priest to leave it in her vows and to add it to his.

They would just have to see who obeyed whom more, she thought.

"*Now* you may kiss your bride," the priest told Rafe with a light chuckle, and Rafe didn't hesitate, pulling Ari into his arms.

After a few heartbeats, he drew back and looked into her eyes. "I'm a very lucky man, Mrs. Palazzo."

"And I am one lucky woman, Mr. Palazzo," she said, holding him tight, and praying this wasn't just a dream.

"Mmm, how soon do you think we can ditch the party and leave for our honeymoon?" he asked, his hand resting low on her back and sending a myriad of chills through her body.

"Right now?" she asked hopefully.

The look in his eyes told her he might just whisk her away.

"Not a chance, lover boy," Shane whispered from behind as he nudged the two of them to take their walk down the aisle as man and wife.

Rafe sent an irritated look his best friend's way, but then he turned back toward Ari, releasing her body only to grab her hand.

Leading her down the aisle, he whispered in her ear just before they left the church. "I can't wait to enforce the *obey* part of our vows."

Ari gasped and looked around. But she turned back to him and said, "And neither can I. Get ready."

Oh, this would be one very passionate honeymoon.

CHAPTER TWENTY-NINE

"CONGRATULATIONS, RAFE. I'M happy for you," Shane said, then took a deep draft from his bottle of beer and clapped his best friend on the shoulder. It was good that Rafe had found "The One." Now, if only *he* could convince Lia that the two of *them* were meant to be together forever, life would be perfect — complete even. "This has been one hell of a party. The king really knows how to pull off an event on a short notice," he added with a laugh.

Rafe wasn't thrilled to allow any praise to go to Adriane, not after what the man had done. Nevertheless, he had to soften just the tiniest bit because it was obvious that his sister had feelings for the man. Still, the creep shouldn't have forced her to stay.

The direction of Rafe's thoughts brought on the return of a twinge of guilt that pierced his heart. What he'd put Ari through that first year of their relationship. How could he have been such a fool?

But that was in the past. They'd both moved on, and there was no use in dredging up the bad memories. He had the rest of his life to make it up to her — and make it up to her he would indeed.

"When do you leave again, Shane?" he asked. Rafe would rather talk of that than voice his opinions about Adriane and his sister, or about this lavish event, one he hadn't asked for.

"I'm on leave for an undetermined amount of time right now. The last mission didn't go well," Shane said, tensing as he thought about the friend and teammate he'd lost.

"Maybe it's time to retire," Rafe remarked.

"I'm considering it," Shane had to say.

Rafe was taken back. He looked up at his friend and noticed the stress behind his eyes. This was something new.

"Does this have anything to do with Lia?"

"Yes and no. I want to be with Lia — like a 'white picket fence, two dogs and some rug rats running around' kind of being with her — but I wouldn't make a decision like this solely because of a woman, not even a woman I care the world about. I think the old job has just lost its appeal. Caring about someone so much has put the dangers into perspective. I think I may want to just focus on my businesses, and let go of being GI Joe," he said with a forced laugh.

Rafe knew better than to accept the joke. But he also knew he couldn't push his friend. Though Shane was obviously going through some sort of private hell, it was also obvious that he had to deal with it on his own. Rafe would be there when and if Shane was ready to talk about it, but only then.

The two men looked silently out across the crowd. Rafe sought out Ari, who was gossiping in the corner with Lia and Rachel. Shane was looking in the same direction, but his eyes were all for Lia.

Rafe could feel for his friend. Not being with Ari every day had been rough. At least that problem was solved. She was now his wife and he would prove to her every single day that she'd made the right decision.

Even so, he had to admit, a fight now and then could lead up to some incredibly good makeup sex. Just the thought had his body stirring as he anticipated all their nights together.

Let the honeymoon begin!

Snagging a passing waiter, the two men set their empty bottles on his tray and grabbed cold replacements. It had taken some doing, but Rafe had managed to get some good beer ordered for the reception, much to the king's disapproval. Yes, the party was nice, but it was just about time to be alone with his bride. He couldn't wait to strip off her exquisite wedding gown, and what was on underneath...the latter with his teeth.

It was like Christmas and his birthday all rolled into one. Shaking those thoughts away before he got himself into trouble, he turned back to face his friend.

"You know, I'm here anytime," Rafe said. Neither of them was good at sharing emotions, but he'd been there for Shane in the past when things had gone wrong on the field and Shane had needed to vent.

Shane turned toward his friend.

He didn't think he was ready to talk about it. Not yet.

"I know, Rafe. But today is your wedding day and you should stay focused on that bride of yours. If I were you, I'd be over there claiming her right now." Shane sent a wink Rafe's way, followed by a smile, though Rafe could easily see past the cocky façade.

He didn't call him on it.

"I think you are right, my man. It's time for a dance," Rafe said, punching Shane in the shoulder before draining his bottle and setting it aside.

As Shane watched Rafe walk toward Ari, eagerness evident in his every step, he let out a sigh. When would his life get just a little bit more simple?

It wasn't as if he wanted to throw a pity party. It was just that whenever his life seemed to even out into some sort of normalcy, something would come along and knock him back several paces. He and Lia had been together for the past three days, incredibly amazing days, and now that they were out in public, she seemed to be pulling away again. He couldn't allow that to happen. Plus, whenever he allowed himself a few minutes to breathe, all the pain of the past few months flooded back.

When would it stop?

When would the pain of losing his friend ease? When did he get to have the girl for more than just a few nights of passion-filled pleasure?

Well, at least that last part was much easier. She was here in all her glory, and it was time to claim her for a dance.

She'd avoided him since taking off from his hotel room and rushing back to the palace to get ready for the wedding. But if she thought he was going to allow her to withdraw from him again, she had a lot to learn.

If he'd learned nothing else over the last few days, he knew beyond any doubt that they were truly meant to be together. When they made love, it was simple, erotic, satisfying — and, yes, it seemed odd to say it to himself, but it was easy.

Their bodies molded together because they'd been created to fit perfectly to only each other. But what came afterward was what had at first terrified him to his very soul.

As he used to be, after sex, he was done, ready to get the hell out of there and move on. But Lia changed everything. He could never be done with her. The moment he pulled from her, he felt an emptiness — a loss. The only way to curb that feeling was to gather her into his arms, and hold on tight.

Falling asleep in her arms felt right.

He wasn't letting her go again — there was no way he could. Maybe Adriane had pissed them all off, but the man seemed to have the right idea.

Maybe it was time to just take Lia and damn the consequences.

The thought of doing just that put the first real smile on his face he'd had since Delzado's death. Being with Lia over the last few days had eased his body, but thinking of having her forever eased the pain in his heart.

Shane turned in Lia's direction again and their eyes met. He could see the way his gaze held hers captive, the way her chest heaved. He sent a clear message her way. *You are mine, and I'm not letting go.*

She bit down on her lip before a secret smile crept up as she seemed to send her own message. *I don't belong to anyone.*

Her curls hung loose around her slim neck, and her eyes sparkled as she gazed at him. The slight flush to her cheeks made her look as if she'd just climbed from his bed.

Oh, and the dress.

My, my, the dress was enough to have his body hardening instantly as he imagined peeling it from her incredible curves. He had to thank whoever had picked it out, because it molded to her body like a second skin and wasn't hiding anything from his view.

Yes, he was ready for whatever excuses she had to throw at him, and this time when they played ball, he intended to win. Not just for the night or the weekend, but for the rest of time.

Lia was going to be his wife. No matter what it took.

With determination and a firm resolve, Shane set down his bottle and took a step in her direction.

The hunger in her eyes was his guiding light.

They were now in overtime, and he was calling a foul. She wasn't getting away this time.

CHAPTER THIRTY

*M*S. PALAZZO, TEAR *down that wall.* That, it seemed, was the unexpected result of Lia's talk therapy.

As her eyes locked with Shane's, she wondered what her next move was going to be. Ari and Rachel had finally dragged the entire story from her, and, no, it didn't help close her off to Shane's attractions. Instead, it speedily increased her need for him — releasing the floodgates of passion.

While she'd talked about him, she realized that in keeping him at bay, she was mainly trying to protect herself. Maybe because she'd wanted him for so long without him wanting her that she'd built some sort of fortress around her heart.

Whatever the reason, she could no longer keep that solid wall from crumbling down around her feet.

He was the man she loved; maybe it would be best if she just gave in to both his and her own desires. Maybe it was time she grew up and took what was being offered to her. She didn't need to look for all the reasons they couldn't be together. It was time to appreciate what she had right in front of her.

Surely she wouldn't lose herself that way. Her life would gain another person.

But she couldn't keep from dwelling on her unhappy fears. What if she gave him her entire heart, and the next day he shipped out, only to be taken away from her forever? What would that do to her in the long run?

Could she ever pick herself up off the ground after such devastation? And yet, would it really make a difference at this point? If he were to go away and never return, wouldn't her heart shatter, even now?

Yes, yes, it would.

Whether she wanted to love him or not, she already did. And if nothing she did at this point would change the way she felt, why not just jump in with both feet?

"Hello, beautiful. Are you avoiding me?" Shane had walked right into her personal bubble and she was glad to see him, her heart instantly picking up speed.

"I was. I decided just now, though, that I want to take you off into a closet, unbuckle your belt and show you how very much I want you inside me."

Shane's eyes grew wide, then narrowed sharply. He looked around to make sure no one was listening.

Lia found that she enjoyed shocking Shane. She enjoyed making him blush, making him shuffle nervously from foot to foot. To make this big man uncomfortable seemed to be a mission of hers in life. It was not only amusing, it was also very much an aphrodisiac, at least when she looked down and noticed the effect she'd had on the fit of his trousers.

He wanted her, even after three days of nonstop lovemaking.

Lia was going to give both of them pleasure, and she was going to do it right now. She took his hand and started pulling him from the vast ballroom.

"Lia, we can't do that here," Shane said, trying to put on the brakes as she reached the door.

Lia turned, a smile on her lips. "What's the matter, Shane? Are you worried about what the other guests will say if they see you sneaking off?" she asked with a laugh.

"I don't want to seem rude," he said as he shifted uncomfortably, firmly planting his feet.

"Oh, you are a beautiful man. But that's not it, is it?" She gasped in shock. "You're worried about my reputation, aren't you?"

"You're a lady, Lia. I don't want anyone to assume anything else. I also don't want them to think you are simply a booty call for me. You are so much more than that," he said, his tone very serious.

"Oh, Shane, I didn't think it possible, but you have just made me want you even more. I am going to pleasure you so well that you won't be able to walk straight for a week. And after I've made sure you're nice and plea-sured, I'm going to throw my head back and receive my own pleasure — over and over and over again."

Shane couldn't protest any longer. Lia tugged on his hand and dragged him through the palace, right onto the guarded grounds. Nei-ther Shane nor Lia said a word to the guards as the two of them jogged past.

They made it around a corner, away from any watchful eyes, and Shane couldn't stand not to feel her lips against his for one second lon-ger.

He hauled her into his arms and their mouths collided. No question now, if there'd ever been any, that he was turned on.

Lia enjoyed what she was doing to this strong man. She surrendered to him with no hesitation, her hands grabbing hold and refusing to let go. When he moved his arms lower and clutched her backside in his hands, she groaned into his mouth.

"Mmm, Mr. Grayson, it seems that you are the impatient one now. I thought this wasn't a good idea," she teased him.

Shane smiled slowly, then pulled gently on her hair to remind her that he had her trapped against his solid body. Fire danced in her eyes, and he decided he'd best back off. He was getting far too revved up, and there was nowhere for them to finish this.

It was a fun game to play, but he wouldn't risk someone seeing her delectable curves, not even if that meant he would be sporting a painful erection for the next few hours. It was better that he be the laughing-stock.

Lia didn't give in as easily. After looking purposefully around, she tugged against his hold. When he saw a new sparkle enter her eyes, he looked in the direction they indicated.

"No way," he said; she reached up and kissed him hard on the mouth.

"Follow me." Lia escaped from his grasp and led him across the large expanse of lawn.

A small storage cottage stood among a few tall trees, and Lia strode straight toward it, dragging Shane behind her. He knew what was on her mind, but he wasn't going to give in, no matter what, he tried tell-ing himself. What if the guards did a patrol? What if the wedding party came searching for them? They absolutely couldn't do this.

Somehow though, he found himself losing all resolve and allowing Lia to take him closer to the building.

It was OK, he assured himself. Surely the building would be locked.

When she got the door to open on the first try and then slipped inside the dark, musty storage shed with him, Shane tried to concentrate. This had gone too far.

This little game needed to end right now.

"Now, Mr. Grayson, what can I do to ease your discomfort?" Lia asked and then kissed his throat, slowly running her tongue across his skin as she reached for the buttons of his dress shirt.

"Lia…" he warned, his body on fire, much as he tried to remain strong and to distract her.

"Yes, Shane?" she asked as she reached the final button and smoothed her palms across the hard expanse of his chest and stomach before dropping to her knees and licking his abs.

"Oh, holy hell, Lia, you have got to stop," he begged. But he was unable to push her away.

Her answer was to slide his belt free before undoing the button on his pants. When he heard the zipper go down, all he could do was lean against the wall while her hand reached inside his boxers and pulled out his throbbing manhood.

"Really? You want me to stop?" she asked with a sweet innocence in her voice as her hand gripped him tight and her mouth came forward, her luscious red lips circling the head of his arousal.

He groaned low in his throat. "No… I mean yes," he gasped as she positioned herself, taking him deeper into her mouth while her tongue licked up and down his shaft. Then, much to his dismay, she pulled back and nibbled on the tip.

"I don't think you want me to stop," she taunted, looking straight up at him while she sank down on him again, taking him all the way to the back of her throat.

"Damn, you are sexy," he groaned, his hands fisting in her hair as he held her to him. No, he didn't want her to stop.

In no time at all, it seemed, he was far too close to releasing in her mouth. She could bring him to the brink of madness with so little effort even after fully satisfying him for three days straight. That she held such power over him was frightening, but not scary enough to drive him away.

"Enough," he demanded, tugging on fistfuls of her hair, forcing her to release him.

The sight of her kneeling before him, her lips swollen, her eyes glowing, and his shaft glistening from her attentions, had him nearly trembling.

"I need you, Shane Grayson," Lia whispered. "I can't get enough of you. We aren't leaving this place until you make me scream in ecstasy."

She stood up and pulled her gown up to her waist, exposing her beautiful womanhood.

The battle was lost. He was just thankful he hadn't known, while the wedding was taking place, that she wasn't wearing any panties. He never would have been able to stand beside Rafe for even the half hour the ceremony had taken.

"I'm never letting you go," Shane growled before grabbing her and lifting her up. She immediately wrapped her legs around his waist.

Shane didn't hesitate any longer. Backing her up against the wall, he plunged deep inside her in one solid push, nearly exploding from the tight grip of her beautiful body surrounding him.

"As many times as we've come together, it's still not enough," she gasped. "I crave the feel of your hands caressing my body, the touch of your fingers on my face, the taste of your lips. I don't think this will ever go away." She spoke as if coming to a realization.

"No, Lia. It won't," he promised as he began sliding slowly in and out of her heat.

"Oh, Shane, please make me come," she begged, no longer wanting the moment to stretch out. She needed release, and she wanted it right now.

"I can't resist you," he said. Bending closer to her, he took her lips with his.

"Then stop trying," she called out as she reached higher, so close to completion.

He held on tight and thrust in and out of her, his mouth ravishing hers while his hands cupped her firm behind. She cried into his mouth, the sound drowned out by his own groans of pleasure.

When she convulsed around him, Shane reached his peak, his body shaking inside her while she gripped him tightly.

It was too much and yet never enough.

He knew he wouldn't let her go.

She could play all the games she wanted, but she needed him, and he would prove to her just how much.

CHAPTER THIRTY-ONE

A DRIANE'S BRILLIANT PLAN was backfiring badly. Yes, having Rafe and Ari's wedding in Corythia had ensured that Rachel stay in the country for a while longer. But Adriane hadn't had much time alone with her since their arrival. Rachel's family had swarmed around her and now she was pulling further away from him. This could end up being disastrous.

No matter what it took, he couldn't allow her to leave with his children.

Surprisingly, it wasn't only the children she carried whom Adriane didn't want to leave. Rachel was becoming too big a part of his life. That was good, wasn't it?

Only if he trusted her not to run.

He was beginning to fear the hold she had over him.

It was better for them both if she understood that he was the one in charge — the one she must submit to. No, he wasn't going to be cruel to her, or make her life in Corythia a hardship, but he did need her to understand that when he expected something to be done, it was the way it would be.

So far, he hadn't had much luck in convincing her of that.

"Rachel, we need to speak," he said when he found her alone by the dessert table.

"This isn't the best time, Adriane. Ari is going to cut the cake soon, and I don't want to miss out on the bridal bouquet toss." She bit down on a soft pastry and moaned her approval.

The sound escaping her lips instantly sent his blood into boiling mode, and he was worried his secrets below the belt would be quite visible to everyone at the reception.

Shifting to try to hide his reaction, Adriane took her arm, making her look up in surprise.

"You don't need to catch the bouquet," he said, his lips near her ear.

"Please don't start in on the marriage talk again. You promised," she snapped, pulling against his hold.

"Of course," he said, though it was only to appease her for the moment. Soon, her family would be gone, and then they would be back on track to their wedding.

"Now leave me be for a while. I'll speak to you after the reception is over," Rachel said, quickly moving away from him as she licked chocolate off her fingers.

Adriane's groin tightened even more. Soon. Very, very soon he would have her back in his bed. Could having a permanent erection without release prevent him from having more children? There was no possible way he would ask his physician.

He'd just have to take his chances.

Picking up a drink, he watched as Rachel approached her brother, who was now smiling and relaxed with his arm wrapped around his wife. Adriane couldn't believe it, but he found himself feeling a twinge of jealousy over the other couple's marriage vows.

Rafe had it much easier now than Adriane did. He'd managed to secure his bride to him permanently. But it would be Adriane's turn soon enough.

*****

Rachel's stomach stirred as she walked away from Adriane. She'd been avoiding him after their almost intimate encounter at the musical performance.

One reason was the utter delight of being with her family again. The other was that Adriane made her feel strong emotions, ones that she refused to dwell on too much but which she found disturbing.

She absolutely didn't want to marry him. And be queen? Get real. She was half American and there was no royalty in America. She wasn't queen material.

"We're leaving in a couple of hours, Rachel. Are you coming home?" Rafe asked as she approached.

Rachel had made a firm resolve to stay for a month, to really get to know Adriane. But now that she had the opportunity to leave with her family, she was wavering.

If she left right now, she feared her children would never know their father adequately. That wasn't acceptable. Rachel had grown up with incredible parents, and she wanted all children — particularly her own — to grow up the same way.

Though she wouldn't marry him for any other reason than love, which wasn't in the cards, she did hope to be his friend.

"No," she told her brother. "Now that you know where I am and can come rescue me the minute I call, I'm not worried by being here. I need more time with Adriane, time to find out if he's a good man. We've fought so much these past two weeks that I don't know him well enough. The week we were together in Florida seems like another lifetime ago. Then, he'd been attentive and such an amazing—"

"Stop right there!" Rafe demanded, his eyes widening in horror.

Both Rachel and Ari laughed as his mouth flopped open.

"OK. I won't torture you, dear brother. But I do appreciate the cell phone. I will keep it well hidden, so if Adriane acts up again, I'll call immediately for a rescue," she promised.

Rachel had no doubt that she'd have to plan a sneak escape if she decided to leave. Adriane wasn't going to allow her to depart easily, even though they did have an understanding. He was determined to have his children grow up in Corythia.

That just wasn't acceptable. She would share the kids with him, but she refused to be told where she could live. She refused to be told what to do — ever!

"Thank you for all you've done, Rachel. I know your life has been chaotic and frightening of late, and still, you put all of that aside to give me the perfect wedding. I *love* you, dear sister," Ari said as she left Rafe's arms and enveloped Rachel in a happy embrace.

Both women's eyes filled with affectionate tears.

"I have to give Adriane credit for a beautiful wedding," Rachel said. "He really went out of his way. I am worried that I'm going to gain a thousand pounds during this pregnancy, though. I've practically moved in by the dessert table, and have to bite my tongue when someone comes up and takes one of my precious delectables. It's ridiculous. I'm surrounded by mountains of food, and I want to hoard it all, not let a single morsel be consumed by anyone else." She had to laugh.

"I wouldn't worry too much, Rachel. You're stunning, and even when your belly is sticking out a mile, you'll still be the hottest woman in Corythia," Ari assured her.

"Thanks. We'll see if you still feel that way in about four more months," Rachel replied.

"I don't want to leave you here. It worries me," Rafe interjected, looking around the room as if searching for danger.

"I'll be fine, Rafe. I really will. If it gets too bad, just send mother back in. She can get me out while still maintaining peace. I swear, if they'd had her around before any of the major wars, they would have never started. All the generals would have just come together and smiled, singing campfire songs as she passed out cookies and her famous coffee."

"I have to agree with you there," Rafe said, reluctantly grinning at the thought.

"I want you both to go on your honeymoon, and I demand that you have an exceptional time. Do you understand?" Rachel said, pulling away from both of them to stare them down.

"Yes, Rachel, we will have a spectacular time," Rafe said before turning a solicitous look on his wife. "We may even start to work on a cousin for your children," he added.

Ari's eyes widened before her lips turned up in a smile. "Do you mean that, Rafe?" she asked, as if afraid to hope.

Rafe's grin fell as he saw the uncertainty in her eyes.

"We spoke of having children earlier. You still want them, right?" he asked as he pulled her close. Both of them forgot all about Rachel, who was standing there awkwardly, feeling that she was intruding on a special moment.

"Of course I do. You know that. I just didn't think it was something we would be doing so soon. I thought you would want to wait until..." She seemed unsure how to end that sentence.

"Ari, I love you. More than I can ever express. I want you to have my children. I want to watch your stomach grow, and be at every doctor's appointment. I want to run to the store for your midnight cravings...I want to do everything a doting husband is supposed to do," he said, his hands moving down her sides, his thumbs caressing her very flat stomach.

"I think the honeymoon is a great time to start trying, then," she said, joy radiating from her.

"Then we'd best use the new...items I've ordered...before you can't fit into them," he said, waggling his eyebrows.

Rachel turned away, horrified. She didn't know whether he was kidding or not, and she didn't want to know. Her only thought was to get the heck away from him before she heard anything more.

Passing by Adriane, who must have had a target painted on her since he kept staring her way, she looked down, figuring that if she didn't make eye contact, he would just leave her alone.

No such luck.

"Rachel, you can't hide from me forever," he said, his voice barely above a whisper. She was shocked at how quickly he could move to her side.

"I don't want to hide forever — just for tonight." She passed on by and left the room.

Forget about watching the cake get cut. She needed five minutes alone.

The next week was going to be a long one. That was all the time she now decided she would give herself to learn more about Adriane. She couldn't handle a full month. If she still didn't have answers by that time, to hell with it. She'd just have to get to know him after the babies were born. Her hormones were too chaotic for her to even think right now, much less make wise decisions.

Mr. Do-It-My-Way-Always would just have to learn to compromise and come to her in the States.

Stepping into her room, Rachel shut the door with a relieved sigh. Then she shuddered. That was too much information to learn about her big brother — *way* too much information.

CHAPTER THIRTY-TWO

ADRIANE DIDN'T LIKE to ask for help. It went against everything he believed in. He was the king. He was respected and revered. He shouldn't have to ask anyone to help him.

But Rachel obviously wasn't cooperating at the moment, so that left him with little choice but to suck up some of his pride. He spotted Ari alone, which was a miracle, since her newly minted husband hadn't seen fit to remove himself from her side most of the day.

He was going to go for it.

"Hello, Ari. I hope the day has been pleasant for you," he said after he'd made a quiet approach.

"Oh, Adriane, you startled me," she gasped as she took the glass of champagne from her lips.

"I'm sorry; that wasn't my intention. Are you enjoying yourself?" He hated to waste time on pleasantries, but trying to soften her up.

"It's been absolutely lovely, Adriane. I really appreciate all that you've done to make the day special," she said in all sincerity.

"Wonderful. Would you mind taking a walk with me? I would like to speak with you alone," he asked, offering his arm.

Ari hesitated for only the briefest of moments before accepting. As they walked outside, she looked him straight in the eye. He found it highly disconcerting. Could she see his very soul, if he had one? Though Adriane didn't squirm, he found himself wanting to.

"How is life treating you as king?" Ari asked as they reached an ornate water fountain, the sounds of its cascading waters soothing in the twilight.

"All is well," he said, his standard answer. Her eyebrows rose as she waited for him to continue. "Mostly, it is wonderful. I love my kingdom, love my people. Of course, I am responsible for a great deal," he had to admit. There was a lot on his shoulders. Most of the time, it wasn't a burden, but while dealing with this strange situation with Rachel, it was all a little bit much. Add to that his problems with Gianni, who had been strangely quiet the last couple of weeks, and he was about as highly strung as he could possibly be right now.

That his brother was not making a move was more frightening than his threats had been. The man wouldn't just disappear — Adriane knew that — which left him wondering what Gianni was plotting next.

How he would love to have nothing more to focus on except for his business ventures. In years past, before his father's final illness, Adriane had been carefree, worried only about making a few billion more to add to his and his country's portfolios.

He missed that rush.

"It won't take long for my husband to seek me out, so why don't you tell me what's on your mind," Ari said.

Adriane was impressed with this best friend of Rachel's. Ari had grown since he'd first met her; she now oozed confidence and faced challenges head-on. She was a good match for Rafe. Adriane wondered whether he and Rafe would ever again share an easy friendship, the way they had before Adriane had met Rachel. At the moment, it seemed doubtful.

"How do I make Rachel see there is no other choice but for us to marry?" he asked. If she was going to be blunt, then so was he.

Instead of being horrified by his words, Ari laughed, a deep, highly amused laugh. Adriane wasn't sure whether he should be offended. He was pouring his heart out and she was almost doubling over with laughter.

"I'm sorry, Adriane," she gasped in between giggles while she tried to pull herself together.

Should he just walk away? It was obvious he wasn't going to get any information from the woman. He turned to do so and her hand shot out and grabbed his arm.

"I really am sorry. It's just so like a man to put a question that way. Can't you see that women don't work like that? You kidnapped her, told her she had no other choice but to marry you, and then you haven't given her a reason to want to stay. Do you care about her?"

Her giggles stopped and she looked at him closely once again. Adriane didn't want his soul under her microscope. That was closed, to everyone.

"Of course I care about her and my children," he said stiffly.

When Ari continued staring him down, Adriane found himself wanting to loosen his tie.

"I think you do care, Adriane. You'd be a fool not to, for Rachel is a very special person. I will tell you this — she won't stay for anything less than love. If you want her to accept your proposal, then you have to give her a reason to do so." Ari didn't blink once as she threw out her challenge.

"Love is messy and unnecessary. There are better reasons for us to marry — the two babies she carries, for one," he said.

"That's not a good reason, Adriane. That would only lead to dissatisfaction and a feeling of being trapped. You have to love each other, be passionate, and like being in the same room together. Marriage is about more than convenience," she warned.

"Arranged marriages have worked for centuries," he pointed out. "Millennia, in fact."

"That was duty, not love, and the world was a different place. Women had little choice, you know. But now they do. I know Rachel, Adriane, and she would die a little bit more each and every day if she married you for the sake of her children and nothing else."

"I disagree. I think without messy emotions, a marriage has a far stronger chance of surviving." He wasn't about to give up on his beliefs.

"Why did you come to me and ask my advice if you're unwilling to listen to what I have to say?"

That was a good question. Why had he come to her? He didn't need her approval, or anyone's approval for that matter, to move forward. He was just tired of hitting brick walls with Rachel. The two of them needed to wed — and he needed her lying beneath him. He was just trying to speed the process up.

"You are her best friend. I thought you might be able to make her see reason," he answered.

Again, Ari laughed. "Oh, Adriane. You are in for a world of hurt if you maintain that attitude. I hope you figure this all out before it's too late," she said.

The worst part was the sympathy in her expression. Adriane didn't need *anyone's* sympathy. He was the king of Corythia! That meant something. Didn't it?

"This will work. She will see reason," he insisted. He and Ari were just going in circles.

"I hope it does work out, but I have a feeling you're up for a bit more heartache, because you are just so damn stubborn — a lot like my husband, actually. But the thing is, Adriane, it just doesn't matter. The more you fight it, the harder you will fall. I'm sorry for what you are going through, but you honestly need to pull your head out before it's too late," she warned.

"I don't need your sympathy," he said.

"Yes, you do," Ari told him, and squeezed his arm. She gave him one more pitying look and then she sauntered confidently away, leaving him alone outside.

What was he going to do about his spitfire fiancée? And, yes, she was his fiancée, whether she wanted to accept that or not.

Dropping down on the edge of the fountain, he listened to the tranquil sound of the water flowing behind him as he tried to decide his next move.

A determined glint suddenly entered his eyes and he stood back up. It was time they came head to head.

He was going to make her his again. That would cut through everything. If the two of them had one thing right together, it was chemistry.

Adriane had to remind Rachel exactly how good the two of them were together. He'd make her remember.

He marched inside the castle with a purpose and a smile of anticipation. Tonight was going to satisfy them both!

CHAPTER THIRTY-THREE

L IA AND RACHEL skidded around opposite ends of the room as they rushed forward just as Ari was standing on the balcony looking out over the audience. Her eyebrows rose and she sent a questioning look the girls' way before turning around.

They were both a bit shamefaced at having left during Ari's reception. Rachel, because she wanted to think, and Lia because she'd wanted to… Well, she wasn't even going to justify her reasons to herself.

When the bride launched the wedding bouquet into the air, Rachel and Lia's eyes met, and then both girls took a step back as the other women in the room rushed forward, everyone trying to catch the bouquet, hoping for luck in capturing their future husband.

To Ari's delight, when the crowd cleared, it was her mother, Sandra, who was holding the beautiful bunch of flowers, her cheeks blushing pink as the other women grudgingly congratulated her.

She thanked them before slipping away to help her daughter change for her ride to the airport. Lia stood by with a smile on her face. With the great-looking man Sandra had come to the wedding with sporting a mysterious smile on his face, Lia had a feeling the magical powers of catching the bridal bouquet might just have some meaning this time.

The party moved outside, and the guests formed a double line for the newly married couple to walk through. Everyone was armed with rice to throw over the heads of the happy pair as a symbol of fertility and prosperity, though with Rafe's billions, they didn't need any luck in the latter department.

When Ari reappeared with Rafe at her side on the other side of the rice throwing wall of people, the newlyweds made sure to give Rachel a parting "gift": yet another firm lecture, letting her know she was to call them the moment she wanted to leave Corythia.

Though Ari hoped that Rachel and Adriane could work through their differences, she wasn't taking any chances. The king had already held her dear friend captive once. He wouldn't be allowed to do it again.

The women shed goodbye tears; the men stood by somewhat uncomfortably and shook hands. Rafe certainly didn't trust Adriane, but he was going to respect his sister's wishes.

As Rafe and Ari left, a silence descended on the other two couples. Rachel wasn't even looking at Adriane, and then in a flash, she disappeared once again, feeling that her room was the safest place to hide for the moment.

Shane and Lia were left alone when Adriane stomped off. The rest of the crowd began to leave the palace, their stomachs full and their smiles genuine. It had been a lovely wedding and reception.

"Does this mean we are together now, Lia?" Shane asked as he grasped her hand and led her to a more private area in the palace. As exciting as their earlier lovemaking had been, he was eager to be where he could slow things down and make love to her the way a woman deserved.

"It means that I'm tired of fighting how I feel. I don't know what the future has in store, but I just know I want to be with you right now," she admitted.

Shane was surprised when a blush stole over her cheeks. Lia hadn't been the blushing type in more than a decade. Her years of shyness had been pushed away, and Lia had never looked back, liking the woman she was now so much better than the shy teenager she'd been. Now she was confident, brave and ready for any new challenge thrown her way.

"Marry me, Lia."

Shane was shocked when the words popped out of his mouth, but when he had no desire to take them back, he knew it was the right thing to say, the right time to ask her to be his wife.

She turned and looked at him, her expression dazed, but not horrified. That was a start.

"You're just carried away by the moment, Shane. We haven't solved any of our problems yet, just masked them in a flurry of lovemaking," she warned.

"I don't care. We can get through the problems, work them out as we go along. I don't care if we fight or don't agree on everything. I don't care what tomorrow holds. As long as I know I'm coming home to you, I can face anything," he said.

She was silent as she looked into his eyes, just the two of them standing together in a large palace ballroom as the lights were dimmed and the music from the joyous party played back in Lia's head.

"Shane…" She seemed to not know what to say.

"Don't give me all the reasons it can't work. I've known you half your life. I love you, Lia — more than any other soul on this earth, past or future. You have admitted you love me too, so why can't we just stop playing games and be together? The two of us can jet off to Las Vegas and get married right now, then tell our families about it later. I just want you by my side for the rest of our lives."

She looked at him with wide eyes before a beautiful smile overtook her features. "I do want to marry you," she said before throwing her arms around his neck, pulling him down to her and kissing him with an unquenchable and fathomless need.

Shane reluctantly pulled back from her. "That wasn't a yes, Lia. Are you saying yes?" His eyes gleamed.

Did she want to say yes? Of course she did! Was she going to let her fears stop her? Lia thought about it.

"Yes, Shane. That's a yes. I may change my mind, think this is a bad idea, but right now, all I can think about is marrying you," she said, beaming up at him.

"Then I had best hurry," he said, abandoning the idea of going back to his hotel as he called a driver to pick them up.

Before Lia had time to think, he had her in the car and was driving to the helipad, where they could immediately be transported to his jet.

"What about our bags?" she asked with a laugh as she stepped from the helicopter and it flew away, zipping across the dark sea.

"We can have them shipped to us. I'm not taking any chances that you'll change your mind again," he said, pulling her close to shield her from the sharp wind picking up around them.

Lia snuggled close in his arms, drunk on what she was feeling in these moments. She did love him. All of the worries she had were still there, but they were tucked away. She wanted to be this man's wife. She might end up losing him tomorrow, but at least she'd have him now.

Their travels went quickly, and soon she was in a jet, lifting into the air — destination, Las Vegas. She felt only a twinge of regret that she was sneaking off to elope. Her family would forgive her — she hoped.

As the jet flew smoothly across the dark, starlit skies, Lia nestled into Shane's arms, falling asleep with her head resting comfortably against his steadily beating heart.

This was where she belonged, and nothing the two of them could do from this moment on would be wrong.

How could it be anything less than perfect when it felt so right?

Shane knew their problems would still be there when they woke up after this act of impulse, but he didn't care.

When they faced tomorrow, they'd be man and wife.

Sure, Rafe might try to throttle him, but it would be well worth it.

Holding Lia close, he relaxed, feeling good for the first time since he'd lost his friend. Maybe it was time to turn in his resignation to the military.

He'd loved his time of service, felt he'd done a lot of good over the years, but now he had a new life to forge, a new life that would include his very beautiful wife.

First, he'd marry her, then take her to buy the biggest diamond he could find. He wanted the world to know she belonged to him — forever.

Shane fell asleep with his head against the seat of the jet's superbly comfortable couch and with a very content and warm Lia held securely to him.

CHAPTER THIRTY-FOUR

"SIR, I THINK the king has had a…um…a breakdown."

Nico sent a withering stare at the servant as he waited for the man to go on. "Do not forget you are speaking about your king," Nico warned him.

"Well, it's just that the king is in the throne room…" the man started.

"And?" Nico asked, though he wondered what Adriane might be doing there.

"Um, it's just that he's in there pacing and talking to himself. No one but the cleaning staff has been in there in months. No ceremonies, no reason for him to be in there."

"The king can be in any part of his palace he chooses to be in. I had best not hear of you spreading rumors," Nico said before dismissing the servant.

Nico walked down the palace hallways to check on his king. What in the world was going on now?

*****

Adriane paced his throne room — alone — by choice.

He'd growled at everyone when he'd been in his offices to get out and then he'd wandered the palace, finding himself in front of the ornate doors leading to the grand throne room. Walking inside, he'd looked at the cold room with its high-backed thrones, gold decorative walls and little else. This was a place for ceremonies, the place his wife would be crowned queen. That thought had stirred his blood. *If* she became queen. He'd remained in the room ever since, for almost two hours, while he came up with the details of how he was going to get Rachel into his bed.

He wasn't going to beg — he'd done enough of that. He was going to seduce, though so far that had failed as well. Maybe he was going insane; he just didn't know anymore. Damn. Their time in Florida wasn't this complicated. It wasn't complicated at all. He'd asked her to dinner, planned on a night of hot sex, and had gotten a week instead. Now, he was pacing like a madman in a place of formal ceremonies and talking to himself.

Adriane laughed aloud, the sound echoing off the walls.

That's it. He was losing it — really losing it. It was a good thing his staff couldn't see him right now.

Why couldn't his time with Rachel be just as easy as it had been back in Florida?

He didn't think he was asking for too much.

Finally finished with sulking on his own, he grabbed some of the fresh-cut flowers that were in a vase on a nearby table and made his way from the room.

He knew how to seduce; he just hadn't been putting in enough effort. A good king knew such things. Seduction was the essence of diplomacy, after all.

As he made his journey to her room, no nerves assailed him, no doubts of his victory this time.

Granted, his desire to have her like him as a person puzzled him. To have her love him, too? He wasn't going there. He didn't need her affection; her compliance was enough — well, that and her lying beneath him. He wasn't going to be married without reaping the benefits of hot sex, and with Rachel, the sex was always hot. He couldn't remember another lover turning him on anywhere near as much.

Just the thought of her sweet ass cupped in his strong hands while he plunged into her heat had him instantly hard and ready to throw her across the bed.

Tonight was going to be good.

As he reached her door, he raised his hand, knowing she wasn't going to admit him easily. But part of her appeal was that he enjoyed chasing her so much. He hoped she didn't lose that appeal once he finally captured her, but he suspected that wouldn't happen.

Still, he enjoyed her fiery temper and the lashing from her tongue, at least on occasion. It would definitely make for an interesting life.

Once he threw the full arsenal of his charm her way, he'd win her over with no problems. He pasted an arrogant yet seductive smile across his lips when he knocked. After several moments, when there was no answer, he knocked again, his smile faltering just the slightest bit.

He didn't expect her to be so rude as to ignore him entirely.

"My little wildcat, I'm not leaving until we speak this evening," he said, his voice low and sexy.

Still no answer.

"I won't leave, Rachel. I can wait at your door all night long. I can last until morning and then some. You should know that well, since I did a lot more than just stand outside and serenade you during that week in Florida," he said loudly. "Yes, I made you come over and over and over..." He knew he'd get some sort of reaction. Hell, he *hoped* she came to the door in a stormy, fiery mood.

Dangerous, of course. He'd have a hell of a time restraining himself, and not shocking the servants by simply pushing her against the solid wood of her door and thrusting inside her. Her temper really fueled his lust.

"I plan on proving my abilities later by stripping off your clothes, spreading your thighs and—"

Before he could finish the sentence, the door was thrown open and a furious Rachel stood before him, sporting an appealingly short silk robe, hair that was mussed, and a scowl on her lips.

She must have been in bed, and he'd gladly escort her back to it.

Rachel looked up and down the hallway to see if anyone else was out there.

"What in the hell are you doing, Adriane? I don't need your staff to hear this sort of talk and think I'm a complete tramp," she hissed, blocking the entrance into her room.

Adriane had to fight back a giant grin. He'd gotten her to open the door. That was the first part of the battle. Now, he just needed to charm her into letting him through, and they could come together and then sleep until morning. He needed both release and a good night's rest, and he was sure she wanted and needed the same.

"I needed you to open the door. It seemed my knock wasn't doing it," he said easily, leaning against the doorjamb, making her take a step back. She still didn't let go of the door, however; nor did she invite him inside.

But he wasn't worried. He had her right where he wanted her.

"Maybe I wasn't answering because I was in bed and didn't want to talk to you tonight," Rachel said tightly. "We can talk tomorrow, *in the morning*." She tried to push the door closed.

Adriane easily blocked her move.

"I think tonight is better. I've missed you, Rachel. Why don't you invite me inside, so we can talk privately and then…um…rest?" he asked, careful with his choice of words.

"Rest? Really, Adriane? That's the best you can come up with? I don't think so. But knowing you, you probably spent hours working up this brilliant attempt at seduction. Am I right?"

"You wound me, Rachel."

"Don't tempt me," she said, deliberately taking his words literally. "We will wait until tomorrow, when you haven't had so much wine, and *then* we will talk. I could have left your charming little country, but I chose to stay to get to know you. If you are going to give me these cheesy pickup lines and try tempting me with your…charm—" Rachel broke off for a second to chortle at the idea, "—then you will simply annoy me and I'll hop on the first flight out of Corythia. I'm trying here — for the sake of my children — but don't push me beyond what I will tolerate." Rachel spoke with a sweet smile, but also with steel in her voice.

Adriane was taken aback by the fire in his little minx.

Damn, he wanted her even more now.

Still, his plans for seduction were going right down the drain, and that hadn't entered into his plans as he'd paced for hours. He wouldn't force her. No, that wasn't his style. But that didn't mean he wasn't willing to do a bit of cajoling.

Looking down, he noticed her bright red toenails, sparkles included. Never before had he been turned on by toenails, but tonight was yet another exception in a long line of them brought on by Rachel Palazzo.

Everything about her, it seemed, got his blood racing and his manhood pulsing.

Yep, permanent damage. He now expected it.

"Why not just invite me in? We'll have a drink by the fire. I can rub your feet," he said. He suddenly wanted to do nothing but that. No, that was something else he'd never had a desire to do before. Damn!

Her expression softened as she considered his words. Ha! He'd found a weakness in her armor. Who would have known?

Adriane smiled with renewed confidence as he held up the flowers he'd so thoughtfully picked up for her. Of course she'd let him in, and then he'd get her in bed easily.

His arousal pulsed at the thought.

"I'll take a rain check on the foot rub," she said as she pointedly looked at the flowers but said nothing.

But he sensed reluctance in her voice and eyes.

"Come on, Rachel. You were wearing heels all day today. A good foot rub is just what you need," he said, slinking forward another inch.

He really wanted to get his hands on her delicate feet. He wasn't sure whether it was more for her or for him. No, that wasn't true. It was certainly more for him.

"Go away, Adriane, before I change my mind about our talk tomorrow. I need to sleep," she said, pushing at the door again.

Double damn!

"You are contradicting yourself, Rachel," he said, some of his charm fading as he stared at her. She confused him and he didn't know how to deal with it. "I am only trying to know you more, which is what you say that you want, yet you keep pushing me away. What do I need to do to get you to talk with me? I even brought you flowers," he added as if he wanted a pat on the back.

"Oh, how sweet! You so thoughtfully grabbed some flowers from a vase that your staff picked and brought in," she said with unmistakable sarcasm.

"I was thinking of you when I grabbed them," he defended.

"Think bigger," she said.

"I'm trying here. Do you want a small island, diamonds, gold? What else can I do so we can…talk?"

She hesitated before speaking. "I don't want material things, Adriane. Don't be so dense. You only want me lying beneath your body again. At least I know how much you're willing to sacrifice to get what you want," she said, her eyes narrowing.

"If you want to be on top, I'm fine with that, too," he said, thinking it was a good compromise.

And that's where he lost the battle.

"Move now!"

Adriane took a step back at the fury in her voice.

Then the door slammed in his face, barely missing his nose with the violence of her thrust. She was quite strong in her anger.

Adriane stood there for several moments, trying to decide whether or not to barge through the door and teach her a lesson on how to speak to a king, how to speak to her future husband.

But he was trying to win a war, not every battle. Maybe he had approached this all wrong. As he turned away, he noticed the flowers still clutched in his hands. With a sigh, he laid them in front of her door and turned away.

Tomorrow was a new day. He'd have to come up with a better battle plan if he wanted to take her to his bed. One way or the other, it would happen soon. It was either that, or... There really wasn't another option. He just had to get her into his bed.

Rachel would learn that he never, ever gave up! Not once in his life had he given up on something he'd decided to go after. If it was something he wanted in the first place, it was worth fighting for.

Still, this was by far the hardest he'd fought for something — or someone, he should say. Never before had he needed to chase a woman. And he didn't appreciate having to do it now. Well, that wasn't entirely true. He was quite enjoying himself, even if he was also frustrated and dealing with a permanent erection.

Rachel was his. She just needed to realize that.

Tomorrow she would be his — body and soul, in his bed.

Poor fellow. It never crossed his mind that this wasn't the first time he'd made this vow. When would tomorrow actually come?

CHAPTER THIRTY-FIVE

ANOTHER DAY, ANOTHER squabble. Rachel had a raging headache the next morning, and Adriane was in a less than perfect mood. She'd ended up storming from the room and slamming the door of her suite in his face…again.

When was this going to get easier?

Maybe she should just leave with her parents.

Today was their last day in Corythia and she was almost in tears. Maybe leaving would actually help the situation between her and Adriane. But she didn't expect him to be thrilled about it, and if she and Adriane entered into a full-scale battle, her protective parents would join in. She definitely didn't want them to get caught in the cross fire.

Lying down on the couch, she held a cold compress to her forehead and waited for the Tylenol to kick in. Someday soon, this pregnancy had to become more manageable.

A slight smile crossed her lips as she lifted her shirt and rubbed along her belly. The bump was more noticeable now. Not enough that you could see it when she had her clothes on, but when she looked in the mirror and turned to one side, she could see the signs of life growing within her.

All her fears about the pregnancy and impending motherhood had gone away, and now she just felt excitement when she thought of holding her twin babies. OK, OK, that wasn't entirely true. She did feel *some* fear. How was she going to handle two of them at one time? She'd just have to figure it out after they were born.

Her head was beginning to clear, and she was starting to feel a little more human when a hand landed on her arm, making her sit up too quickly. She felt nausea fly straight to her throat as she let out a squeak of fright.

"It's all right, darling, it's just me," came the sweet voice of her mother.

Her heart pounding, she opened her eyes and turned her head. "You scared me to death, Mom," she gasped, then laughed when she realized how stupid it was to be afraid. The palace was literally surrounded by guards. The chances of someone getting in there to hurt her were slim to none.

She looked around, found her compress on the floor, picked it up, then lay back down and put it back it on her forehead.

"I'm sorry. Your father and I are leaving soon, and I just wanted to make sure you were OK before we left. But you're not, darling. You're obviously not well. You can come with us, you know," her mom said for the hundredth time.

Rachel understood her mother's unhappiness at leaving without her daughter. But the king wasn't likely to do anything rash a second time. Though he still didn't want his "baby mama" to go, Rachel didn't see him risking a major diplomatic incident to keep her there, and now, with the cell phone her brother had given her, she had communication beyond the palace walls.

When it came time for her to leave, she would do so, whether he was ready for her departure or not.

"Besides having this killer headache, I'm fine, Mama. I promise," she added when her mother looked at her skeptically.

"You realize I've always been able to tell when you're fibbing to me, right?"

"Yes, Mom. None of us has ever been able to get anything past you. It's always been quite inconvenient," Rachel said with a fond smile.

"A good mother knows her children, knows everything about them, the good and the bad. A great mother loves them regardless. I love you and your sister and brother and would do anything for each of you — including supporting you even when I think you are making a wrong choice. I am not saying that I think you're making a bad choice right now; I just think you need to take care of yourself, or let your parents take care of you. No matter how old you get, Rachel, you will always be my baby."

"Oh, Mom, I love you so much." Rachel sat up and wrapped her slender arms around her mom's neck, with tears beginning to stream from her eyes. "Dang hormones," she grumbled.

"I love you too, sweetheart, and I'm so sorry that you're going through such a terrible amount of pain right now. If I could take it away, I would," she said, tenderly rubbing the length of Rachel's back in comfort, the way she'd always done since Rachel could remember.

"I'm just so confused," she admitted.

"Then tell me about it. Let's see if we can figure things out together," Rosabella said.

Rachel hesitated for only a moment longer before sitting back and clutching the blanket beside her to her chest. This was her mom, the woman she'd always told everything to. Of course she was the one who would give her the best advice.

"I know Ari filled you in, but I don't know exactly what she told you, so I guess I'll give you my version of the events. You've probably been told that I had a weeklong affair with Adriane in Florida," she began, feeling bad when her mom winced. Though she'd heard it already, no mother liked to be told about her daughter having an illicit affair with a man she didn't know.

"I'm sorry, darling. I know you're an adult now, but it's still something hard for a mother to hear, especially when I've heard it twice," she said with a chuckle.

"Yeah, I know. The thought of my children growing up and behaving the way I did fills my heart with terror," Rachel admitted.

"You followed your heart and you've always been responsible. I'm not faulting you for that. I just wish you'd been more careful this time. Adriane could have turned out to be a serial killer," Rosabella admonished her.

"Worse! He turned out to be a flipping king!" Rachel countered.

"We will have to disagree on which of the two is worse," Rosabella said with another laugh.

"Everything was great with Adriane. I only knew him as Ian at the time. We laughed, talked, and, well...had fun. Then, it was just something carefree and exciting. Now, I realize how irresponsible I was," she said, not quite willing to tell her mom that she'd had the best sex of her life. Not to mention the only sex of her life, but who was counting? Anyway, Rosabella seemed grateful for her discretion.

As Rachel repeated her story, her mother sat there patting her leg, listening without interruption. Though Rachel hadn't been listening to anyone recently, she was eager to hear her mother's advice.

"Have you decided if you want to stay with him?" Rosabella asked when her daughter finished her tale. "It is to Adriane's credit, I hope you know, that he wants to marry you. Many a royal man wouldn't be so principled."

"I am honored by his offer, Mom, but no. I'm not going to marry him. I learned from watching you and dad that a marriage can only be about love, and anything less would be settling. I deserve better than that. I do, however, want to know him. I want to be able to tell my children good things about him, and I hope we can be friends for their sake. I think the reason I want to know him so much is because I feel that after we leave, that will be it, that he'll move on, get married to a proper woman, and the kids will never see him again. At least if I've spent time with him, then I will be able to share with them who their father is. When I read them fairy tales, I can tell them that their father is a real live king. I would have been excited to know I was a princess when I was a little girl."

"I'm so very proud of you, Rachel. The choices you're making aren't easy ones, and the way you are already putting your children ahead of anything else shows me that you are more than ready to become a mother. A lot of young women think being a mom is all glory and nothing messy. Many teens think they will have this child who will love them always. The reality is that children are difficult. They are demanding and it's all about them — always. We make sacrifices as a mother, and those sacrifices are well worth it, because then when our children grow into fine young men and women, we get to sit down with them and share their life. I wouldn't change a thing about being a mother — well, I might change those sleepless nights."

"Thanks, Mom. Sometimes it scares me to do this alone," Rachel admitted.

"You will never be alone; you have your family. Plus, you never know. Maybe Adriane is the one — maybe you will fall hopelessly in love," she said with a twinkle in her eyes.

"I will never fall in love with that man. He is too pompous and he thinks he's always right. He would drive me insane!" she cried, narrowing her eyes at just the thought.

Rosabella chortled as she looked at her daughter. "That's what I said about your father. He stormed into Italy like he owned the country. I wanted nothing to do with him. But look at us now. Married for almost forty years, and I love him now more than ever before."

"That's because you and Dad are perfect together," Rachel said, only hoping she could someday have a marriage even half as beautiful as her parents had.

"We weren't in the beginning, darling. I kept turning him down flat when he asked me out. *Not interested*, I kept saying. It took some time, but he was so persistent that eventually I agreed to a date, thinking he would grow bored after I spoke in a monotone and refused any of his advances. I was wrong. He stirred my blood that night, just as he does now," her mom said with a dreamy smile.

"Ugh, mom. I don't even want to think about dad stirring your blood," Rachel said with a fake gag, but her cheeks turned pink at the thought.

"I'm not in the grave yet, Rachel. I still have feelings."

"OK, you can still have feelings. I just can't hear about them. That's my *dad* you're talking about," she said with a grin.

"I will miss you so much, cara. I want you to come home soon, OK?" Rosabella leaned over and embraced Rachel with the magical comfort of a mother's love.

"I will miss you too, Mama. I promise I won't be gone much longer. I can't give birth to these babies without you by my side."

"I want you to be strong and stand on your own two feet. I raised you that way, but I do want to be there. Some events are just too important for a mom not to be a part of them with her own baby," Rosabella said.

"I agree. You raised me well, Mama, but I will always still need you."

Rosabella held her for several long moments, and then it was time for her daughter to walk her out. Saying goodbye to her mom and dad together was going to be even harder, and Rachel took several long breaths before she met them at the front entrance to the palace.

"You are both welcome here at any time," Adriane said as he joined them there.

"Thank you, Adriane. We appreciate the invitation," Martin said as he shook Adriane's hand.

"It was my pleasure to have you both," Adriane said as he turned toward Rosabella and lifted her hand, kissing the back of it before smiling. "Your daughter certainly received her beauty from you."

Oh, the man was smooth.

Rosabella giggled and a slight blush entered her cheeks as she moved in front of Rachel.

"I love you. Call me the minute you need anything. Or just call to tell me about your day. I look forward to your coming back home," Rosabella said, and Rachel noticed Adriane's body tense as if afraid she would just run away with them right now.

Tempting.

But no. She was committed.

"I will miss you, baby girl," Martin said as he pulled Rachel gently into his arms.

"I will miss you, too, Daddy," she said, leaning into his embrace and allowing a few tears to escape, though she'd promised herself she wouldn't cry. It wasn't as if she were losing her parents forever. But they'd just be so far away.

"I will take good care of her and our babies," Adriane assured them as he walked up and put his arm around Rachel as soon as Martin released her.

Rachel stood there with Adriane and watched the two walk from the palace and get into the awaiting car that would take them to the helipad.

"I won't make you feel trapped ever again," Adriane said as he turned her and looked into her eyes.

Rachel wiped her tears away as she looked at him with suspicion. What was he doing now?

"It was wrong of me. I'm truly sorry, cara. You have free rein to speak to all of your family. I can admit when I've done wrong," he said with a rueful grin.

"I may need to record this," she said, her heart clattering just a bit too much at the gentle way he was speaking to her. She was a bit too vulnerable right now.

"How about joining me for lunch?"

"Yes."

Rachel didn't hesitate. The thought of going to her room and being alone at this moment was unbearable. It was time to let down her guard and really try to know this man, try to tear down some of the walls that both of them had in place.

"Thank you," he said so quietly, she almost missed it.

It seemed he was feeling the same way as she was. When he took her hand into his, she didn't pull away, just followed him deeper into the palace.

CHAPTER THIRTY-SIX

BETRAYED.
Deceived.
Devastated.

Rachel was also disbelieving as she looked down at a message she was sure had been sent to her in error.

How could Adriane do this to her? She'd stayed to get to know him, had let her family leave her there even though they hadn't wanted to. Despite everything, she'd even started to believe that he wasn't the monster she had originally thought him to be.

She'd been wrong.

Fury and fear mingled inside her, making her stomach roil with nausea. This couldn't be good for the twins. It certainly wasn't good for her.

I am sorry to have missed you, Ms. Palazzo. Your dress fitting has been pushed back an extra week, but we do need to have your measurements as soon as possible to ensure that your gown fits properly on your wedding day. Remember that two weeks goes by quickly, and we only have your best interest at heart, since the wedding will be televised.

Thank you,

Mariana

Rachel reread the note that had been left on her dressing table. And still she couldn't believe what it was saying. Adriane had never canceled the wedding plans. He was simply humoring her until he could march her down the aisle. How could she have been so blind?

Although he'd offered to play by her rules and taken her out on a few outings where the two of them could talk, she clearly didn't know him any more now than she had back in Florida a few months ago.

And she'd so wanted to have faith in him, so wanted to believe he was a good man. The alternative was unacceptable — that the father of her children was an egomaniac.

This was a nightmare and she couldn't seem to wake up from it.

As the tears welled up, she twisted her hands in her lap, digging her nails into her flesh. She would not cry again, hormones or not.

Anger was the only emotion she wanted to feel at this moment. She closed her eyes, and reveled in it. Let it build. The angrier she was with the man, the less he could hurt her.

She suspected she was going to hurt plenty, anyway. Without rhyme or reason, she found herself growing attached to Adriane. Maybe it was the way he looked at her with so much need burning in his eyes. Maybe it was the few times he let down his guard and shared his feelings with her. Maybe it was just because she was a fool.

Whatever the reasons, she cared about him.

But it was a one-way feeling.

He desired her; that was more than obvious. He wanted to marry her — but not for the right reasons. He wanted his heirs to live there with him, to be raised the way he wanted them raised, and he wanted not to lose any time with them.

He also had implied — how generous! — that sharing her bed wouldn't be a hardship for him.

That wasn't enough. It never would be. She wanted love or nothing at all. And even if he did give vows of love, she wouldn't be able to trust his words, certainly not after he'd just proved himself to be such a scheming liar. He'd never planned on canceling the wedding. It had all just been a big smoke screen for him to woo her into his way of thinking.

He was going to be highly disappointed.

Rachel had no doubt that he would say or do anything at this point to keep her in Corythia. So what was she going to do? Did she leave right away?

That was what she wanted to do. She wanted to run far from him and not look back. But if that's what she really wanted, why did her stomach turn at the thought?

Because she was falling in love.

"You stupid, stupid fool," she berated herself aloud. "But maybe, just maybe he's trying to protect himself," she said to the mirror.

Letting out a groan of disgust, Rachel stood up. She couldn't even look herself in the eye anymore.

She'd heard that prisoners sometimes developed feelings for their captors. Maybe that's all this was about. She might be misunderstanding her emotions because she felt trapped and dependent on Adriane.

The thought made her feel slightly better in a sick sort of way.

One thing she did understand completely was fury, and right now, anger was her number one emotion. Her stomping back and forth in her room wasn't doing the antique Aubusson carpet any favors, but she didn't care.

She'd called his right-hand man an hour ago, demanding an audience with the king, but Adriane was sure taking his time getting to her. For someone so insistent that he wanted to spend more time with her, he wasn't in any hurry to arrive now. Maybe he'd had a premonition of what was to come.

He was going to get hit with everything she had the moment he walked through the sitting room door. Hell hath no fury like a woman burned by some two-bit king.

"Nico said it was urgent that I come to see you."

Rachel turned to find Adriane in the room with her. Before she had a chance to jump at him, she noticed that he wasn't at his best. His eyes had dark circles, and he looked as if he were entering hostile territory. Maybe he wasn't as stupid as he acted.

Looking down at the note from the seamstress, she quickly changed her opinion. Yes, he was that much of a fool.

Even in his obviously exhausted state, he still looked good — way too good, in her opinion. It wasn't fair or right. Why couldn't he look like the control freak that he was? Then, she could have had some warning.

Of course, then she wouldn't be in this mess, because she never would have slept with him to begin with.

Turning back around, she took a deep breath. If she began screaming at him, he would just walk from the room and nothing would get solved. She had to decide right now whether she wanted to give him a chance to explain, and whether she wanted to continue her mission of trying to befriend him.

Anger wasn't going to do her any good. Yet it was all she seemed capable of feeling at the moment.

Grabbing the note that the seamstress had left, she approached him and handed it over. He took it warily and read the words, his eyes narrowing just a hair.

She waited.

Finally, he spoke. "You weren't supposed to receive anything like this."

"Are you kidding me, Adriane? *That's* all you have to say?" she snapped, ready to start pummeling. She took several more breaths as she tried to calm her rapidly beating heart.

She was in fight-or-flight mode right then, and if the man wasn't careful, he would be wearing a black eye in about three seconds.

"I'll have to speak to Nico," he said.

"This has nothing to do with Nico. This is about you lying to me!"

"I haven't lied," he protested.

"How can you possibly say that? We agreed that we'd get to know each other, that you would drop these foolish plans for a wedding," she shouted, then took steadying breath as she tried to get herself under control. She'd promised herself she wouldn't yell.

Well, he'd broken his promise, and she'd just broken the one to herself.

They were even in that regard.

"This isn't worth so much drama, Rachel. It's a minor matter, and you're turning it into something it isn't," he said in a calming voice that only infuriated her more.

"You arrogant pig. How can you stand there and call it 'a minor matter'? I'm trying to know you, trying to make an effort for the sake of our children. You don't seem to get that. Or you simply don't give a crap."

"I very much care. That's why I'm trying to marry you!"

His voice rose as he stalked toward her.

This time, she refused to back down. She was sick of doing that.

"And I told you that I wouldn't marry you. I thought we understood each other," she said as he reached her, stopping only inches from where she stood. She wanted to take a step back, but she wouldn't give him the satisfaction of seeing her rattled.

Her pride was at stake here.

"I told you I would give you time for us to get to know each other more. I never said the wedding was canceled. I simply told you that I wouldn't mention it anymore."

He looked down into her eyes as if that explanation should appease her.

"I have never, *ever* in my life wanted to hurt a person as badly as I want to hurt you right now. Do you really think these games will win you a bride? I am not a toy that you can play with. I am not going to sit submissively in the corner and obey your every command, and most importantly, I am *not* going to marry you! Not today. Not tomorrow. And not in a couple of weeks. Do I make myself clear!"

Rachel lifted her hand as she was saying each sentence and punctuated every point by poking him hard in the chest. If she didn't get her words through the thick shell of his skull this time, she'd give up trying to speak to him.

He'd best pull his head out of the dark place he'd managed to get it stuck in and start giving her the respect she deserved, and not just as the mother of his children.

If he was unable to manage that on his own, she might have to give him a swift kick to his ass to help him out.

"I have done everything you've asked. I have taken time out of my busy schedule to court you, taking you to see the country you will live in as queen, attending dinners with you, giving you attention. I have given you all you want — and still you refuse me night after night. If anyone is being unreasonable here, it is you!" he snapped, grabbing her arms and yanking her into his embrace.

Rachel gasped when he ground his hips against the lean curve of her stomach, showing her that even in anger he wanted her.

Much to her horror, her body reacted to his touch. Her blood heated straight to her core, her nipples hardened, and her breath seemed to rush from her.

How could she desire him when she wanted to kill him? It was impossible.

"Get your hands off me right this minute, Adriane. I swear I will scream so loud, the walls of this palace will crumble," she hissed, pulling from him and the hold he had on her, both physically and emotionally.

"Why should I? Your body knows what you want. I could easily take you, make you scream out my name in pleasure. Why should I consider your demands when you are uncaring of my needs?"

This time, as she struggled against him, he let her go. Spinning away, she took a moment to compose her features before turning back around.

"Yes, Adriane, you could probably seduce me. You could make me want you. Go right ahead. Do it. I will despise you forever when it's over."

The gleam in his eyes told her he was considering it.

Rachel needed to find out what kind of man he truly was.

"Maybe your hatred is worth getting both our needs met," he said, his voice low and almost menacing.

"Fine, Adriane. Is that what you want?" Rachel said as she lifted her hands and began unbuttoning her blouse. "Do you want to sink inside me, take your pleasure?" She removed the garment, her chest heaving as she stood before him.

His eyes widened as his gaze zeroed in on her barely covered breasts.

"Let me make this easy for you, shall I, my king?" She undid her pants and slid her hands into the waistband, scooting them downward so they pooled at her feet. She kicked them away and stood before him in nothing but her minuscule bra and panties.

"Don't you want me, Adriane? Don't you want to take what you think belongs to you?" she said, her voice close to tears, which only infuriated her more. "Here I am. You can prove what a man you are!"

Adriane stood stock still as he took in her nearly naked body. Below the waist, he offered clear evidence that he wasn't unaffected.

With deliberate steps, he approached her, and Rachel's heart shattered. He *was* a monster. How could he possibly do this? The worst part was that, despite her fathomless pain and horror at his callous approach, she also knew he would most likely bring her pleasure.

No matter what, she would despise him, never be able to look at him the same way again. Maybe that's what she needed. Maybe this was what had to happen for her to give up on him.

Adriane's arms slipped around her naked back, making her flesh quiver. Yet she refused to back down. Lifting her chin defiantly, she peered up into his eyes, waiting for the attack she knew was coming.

"Even in fury, you heat my body, nearly make me come undone," he said, the corners of his lips turning up as he gazed at her. "I am furious with you right now, but I am no fool. I won't play your game, though I will burn all night because of it. To make sure you burn just as much, I will leave you with a little something." He bent his head and locked his mouth with hers.

Rachel lifted her arms, intent on pushing him back. She couldn't do this, couldn't allow him to touch her, no matter what she'd said, no matter what she'd done in the heat of the moment. Why had she performed her impulsive striptease?

As his tongue demanded entrance into her mouth, she held out, keeping her lips locked tightly together. He didn't seem fazed.

He slid his fingers down her back, gripping her buttocks and pulling her tightly against his thickness, centering her core on his arousal and making her gasp as he bit down on her bottom lip. His tongue achieved its objective.

After seconds, hours, days — who knew? — he pulled back, steadying her before he let go and stepped over to the refreshment cabinet in her room. He poured himself a full glass of whiskey, quickly downing it before he turned back around.

Much to her shame, she could feel the hardness of her nipples straining to be free, and she also felt her panties grow wet. She only hoped he couldn't see how turned on she was.

"I'll be in my chamber. One call, and I can end the torment you're putting us both through. As for the wedding..." He smiled — actually smiled at her. "It's going to happen. You can come willingly, or you can fight it, but you will be my wife."

With those words, he turned and walked toward the door. Rage filled her to the breaking point. She didn't know if it was his rejection or his threat, but fury fueled her.

Stepping forward, she grabbed the glass he'd just set down, the ridiculously expensive crystal glass, and threw it, without taking a single second to think about what she was doing. It shattered against the door, inches from his head.

Adriane jumped back, then turned around and looked at her with shock. And then, much to her horror, he laughed. A real, deep, stomach-jolting kind of laugh.

Rachel debated launching herself at him and scratching his eyes out. As if he could see what she was thinking, he stopped laughing, though the spark in his eyes didn't fade in the least.

"Thank you, Rachel. You have made my night." He turned away and twisted the doorknob, his foot crunching on the recently broken crystal.

"Don't you dare walk from this room until we are finished!"

"Unless you plan to follow through on your offer of going to bed with me, I'm leaving now. What will it be, Rachel? Do we finally make love again, or do I walk through this door?"

"It's not making love when you hate the person!" she snapped, stooping down and grabbing her blouse and flinging it around her shoulders. She suddenly felt far too exposed.

"Ah, baby, something that feels as good as it does when we come together is always making love." His eyes scanned her torso before she snapped the edges of the shirt together, covering that part of her body from his view. "Pity. You should always just...stay naked," he added.

"You really are a pig, Adriane."

"I haven't claimed to be anything else."

With that he opened the door.

"The wedding won't happen," she shouted before he could shut the door.

"It will. One way or the other, you will be standing at the altar with me."

And with that, he turned away and walked out, closing the door behind him, leaving her standing there trembling.

From rage.

From lust.

From so many emotions, she couldn't name them all. She was leaving. That was the last straw.

CHAPTER THIRTY-SEVEN

ADRIANE THREW OFF his tie, unbuttoned his shirt and paced. More pacing. He was always pacing nowadays. What was wrong with the woman? She wanted him, it was obvious, but she continued to fight herself.

Yes, she'd done her little striptease, but he wasn't a fool. Had he taken what she was deceptively offering, she would indeed have hated him forever. Walking away had been one of the hardest decisions he'd ever had to make — literally and figuratively, he thought as his erection pulsed.

He felt only a tiny bit better with the knowledge that he'd left her aching almost as much as he was. He hoped he had, at least. The signs of her aroused body had been staring him in the face, making it even harder to leave her room.

She infuriated him! If that were all she made him feel, he would be able to move on, focus on other tasks at hand. But, no, that wasn't the only emotion she unleashed inside of him. He also felt passion, joy and other feelings he couldn't even begin to name.

She was quickly turning into the most important person in his life.

How had that happened?

When had it occurred?

The more pressing question was, what was he willing to do to capture her?

He'd tried kidnapping, cajoling, seducing. What else could he do?

How about being honest?

The thought stopped him in his tracks, right in front of the wide windows of his sitting room. Staring down at the stormy day, the water churning, waves splashing against the shore, Adriane was at a loss.

This was all new territory for him, but the one thing he did know was that he didn't want her to walk away. He could hold her captive for only so long. His threats were all empty and they both knew it.

Maybe it hadn't been his best idea to tell her she was going to marry him whether she liked it or not. It might be time to try a bit more cajoling. Why couldn't this be less complicated? Why did messy emotions have to get involved? They were good together. They'd proved that in Florida.

If she'd just get past this little squabble, they could be in bed together right this very minute, and be on their way to a wedding. All their problems would be solved in a trice. Why couldn't a woman be more like a man? Couldn't she learn to use her head?

Adriane was quite proud of himself for being so logical.

Now, he just had to convince her that he was in the right.

That shouldn't be too hard a task, he thought smugly.

With a new resolve, he stepped into the shower and found himself whistling one of his favorite show tunes. Yes, he still had an aching arousal, but he was sure that after he spoke rationally to her, that problem would be solved and all parties would be happy.

Yes, his mother had told him to try being more romantic, but hadn't he been? He'd taken her on romantic dates, showed her they were compatible. He'd done what had been asked of him. Yes, he gave her romance. But love? That was going a bit too far. Love didn't have to be a factor in their relationship. Logic was the only way to make a lasting union. He was sure he could get her to see this. She was a smart woman, after all.

*****

Adriane's confidence faltered briefly the next day. Where was she? Had he pushed her too far and caused her to run away?

But she hadn't gone. He happened to find her sitting in one of the garden gazebos. He was about to saunter up to her with a winning smile, but he was stopped by the gloomy expression on her face as she gazed off into the distance. It tore him apart knowing he'd been the one to make her feel that way.

He would make this better.

He approached her cautiously. "Can we talk?"

He watched her struggle to mask the wounded look in her eyes, and he vowed to quit hurting her, vowed to consider her feelings more.

"I'm not sure you know how to talk — you just yell and snap orders," she said, turning away from him and looking once more into the horizon.

Ouch.

"What if I work on that, and you accompany me on a walk?" he said in his best diplomatic voice.

Her eyes narrowed at his tone, but she wasn't refusing him. That was a start, at least. Without actually accepting his invitation, she stood and then they were strolling through the gardens. It just felt natural when his hand brushed against hers, and her fingers were suddenly entwined with his.

The feel of her skin sent a thrill of passion through him, as always, but also a feeling of warmth, of rightness. This was the way they were supposed to be — hand in hand.

As the storm clouds brewed overhead, they walked in silence, the invigorating smell of the gardens drifting around them, the sea air warm as the breeze stirred her hair.

Adriane had always considered Rachel stunning, but he saw her now in a new way, a way he hadn't taken the time to notice before. There was a vulnerability about her, but a deep strength, as well, and the combination made her compelling to behold. She had the presence and the character to make an outstanding queen. She just needed to realize it.

"What can I do to make this better for us?" he asked, his tone gentle, as they paused by the beach and looked out at the threatening skies.

"I don't know. I want to know you, but we keep hitting walls."

"I will do whatever you want," he replied.

"Then quit insisting we marry. That would be a good start."

"But there's no other option; you carry my heirs," he argued. His frustration was mounting again, though he desperately wanted to bury the emotion and keep their conversation on an even keel.

"To me, love is paramount when choosing a mate. It will stand the test of time when the winds blow and the tempest of the outside world tries to tear the marriage apart like the shifting of the waves of an ocean crashing to shore. Love has to be the driving force or the marriage will not last in today's world. I've vowed to myself that I would never settle for anything less than the marriage that my parents have. Their love and respect for each other forms one of the most beautiful unions I know. I want that for myself...and my husband," she said, hoping he would truly listen to her.

"Your fairy-tale view of love is surely commendable for a woman, at least when she's in normal circumstances. If she can deceive herself into happiness with such an enchanting illusion, fine and good. But we're not in normal circumstances. And I don't see any need to plaster such a fantasy over an animal instinct. Why can't we treat this rationally? Think about what really happens: People meet, feel attraction, make love, and then proclaim undying devotion. And what is it all really? It's a game that allows the participants to feel better about themselves because they said those three magic little words."

"Very inspiring, Adriane. I applaud you."

"I understand you feel strongly about this, Rachel, but I cannot comprehend why. Isn't companionship enough? Can't you understand that I want to take care of you? That I enjoy your presence? Why trick it out in fancy dress? I don't believe love is real. I *do* believe desire can be for keeps. I haven't looked at another woman since you, not once in over four months. Can't that be enough, or do I need to say those words to you. Is that what this will take? Will you finally quit fighting me and become my wife if I say, *I love you*?"

Rachel gaped at the audacity of the man. Did he really think she would bubble over with joy if he expressed fake emotions? Who or what on earth had made him so cynical? This wasn't a man she could fall in love with — this wasn't a man she could even speak to.

"I think we're wasting our time here," she said, and she turned away from the crashing waves and headed back toward the palace. She knew now that he would never understand how she felt.

Not that *she* really knew how she was feeling.

Knowing he was going to regret being impulsive, Adriane nevertheless grabbed Rachel's arm and spun her around before she was able to get far away.

Without giving her time to protest, he pulled her against him and kissed her deep and long, trying to show her how much he wanted her, needed her, would do anything to have her. Words obviously weren't working, so he decided to speak in the only successful way he'd been able to communicate with her — through passion.

She growled in agitation as he captured her lips, his hands sliding down her back and cupping her delicious backside. As he'd hoped, she melted into him without much of a fight — the intensity of their chemistry couldn't be denied.

This was the way to heal the rift between them. This was the white flag that would set them free. With this reminder of the taste of her, the feel of her subtle curves, the passion of her embrace, he could think of no other woman.

Only Rachel.

His future bride.

By the time he pulled back, they were both breathless and in need of fulfillment. Naturally, he expected to take her back to the palace, make her his again.

After all, it was what both of them needed and wanted.

He smiled down at her, a gentle, reassuring smile. Rachel's eyes flashed with desire, her breasts peaked with arousal. He knew he'd finally won this battle of wills.

Then she lifted a hand and slapped him across the face.

"Learn to ask," she said, her tone low, threatening.

While he stood in absolute confusion and shock, his mind racing for answers on what had gone wrong, she slipped away.

It looked as though he'd struck out again.

If he were a quitter, that would have been his cue to give up.

But he never gave up.

Tomorrow he would win this game; tomorrow would be a better day. One of these times that he said those words, they would come true. It was the power of odds.

CHAPTER THIRTY-EIGHT

I T WAS TIME to go home.

Rachel hadn't heard a word from Adriane in three days. At first she'd been relieved, believing that he was coming to terms with the futility of their situation. Not quite, she found out. He'd been off on business — some complication with his brother that she knew nothing about.

So it was more time with no progress, and she'd given up hoping for any. Loneliness was consuming her and she wanted to be with her parents and the rest of her family. She had to accept that it just wasn't going to work out, no matter how much she wanted it to.

Clutching her cell phone in her hand, she hesitated. Should she dial her brother and have him send a jet for her? She had no doubt that if she left, she wouldn't come back, that she and Adriane would never come to an agreement. And she'd never get to know her children's father.

Is that what she wanted? Could she accept that?

Did she have a choice?

For a short time, she'd thought that maybe there was a spark between them — something more than just a friendship. A slight shade of pink stole across her cheeks at her foolishness in feeling that way.

Though she fought to admit it, she was finding that it would be so much better if they could be…more.

Wouldn't it be ideal if the two of them could fall in love? Indeed, but love didn't work that way. She couldn't just flip a switch for the two of them to simultaneously fall into a lovers' trance without end. If only things were so easy.

Rachel's silent torment was interrupted by an urgent knock. As she rose and approached her bedroom door, her heart picked up speed, and she wanted to kick her own ass for hoping it was Adriane on the other side. When she discovered Nico instead, she couldn't help but feel let down.

With that raw emotion evident on her face, he offered her a sympathetic smile, which only underlined how pathetic she'd become.

"Good morning, Ms. Palazzo. The king would like to invite you to a ball tonight," Nico said, and he held out an invitation bordered in dark blue and engraved with gold letters.

"Tonight?" she asked, glancing over at the clock and noting it was already eleven in the morning. This was late notice. And why should she accept when he'd been such an assuming ass of late? Plus, she'd already decided to go home. That was the right choice — she knew that.

"Yes. He apologizes for the delay in asking you, but there were back-to-back meetings he couldn't step out of, and he wasn't sure he would be able to attend the event until just a little while ago," Nico explained.

Rachel hesitated for a moment, automatically ready to refuse because of such an inconsiderate last-minute invite on top of everything else. But what would saying no accomplish? Nothing. Maybe this was the last inning of the game and she could gain something — anything from him. Didn't she owe this much to herself?

She wanted to *bridge* the gap between the two of them, not increase the miles that currently separated them. She'd never know whether she made the right decision if she didn't give this her best effort.

"Tell him I would be pleased to meet him," Rachel said, giving Nico a big smile.

He let out a relieved breath, and she smiled even wider.

"That is wonderful. I'll send someone over right away to assist you in choosing your gown," he said, efficient as ever.

Rachel normally would have rejected such assistance, being perfectly capable of dressing herself. However, she was going to an event she knew nothing about, and she didn't want to be under- or overdressed, so she nodded her acceptance, and Nico turned to leave.

"Nico," she called out, and he respectfully turned back toward her.

"Yes, madam?"

"Am I a fool for hoping for more?"

Rachel was surprised by her question to this man, one who hadn't been overly friendly with her. But if anyone knew Adriane, it was Nico, as he'd been his assistant for many years. She knew he wouldn't betray his king, but maybe he would give her just a touch of honesty.

"I would never take you for a fool, Ms. Palazzo," he said before a slight smiled split his lips. "You are adapting quite well," he added.

It wasn't an answer, but for some reason his response made her feel better.

"The car will pick you up at seven," he said with a slight bow, then left her.

The next few hours were a blur of activity as she bathed, dressed with some assistance, and did her hair and makeup, taking her time in getting ready, anticipation flowing through her.

Nervous tension filled her stomach as she made her final preparations for what felt like a defining moment in her relationship with Adriane.

If he still showed no interest in her as more than a body, and when in the public eye he was cold and distant, nothing more than a king speaking to a peasant, another obligation in a long line of obligations, then she was throwing the game and walking away.

She would contact him once the twins were born.

But if... This was a frightening thought. What ifs always were. But still, maybe the two of them could really see each other for the first time; maybe they could take a step in the right direction and be more than the parents of these two babies.

Looking in the mirror, Rachel almost didn't recognize herself. The gown did a spectacular job of accentuating her curves, while hiding the slight bump on her stomach, focusing the attention all on her and not the babies she carried.

Her hair was left to flow down her back, strands whispering around her face and framing her expertly done-up eyes. Even her lips screamed seduction, painted blood red and glossy as they were, imitating the flare of color they took on when in the throes of passion.

This evening should be a tell-all for what she needed to know.

For, after all her going to and fro in confusion and anguish, she had decided on a bold action. She was going to make love with him. Then, when morning hit, she would have her answers. She hoped, at least, that they lasted till morning. If he walked away from her when he was finished, she didn't think she could bear it.

Trying to calm her nerves, Rachel stepped from her room at ten minutes to liftoff, and began the long walk to the front of the palace. This was it. She was giving her all, and she prayed that Adriane was willing to accept her offer.

There was no sign of the king when she stepped into the palace foyer, and Rachel's nerves became even more frayed. Had he changed his mind after she'd spent the entire afternoon preparing for this night?

The thought was too much to bear.

"Ms. Palazzo, King Adriane's meeting ran over," Nico said, "and he has asked me to escort you to the ball, to ensure your safe arrival. Please, this way." He held out his hand, smiling at her and offering a bow of respect.

"I'm sure I can get there on my own," she said, knowing Nico wouldn't enjoy spending his time in her presence.

"A lady as beautiful as you cannot be out alone. You would never arrive, as suitors would be stopping you each step of the way," he said, taking her hand and pulling it through his arm.

"You are quite the charmer, aren't you, Nico?" she said, loving the softening he was showing toward her. Maybe he didn't think she was the stupid American he had originally thought her to be. No, he'd never treated her with disrespect, but it had been obvious from day one that he didn't find her suitable to stand alongside his king. Maybe, just maybe, his opinion was changing. It was odd that she cared, though.

"How can I resist a man who bestows such lavish flattery on me?" she said, laughing as he led her through the massive doors and down the steps to a waiting car.

Nico assisted her inside, then joined her, reaching for a bottle of chilled cider and pouring her a glass. The cool liquid sliding down her throat helped ease a bit of the tension in her stomach.

She and Nico chatted on the extended ride to the Fiorito mansion, and as they drew near, Rachel felt her nerves jump. The closer they approached, the more nervous she became.

What if this night was a failure and she ended up feeling like an idiot?

Then, she would go on with her life. It wasn't the end-all, and she was too strong to wallow in pity.

"The ball is being held by a longtime friend of the royal family. It is to honor the fallen soldiers of our land, and is quite a big event each year. It would be a disgrace if some member of the royal family did not attend, which is why the king was so upset when he didn't think he'd be able to make it. By bringing you here, he is announcing to the country that you are a very important part of his life," Nico said as the car arrived in front of a stately residence.

It was impressive in its old-world charm, made from stone like that used at the castle, and from exquisite marble.

The driveway was lined with a canopy of lush trees, and it wound around a fountain showcasing two cupids dancing within its waters' mist. Though Rachel had grown up with more money than most, she still found it all a little intimidating.

This was different from what she knew. It was a world of ancient bloodlines, of authority and prestige — a world that wasn't hers.

Rachel cast off the thoughts as she accepted Nico's hand and climbed the steps with him. Soon, she'd see Adriane, soon she'd know whether she was giving their relationship a chance, or running away.

Either way, she'd be out of the quandary she'd been in since the day he'd told her she'd be his wife.

As they walked inside the large ballroom, Rachel clung tightly to Nico's arm and looked around with insecure doe eyes, wondering where Adriane was.

The crowd parted, and suddenly he was there, throwing his head back and laughing at something his companion must have said. The king looked so carefree for a moment that she was rendered motionless.

As if he could sense her, he turned his head, and their gazes locked. Without a word to the man he'd been conversing with, Adriane moved swiftly through the crowd, his eyes never breaking contact with hers, not for even the briefest of seconds.

An unsatisfied ache flared within the recesses of her womanhood as he reached her side, his gaze drifting down the feminine lines of her body. She felt as if he'd touched her, for his look was so intense as his eyes drank in her revealing but elegant golden gown.

When his gaze returned to her eyes, his expression was unreadable, and Rachel wondered if she'd just made an idiot of herself. She suddenly wanted to turn around and flee.

"My deepest apologizes for not accompanying you on your ride here. I only just arrived," he said as he held out his arm.

Did she take it and swiftly move forward on her mission, or did she bolt the way she so wanted to do?

She took his arm.

"Nico has been a fine escort. Thank you, Nico," she said, impulsively leaning over and kissing the man's cheek. Much to her amazement, the king's always confident adviser blushed deeply as he looked down and cleared his throat.

"The pleasure of escorting you here was all mine," he murmured before looking back up and smiling.

"Thank you for bringing her safely, Nico. You may take the rest of the night off," Adriane said.

Rachel wanted to grab the man and prevent his departure, suddenly feeling safer in his presence. But the moment the words left Adriane's mouth, Nico obediently turned and left her alone with the man who wanted to marry her.

They were silent as Adriane led her to the center of the room, where couples were floating around the floor in a traditional Viennese waltz. Without a word, he pulled her into his arms as the music enveloped them. Rachel melted against his chest; they spun slowly in a circle.

"I don't know if I can last this entire event. The way you look in that dress has taken my breath away. I want nothing more right now than to take you back to the palace, carry you to my room and slowly peel the fabric away from your flushed skin and reveal your curves in all their glory. I want to bury myself inside you, and then, when it's all over, I want to begin again, and pleasure you all through the night."

Rachel couldn't say a word as she looked at the raw hunger on his face, in his eyes, and in the tenseness of his mouth, and felt his arousal pressing insistently against her stomach.

After several heartbeats, she nodded her head.

For a moment, he did nothing, as if he didn't know what she'd just said to him with her silent gesture. When she nodded again, the breath he'd been holding exploded from his lungs; his feet stopped moving, and he bent down and claimed her sweet mouth.

Rachel didn't care that they weren't alone. She clung on tightly and accepted his passionate kiss. Finally, tonight she would get to feel the pleasure of lying in his arms again.

The ball couldn't end soon enough.

CHAPTER THIRTY-NINE

"WE'RE LEAVING!"

Trembling from the power of his kiss, Rachel didn't realize for a moment that he'd pulled back from her and now had her hand in a viselike grip as he led her through the crowded room.

"Leaving?" she asked.

"Yes. I want you in my room, on my bed, naked and wet for me," he said, picking up his pace even more.

Suddenly Rachel's clothes felt like a straitjacket. She wanted them off immediately.

"Oh, don't worry, I'm plenty wet," she whispered, relishing the instant power she felt as his steps halted for an instant. He didn't dare turn in her direction, but instead picked up speed again and led her through the front door.

When he called his car around, Rachel looked back. "Shouldn't we tell someone we're leaving?"

"No. I made my appearance; they won't notice that I've gone," he said in a strained tone.

She doubted that — everyone notices what a king does — but she was too excited to argue. She didn't even care that she'd spent hours getting ready only to stay at the ball for about ten minutes.

After all, what she'd really been doing was preparing for a night of lovemaking, and it looked as if she was going to get exactly that.

As the car approached, he didn't wait for his driver to open the door, but just flung it open and helped her inside, and then slid in next to her. As rushed as he was, he was surprisingly gentle.

Before the car pulled from the drive, Adriane grasped her, lifting her onto his lap as he guided her mouth to his face and meshed their heated breaths together in a tantalizing kiss that didn't quit.

Rachel inhaled his sweet, musky scent as he ran his tongue along her lips. When he bit down softly on her lip before sucking it into his mouth, she felt her blood rush straight to her core, demanding him, now.

Her hands lifted, grabbing and tugging a fistful of his thick short hair, craving more from him. It was never enough — nothing was enough. She wanted him buried inside her while his hands stroked hungrily up and down her back. She wanted a mutual feeling of complete possession in each other's arms.

She wanted to be held and never let go.

"The sight of you in this dress...oh, Rachel, I've been hard and aching since the first glance," he gasped. "But you can wear anything and my body responds. I've never desired a woman so much. Never. I will make love to you long into the night. I don't think I will ever release you from my bed." His lips trailed down her throat and sucked on her erratically beating pulse.

Rachel tried to keep some semblance of her sanity — tried to remember that this was about more than sex — but the more places he touched her, the more he spoke, the less control she maintained.

Need.

Raw, exhilarating, thrilling need raged within her in waves and she hoped it would never, ever end.

Adriane was silent when they finally entered the palace. He shot a single look at his servants, and within seconds, he and Rachel were alone.

"I won't stop," he warned, as if giving her a last chance to back out.

Rachel didn't understand why he would give her an out after he'd been waiting for so long, but she was grateful for the consideration. A man who didn't care wouldn't have given her the chance to change her mind, would he? She didn't think so.

"Why are you still talking?" she asked, batting her eyes and letting him know with nothing other than the intense yearning in her features how much she wanted him.

Victory flashed in his eyes for the briefest of moments, replaced by a molten need. She'd given him an answer to his unasked question. She wasn't going to pull away from him this time.

Without even giving her time to blink, Adriane lifted her into his arms and then began up the staircase, quickly ascending and then winding his way through the hallways, breathing heavily, though not from exertion, as he reached his massive bedroom doors, so lost in his haze of passion, he forgot all about his promise of not taking her to his chambers until after the wedding.

Leaning in against him, she couldn't resist running her tongue along the salty skin of his neck and delighting in its erotic tang.

"I can barely walk," he groaned as he dashed through the sitting area and made a straight path to his sleeping chamber, stopping only when he reached his bed.

Had Rachel been able to look around her, she'd have taken in the bold red of his curtains, the matching duvet and the lavish antique furnishings he'd chosen — if he had in fact, chosen them. How foolish. He had servants to do such tasks, of course. Still, she wanted to study it all, but afflicted by passion-inspired tunnel vision, she could see only the man still holding her securely in his hard-muscled arms.

"I want you, Adriane," she whispered, feeling a shudder pass through his body.

He released her, and she slid down the hard planes of his chest, her stomach trembling as she felt his manhood pulse against her.

Undoing the top of her dress, he dropped to his knees as her skin was bared to him, letting the dress pool at her feet. He grasped her hips with his hand and leaned forward, breathing in her very essence.

With fierce impatience, he ripped her panties away, grabbed her thighs and spread them roughly apart, not giving her time to even gasp before he buried his face between the juncture of her legs. Her knees trembled while he began licking along her upper thighs, inching toward the place where she was aching the most.

With expert technique, he penetrated her moist folds with his tongue as he continued pushing her legs apart, and when neither of them could stand the foreplay any longer, he clasped her throbbing womanhood and sucked. She cried out when he drank from her, sliding one hand up her thigh and inserting his long fingers into her heat, making her gasp and moan in pleasure.

"Yes, Adriane, more!" she cried as she held on to his shoulder, wondering how she was still standing.

Only a slight groan exited his mouth as he continued devouring her core, his tongue torching a path along every inch of her womanhood.

More! She wanted so much more. She wanted him — only him.

"Please," she pleaded, wanting it all.

His lips circled her most sensitive area; his tongue swirled and his fingers pushed deep inside of her. She exploded, slumping forward against his face as tremors shook her body.

"Oh, Adriane," she groaned, unable to move at all, still upright only because she was leaning against him.

What a fool she'd been to wait so long to do this with him!

When he stood up, she nearly fell to the floor, but he caught hold of her, turning her body so she fell on the bed, her limbs weak, her rounded behind in the air.

Trying to turn, she didn't have a chance as he grabbed her legs and pulled her back to him. "I need you now!" he said in a strained voice before lifting her hips, then gripping her as he slammed into her, burying his burning manhood deep.

Rachel cried out as another orgasm ripped through her, taking her by shock as she pulsed around him, his staff filling her completely.

"Too long," he groaned as he pulled back, and then surged forward again, making her orgasm continue on and on. "Way too long. You are mine, Rachel Palazzo, mine forever. No other man will touch you again; no other man will have what's mine," he said, slamming into her again and branding her with all he was.

"Yes, Adriane," she cried, not caring what she agreed to, just desperate for him to continue.

He paced himself, moving deep within her body before retreating and then starting all over again, moving slow and then fast, his thick arousal filling her, stretching her, building her ever higher in her need for him.

He'd already given her a surfeit of satisfaction, and still, it wasn't enough! She felt like a sexual glutton.

"Now, Rachel. Let go now!" he demanded.

As if attuned to his every desire, she prepared to climax again, her body responding to his movements, to the sound of the ardent groan deep within his chest. As he emptied himself inside her, her pleasure overwhelmed her, and she shattered, then floated away into a sea of blackness.

Rachel quickly returned to consciousness, surprised when she realized she'd passed out.

"Rachel, are you feeling all right? I should call the doctor. I was too rough; I wasn't thinking about the babies at all. I'm sorry," Adriane said as he ran his hands down her body, stopping on her stomach as if he could tell whether the babies were healthy just by feeling her.

Some of her euphoria faded as she saw him focused solely on her stomach.

How could she forget even for a single moment what his ultimate goal was? He had to protect his heirs no matter what.

Would nothing she did make him focus only on her?

If the sex hadn't been enough to knock his socks off and have him thinking of her as a woman and not a human incubator, then she didn't possibly know what would catch his attention.

Pushing his hands away and pulling the blanket up to her chin, she sat up, suddenly feeling overly exposed. Where were they going to go from here? He'd gotten her into the sack; now was he going to leave her alone?

She didn't want that. She wanted to be held.

Impossible as it seemed, just the feel of his hands caressing her flesh had begun stirring her up again. Even with the confusing thoughts fogging her mind, she wanted him — as she feared she always would.

Maybe it was because it had been too long since she'd been held; maybe it was just because he was such a fantastic lover that it was easy for her to forget why she was here in his palace — and in his bed.

"I'm fine, Adriane. Pregnant women all over the world have sex. I highly doubt anything could happen. The children are locked up safely inside my womb," she said, trying to disguise the sting she felt, trying to focus on the positive fact that at least he was concerned.

After a pause, while he tried to determine if she was telling him the truth, he began shedding the rest of his clothes and dropping them to the floor — the clothes he hadn't removed in his haste to claim her.

"If you're sure…" he said, hesitating before lifting the blanket on the bed.

"I know how I feel. I'm fine," she said, her voice confident. But if he dared ask about the babies again, she wouldn't be at all OK.

"In that case, I will just make sure to be more gentle from here on out."

"Oh," she said. "There's more?" She couldn't deny that her blood was already heating at just the thought of him making love to her again. That round had been undeniably satisfying, but it was still over too quickly. He'd promised her till the sun rose.

She didn't think she'd get that much lovemaking, but she'd gladly take another hour or two.

Climbing beneath the covers, he immediately reached for her, pulling her into his arms and positioning her body on top of his.

The heat of his skin scorched her from breasts to toes, and it was a burn she reveled in.

"Plenty more, Rachel. It's been entirely too long since we've come together," he said, letting his hands glide across her skin, running from the smooth indent of her calves all the way to her collar bone before moving lazily back down.

"Adriane," she moaned, unable to keep still as he caressed her.

"The shape of your body takes my breath away. Every single curve on you is perfect, fits beautifully in my hands, or softens beneath my touch. You were made for me — and me alone," he said as he leaned into her and trailed kisses along the path he'd forged with his fingers.

Each kiss brought her intense pleasure that pooled in her core and made her ache for his touch. Reading her mind, he let his fingers rest there, and she leaned back, giving him better access.

His arousal grew beneath her backside, and she wiggled against him as his fingers sank inside her, time fading away as she cried out in pleasure with each sure stroke of his hand.

After she peaked again, she turned, capturing his mouth with hers and kissing him in appreciation.

"You make me feel so good," she said, pulling back to kiss his neck. Moving downward, she first swirled her tongue across his hard nipples, nipping the dark peaks, before kissing his trembling stomach.

"Rachel?" he asked, but she ignored him as she reached her favorite place on his body.

Not giving him time to stop her, she cradled his thick member in her hand and sucked him inside her mouth, moving slowly on him as he cried out.

His hands reached downward, grasping her head and guiding her up and down his shaft, teaching her exactly what he wanted.

When he came close to coming in her mouth, he moved her head away and then grabbed her hips, pulling her up his body until she was sitting on his face; his mouth began to work its magic on her core again.

Soon, time had no meaning as he pleasured her over and over again, trailing tender kisses along every inch of her skin before singeing her body as he touched her everywhere.

Just as the sun was beginning to rise in the sky, he sank deep inside her with a sure, strong thrust of his hips. Gripping the back of his head, she held him close as he pushed against her. Lifting her hips, pulling him deeper, Rachel held on as he stoked her fires ever higher.

When she climaxed around him for the final time that night, he collapsed against her, both of them too spent to move a muscle.

It had been needed, this night of lovemaking, but she was more worn out than she'd ever been. Adriane was a considerate lover, and her body had tensed many times as she reached her peak over and over again.

"I want to take you back to the private hideaway soon," he whispered as he shifted off her, only to tug her into his arms.

"That sounds nice," she sleepily murmured.

"Then it's settled," he said, a smile in his voice.

Rachel drifted into a dreamless sleep, secure in her lover's arms.

CHAPTER FORTY

"**D**O YOU LOVE my son?"

Rachel stared at Adriane's mother, Queen Octavia, and was at a loss for words. She'd managed to avoid a conversation like this with his mother before now, since she'd never been alone with the queen before. This luncheon wasn't going well, and she was praying for a natural disaster to intervene.

It seemed she'd prayed for a lot of those since meeting Adriane.

That should be a sign that she should run as fast as she could, but the last few days had been about as perfect as they could be.

"Adriane and I haven't had a lot of time to get to know each other," she replied diplomatically, then picked up her cup of herb tea and took a sip.

"Time is irrelevant when you're with 'the one,'" Octavia countered.

This queen wasn't giving up. Rachel was sure the woman hadn't sat by her husband's side for more than thirty years without learning how to interrogate people. Could Rachel be thrown into the dungeons for not being loyal enough to the king of Corythia?

Though she was joking to herself, a shudder still passed through her at the thought. Still, she was raised not to lie.

"I don't dislike him anymore," she said.

"You are guarded, aren't you, Rachel?"

What was she supposed to say to that? She picked up one of the small tea sandwiches and took a bite, thrilled when her stomach didn't rebel as the salmon and watercress traveled down her throat. The last few days, she hadn't felt a lick of morning sickness. She so hoped that she was over it.

"I just know I deserve to be in a relationship where the man wants *me*," she said.

"I think you are good for my son. He needs a woman unafraid to stand up to him. The responsibilities of ruling a country can be taxing, and a confident woman he can share his worries with and hold tightly in his arms can make the difference between Adriane being a mediocre king and a great one."

Rachel gazed at Adriane's mother, pretty sure she'd just received a compliment. "But Adriane doesn't love me. How can I help him do anything if he looks at me as only another one of his duties — as simply a responsibility he has because of my condition?"

Queen Octavia hesitated as she stared at Rachel, making her want to fidget in her seat. The woman's piercing black eyes were enough to penetrate Rachel's skin. But she was a Palazzo, and no Palazzo would cower, even before royalty.

"I think you would be surprised at how Adriane truly feels. You are a special woman, Rachel, and you carry my grandchildren, so I am very pleased with the way this relationship is progressing. Don't underestimate the loyalty of my son. He will make a fine husband and father."

"I'm sure he will, Queen Octavia. But I need to be loved," Rachel said, almost pleading with the woman to understand.

"So you do love him?" she pressed.

As Rachel sat there, locked in this woman's knowing glance, her stomach heaved. Her sickness came back with wrecking-ball force.

How could she possibly be in love with Adriane? Their relationship had started off as a brief no-strings affair between strangers, followed by three months with the two of them not seeing each other. Then he'd suddenly appeared in her life again, demanding marriage, kidnapping her, and then coldly "courting" her.

To have fallen in love with him was impossible.

But it seemed as if that had somehow happened.

Somewhere along the line, his moments of kindness, his softer smile, his loyalty and compassion for the people of his kingdom — all of it had added up to his winning her heart.

How could she have left herself so unprotected?

They'd boated around the island, with him pointing out the small fishing villages and independent landowners. He had driven her through the land, stopping in quaint towns where the people had rushed to visit their king. He'd talked to her for hours about his plans for the kingdom, and about what would be expected from her as queen.

She'd slowly fallen under his magical spell, and now she was apparently in love with a man who hadn't made a single declaration of any emotion toward her beyond lust and duty.

This was going to end up hurting her — maybe inflicting a wound that was irreparable.

"Ah, it appears that you have deeper feelings for my son than you want to admit. I am pleased, Rachel, very pleased. I will leave you alone now to sort through your thoughts. Thank you for taking the time to meet with me today."

Queen Octavia stood and quietly left the room. When Rachel was sitting glued to her chair several moments later, she realized she hadn't said a word. She hadn't even stood up when the queen had exited. That had been unpardonably rude.

Yet too lost in her thoughts to dwell on it, she finally rose and walked from the palace, her stomach still heaving. She had to get some fresh air, calm the churning within. It seemed the ocean was calling to her, for her feet moved that way of their own accord.

She needed to clear her head and figure out what she was going to say to Adriane. Should she tell him how she felt — see whether there was any chance of him loving her back?

Reaching the white sandy beaches, Rachel slipped off her shoes and walked on, anticipating the feel of the gentle waves splashing against her legs.

The clouds were rolling in, but far enough off in the distance that she wasn't concerned. The fine sand squished between each toe soothed her as her mind continued racing with her newfound knowledge.

When she turned her head and saw Adriane walking toward her, she tensed, not ready for this talk with him, not sure of what she wanted to say to the man who had dominated her life over the past month — the past four months, in fact, if she went back to the beginning.

It was almost ironic that she would be realizing she was in love with him while standing on a beautiful beach. It was, after all, where their journey had begun. Of course that had been in another country, and at quite another time.

The wind blew his short black hair as he stepped closer, and his eyes crinkled slightly at the corners as he smiled her way. He looked relaxed and sure of himself, something she couldn't say for herself right then.

When he reached her, he pulled her immediately into his arms, his skin warmed from the hot sun and easily heating her body as he held her close.

Rachel leaned against him, inhaling his all too familiar scent. What a handsome and dangerous man he'd turned out to be. Their thoughtless weeks together had altered the course of her life forever.

She closed her eyes as she remembered when she was seventeen and thought she was in love, and what her mother had said to her:

Never do anything irrevocable with a man you don't want as your husband. You must be sure that you can live with yourself, and with him. It may seem like only a moment, but you will be forever locked to him — emotionally, physically, or even more.

Rachel hadn't thought of those words for a long time. She hadn't been able to go all the way with the boy she'd been dating back then, and she'd been grateful she hadn't, because soon afterward, he'd broken up with her. That was when Rachel had found out he had two other girlfriends in neighboring towns. They'd been giving him what she hadn't, all along.

She would have given her heart to him, along with her virginity, for nothing.

She probably would have been much wiser to take her mother's advice the day she'd met Adriane. But nooo. She'd thought only of her own immediate pleasure. Now she was *forever locked* to Adriane, both because of the twins she carried and because of her love for him.

As Adriane leaned back and lifted her chin, she met his eyes before taking a moment to admire the strong shape of his high cheekbones, the perfect angle of his nose, the beauty of his tanned skin, and the sensuousness of his full lips.

He was beautiful, on the inside as well, she was discovering. He was just very good at hiding that man deep beneath a thick skin.

He was also a king. He would do his duty and marry her, but would he ever love her? Was he even capable of that? From the time he'd known he would one day rule Corythia, he'd been groomed to find a princess, marry her, and continue his royal line, as the kingdom expected.

Instead, he'd ended up with her.

How could they possibly have anything more than a marriage of convenience? Sure, he was most likely fated to a marriage of convenience, but at least if the woman was of royal blood, the royal lines would stay pure. Her children weren't fully royal, not with her as a mother.

Before she was able to dwell too much on that thought, she began thinking again of their nights of lovemaking. He was a phenomenal lover, taking her to a new level of luxurious satisfaction each time he pleasured her body.

Maybe that was enough. Passion and loyalty.

Rachel didn't think Adriane would betray her by taking another woman. He just didn't seem the type of man to do something so horrendous. This was a new age where kings didn't need concubines anymore, right?

"My mother said the two of you had lunch. I am glad she returned home from her trip. You will spend a lot of time together, and the two of you have much in common."

"Your mother is a beautiful woman and was very kind to me," Rachel told him as she lowered her head to lean it against his chest.

As the sea swirled around their feet, Adriane's hands moved slowly up and down her back. Feeling unstoppable, Rachel lifted her chin as Adriane's mouth descended and he gently caressed her lips.

His smooth touch only confirmed her love for him. Tears filled her eyes as he nibbled on her bottom lip.

It was too much.

She had to get away from him for a while, had to gather her thoughts, figure out what she was going to do with this new information.

"Do you want to go back to the room and lie down?"

She knew he was offering her more than just a nap. She knew he wanted to take her again, and her body ached to accept his offer, but she couldn't, not right this moment. She had to reel her emotions in and figure out what to say to him.

"I'm not a child, Adriane. If I am tired, I will let you know," she said, purposely misinterpreting his words.

She felt like a monster as he flinched, showing hurt in his eyes for the barest second before he masked his expression.

He was a master at aloofness, which explained her complete cluelessness about what he was generally thinking or feeling.

She began to shake in his arms, and the anger he'd briefly shown seemed to fade away instantly as he looked down on her flushed face, and the line of sweat beginning to bead on her forehead.

"You look unwell, Rachel. Let me get you to your bed and call in the doctor. I want to make sure you aren't catching something," he said, and he leaned down to pick her up.

"I will not break just because I have a slight ache, Adriane. Are you really so worried about your heirs that you won't give me five seconds to work it out on my own before alerting the doctor?" she asked in exasperation as she pulled back from him.

This time, he didn't show any expression as he allowed her to take a couple of retreating steps.

He wasn't letting her get too far, however.

"Please, Rachel…" He broke off, at a loss for words because of her instant change in mood.

"I will get back to my room alone. I can take care of myself. Just leave me be," she snapped, putting a further divide between them.

She knew she was making the situation worse, but if he'd just allow her to go, she told herself, she would stop saying hurtful things — and start worrying about what she was going to say to him next.

Would he even want her love, this gift she was willing to give him for no more than the small price of him allowing her access to his heart?

"If it weren't for the fact that I'm carrying your twins, you never would have called me again, would you?" she asked, needing to hear him say it.

He hesitated as if he knew this was a trap, but his honest nature wouldn't allow him to lie.

"We won't ever know that, Rachel. The fact is, you *are* carrying my babies and you *are* here with me now. Why don't we just focus on that?"

"I can't, Adriane. I can't…" she said, almost on a sob. "I need to go," she said again, this time moving up the beach, bending down to grab her shoes and then making her way to the path that led to his palace.

This wasn't her home.

It could be if she accepted his proposal, but though she'd be his lawfully wedded wife, wasn't that all she'd be? They'd have great sex and she'd give birth to his babies, and then what? Without love, he'd lose interest and she'd become bitterly alone.

"Rachel, we need to talk more," he said, quickly catching up to her as they entered the palace.

"Can you ever love me, Adriane?" she asked, stopping him cold as she faced him in the cool, dark hallway.

He weighed his answer before opening his mouth. "Love doesn't matter, Rachel. Why do you keep bringing it up? Haven't these past nights been good for you? We can have that every night."

"Yes, Adriane, love does matter. Since I do keep bringing it up, don't you think that it's important?" she argued, angry and hurt-filled tears blurring her vision.

He didn't say anything to that, which Rachel felt was an incredibly painful slap in the face.

She walked away from him again, and this time he let him go. When she reached her room, she knelt beside her bed, and said a fervent prayer.

"Please help me to make the right decision, no matter what that decision may be. And please help me not to be such a fool as not to listen when I am given the answers."

Her prayer finished, Rachel stood up and crawled into bed.

Adriane had to think she was crazy now. One minute she was holding him as if she would never let him go and the next minute ranting at him to leave her alone. Had she not had that revelation while with his mother, her day would have gone a lot more smoothly.

She'd most likely be lying in his arms right this very minute.

Damn her stubbornness, and damn her inability to decide what she should do next.

CHAPTER FORTY-ONE

THEY WERE BACK to the real world, and Ari was scared.

Disaster had to await them, didn't it?

After all, their honeymoon had been perfect, everything she'd ever imagined and then some, thanks to all of Rafe's romantic surprises. They'd played on the beach, watched as whales and dolphins danced in the waters, lain in the sun for hours, and made love more times than should be physically possible.

But their jet had landed, and they were already back home. Would everything change now that the honeymoon was technically over? Would the honeymoon truly be over as they resumed their normal lives? Whatever the reason, Ari's nerves were gnawing away at her.

As Mario drove them toward Rafe's house, she felt a little sick.

This was his home, the home he'd had before she was a part of his life, the home he'd built for himself. The home he'd broken her heart in. She knew she shouldn't be upset, but they were starting a new life together and she wondered whether she'd always feel that this was his place, never feel that it was equally hers. Never get over the night she'd bared her soul to him and had been so completely crushed.

She would never say anything to him of the sort. It was petty of her even to think of asking him to move, but although it was a fine home, it wasn't a place she would choose for herself.

227

She wanted something with a large yard, a place where she felt comfortable getting to know her neighbors. She knew Rafe needed a large home, since he entertained clients in it, and he worked from his home office at times, but this setting, his bachelor mansion, was just not what she envisioned spending the rest of her life in.

Maybe at some point she would feel safe in bringing up the subject.

Not today, though. Today was their homecoming day. Today was their first day back in the real world — as man and wife.

They pulled up to the house with all the lights burning bright, a welcoming gesture from Rafe's efficient staff. As she emerged from the car, Ari looked at the imposing front door and hoped to feel a modicum of pride — a feeling that this was her home now, too.

Nothing.

"Welcome home, Mrs. Palazzo," Rafe said before scooping Ari up into his arms and carrying her across the threshold. At least he didn't stumble, but she didn't expect him to.

Her worries temporarily forgotten, Ari laughed with delight as he nuzzled her neck and made his way to the kitchen. Then she melted a little when she saw the gigantic bouquet of stargazer lilies waiting for her on the table.

"My favorite flowers," she sighed.

"I could never forget. I will have a bouquet for you every week for the rest of your life," he said before kissing her breathless while letting her body slide down his as he set her on her feet.

"Did you order them yourself, or have Mario do it?" It shouldn't matter, but it did. If they were from him, the gesture meant so much more.

"I ordered them," he said, and kissed her again.

"I love them, then," she said before kissing his neck, tasting his skin as she reached toward one of his buttons.

"I'm starving, woman, so quit distracting me," he said with a grin as he pulled back after leaning in for one more lingering kiss.

"Mmm, I'm not the one who started this," she reminded him while looping her arms around his neck and nibbling on his lips.

"I can't seem to keep my hands off you," he said before deepening the kiss, making them both lose sight of the meal they needed to have.

"I like that very much," she told him when he came up for air.

"You are going to have to sit on the other side of this island so I'm not tempted," he said, finally extracting himself from her arms.

Ari pouted as she took her seat, but quickly lost her moue as she watched him take food from the fridge. She hadn't seen him cook before. This would be interesting.

"What are you making?"

"For our first night together, I thought a salmon-topped salad, lots of wine, and ice cream for dessert."

"That's not very creative," she teased him.

"I've never claimed to be a culinary master," he said, unwrapping the already prepared items and putting the salad together.

"You have many other talents, so I suppose I shall forgive you."

"Why, thank you ever so much," he said as he set a plate in front of her. It was so nice to be alone with him, with no staff interrupting them as they enjoyed their first meal back in the States as man and wife.

It still seemed unreal, even after their time on honeymoon.

"I love you, Rafe," she said, halting the progress of her fork halfway to her mouth.

"You are my world, Ari," he said as leaned over, gently caressing her lips with his before lifting his hand and running his thumb across her swollen bottom lip.

"Who needs food?" she asked. The bedroom beckoned, saying "Now!"

"Oh, woman, don't tempt me," he scolded gently. "Eat up. You will need the fuel," he continued with a wink, making her stomach tighten in anticipation.

"You have a strenuous night planned?"

"Oh, yes, yes, I do," he promised.

Further anticipation filled her as she picked her fork back up and nibbled on her salad. They'd had romantic, amazing, take-her-breath away sex on her honeymoon, but now that they were home, she couldn't wait to see what he had planned next.

"Before we retire to our bedroom, I want to show you something," Rafe said as he cleaned up the dishes and set a bowl of ice cream in front of her, topped with extra whipped cream.

Ari filled her spoon with vanilla ice cream and syrup, enjoying the cold on her tongue. He grabbed a folder and placed it before her.

"What's this?" she asked, picking it up and opening it.

Then her eyes widened in delight. Listings. Home listings.

"I wanted to surprise you with a new house, Ari, but then I thought this was something you would want to be involved in. I know you haven't said anything, but I want us to start our life together with a home you can love. Here are some choices for you to thumb through. If you hate them all, then we'll meet with the Realtor and keep looking. I spoke to your mother and she told me what she believed you would like." Rafe spoke almost nervously.

Ari glanced through the listings, and on the third one, she stopped, entranced by the pictures of a beautiful colonial-style home with a wrap-around porch and bamboo flooring. And then the pièce de résistance, at least where she was concerned: a giant backyard, with a pool and a variety of giant trees providing shade and privacy.

It fulfilled her dreams.

"Oh, Rafe, I don't know what to say," she gasped, feeling as if it were already home without ever having set foot inside the double front doors.

"Do you really like it? This was my pick. I put down earnest money to hold it," he said, smiling as if he'd done well.

"I love it, but are you sure? You've lived here a long time." She suddenly felt guilty over not loving the place he'd called home.

"This is just a house, Ari. It's just a place I have rested my head. I've been waiting for you to come into my life to actually have a home — the place I can see myself living forever. You are what will make it a place of comfort, you and our children. If you're happy, then I will be too."

"Oh, Rafe, I am going to make you a very happy man tonight," she said with a watery smile as she rose from her seat and positioned herself between his legs. She leaned forward and kissed him.

"Mmm, it's too late, Ari. I'm already the happiest man alive," he said, when speaking was possible.

She grasped his face, her thumbs rubbing over his high cheekbones. "I can't believe I get to spend the rest of my life with you." She kissed him again, trying to convey all the emotion she was feeling, and she held on tight as his hands drifted down her back and cupped her behind, pulling her against his already aroused body.

When he pushed her back, she whimpered until he reached into his pocket and pulled out a bright red sash.

"What's this for?" Though she asked, she already knew, and her body tingled as she realized the games were about to begin.

Without saying a word, Rafe turned her around and lifted the sash, securing it across her eyes and tying it behind her head. Then he leaned forward and ran his tongue along her throat, making her core heat up. He wrapped his arms around her, and slid his hands up her stomach to surround her breasts, making her breathing deepen and her nipples harden painfully.

Ari felt herself being lifted. She quickly looped her arms around Rafe's neck as he made his way through the house and began ascending the staircase.

"What—"

"No speaking," he said, leaning down and silencing her with a hard kiss that made her body throb. Mmm, she loved this commanding Rafe, loved it when he came out to play. He'd been too afraid to for a while, too afraid of frightening her after the way things had ended for them before she'd taken him back. She didn't want to admit how much this man turned her on when he took control, but when he was in full command, her entire body pulsed with arousal.

He reached a room and laid her down, but not on their bed — the surface was too hard — and within seconds, he'd stripped her clothing away. Curiosity made her want to reach up and pull off the mask, but as she thought about doing that, Rafe grabbed her hands and lifted them above her head, quickly securing them.

"Rafe..." Ari's voice was unsure. Nonetheless, she realized that not even an ounce of fear was flowing through her veins, just pure desire. Whatever this new game was, she was enjoying it immensely.

"Shh," he said. After running his tongue across her lips, he spread her legs and secured them, too, leaving her wide open for his pleasure. And hers.

When she was fully tied up, he climbed back up her body, then let his mouth blaze a heated path down along her skin, grazing her jaw, kissing her neck and then in between her breasts. She shook with need. Her inability to see anything heightened her other senses.

He reached her stomach, gently nipping the skin below her belly button, and then his hands gripped her thighs and he lowered his mouth. As he kissed the outer edges of her core, she struggled to shift, wanting his mouth everywhere at once.

He gave her what she wanted, moving his mouth further down, kissing the inside of her thighs, while he moved his hands up to caress her hips and then smooth along her shaking stomach.

"Please, Rafe," she begged.

He said nothing. His tongue swept out and caressed her core with only one slow lick, making her back arch in the air. Then he began to move upward again, making her whimper.

This time he planted kisses up the slope of her breast and circled his tongue around the outside of her pebbled peak before sucking her nipple into his mouth and gently clamping his teeth down, making her cry out.

His hand found her core and he thrust two fingers inside, making her juices flow as she came close to falling over the edge.

Begging him did no good. He took his time kissing her all over; his hands followed the path of his mouth and he glided across every surface of her skin.

Finally, he bent down and opened his mouth to her core, sucking her throbbing pleasure point into his mouth and making her scream as an orgasm ripped through her, pulsing on and on, endlessly.

His tongue soothed the area, drawing out her pleasure; but then, suddenly, he was gone. She wanted to see what he was doing, but she couldn't shake off the blindfold.

"Rafe?" she asked when several moments passed and he didn't touch her, didn't slide his body into hers.

The room was utterly silent and she started to grow nervous. Yes, the orgasm had been insanely good, but she wanted more — she wanted his body to sink into hers now, needed him to join them together to make everything complete.

When she was really starting to worry, she felt something silken and velvety against her lips, and she swept out her tongue to taste his excitement as he pressed his arousal against her mouth.

She gladly opened to him, her core beginning to pulse again as he slipped his manhood into her mouth, sliding slowly deeper as he grasped the back of her head.

She hadn't done this before — hadn't sucked him inside her mouth while tied up and blindfolded, with him in complete control.

She was amazed at how turned on she was.

He still said nothing as he pushed himself deeper, quickening his movements as he touched the back of her throat, his pleasure lubricating his thick staff and dripping on her tongue.

Pulling out, he ran the head of his arousal across her lips and she swept out her tongue to taste him again, to feel his texture. The only sound in the room was a mixture of their excited groans.

He pulled away from her and she whimpered until he leaned down and kissed her, his tongue possessing her mouth, demanding her submission.

She was his. Unquestionably his.

He moved again and she whimpered until she felt him pressing against her core.

Finally!

She was more than ready for him to fill her. With a solid thrust, he drove inside her body, rocking her forward on the table as he groaned. "So hot," he called out as he stilled, buried fully inside her.

Then Ari blinked as he ripped off the blindfold and looked into her eyes. "I want to see your eyes dilate when I send you over the edge again," he gasped as he began moving.

Ari couldn't take her eyes from his as he thrust in and out of her, building her higher and higher as his body possessed hers.

She shook as he brought her close to the brink before slowing down and pausing, making the orgasm so close but just out of reach. "Please don't stop," she begged, and he sped up again.

Rafe smiled at her as he lifted a hand and cupped one of her swollen breasts, taking her nipple between his fingers and pinching hard.

That was all it took. As he thrust against her while squeezing her swollen peak, she came apart, her body holding his manhood tight as she convulsed around him.

"Ari," he cried, pulling almost all the way out before slamming back inside her, then shaking with the power of his release.

He now moved slowly within her, squeezing her hip bruisingly hard with one hand and her breast with the other. She didn't care about the marks he was sure to leave. All she could focus on was the pure pleasure in his face.

When the last of their orgasms eased, he gave her a look of complete satisfaction, then leaned forward and kissed her lips.

"I will never get enough of you, Ari."

"But it will sure be fun if you try," she told him.

Rafe released her from her binds and picked her up in his arms. She turned her head to look at the newest toy he'd bought, a wooden table with movable areas for the arms and legs, and with soft leather straps that he'd used to bind her with. Oh, the fun they would have with that.

One of these times, she'd turn the table on him. She was already plotting the wicked things she'd do to him once he was tied up there.

That was for tomorrow, or maybe the next day. With a contented sigh, she nestled against his chest as he carried her to their bedroom.

CHAPTER FORTY-TWO

ARI RAN TOWARD her mother with her arms out. There was so much to tell her, so much to fill her in on.

"I missed you," she said as she threw her arms around the woman who had always been her confidante, her best friend.

"You know I always miss you, darling," Sandra said. "How was the honeymoon?"

"It was perfect in every possible way. We took a tour of Scotland and went through old castles, and then lay on the beach for hours. I even got to watch dolphins dance, and saw some giant whales. The best part was just being with Rafe. I can't believe how much he has changed from the man I met a few years ago. It seems so unreal that we almost didn't get our happily ever after. We're going to have to go there again with you and Rafe's family."

"That sounds divine. But would you mind one more person joining our group?" Sandra asked.

"Who? Oh, wait, that was a stupid question. Things must be going well with you and Marco," Ari said with a teasing grin.

"He asked me to marry him." Sandra grew quiet, as if unsure how Ari was going to feel about her mother marrying.

"Oh, Mom, that is so great!" Ari exclaimed, catching her mom up in another embrace.

"I'm glad to hear you're happy about it, because we went ahead and eloped three days ago," Sandra said. She held up her hand and showed Ari the platinum band with an exquisite design of diamonds circling it.

Ari replayed her mother's words in her head. Her mom had gotten married — without her. Finally she found her voice again.

"I can't believe you would get married without me there," she managed to say.

"I'm sorry, baby, but I knew you would want to make a big fuss about it, and you are a new bride. I wanted you to be able to focus on your marriage and husband and not worry about me. I'm just an old woman who's been lucky enough to find a great love late in life. We'll have a big celebration dinner. How does that sound?"

Ari wasn't thrilled that she'd been excluded from the ceremony, but she also didn't want to cast a shadow on her mother's happiness, so she sucked up her disappointment and smiled.

"That sounds wonderful, and don't you dare call yourself old again. You are as beautiful now as you were twenty years ago."

"Aw, you are my sweet girl. Now what are our plans for the day?"

"I'm going to show you my new house after we do some shopping," Ari said with excitement, quickly getting over her disappointment.

"You got it? Which one did you decide on?"

"The colonial. Thank you for helping Rafe find me the perfect house," she said,. It was a day of all holidays rolled into one. If she never got another present, she wouldn't care. This was security unlike anything else she could imagine. She'd been lucky enough to grow up in one home and she wanted to give her future children the same comfort.

"I am so happy for you. I'll never forget the day I signed the papers on my house. It was a dream come true. There is just such comfort in knowing it's yours and no one will take it away. It's been a good house for me. Marco and I have decided to start fresh, both of us selling our homes and getting a new one together where we can make new memories, but I will always hold my first home close to my heart," Sandra said as the two of them got into Ari's brand-new Lexus, a wedding gift from her husband.

Ari would usually have been irritated he'd spent so much, but since it wasn't in the six-figure range, and as the day was clear and sunny and she was driving with the top folded down, she couldn't be upset. She loved the car way too much.

"This is wonderful," Sandra said, relaxing in the passenger seat as they began moving slowly through the city.

"I know. Rafe spoils me," Ari said with a smile as they pulled up to a store. "I love how much he loves me, Mom. That makes everything seem perfect, though I know it won't always be that way. We will have our fights, but I believe we can make it through anything that comes our way."

"Just remember that, and the two of you will have a good marriage. A lot of relationships fail because one or the other in the relationship tries to smother the other one or they don't listen to their partner. That can only lead to resentment."

"Is it difficult to marry a man when you are so set in your ways?" Ari asked.

"You would think so, but Marco and I have dated a long time now, and we both understand that we have businesses that are important to us. We get to share our days when we get home in the evening and it's almost effortless. I truly love him," Sandra said, a sparkle in her eyes that Ari hadn't seen in years. "He can't wait for us all to get together, but he went to a convention in Las Vegas. He'll be home tomorrow and then we will all have dinner."

"I'm so glad you have someone, Mom. Truly I am. I really like Marco. He's a good man with a big heart. I love that he puts a sparkle in your eyes. Not to mention on your ring finger."

"Thank you, Ari. That means a lot to me. *You* mean a lot to me, and don't you ever forget that."

They spent the rest of the day going to different stores and buying items that would make her feel at home, and then ended it by getting manicures and pedicures and having dinner together at their favorite Mexican restaurant. The food was greasy and cheesy — a perfect way to end their day. It was just what both of them needed; since they'd been so busy of late, they hadn't spent nearly enough time with one another.

Ari had missed her mom. She was grateful that they lived in the same city, so they could visit often. Too many people failed to value the importance of family. Ari was lucky enough to have married a man who loved his family and understood how important her relationship with her mother was.

By the time their evening came to a close, Ari wasn't quite ready to say goodnight, but she knew they'd see each other soon enough. After letting her mom tour her future home, she dropped Sandra off and then drove back to Rafe's place. Soon, she'd be in the new house and she couldn't wait.

"Mom absolutely loves the new house," Ari said as she stepped from her car, seeing Rafe standing on the front steps to greet her.

"I hope you had a good day with your mother. It's been a while and I can't wait to see her again," he said, coming down the steps so he could escort her inside.

"She feels the same about you. And it was a perfect day. I really enjoyed driving my sleek new car. I don't think Mom wanted to get out of it," she said, making him beam.

"I knew you would love it," he said before kissing her, unable to hide the contentment he felt that she liked her wedding present so much.

"Yes, you know me well. We spent the day shopping and I picked out some great decorations for the house. They will look fantastic."

"I can't wait to see everything," he said, taking her hand and leading her inside. She knew it would bore him to pieces, but she appreciated that he said it anyway.

They walked inside as the telephone rang, and after putting her bags in the living room, Ari stepped into the kitchen and sat at the island with a cool glass of wine while she waited for Rafe to join her.

When he entered the room, his smile was gone and she stood up, instantly concerned.

"Is everything OK?" she asked.

"No. That was my mother. She hasn't heard from Rachel all week and she's worried."

"Have you tried to call her?" Ari asked, instantly on alert.

"No, but Mom has with no success. I think it's time we head back over there. I don't like this," Rafe said.

"When do you want to leave?" Now that the euphoria of her wedding and honeymoon were over, the worry for Rachel came crashing to the forefront of everything. It was obvious that Rachel cared about Adriane, but maybe the king wasn't capable of caring for Rachel in the same way.

Of course Ari would respect whatever decision Rachel made, but she had a feeling her sister-in-law needed her, needed all of them. If Adriane did reject her, it was going to hurt. Ari knew how much it hurt not to have the love of the man you were giving your heart to.

"Tonight?" Rafe said as he looked her way.

"Let me pack a bag."

Family came first. Of course they would go to Rachel. There was no question where Ari's priorities lay.

"What about Lia? Have you heard anything from her since she and Shane took off?"

"Nothing more than the email telling me they eloped. Shane has some explaining to do," Rafe said, his eyes narrowing.

"It seems that eloping is the thing of the hour. My mother and Marco eloped, too."

"That's wonderful, Ari. We will send them a wedding gift," Rafe said, though the smile didn't reach his eyes. The call from his mother must have really shaken him up. She squeezed his arm as she tried to distract him.

"Mom did love my car..." she said with a teasing grin.

"Done."

"I was kidding, Rafe. She will beat you over the head with a cast-iron skillet if you buy her something so extravagant," she said. She should have known better than to make that kind of joke around her husband.

"Then I'd better get a helmet."

Ari knew she wouldn't be able to talk him out of it. Secretly, she was pleased with his generosity, but she didn't want him thinking he had to do things like that. Still, her mom had given up a lot to raise Ari, and Ari could hardly deny her such a wonderful gift.

"You know, you should give Lia a break. She loves Shane and he loves her."

The two of them were moving to the stairs as they spoke. Getting to Rachel was important, but they didn't think that she was in danger, just that she needed them to be there with her.

"I have no issue with them marrying. But my mother is crushed that she wasn't there. She would have liked to help Lia plan the wedding and to see her walk down the aisle."

"Some women don't want a fuss made," she told him as they entered their bedroom.

"When you have a family as big as ours, that just isn't an option," he said.

"You'll forgive her because you love her and Shane." She leaned up on her tiptoes to nuzzle his neck.

"How can I stay irritated when you keep touching me?" he asked, finally softening just the tiniest bit as he wrapped his arms around her.

"You can't. That's the plan," Ari told him. She reluctantly pulled back, loving that she'd been able to pull him from his dark mood.

"Thank you, Ari."

"For what?" she asked as she reluctantly let him go and moved toward her closet.

"For knowing exactly what to say to take my stress away. You are good for me in so many ways."

She turned and faced him. "I'm a better person for having you in my life. Now, you call the jet and have your staff ready it, and I'll gather our clothes."

Rafe smiled and grabbed his phone. They had a long night ahead of them, and he wasn't about to waste it.

CHAPTER FORTY-THREE

ADRIANE STORMED INTO the palace, heading straight for his study with a scowl on his face. How dare she!

He'd been more than accommodating. He taken time out of his day for Rachel, much to the distress of his council during a time that his brother was making a bid for power. He had shown her his country, taking her deep into the heart of the island, showing her the farms, the small factories, the people. He'd showered her with gifts, attention, and anything else her heart desired.

Why did she have to be so contradictory? Why couldn't she just accept that this was her life now, this was the way it needed to be?

Because she was a woman — irrational.

Adriane was glad his mother wasn't around, and very grateful he hadn't said his thoughts aloud. If his mother overheard him now, she'd wither him with a single look.

Rachel was in no way being abused, so what was wrong with her that she couldn't just accept they were to wed?

He *would* raise his children!

Through with his chaotic thoughts, Adriane decided to douse his foul mood with a few shots of whiskey. Walking to the nearest liquor cabinet, he poured himself a generous amount and moved over to the couch.

This would all be so much easier if he could keep his feelings separate from the situation. But he couldn't seem to do that; he couldn't stop thinking of her, day and night.

The past few nights had been spectacular. Sex was certainly not something they had any trouble with. Quite the opposite, in fact.

All Rachel had to do was enter a room and his body hardened and his heart rate accelerated. Even after their passionate encounters, several times a day over the last few days, he hadn't had enough — not nearly enough.

Even with anger wreaking havoc inside him, he was still hard for her, still wanted to haul her off to bed and ravish her again and again. Perhaps it would be easier for him to tie her up in the bedroom, the only place he seemed to have any control over her.

Would their children suffer if he continued to insist on this marriage? Was she really that unhappy with him? He'd thought he was being good to her, but maybe she still believed him a monster.

How could she make love to him night after night if she despised him?

Even as the thought flitted through Adriane's mind, he knew he had used women before. He'd lain with many — a long line of nameless faces — just to have his needs met.

Walking away from those nameless faces hadn't been difficult to do, not even a little.

So was that what *she* was doing? Was she scratching her itch, so to speak?

The thought made his chest feel hollow. But why should he care? If it made her stay, he didn't need to have her be in love with him. Love could end in hate; it could end in bitterness and divorce. Wouldn't it be even harder for him if he got to spend every day with his children for a few years only to have them taken away when she decided she'd had enough?

No, it was wiser to not involve love.

He felt confident in his conclusions.

But as he stood there, he felt somehow empty at such a thought. Gazing out the window, he realized it was too late for him. He didn't know if this was love, but he did feel something for her. It wasn't just friendship, and it wasn't just great sex.

There was more to what he was feeling for this woman who defied him every chance she got. Was this what love was all about? Was this that mythical emotion people spoke of?

It couldn't be, could it?

How could he be in love with her? She exasperated him — tormented him — angered him almost as much as she heated his blood. If she weren't carrying his children, he wouldn't even think of marrying her, would he?

That thought caused physical pain to rip through his stomach.

What was going on with him? Adriane took another long swallow of his whiskey, hoping it soothed this strange emotion inside the hollowness.

"I see my sister isn't making life easy for you."

Adriane turned to find a smug-looking Rafe standing in the doorway, looking pointedly at Adriane's nearly empty glass. How the man had managed to charm his staff enough to get in to his private study unannounced, he didn't know.

"Your sister is certainly a handful," Adriane said as he moved back to the cabinet and refilled his glass before offering one to Rafe.

"Don't mind if I do," Rafe said, stepping up beside him.

A deep panic started in Adriane's stomach as he began to wonder why Rafe was there. Had Rachel called him — asked to be picked up? Hadn't he decided that if she refused to stay past this point, he would let her go? What else could he do, after all?

Just the thought of her leaving stirred him up within. No!

"What are you doing back here so soon?" Adriane asked, trying to control his tone.

"Can't a friend stop by for a visit?" Rafe asked instead of answering.

"I'm not in the mood, Rafe," Adriane said.

Rafe studied him for several long moments before downing the contents of his glass and walking over to the sofa to make himself comfortable. Adriane couldn't sit, not with the way his gut was churning. He almost wished it were olden times, and he could hop on his trusty steed and ride off to do battle with the enemy.

Even going mano a mano with modern-day terrorists seemed pretty appealing at this particular moment. Anything to work off this frustration.

"Do you love my sister, Adriane?"

Stunned that those words had come from Rafe's mouth, Adriane turned toward the man who had been his friend for so many years — actually, he'd really been more of a cold and calculating business acquaintance. Rafe had changed.

Yes, there was still the gleam of the ruthless businessman in his eyes, but if you looked a little deeper, there was a peacefulness there too. Adriane didn't know what to think about that, but obviously Rafe had been hit by Cupid's arrow.

"We're having twins together," he said, avoiding Rafe's question.

"That's not news, Adriane, and also not what I'm asking, as you're well aware."

"I don't love anyone," Adriane said, though that was possibly a lie. His feelings were none of Rafe's business.

Rafe was silent as he studied Adriane, who suddenly felt as if he was being carefully scrutinized beneath a high-powered microscope.

Adriane was king of Corythia. He didn't squirm!

Standing tall, he squared his shoulders and owned his answer. It might not be the answer Rafe wanted to hear, but at least he was being honest. OK, a nagging thought in the back of his mind told him he was being anything but honest — which was the heart of his problem.

"I don't think you're telling the truth, Adriane. I think you have deeper feelings than you care to admit. Whether or not you want to share them with Rachel is up to you. Man to man, though, I'll be honest with you. If Rachel wants to go home, nothing will stop me from taking her with me."

"I appreciate the warning," Adriane said, his voice dull. "It is her choice to leave or not."

With that, Adriane walked from the room. He couldn't stand there with her brother any longer. He couldn't face being reminded that she might leave him.

He was sure his strange reactions were really nothing — a temporary spike of insanity brought on by the strange and fraught circumstances.

If only he could convince himself that's all it was.

CHAPTER FORTY-FOUR

TAKING A BREATH of courage outside of Rachel's door, Adriane felt his irritation grow. Why should he fear speaking to her? They were both adults.

Maybe if the two of them had been more honest with each other from the start, he wouldn't be standing here afraid she was going to leave. He'd tried to be honest, surely he had, but what he was feeling was overwhelming. He didn't understand it, didn't trust it.

The two of them would have a wonderful existence together, raising their children, and enjoying a healthy sex life. They had that department nailed down. Why couldn't that be enough? Why did these strange emotions have to seep in and make him worry?

When he opened the door, she was in the middle of the room, her eyes slightly puffy — he assumed from lack of sleep. It certainly couldn't be attributed to crying. She was strong and had nothing to cry about. Up until their fight earlier, they'd been getting along perfectly, for the last few days, at least.

As he moved near her, the scent of her shampoo drifted around him, making him lose track of what he'd just been thinking about.

Damn!

Focus, he ordered himself silently.

Rachel didn't say anything; she just waited to see what he'd come to her for. Her expressive eyes seemed almost haunted, afraid. He couldn't understand what had happened this afternoon, why she'd had such an about-face in moods.

He could understand her silence after their fight, though he still didn't understand the fight itself, or how it had started. Why was she so angry with him for caring about how she was feeling? If she was sick, he wanted her treated. It was ridiculous that she should take offense at his concerns.

"Your brother is here."

That isn't what he'd intended to say, but it came out anyway. Walking to her wide windows and looking down at the grounds below, he told himself to breathe deeply and remain calm. It didn't behoove a king to feel such a lack of control.

When he turned back to face her, she wore an impenetrable expression. Normally, he could read her fairly easily, but not now. Fear still shone in her eyes, but he didn't understand what she was afraid of. Surely not him.

"I know. I just got done speaking with Ari, but I appreciate that you came here to tell me," she finally said, with just the slightest hitch to her voice.

"I'm sure he would enjoy your company when you feel up to it." They were both being so formal, it was ridiculous.

If killing someone with nothing but a look happened outside myth, his problems would be over. Her eyes flashed lethally, and yet he was almost grateful to see light coming to them.

"Thank you. Let him know I'll be down in thirty minutes."

With that, she turned away.

Adriane's shoulders stiffened as he faced her back. This had to stop; it was time she got over her snit.

"I'm sorry if I offended you this morning. I still don't understand what went wrong, but upsetting you was certainly not my intention."

There. He was being the better man and apologizing, though he didn't see what he needed to apologize for. Still, if it would get this fight over with, his apology was worth it.

"There's no need to apologize, Adriane. I just need some time to think," she said, walking to her closet and grabbing a coat.

"Where are you going?" He hated the anxiety that kept assailing him. With her brother there, it had grown worse.

"I'm going to walk on the beach. I need to clear my head — make some decisions."

The decisions had to be whether to leave with her brother or not. Adriane couldn't let that happen. If he did, he knew he would always regret it.

"A storm is brewing and the wind's picking up, so please don't be gone long."

"I'm not worried, and I won't go far," she said.

"Rachel…"

She paused as she turned to look at him. What did he want to say? Was he going to beg her not to leave? He took a step forward, but his pride prevented him from acting.

"What, Adriane?" She seemed impatient.

"We're going to be fine, Rachel. I know you're upset today, but everything is fine between us. I enjoy being with you." He was almost surprised by his confession, but he wasn't unhappy he'd said it.

She paused as she looked at him, gazing into his eyes as if trying to read into his words, trying to see if there was a deeper meaning behind them.

She said nothing, so he continued. "Our marriage will be good. We will please each other. I won't have another woman in my bed — I won't cheat. And I will be a good father."

"What exactly are you telling me?"

What *was* he telling her?

He didn't know. He was giving her all he knew how to give her. He was trying to make her stay.

"I don't want you to leave."

It was unbelievable how hard that was for him to say.

Her face grew sad, as if he'd disappointed her. What was he doing wrong? What would make this all better?

"I know, Adriane," she finally whispered as she came close to him and lifted her hand, rubbing her fingers against his cheek. He lifted his own and pressed her fingers to his face, not wanting to lose her touch. It was almost as if she were saying a goodbye. "I need to walk."

With that, she pulled away and stepped past him, and he found himself alone, enveloped by her scent.

Unable to stand being in there without her, he left the room and closed the door. He had to collect himself and figure out what he was going to do if she decided she just couldn't be with him anymore.

It was an unbearable thought.

CHAPTER FORTY-FIVE

A S IF ON cue, the storm picked up speed. As Rachel stepped from the warmth and security of the palace, she was hit with a gust of wind so strong, it nearly blew her over. But she had to think, had to get away from the stagnant air she'd been breathing inside.

What was he saying to her? Did he care? It seemed that way to her each time they made love.

She'd been a fool to think she could ever just be Adriane's friend. She'd wanted that for the sake of the children she carried, but how could she not fall in love with the man when she made love to him? Though some women might be able to have meaningless sex, she wasn't built that way.

At least she had accomplished her goal — so to speak. She'd gotten to know Adriane about as well as anyone could. He wasn't easy to know: he was too closed off to the world. Maybe that was from being born royal. Too many people sought only to use him.

She wasn't one of those people. But did he know that?

And how long could she continue hoping he would give her all of himself? She deserved that; she didn't deserve to be kept there waiting, waiting, and waiting for the day he'd profess his undying love.

But at this point could she simply walk away? Give in so easily? He seemed so close. If she hadn't realized her heart was involved, the decision would be so much easier. She was terrified, though, that if she stayed now and he never felt anything more than a fondness for her, she would slowly wither away.

Her gloomy thoughts accompanied her to the beach, where she looked out at the ocean as the waves crashed dangerously close to the shore. She didn't care; the looming tempest matched the way she felt. As she drew farther and farther from the palace, the storm clouds grew angrier and blacker in the sky.

Just as the first drops of a pounding rain started, Rachel was pushed to her knees by a large gust of wind. She fell to the sand, her hands digging in as she fought to find her breath.

When she looked back and realized how far she'd wandered, she decided it was time to go back. The sea was tossing and flailing about, and the wind blew strongly, strongly enough to carry her off into the waves if she wasn't careful. No matter how emotional she was right now, she couldn't put her babies in jeopardy. Now was a good time to face Adriane and demand answers from him.

He was going to give her all or nothing. And all was the only thing she would accept.

Pushing against the wind, she struggled to her feet and turned. Her breath hitched when she discovered a man looming nearby. Feeling strangely afraid, she looked for the path, seeking the palace in the distance. She really had walked too far.

When this new fear clawed at her chest, she had to remind herself that this was Adriane's private beach — no one who didn't belong could be here. This was most likely a new guard.

Still, she just wanted to get away from him.

"Hello, Rachel. I've been waiting to get you alone."

The sound of his voice sent a chill straight through her body.

"Who are you? How do you know my name?"

She automatically took a few retreating steps from him.

"I know all about you and the children you carry — the supposed heirs of this kingdom. You are an inconvenience that must be disposed of if I'm to gain my throne."

It took a few seconds for his words to sink in.

"You're…" her words failed her.

"Yes, I'm Adriane's brother, Gianni. You and I are going to take a little trip together, Rachel."

He reached over and grasped her arm, tugging at her.

Hell, no!

Rachel kicked at him, and in his surprise, he released her. She took off running, screaming at the top of her lungs for help, but she knew it was a long shot that her voice would be heard over the thunder and lightning roaring across the sky. Add to that, the crashing of the waves, which were only growing in violence as the storm gathered force.

Suddenly she was flying through the air, her feet kicked out from under her, and she fell hard against the wet sand. A slicing pain ripped through her abdomen and side.

"No!" she screamed as her stomach cramped. This man wasn't going to make her lose her babies. Pain almost consumed her, but she still fought him, trying everything in her power to escape.

He bent down to grab her, and her hand shot out, scratching his face. The look of hatred in his eyes frightened her; screaming again, she kicked out, despite the pain she felt lancing through her stomach. She knew that if she gave in, if this man captured her, she didn't have a chance.

When he reached for her again, her foot connected, forcing a shout of rage from his throat. She got to her feet and stumbled a few steps before he grabbed her hair and yanked her back. Tears leaked from her eyes at the pain, and she lost her ability to fight. When his fist shot out and struck her cheek, it was all over. Rachel succumbed to a vortex of blackness as dark as the waters crashing around her.

CHAPTER FORTY-SIX

THE PEOPLE WHO took care of the inlaid wood flooring wouldn't thank him for the punishment it was receiving as he tried to sort through his conversation with Rachel. Approaching his window, as if to find answers there, Adrianne looked out at the flashing thunderclouds and the leaves being thrashed around by the angry wind. The branches of the trees were bending dangerously low, and worry rose high within him. Surely she had changed her mind.

She wouldn't be so foolish as to stay outside in this storm.

His guards would be smart enough to go after her and bring her back if she hadn't returned quickly. If not, they would be let go for endangering her life and that of his children.

As he was reaching for his phone to make sure she was inside the palace, a knock sounded on his door. Pausing, he turned angrily toward the intruder. He wasn't up for visitors right now; he couldn't even seem to think straight, much less talk civilly to someone.

"Leave me," he snarled.

"Sire, I need to speak to you."

Adriane turned to see his adviser practically shaking. It wasn't often that the man disobeyed a direct order. With the phone clutched in his hand, he gazed at Nico and lost his train of thought.

"This isn't the time," he snapped again. He had to pull himself together so he could find Rachel, speak to her before she decided to leave the country with her brother. The thought of it made his chest ache. He took his free hand and massaged the offending area.

But he had just a muscle in there, for God's sake. The thought of her leaving him shouldn't make the inside of his chest hurt. He let the phone dangle in his other hand as he pondered the riddle.

"Sire. There is news I need to tell you."

Adriane turned incredulous eyes on Nico. The man had never defied him to this extent.

"I said this isn't the time, Nico. Leave."

He didn't even bother turning to face the man, expecting his orders to be followed this time.

He felt as if he were being kicked in the gut. What was happening?

He couldn't focus, couldn't think straight. Nothing seemed to be holding a place in his mind except Rachel's face, the look in her eyes right after he pleasured her, the laughter that spilled from her when something delighted her, the display of pain in her expressive eyes when he hurt her.

Adriane realized that he thought about her all the time. During his meetings with his council, while he was awake and asleep, she haunted him. Her smile, her touch, her voice...even her smell. There wasn't a moment that went by when she wasn't on his mind.

Not just as the mother of his children, not just as a lover. He cared about her as a person. The thought of her leaving him was like taking a knife to his chest. Was this love? Had he found this thing he had never believed in being real? Was this what his mother had spoken of? Was this what Rachel was demanding of him?

Suddenly, the aching in his chest and midsection vanished. What a fool he was. Why would he fight against something that felt so right? Why had it taken him so long not only to take the advice of his mother, but to listen to his own heart?

He could have saved a lot of pain, pain for both him and Rachel. Surely it wasn't too late, though. He just had to catch her before Rafe whisked her off to America.

"I love her," he said aloud. He needed to put his emotions into words.

If Rachel left him for good, if she ran away, he would lose a part of himself. He wouldn't have the same purpose in life — just empty days and lonely nights. This must be what people meant when they professed their love. Without the person you loved by your side, a vacant nothingness of days lay ahead.

He turned, surprised to see Nico still standing uncomfortably by. The man obviously wasn't leaving until he said whatever he'd come in to say.

"It's about Rachel."

Adriane's heart stopped for a beat before resuming at a much faster pace. Had she left with Rafe? Was he too late?

No! Even if she had left, he would find her — beg her to come back to him, humble himself before her.

"Tell me," he said.

"One of the guards saw her running from the palace out to the beach. With the weather so turbulent, he grew concerned, and after she didn't return right away, he followed her path. He got there just in time to see her being tossed into a boat and taken from the island."

Nico's voice trembled as he spoke. Adriane was afraid to ask the next question.

"This wasn't consensual?" Whether it was or not was a moot point. No one should be out on those rough waters at this time. The sea was a dangerous place at any time, but during a storm, it was practically suicide to be on the ocean.

"No, Sire. She was being carried over the man's shoulders, and was placed in the boat in a rather unpleasant way. The guard called back to the palace and immediately began a foot pursuit after the kidnapper, but it was too late. The boat was long gone before they were able to reach the dock."

"Who took her?"

Everything in Adriane froze as he stared at his trusted adviser. There was deep worry in the man's eyes.

"The guard made eye contact with the man. There's no doubt about who it was," Nico said, hesitating.

"Tell me!" Adriane shouted, fury filling him because he already knew the answer.

"Gianni." The name was barely a whisper from Nico's lips.

Adriane felt his face drain of color, felt his blood turn cold. She was out there with his brother now because he'd been unable to speak to her — unable to tell her how much she meant to him.

He was a coldhearted bastard and Rachel was going to be the one to pay for his sins. Gianni was making the ultimate play in a long struggle against Corythia, and Rachel was nothing more than a bargaining chip. His brother would have no problem killing her and the children she carried.

"Get Rafe up here immediately," he said, the dead sound of his voice unrecognizable even to him, and he picked up the phone to call his guards.

Seconds ticked by like hours as Adriane stood before his large windows, looking out at the thrashing ocean, praying that the boat wasn't overturned, that Gianni was able to navigate to a place where Adriane was sure he had a crew waiting for him.

"What is it, Adriane?"

Rafe sounded irritated. He was about to become enraged.

"Rachel has been kidnapped." Adriane was barely able to get the words from his mouth.

Suddenly he was being pressed up to the glass he'd been looking out as Rafe's eyes flashed before him.

"You'd better talk fast," Rafe thundered, fury transforming his features, fear just as apparent behind the fury.

"My brother was seen grabbing her on the beach less than an hour ago. My guards were too far away to get to her," he said, his throat closing at the thought of what could be happening to her.

"Do you have any idea where he'd take her?" Rafe asked, his fury dissipating to be replaced with anguished concern. He released Adriane and began to pace the office. Adriane almost wished Rafe would just punch him. He'd rather feel the ache from physical pain than this strange burning in his chest.

"I think so. I'll have the guards prepare transportation right away."

"Why would he do this?"

This was the question Adriane had been afraid he'd ask.

"He's making a play for the throne. As you know, he was supposed to be Corythia's next king, but he gave up the title years ago. He wanted nothing to do with the kingdom. A few years back, he changed his mind, but it was too late. Father told him he was disinherited and not allowed back in Corythia. He hasn't stopped seeking revenge since then. I'm afraid this is his ultimate showdown."

"Will he hurt her?"

"Honestly, I don't know. The brother I used to know is long gone. I think at this point he is capable of anything. That is what frightens me the very most."

"Then we can't just go in with guns blazing. We have to come up with a solid plan. If he's using my sister as some sort of pawn and sees us coming, he will shield himself with her. We can't let that happen," Rafe said, clearly the one thinking out of the two of them.

"He has a compound in America. That's where he went after renouncing the throne and leaving Corythia. He doesn't know that we are aware of his hideout. My father had Gianni investigated when he first came back into our lives. The place is in rough country in Montana."

"Can we reach him before he gets her on a plane?"

"I have no idea where he would fly from. My guess is that he's been lying in wait, and had it all arranged. I think our best guess is to get to that compound."

"How do we know for sure?" Rafe asked, hesitating before making an irrevocable decision.

"We don't know. All I can do is go with my instinct. At one point in our lives, Gianni and I were close. We loved each other. He's been attempting to form armies for months, but Corythia's forces have quickly disbanded them, having no trouble staying one step ahead of him. I'm afraid that now, he is desperate. He would want to regroup where he feels stronger, feels he has more power. That wouldn't be here in Corythia, where he has no one loyal to him."

"I will trust your judgment, then," Rafe said, though Adriane was sure they were equally terrified that Adriane might be making the wrong move.

"Thank you. I already have men out combing the waters and the land here, too, just in case, but I truly think he's taking her from the country." There was nothing else he could say until they knew for sure where Rachel was.

"I'll call Shane. He can be there before us, since he's currently in the United States. Give me the exact location."

After the calls were made, it didn't take them long to collect Ari from the sitting room and for them to arrive at the airport. They would have to drop her in a safe location when they got to the States, because they weren't taking any chances of her getting caught in the crossfire. It was bad enough that Rachel was in danger.

The weather was such that no one should have been thinking of flying, but none of them said a word as they made their way to the airport. They would reach Rachel, or die trying.

"Sire, I'm sorry, but we can't get authorization," Adriane's pilot said.

"I don't care what it takes; you will get this damn jet in the air," Adriane thundered.

"A hurricane is about ten miles off the coast of the island, Sire, threatening to turn at any time. We won't even get liftoff," his pilot told him.

Rachel had been out on that water, far too close to the dangerous winds and waves of the hurricane. What were the chances that Gianni and Rachel had even made it to Gianni's safety point? It wasn't looking good.

Instead of coming unglued and berating the pilot, Adriane, Rafe and Ari waited, counting down the hours for the storm to pass. The walls of the hangar shook as the wind did her best to wipe out the entire building, but none of the people inside had a single thought of waiting elsewhere.

If they made it through this storm, they would head out the second the jet was able to lift into the air.

As the tense night progressed, the storm continued to grow in its fury, threatening to lay waste to Adriane's country. He didn't even care. All he cared about was finding Rachel.

Homes he could rebuild; crops could be replanted.

Rachel. There was only one of her.

If it took his death, that's the price he would pay. As long as she lived, the world would be righted.

Finally, the winds abated.

Now, for the long journey, with only the hope that she was where they thought Gianni had taken her.

CHAPTER FORTY-SEVEN

"TAKE A BREATH in and then push it back out." Rachel continued to repeat those words to herself in a low whisper as she sat on the filthy cot in the pitch-black room. The last thing she needed was to panic.

Two days she'd been there.

She knew that only from the remarks made by Gianni's minions. They'd hauled her by her ropes from the filthy room, bringing her into the main part of the house to question her about Adriane, trying to force any information they could from her that they thought would help them in the takeover of Corythia.

She didn't know anything of that sort, and if she did, she certainly wouldn't tell them! She'd closed her eyes as they'd tried terrorizing her by making lewd comments about what they planned to do to her once Gianni felt her no longer useful to him.

She was nothing to them — less than nothing — and they weren't afraid to remind her of that fact, over and over again.

She'd woken up when she was dragged from the boat onto land and then quickly transported to a helicopter. The wind had been picking up speed as the chopper hurried away, deeper inland, outracing the hurricane that had been on their tail.

A few times she'd thought they'd go down. The man sitting next to her with the cold, dark eyes hadn't even blinked while they'd been tossed about. She'd said a few prayers, hoping they wouldn't end up in a fiery pile of metal.

She didn't know how they made it out, but somehow she'd survived that ordeal only to be moved to a private jet. She'd been in the air all through the night, to somewhere far from Corythia, and had ended up in this new prison. She was sure that hell would be a safer and more comfortable place. If it weren't for the babies she was trying to protect, she would gladly have wished for death.

Her stomach had been cramping up for two days, but the first time she'd been allowed to use the restroom, she'd burst into relieved tears at seeing not a trace of blood in her urine.

As sore as she was, then, so far she still wasn't bleeding. Maybe her children would make it through all of this. She had to keep her wits about her and think if she had any chance of escape.

Closing her eyes, she tried to focus on her twins, on a nice warm bath and a hot meal. She tried to dwell on pleasant thoughts so she could calm her rapidly beating heart.

Anything was better to focus on than the putrid smell surrounding her. The men were barely feeding her, just the scraps they placed before her during their demented meetings. She couldn't afford to lose the few nutrients they'd provided.

She would make it through this. She wasn't one to give up.

Someone would rescue her soon. Either Adriane or Rafe, surely. They wouldn't leave her in this hellhole. But what if they didn't know how to find her? How could they know?

It seemed so hopeless.

No! She wouldn't think that way. If she did, she'd really panic and only make her situation worse.

"Time to come speak to the boss."

Rachel didn't open her eyes at the gruff command. She didn't want to go out there again with those animals. They were too disgusting to even call human.

They were scum.

"Get your ass up now, before I have to come over there and assist you."

The way he said it, he was clearly hoping she would defy him. The last time she had... A shudder passed through her at the thought. Gianni had walked in as the man had her trapped against the bed, and he'd ripped the man off her.

Not that he cared about her safety, but he'd told his minion that now wasn't the time. He was too afraid they'd kill her in the process before he could get information from her. But once she'd served that purpose, she was all theirs.

They planned to do unspeakable things to her on video for Adriane's benefit. She didn't know when the next part of their nasty game was going to begin, but fear seized her heart at the thought of it.

With trembling legs, she rose from the bed and opened her eyes to look at the man's face. She wanted to remember every single feature. When she got out of this — because she refused to believe she wouldn't — she wanted to be able to identify him.

He would pay. They all would.

Rachel followed him down the narrow hallways, the only light coming from the uncovered bulbs hanging every ten feet or so. Layers of dust and grime covered every surface, and the windows were boarded up.

If she'd had a clue where they were, maybe she wouldn't have felt so hopeless, felt that there was no chance of rescue. This was obviously not Gianni's regular abode. The son of a king wouldn't live in such filth.

No. This was a perfect place for him to have her — a place no one would suspect. How had he managed to get American men to work for him? There were a few men from his country there, about five that she'd managed to count. But he also had about ten Americans, to judge by their accents. Why would they help him?

Money. The depths that some humans could stoop to for a few dollars was abhorrent to her. They not only had no problem with torturing a pregnant woman, but they enjoyed doing it.

When they reached the dingy kitchen where she'd been brought a couple of times before, the thug thrust her into a chair none too gently, then slapped a bowl of oatmeal in front of her, its lumps turning her stomach.

"Don't turn your nose up at good food, princess. You will need the energy to get through the interrogation that's coming," he taunted her, and moved off to a corner of the room to watch.

Just then, the door opened and Gianni walked in, his eyes as black and hollow as they'd been each time she had the misfortune of seeing him.

He sat across from her and sneered — his idea of a smile — as he waited to see what she would do. They had mocked her the first time she'd refused to eat what they chose to serve her, telling her she wasn't royalty yet and had better take what they offered.

Then Gianni had spent hours relentlessly questioning her. What he asked her, she didn't have answers for. Even if she wanted to tell him, she couldn't.

A shudder ran through her. She didn't know how much longer she could take it.

It's for the babies, she told herself as she picked up the spoon and took a bite of the half-cooked oatmeal. It was disgusting, but she hoped it would stave off starvation and give her just enough energy not to fall face-first when she had a chance at escape. Because the first chance she got, she was running as far from this place as possible.

If she was going to die, then she was going to do it fighting, not cowering in the corner the way they expected her to.

Only once since arriving had she been outside, and snow had covered the ground. They had huge floodlights all over the yard, making it impossible for her to sneak out beneath the watchful gaze of Gianni's guards. There were woods all around, so if she could get to them, she had a place to hide, but she'd bet there wasn't another house around for miles. If the elements didn't kill her, then wild animals might. It was still a better death than being tortured and raped.

"Have you decided to cooperate yet?"

Rachel looked the man dead in the eyes while she forced another spoonful of mush into her mouth. She said nothing.

"Ah, I see you still think you have choices here," he said, a corner of his lip turning up as he gazed at her, his head tilting slightly as if she were a puzzle he couldn't quite figure out how to solve.

"I can understand why my brother is so fascinated by you. There is fire running through your veins. If we had met under more…pleasant circumstances, I might have fancied you myself," he said. It was a compliment she could do without.

Rachel didn't blink, just tried her hardest not to explode. It wasn't the right time yet. He was a slimy slug and she would have no qualms about gouging out his eye with a fire poker if she could get her hands on one. Unfortunately, these men weren't stupid, and they allowed no possible weapons where she might get to them.

She wanted to scream, but kept silent, conveying her loathing of him loud and clear with just a look.

His hand lifted and caressed her face. When she jerked her head away, he grabbed her hair, yanking it and pulling her forward so her bowl was knocked over the edge of the table. "I think it's time to teach you how a real king gets a woman to behave," Gianni said, his voice deadly. He stood and grabbed her arm, bruising her as he hauled her from her seat.

Rachel struggled against him, but to no avail. Gianni raised his other hand and slapped her hard enough that she nearly blacked out. Her eye began swelling as he moved toward the door.

Within a few seconds, the heavy back door was open and he pushed her outside, making her stumble and sink to her knees in the snow. Two of his men approached and grabbed her arms, lifting her back to her feet as they continued their forward march. She couldn't suppress her overwhelming fear about what would happen next. As she trembled from terror and the cold, they marched her barefoot through the snow to a shed.

Opening the door, they tossed her in. Rachel landed on her backside and scooted away from the men to the far wall.

"Why don't you cool off for a while and see if it gives you a better attitude? When you are ready to speak to me, we'll allow you to come back inside," Gianni said before the door shut, locking her inside.

The shed did little to ward off the bitter cold of winter, and Rachel's thin clothing helped her not at all. So she searched until she found an old tarp under a pile of debris.

Folding it in two, she felt the gripping cold of the plastic material pierce through her clothing and freeze her skin while she wrapped the thing, filthiness and all, around her shoulders. But it was all she had, and she prayed it would help to hold in what little body heat she had remaining.

Curling up in a fetal position on the hard earth floor, she breathed deeply into her plastic cocoon, refusing to let any tears fall.

This wasn't how her life was supposed to end.

She was supposed to be a mother in five months; she was supposed to hold her babies close as she dreamed about tomorrow.

Rachel knew she should try to stay awake, but as sleep began dragging her under, she soon stopped fighting it. She didn't want to be awake. If she didn't ever awaken, it was meant to be.

Letting go, she huddled beneath the tarp and prayed for the comfort of dreams to replace her harsh reality.

CHAPTER FORTY-EIGHT

THE DOOR SWUNG open and Shane was standing there in full military gear, looking like GI Joe come to life. Rachel was trying to analyze this dream. Why would she be fantasizing about Shane? She'd think it would be Adriane, the man she loved, rescuing her.

But, no, not even in her fantasies was he playing the star and the hero. Maybe she'd closed the door on the hope of a happily ever after with her king; maybe she thought it was too much to hope for at this point.

She did think it would be mighty nice if Shane passed his coat over to her, though. If she were going to have a fantasy about him stripping, then she'd really like to have his coat.

Rachel giggled at the thought. The sound of her voice coming out squeaky startled her into stopping her laughing as quickly as she had begun it. Wow, this was a strange dream.

"Put this on," Shane said, rushing to her and placing a bag at her feet, then kneeling down and helping her sit up. Rachel gave him a sweet smile and nodded her head. She tried to reach for the bag, but her fingers wouldn't work.

Maybe she had frostbite. It wasn't unlikely. Maybe she was already dead and this was heaven. But why would Shane be in her heaven?

"Let me help you," he said, then he carefully removed the tarp. She wanted to protest even though it wasn't much protection against the cold.

Within a few heartbeats, a warm coat was being wrapped around her shoulders, sending some feeling back into her arms. Then gloves were being thrust upon her hands. Oh, this dream was getting better all the time. If she got out of here alive, she'd have to apologize to Lia about fantasizing about Shane. At least she could tell her sister that she'd been fantasizing about Shane putting clothes *on* her, rather than taking them off.

She'd never been attracted to Shane, but right now, she could kiss the man.

"Lean on me," fantasy Shane said as he pulled her into his arms, making her stand up on wobbly legs. She didn't like this part of the dream. Her feet ached from walking in the snow and then being clenched stiffly as she'd tried to curl up into as tight a ball as she possibly could.

Soon, warm pants were pulled up her legs, and then, even better, thick wool socks. Before she could blink, Shane was putting shoes on her feet and tying the laces.

Rachel reached out and touched his face, afraid he was going to disappear and she'd find herself huddled in the cold again without the fabulously warm clothing enveloping her.

"Shane?" she asked.

"I'm here, Rachel. I'm getting you out of here," he said, his voice soothing as he wrapped her in an affectionate embrace.

Wait a minute. She could actually feel him. She'd never had a dream this real.

When Rachel realized this was no dream, her emotions released in an avalanche. She began sobbing against his shoulder as the warmth began returning to her aching joints. He must have placed warmers in the clothing, because she could feel real heat penetrating her frozen form.

"Eat this," he commanded, placing a PowerBar in her hand. Rachel didn't hesitate to lift it to her mouth and bite down, and she moaned as the flavors exploded on her taste buds and she knew the lovely calories were headed toward her stomach.

Not caring that she looked like a savage animal, she gobbled the bar down greedily, eating every last bite. She nearly licked her glove-covered fingers, but Shane placed a water bottle in her palm and instead she lifted it to her mouth and guzzled.

"Can you run?" he asked.

"I don't know," she replied. She hadn't had much food the last couple of days and her body was still frozen.

"I need you to run just to the fence, OK? I have to keep my gun out in case anyone tries to stop us. It's dark out, but floodlights are illuminating the yard and I don't know when Gianni's men are going to come check on you. I saw them put you in here two hours ago. I'm sorry it took so long for me to get to you, but the yard finally cleared so I could safely reach the shed. I've counted about fifteen guys in total. I couldn't take the chance of having them hit you while trying to get me."

"That's OK," she said, not really knowing what she was saying.

"No, it's not. None of this is OK. I got here as fast as I could, but it wasn't fast enough. Rafe and Adriane will meet us. Their plane just landed an hour ago and they are moving as fast as they can to reach us. They wanted to be here for the rescue, but I wasn't going to wait. We just have to get past the fence line, and I have a snowmobile ready."

"Sure," she mumbled.

"All right, I'm going to open the door. Hold on to my belt," he said. She took a couple of unsteady steps, testing her legs. They were holding her upright. That was a good sign. "Don't let go," he commanded her.

She acknowledged his order with a nod.

"Trust me, Rachel. I'm going to get you out of here." He leaned down and hugged her again before placing her hand on his belt and cracking open the door. "It's all clear. Don't make a sound. We're going to move swiftly and get the hell out of here."

She didn't say a word as her muscles tensed in preparation. She'd do what he said and hope she didn't fail him. She wanted to survive. She needed to.

Without further delay, they were off. After only a few paces, she heard shouting to her right and then Shane lifted his gun and began shooting. Gripping his belt for all she was worth, she focused on putting one foot in front of the other as she ran behind him. She knew he could move faster, that he was slowing his pace for her. As much as she wanted to leave, she was going as quickly as she could. She was grateful he seemed aware of her limits.

They made it to a wire fence as more shots were fired. She didn't look behind her, but just focused on Shane's back as he opened the fence and thrust her through. She stumbled to the ground and looked behind her as Shane kneeled, holstering his handgun and quickly raising his rifle and firing several shots.

The gunfire had alerted Gianni's other men that there was trouble, and soon doors were opening and more men ran around the house, intent on taking both her and Shane out. Now, they didn't care about information they could obtain from her; they cared only about stopping her escape.

"Run straight ahead!" Shane yelled without turning, still firing as two more men came into view.

She knew she was moving slower than he was, knew she couldn't help him, so she stumbled to her feet and began running as hard as she could. She tried to inhale through her nose so the breath wouldn't freeze in her lungs, but she couldn't help but gasp in her desperation for oxygen.

She didn't know how long she ran, but it seemed each time one foot hit the snow-covered ground, another shot fired off. If something happened to Shane, she wouldn't be able to forgive herself. Maybe she should turn back around and help in some way.

No. That would end up getting him killed because he'd be focused on her, not on the enemy. She staggered forward, face-planting into the snow, but she refused to stay down. She rose again quickly as she told herself to just keep moving, keep heading in the direction he'd told her to run.

"You're almost there," Shane said as he suddenly came up behind her and lifted her up, cradling her to his chest as he kept running.

"Are they dead?" she gasped.

"Not all of them," he replied. The two of them were in the shadows, safe from a direct hit, but a stray bullet could still find them. They weren't safe yet.

Just as they reached his snowmobile, there was a loud explosion, the night lighting up and making her jump as Shane put her down on the seat before climbing on in front of her.

"It's not over, Rachel. We have to move. Hang on to me." Shane started the engine and threw the machine into gear, snow flying out behind them as he jolted them forward.

Rachel held tightly to Shane, though she couldn't help but turn around and look at the mess behind them. The house she'd been held in for two days was nothing but a great ball of fire, and it lit up the night sky, making it easy to see the remaining men scrambling from the windows and flailing about on the ground.

She was safe.

"I'm getting you out of here," Shane yelled over the scream of the whipping wind.

"Thank you, Shane," she whispered, more to herself than to him. She leaned into him as they sped away.

It was almost over.

CHAPTER FORTY-NINE

ADRIANE APPROACHED THE compound with Rafe right behind him. Looking in all directions, they spied Shane rushing through the yard with Rachel clinging to his belt.

Adriane immediately jumped up, ready to run to her, catch her up in his arms and take her away from here — far away. Rafe snatched his coat and pulled him back.

"What in the hell do you think you're doing?" Adriane snarled, prepared to throw a punch.

"Look!" Rafe growled, trying to keep his voice down.

That's when Adriane saw two men come around the corner of the house and spot Shane and Rachel. His breath caught in his throat as the men lifted their weapons, aiming them directly at the woman he loved.

Before the men were able to get off any shots, Shane fired, nailing both men, while he continued moving rapidly toward the safety of the fence.

"We need to help them," Rafe hollered, no longer trying to be quiet as shots rang out in the cold winter night.

Adriane and Rafe raised their weapons and charged forward as Shane and Rachel reached the fence. They were too far away to help in the actual escape, but they could take out the men trying to shoot the pair. Adriane breathed a sigh of relief as Rachel slid through the opening and began running. Then he lost her to the night as he faced the house again and shot a man in a second-story window who was aiming straight in the direction Rachel had just run. The man went down, screaming as he fell into the snow, his blood turning the ground red.

Just as Rafe and Adriane moved through the fence, there was an explosion, the blast so powerful that the waves hit them both, sending them flying backward in the snow as the sound echoed through the mountains.

"What in the hell was that?" Rafe shouted as he staggered to his feet.

"I don't know," Adriane replied, also struggling up.

They looked toward the house, which was now up in a ball of flames, and looked for the source of the blast. They hadn't launched any explosives. Had Gianni destroyed his own place?

Creeping forward, they noticed the propane lines.

"A bullet must have hit the propane tank," Rafe said as he cautiously looked around, searching for any more threats. It seemed the explosion had taken care of the rest of the men.

The next several minutes seemed endless as the house burned bright and the screaming of the enemy men who were still barely alive filled the air.

As Rafe and Adriane, who could count about fifteen men, dead and dying, scoped out what was left of the building, Adriane was torn. He wanted nothing more than to follow after Shane right now, to get ahold of Rachel and never let her go, but he had to make sure the threat was gone.

He couldn't stop until he saw Gianni's cold, dead face.

"Move cautiously," Adriane said; the two of them stood up and crept forward.

They moved through the yard, the house now fully engulfed in flames and casting an eerie glow on the night. Adriane searched the faces of each of the men, frustration mounting when he didn't see his brother among them.

"Gianni! Where in the hell are you! Come out and face me like a man!" Adriane called, his voice echoing through the mountains.

"Careful, Adriane," Rafe warned.

"Time for being careful is long over," Adriane replied, his eyes almost wild.

"I understand, but it doesn't look like he's here. Maybe he never was."

"No. He's here. I can feel it. He'd never have sent Rachel here alone. He trusts no one, not even those he hires. Rachel means less than nothing to him; she is merely a means of getting his way. But still, he wouldn't leave her in the hands of these guys — not until he'd gained his objective."

It had been a long time since Adriane had been with his brother, but he knew the man hadn't changed that much in their years apart. Gianni used those he could and condemned the world as a pack of fools. But this time he was the fool, for he never should have pushed Adriane to this point.

"Come out now, Gianni!"

Only silence greeted him.

"We need to get back to the meeting place," Rafe said, a new urgency in his voice.

"He couldn't have gotten away," Adriane said, frantically searching the yard, not ready to give up. Gianni had to be there.

"What if he did? What if he ambushes them?"

Adriane halted at Rafe's words and turned to face him. "Let's go," he said.

The two men ran from the yard and made their way to the snowmobiles they'd come in on. Time seemed to freeze as they forced their way through the snow to their transportation. It seemed that every step took minutes instead of fractions of seconds.

Adriane needed to get to Rachel right now.

CHAPTER FIFTY

J UST AS THE sun began rising in the sky, casting eerie shadows across the ground, Shane and Rachel rode over a hill on the snow-covered mountain and saw a vehicle waiting ahead on a paved highway road — no more bumpy remnants of mountain trails.

And did that vehicle beckon! Rachel, still freezing, had been fighting against the wind, and now, before her, sat a car that she knew would be blasting heat from its vents.

"Your rescue vehicle, madam," Shane said as he slowed and clicked the doors open.

A shot rang out.

Shane suddenly jerked against her and then slumped forward, leaving Rachel baffled. What had just happened?

"Go!" Shane said, gurgling on his own blood, as he threw himself sideways off the snowmobile.

"Go!" he said again, but Rachel could do nothing but sit there as she watched his blood start to seep out against the fabric of his coat.

"You didn't think you would get away so easily, did you?"

Rachel looked up as Gianni approached. She struggled to get her brain to function, to make her arms move, but fear paralyzed her.

She couldn't leave Shane there, even if that's what he wanted her to do. It was too late, anyway. Gianni was almost beside her, with a gun aimed directly at her head.

"Why?" she said, her voice trembling. She was trying to be brave, but Shane was lying there dying before her eyes and there was no way out.

"Because my brother needs to be taught a lesson. He may think he won something today, but all he did was kill off the men I would have had to destroy anyway. There can't be any witnesses left when this is over. If I'm to take my rightful place on the throne, I have to look like the grieving brother, the savior coming home after the tragic deaths of my brother, his fiancée and his bastard children."

Keep him talking. Rachel knew that's what they did in every crime show she'd ever watched. She didn't know why, didn't know how it worked, but that's what they did, and so would she.

"Adriane said that the crown was supposed to be yours but you didn't want it." Rachel spoke through chattering teeth.

"I didn't know what I wanted when I left Corythia. I wasn't much more than a child. My father is the one who sealed my fate. By the time I decided I wanted the throne that was due to me, he told me it was too late, that my ideas were wrong for Corythia. He's the one who didn't want to modernize. I will make a fine king, a king who will go down in history. This world may look at royal titles as nothing more than a show these days, but a little fear from my people is just what Corythia needs. I have a vision for my country — a vision both my father and brother were too weak to adopt. The people should respect their king — bow down to him — and pay, always pay, for the privilege of his rule," he told her.

"If we promise to leave you alone, will you let us go?"

"You naïve, stupid woman. We both know that's not how this works. You could make all the promises you liked while I had a gun pointed at your head, but the minute you were safe, you would be running to anyone who would listen to your story. I'm not a senseless man. So don't insult my intelligence with your lies."

"Then why not just kill me?" she shouted, growing fed up with this game. She'd rather he fired, took her life, gave Adriane some kind of warning, than force her to keep dancing around him, giving him this time to gloat.

"Good idea." He raised the gun and aimed it right between her eyes.

"I'm so sorry," she whispered, a goodbye to her family — to Adriane. Closing her eyes, she waited. She wished she were brave enough to look Gianni in the face.

The gun fired and an unnerving silence filled the air.

Rachel waited for the pain to start, waited for her knees to give out and for her body to slump to the ground next to Shane.

"Shane!"

Lia's scream startled Rachel into opening her eyes. Where Gianni had been standing in front of her, there was now only empty space. Her body racked with trembling, she looked down and saw the man who'd been torturing her, now lying on the ground, blood trickling down his chin from his mouth as he tried to catch his breath.

Then she saw the blood spurting from his neck. He was clasping the spot with one hand, but the light was already leaving his eyes. His hatred undying, he attempted to lift the hand still clutching the gun, but his fingers failed him and the weapon fell beside him as he stilled.

Kicking the gun away and then turning, Rachel saw Lia rush up from behind, drop to her knees and grab hold of Shane.

"Shane, don't you dare die! Do you hear me! I won't let that happen," Lia yelled as she pulled open his coat and looked at the blood coating his shirt. So much blood — too much. It had seeped through his shirt and coat. How could he survive?

"Rachel!"

Turning again, she watched as Rafe and Adriane pulled through the trees and skidded to a stop in front of her.

Suddenly there was movement all around her, everything happening so quickly. Lia was shouting as Rafe and Adriane picked up Shane and rushed him to the rescue vehicle that Shane had brought to that place.

Rachel couldn't move — she was frozen to the spot.

Adriane rushed back over to her. "Were you hit?" he asked, opening her coat and running his hands all over her body to look for any wounds. Rachel shook her head, but she couldn't get her voice to work.

Shock had taken over.

Adriane lifted her carefully into his arms and carried her to the car. He got in with her on the passenger side and cradled her in his lap, close to his chest, as he whispered soothing words into her ear and rubbed her back.

Shane was lying on the backseat with his head in Lia's lap as she held a wad of material over the bullet wound.

"Where was he hit?" Rafe asked as he threw the SUV into drive and began moving.

"Between his chest and stomach. I couldn't tell if it hit any vital organs. There's just so much blood," she cried.

"Keep pressure on the wound," he called back.

"I am," said Lia, her voice choked but strong. Then she yelled again.

"Stop!"

Rafe lifted his foot from the gas, carefully tapped the brakes and came to a stop. "Why? What's happened?" he shouted as he twisted in the seat, thinking it was too late for Shane.

"This is where our car went off the road. We have to get Ari," she said.

"What?" Rafe asked as his head whipped around as he noticed the skid marks going off the road. Without waiting for Lia's explanation, he jumped from the vehicle and rushed down the short drop, wrenching open the door.

"Are you all right?" he asked, nearly sobbing when he found Ari in the driver's seat.

"I'm fine, Rafe, just a swollen knee. I couldn't climb the hill. Lia heard a gunshot and then shouting, and she knew she needed to go help," Ari replied.

"What in the hell were the two of you doing up here? You were supposed to wait at the hotel," he said, but he was careful as he lifted her in his arms and then quickly began climbing back up the ditch wall.

"We couldn't not help," she said as they reached the vehicle and Rafe set her inside on the third-row seat.

"We will discuss this at the hospital," he warned her.

Jumping back in the SUV, he went flying down the mountain, taking the slick roads far too fast, but somehow Rafe managed to keep them from sliding over the steep edge.

Rachel had no idea how long it took them, but she realized everything was measured in sound. The sound of Shane's harsh breathing, the sound of Lia's words of encouragement to Shane, of Rafe calling out orders, of Ari telling Lia that Shane would be fine, and of Adriane telling her that everything would be all right.

They skidded into the emergency room bay at the closest hospital and doors flew open as Rafe rushed from the vehicle.

"He was shot. He needs medical attention right now!"

"Do you have the weapon?"

"No!"

"Sir, please calm down."

"Don't tell me to calm down. Get him help now!" He looked like a madman.

"Officers!"

"Damn it, I'm not the one who shot him. The guy who shot him is dead!" Those words made the officers approaching look a little uneasy.

All of the words flew over Rachel's head. More people were speaking. Officers were there with their hands on their guns. Nurses were getting

Shane on a gurney and placing Ari in a wheelchair. The officers were talking to Rafe. Adriane continued holding her until someone pulled her from his arms. No! She didn't want to be taken from him. Still, she couldn't speak.

"Rachel, you have to snap out of this!" She turned her head to find Lia in front of her, kneeling on the ground with worry on her face. "We need you back. Please!"

Blood.

So much blood covered Lia.

The sight finally seemed to make something inside of her snap. Rachel bent forward as a sob was ripped from her throat and she grasped her sister tight.

"Why? Why?" she wailed, leaning against Lia.

"I don't know, sweetie, but the doctors are going to fix Shane, and we're going to make sure you're OK, too. The police are questioning Rafe and Adriane right now, and the two of them looked beyond pissed off about being detained, but I'm here with you. Let's go have the doctors make sure my nieces or nephews are all safe and sound, and then let's find Ari as we sit and wait."

"What about Shane?" Shouldn't Lia be with him?

"I can't think about that right now, so I'm going to focus on you. I have to focus on something or I will fall apart. Please, just stay with me," Lia begged.

"You are so strong, Lia. I wish I had even a fraction of your strength," Rachel said.

"Are you kidding me, Rachel! You nearly gave me a heart attack when you told that man to shoot you. What in the hell were you thinking? If I hadn't gotten into position right then, you would have been dead. I heard him shoot Shane, heard the shouts as he threatened your life. I was helpless to stop Gianni. But I wasn't going to just stand by. I was too far away to shoot him and guarantee a hit from where I was. I had to sneak closer. You did really well at distracting him. I'm so proud of you," Lia said.

"We're going to take you to the exam room now, Ms. Palazzo," the nurse said, making both Lia and Rachel turn.

"Have you been hit?" another woman asked Lia, eyeing the blood all over her.

"No. This isn't my blood," she told the woman. "I'm staying with my sister here."

No one argued with Lia. She looked like GI Jane right then with her blood-covered clothes and black hat, and more importantly, the glint of raw courage shining from her eyes. Rachel couldn't be more proud of her.

It seemed like hours before the doctor finished examining Rachel and ran some tests, but by then, Ari's knee had been wrapped and she was in the room, too. They had given Lia fresh clothes to change into, and now it was a waiting game.

When the doctor came back, he told Rachel that, although she had slightly elevated blood pressure, she was suffering from dehydration, and she was underweight, the babies were progressing nicely.

He wanted to keep her at the hospital overnight and hook up an IV to get her body proper nourishment, but he was sure he could allow her release the next day.

When they were finally left all alone, a frightened silence fell as they waited to hear news about Shane. After several minutes, Rachel couldn't stand it anymore.

"He will make it, Lia. You two have just gotten married," Rachel said.

"I was so afraid of this. It was the reason I didn't want to have a relationship with him. I was so terrified that I'd be sitting at home one day while he was out on a mission, and then two uniformed men would show up at my door. But with all that, I never, ever imagined that I would be just around the corner when he got shot — and that I would be the one to kill his shooter."

"I'm so sorry you had to do that, Lia. I don't know how you did it, but I am so very thankful you did. How in the world did the two of you end up there? How did you even have a gun?" she asked as she looked between Lia and Ari, who looked at each other as if they had a secret they'd vowed never to tell anyone.

"Well, what to answer first?" Lia said with a slight smile toward Ari.

"Rafe and I both have family tracking on our cell phones, so once they left, Lia and I got in the car and followed them. We were coming up the road when I lost control of the vehicle and slid into the ditch. My knee slammed into the middle console and there was no way for me to walk, so Lia took off on foot in their direction. I told her I was fine."

"Yeah, I protested at first, but my stomach was churning. I knew I was needed. I didn't realize how needed I was. I hated leaving Ari there, but the car was concealed and I wanted to help. We both wanted to, but Ari's knee was swelling."

"And the gun?"

"Rafe and Adriane left us with one just in case any of the bad guys managed to track us down in our nice and safe hotel room."

"You are both so brave. I couldn't have done that," Rachel said, feeling small and useless as she lay in the hospital bed.

"Don't you dare say that!" Lia said. "I heard you tell that miserable man to take your life. You were willing to sacrifice yourself for Adriane. That's about as heroic as it gets. Stupid! But heroic."

Rachel squirmed, uncomfortable with her sister's praise. "Was it hard to shoot him?" Rachel honestly didn't know whether she would have been able to pull the trigger.

"I didn't think — I just shot. I never thought I could kill a person, never imagined pointing a gun and pulling the trigger. They say that if faced with a life-and-death situation, you can do anything. I guess *they*, whoever *they* are, are right. That man shot Shane and he was planning on shooting you next. There was no hesitation on my part."

"Do you regret it? Will it haunt you?" Rachel asked.

"I would do it all over again," Lia said, lifting her head and looking at her sister with pure love.

"I adore you, Lia," Rachel told her.

"That goes the same for me, little sister."

Lia and Ari scooted closer on either side of Rachel's bed and grasped her hands. Then there was no more talking. They were all thinking of Shane.

CHAPTER FIFTY-ONE

RACHEL LOOKED UP to find Rafe and Adriane standing in her room with identical looks of worry on their faces.

"How was the interrogation?" Rachel's eyes widened as the words popped out of her mouth. How could she make even the slightest of jokes right now?

"Unpleasant," both Rafe and Adriane said with a grimace.

"Well, they must have realized you weren't the bad guys," Lia said as she sat up straighter.

"As a head of state, I have immunity under international law. Rafe, on the other hand, had to do a bit more of a song and dance to get the local cops to believe he really was who he said he was. It didn't help that he lost his wallet somewhere," Adriane said.

"Yeah, that was great," Rafe said, a slight smile coming to his lips.

"Have you heard anything yet?" Lia asked, her eyes shadowed with worry.

Rafe walked over and scooped Ari into his arms, then sat down and held her close. He was furious with her for risking her life, but proud of her, too. Both she and Lia had been so brave. How could he have doubted their ability to help? Before he was able to say something to her, the doctor entered the hospital room. All eyes focused on him as they waited with bated breath for whatever he had to say.

MELODY ANNE

"Mr. Grayson has made it through surgery successfully. The bullet entered his rib cage, cracking a rib, but missing all vital organs. Unless there are major complications, he will pull through this just fine. He's asking for his wife."

Lia didn't hesitate. She jumped from the chair and rushed from the room. The rest of them breathed much easier. Everyone was going to be OK, and this nightmare looked as if it would *finally* have a happy ending.

"I've been so worried about you," Rafe said as he looked over to his sister and held out a hand, gripping hers tightly in his. Adriane gave me the scare of my life when he said you'd been kidnapped by his power-hungry brother."

"Thanks to all of you, I'm going to be just fine, Rafe. It seems you've been rescuing me in one way or another my whole life."

"That's what big brothers do, and apparently big sisters and best friends, too. We protect the people we love."

"Well, you have done a damn fine job of it. Thank you both," she said as she looked from Rafe to Ari.

"We're family. Next time, you get to rescue me," Ari said with a chuckle.

"Sounds like a deal," Rachel said.

"Ari and I will go check up on Shane and let you and Adriane have a few minutes together," Rafe said, then squeezed her hand. He nodded at Adriane before standing up with Ari in his arms and moving toward the door.

"I do have a wheelchair in here," Ari said with a laugh.

"Ah, woman, don't you know that I look for any excuse I can find to hold you tight?" he replied, their voices fading as they moved down the hallway.

Silence had fallen again as Adriane neared Rachel's bed. Sitting on the edge, he took her hand and brought it to his lips, tenderly kissing her palm.

"I've been such a fool, Rachel — such a stubborn fool," he said, his voice so quiet, she almost couldn't hear him.

"You saved my life," she said, unsure what else to say.

"Actually, your sister saved you. She is one very tough woman," he said with a chuckle. "I was the one who put you in jeopardy."

"Please don't think that, Adriane. You can't be held accountable for the actions of your brother. He was a very sick man, and I know he was guilty of evil in his lifetime, but I'm sorry you lost him today."

Adriane stared at her in shock as she squeezed his hand. But all Rachel knew was that no matter what Rafe or Lia ever did, she would love

282

them, and to lose one of them, no matter the circumstances, would rip a piece of her soul away. Adriane *had* to be hurting for his loss.

"It's strange, because there's a part of me mourning him. I had hoped one day to reunite with him, one day to have the brother back whom I used to love so much."

"It's OK for you to mourn him, Adriane. He's your family, no matter what he did," she reassured him.

"I'm just glad you are safe now, so very glad."

"Our babies are healthy, too," she said, and his shoulders visibly slumped as if he'd been afraid to ask.

"I'm so grateful to hear that." His free hand stretched down and rubbed along the top of her stomach.

She was silent as she worried about what to say. Did she tell him how much she loved him — how she was ready to take him on whatever conditions he imposed? Nearly losing her life had made her realize she didn't want to be away from him, even if she didn't have his heart.

Wasn't it better for their family to be together?

"Please forgive me, Rachel, forgive me for everything I've put you through. Forgive me for trying to force you into a marriage for the sake of our children. That was so wrong of me," he whispered, and her heart thundered.

Was he taking it all back right when she was ready to accept?

"I don't want to keep your children from you, Adriane. I know how much you already love them," she said, trying to build up the courage to proclaim her love for him.

"Yes, I love them, but I love you too, Rachel. Even before I knew you were missing, I realized what a fool I'd been in my treatment of you. I was afraid of something because I'd never experienced it before, but love isn't a thing to be afraid of. I don't know why I acted in such a ludicrous fashion, but I do know that if I have to live my life without you, I will only be a shell of a man."

"Is this real?"

Suddenly she was afraid to even hope. What if she really were still back in that shed, frozen and dying, and all this was nothing more than a dream?

"I love you, Rachel, truly, wholeheartedly, with everything that I have. I want to spend the rest of my life with you, not for the sake of our children, but because I can't live without *you*. I want to have these babies, and I want ten more, not because I need heirs for Corythia, but because I want to see you in each of their faces. I don't ever want to come so close to losing you again. These have been the worst few days of my life."

The warmth in his eyes filled her soul. He meant what he was saying. She had no doubt.

With her vulnerability at an all-time high, she wanted nothing more than to be in his arms where she felt safe, where she could be loved. She didn't know how it was all going to work, but none of that mattered. They would figure it out along the way.

"I do love you, Adriane, so much that it hurts to imagine my life without you. I don't want us to be apart for even one more day," she said, choking up as he gently brushed her lips with his.

"Will you marry me, Rachel, do me the honor of becoming my bride?"

She looked at him with wide eyes. "Did I hear correctly? Was that a question, not a demand?" A small smile broke over her lips to take the sting from her words.

"Yes! I am pleading with you on bended knee to accept," he said. "See?" Still clinging to her hand, he knelt down on the cold hospital floor.

"In that case, yes, it would be my honor to accept."

He rose back up and crawled into the bed next to her, pulling her into his arms and taking her lips in a kiss of pure love. Rachel became lost in his embrace, forgetting time or reason. And she reveled in knowing nothing could hurt her now.

Adriane's hand shifted and he rubbed her wrist, making her cry out. So much for her belief that nothing could hurt her! When he looked down and saw the angry welts from the ties Gianni's men had used to bind her, his eyes narrowed to dangerous slits.

She wouldn't want to be his enemy — that was for sure.

"You know you can tell me anything about the last few days, talk to me to get it all out. It will kill me to know what you went through, but I am here to listen," he said, his thumb gently rolling across her bruised and abraded flesh.

Rachel thought back to the thin ropes that had bound her, to the night the man had threatened to rape her, to the taunts they'd thrown her way. Did she want to rehash all of that? No — not yet.

"I will someday, Adriane, but not now. I'm sure I will have to tell the police everything, and for now I just want to lie in your arms. I just want to feel safe."

"But, did they... I mean, were you...?" He couldn't finish.

"No. They didn't sexually assault me. You saved me before that could happen. But the rest of it...I'm just not ready to put it into words right now," she said, hoping he wouldn't push her.

And he didn't.

"Anything you want, Rachel," he assured her.

She cuddled up close to him and let his loving embrace soothe her, let his soft touch erase her fears. She had a good family and a wonderful fiancé, and two babies she would meet in just a few short months.

The day had gone from hopeless to nearly perfect.

"You will make such a fine queen," he whispered. Just like that, fear rushed back, and it felt like strangling hands around her neck.

"Oh, dear. I wasn't thinking about that," she whispered. She was so not ready to be queen. That was something not at all on her bucket list. She'd rather face the terrorists again than face the throne.

"Don't worry, my beloved Rachel, you will be spectacular," he promised.

She had her doubts. She'd voice them in detail when she woke up. Right now, the medicine the doctor had given her was kicking in and she couldn't keep her eyes open any longer. A good sleep would make it all a lot better.

"It turns out that tomorrow just had to wait until today," Adriane whispered.

Adriane laughed at his private joke as Rachel fell asleep, safe within his arms.

CHAPTER FIFTY-TWO

MUSIC DRIFTED THROUGH the cathedral and past its ornate doors to where Rachel stood outside. The morning sunlight seemed to be shooting a ray of light directly on the golden door handles, as if directing her to enter.

She took a breath as she turned to her sister and to her best friend. Did she deserve so much happiness?

"You're getting married today," Ari said, smiling in encouragement.

"And becoming queen," Lia added, making Rachel's stomach knot.

"Oh, please don't remind me of that. I have been telling myself that part is just make-believe," Rachel said with a nervous laugh.

"You will make a wonderful queen. You care about people, Rachel. That's all that really matters," Ari said, squeezing her hand.

"Well, unless I say something foolish and land Corythia in a world war," Rachel said, only half kidding. But though she was terrified of her new role, she wasn't terrified of marrying Adriane. She loved him and couldn't picture her life without him now. Enough time had been wasted and she was ready to be his bride.

Only a month had passed since the kidnapping. He'd rescheduled the original wedding date so they all had time to recover from their ordeal. After she'd said yes, she was ready to marry him instantly, but the wait had been good because it showed her that she hadn't wavered, that she was as sure now as she'd been the moment she'd said yes.

"We'd better get you down that aisle before your stomach grows any bigger," Lia said with a pointed look. Though Rachel was now five months along, her dress hid the growing bump.

"I can't believe the twins will be born in only four more months. I figured I'd be as large as a whale by now," Rachel said with a giggle.

"The last four months is where you'll really start to expand," Lia said with evil delight.

"You will get your turn," Rachel said.

Lia froze as if she'd been caught with her hand in the cookie jar. Both Ari and Rachel turned to her in shock.

"Are you pregnant?" Ari asked, a smile breaking out on her face when Lia silently nodded, tears of joy shining in her eyes. "Me too," she gasped.

All three women stood silent, and then flew into each other's arms, thrilled to share this special moment together.

"How far along are you?" Lia asked.

"Six weeks. I think it happened on the honeymoon," she said.

"Me too," Lia gasped. "Maybe they will be born on the same day. Then it will be like having two sets of twins in the family."

"I'm sorry, Rachel. I was going to wait to say anything so I wouldn't take away from your special day," Ari said.

"I would be so disappointed in both of you had you waited. This only makes this day so much more special," Rachel hastened to tell them.

"We'd better get you in there," Lia said. "They've restarted the wedding march three times now. I bet Adriane is going to come looking for you if we don't get to walking." She adjusted Rachel's veil and directed the guards manning the doors to go ahead and open them.

With a final smile, Ari began walking down the aisle, followed by Lia.

Rachel took a deep breath and waited until the wedding coordinator motioned for her to step inside. As she stood at the back of the church, butterflies swarmed in her stomach, but no reservations about what she was doing made her hesitate.

In fact, she found herself wishing she could skip all of this tradition and simply kick off her shoes and run to her waiting groom. She'd never been known for her patience.

The music changed and she heard the rustling of clothes as the people who'd filled the church stood and turned, waiting for her to make her way down the aisle. She felt as if she were floating as she counted her steps, drifting closer and closer to Adriane, who looked so handsome in his military uniform, the crest of Corythia proudly standing out on the sash that he wore. She halted at the beautiful picture he made, standing at the altar, waiting for her arrival. He was so suave, so devastatingly handsome — and he was all hers.

His smile faltered at her pause, but as her smile grew, she sent him a silent message that he had nothing to fear. She would make no more attempts at escape.

Taking her father by the arm, she ascended the stairs to the altar and found herself facing Adriane. Though the room was filled with hundreds of people, all she saw was her future husband.

"I love you," she whispered, overcome by joy.

"You are my life," he replied.

It took everything in her not to lean forward and kiss his sweet lips. At least in public, she needed to act respectably, as she was soon to be a queen. Awaiting them was a long honeymoon, when they could kiss as much as they wanted.

And that's exactly what they did.

EPILOGUE

"MY SON AND daughter are beautiful," Adriane said to anyone who would listen while he cuddled his baby girl safely against his chest.

"They sure are," Rafe agreed.

"And little Alessandro came out a full three minutes before his sister," Adriane made sure to tell everyone for the hundredth time.

"Oh, how wise you were to predict a son first," Rachel teased him.

He'd been quite pleased when his son was born first, but he'd been mesmerized when Marietta emerged next. Only a month old and already she owned her father's heart.

"I can't help it if the Graziani line is all-powerful," he said, teasing his wife while she cuddled Alessandro to her chest.

"I want to hold my nephew," Rafe said as he walked into the room and purposefully approached Rachel. She smiled and nodded her head and Rafe picked up little Alessandro. "He adores me."

"He loves anyone who smiles at him," Rachel said, though she secretly believed that Alessandro did have a soft spot for his uncle. After all, Rafe had been the one to draw the first smile from her son, making Adriane quite unhappy. Adriane had been blessed with Marietta's first smile, though, so he'd forgiven Rafe.

"He's just practicing for when his baby is born," Ari said as she sat down next to Rachel and rubbed her own belly, which was beginning to be quite noticeable. "This will be the last trip we get to make until after the baby is born, so remember your promise to be there on time."

"I wouldn't miss the birth of my niece for anything in this universe," Rachel assured her.

"Nieces, darling sister. I was just kidding at the wedding, but since we both have the same due date, you may be running back and forth between our delivery rooms," Lia said as she sat down on Rachel's other side.

"It would be much easier if the two of you just had them in the same room," Rachel said.

"That would be far too much screaming to listen to," Shane said, unwisely. All three women glared at him. "I was just kidding," he added, and he stepped away with his arms raised in defense.

"Oh, girls, I almost forgot to tell you. I finished reading the journal of your Civil War ancestor. When you come out into the world, you'll have to read the story with me. It's magical," said Ari, a sigh escaping her lips.

"Why, what happened?" Lia asked as she propped her feet up.

"Their story is just heartbreaking. I refuse to tell you what happens, though. You have to come stay with Rafe and me and read it then. I'm telling you, you won't be able to put the story down."

"It can't be nearly as exciting as our own lives," Rachel said with a laugh as she looked over at Adriane. Her husband, along with Rafe and Shane, had a drink in his hand.

"Yeah, as much drama as we've all gone through, I understand why you'd think so, but really, their story is unbelievable," Ari insisted.

"OK. You have me intrigued. I want to learn about our great-a-million-times-over-grandparents," Rachel said with a giggle.

"They didn't live that long ago. Only about a hundred and fifty years."

"That may as well be a million years," Lia said. "Kind of like how long this pregnancy is taking."

"I know the feeling," Ari said, rolling her eyes with a grin.

"Neither one of you gets to complain until you carry *two* of these little things inside your body," she said, but there was no heat to her words.

"Is it possible to be any happier than this?" Ari asked as she looked across the room and her eyes connected with Rafe's.

"I don't think so," Lia said, as she smiled at Shane.

"Agreed," Rachel added, her arms aching for one of her babies. As if Adriane could read her mind, he brought over her daughter and rested her in Rachel's arms, then leaned down and kissed his beloved wife's lips.

They'd all gotten their fairy-tale ending, and, of course, their happily ever after.

THE END

If you enjoyed the Surrender Series, continue reading for an excerpt from the first book in the new:

Forbidden Series

BOUND
Book One in the Forbidden Series

By
Melody Anne

PRELUDE

"TAKE OFF YOUR clothes."

Jewell looked at Blake as if he'd lost his mind. "What?"

His eyes narrowed. "Take off your clothes. Do not make me repeat myself again." He stood back and looked at her through silver eyes that seemed to see right into her soul.

"I c…can't. We're in a parking garage," she stammered. She looked desperately around at the full lot.

Sure, this corner happened to be dark, but what if someone drove in? What if a police car cruised by again? There was no way she could do what he was ordering her to.

Blake just waited in silence, leaning against the front of his car and watching her pace nervously in front of him.

"Please?" Sheesh. She was reduced to begging now.

"I guess our agreement is finished, then." He shrugged as if he didn't care.

Was he bluffing? Could she take the chance? Her stomach knotted painfully as she weighed her options.

Wanting more than anything to walk away, she closed her eyes and saw her brother's sweet, impish face. What was she willing to do for him?

Anything.

CHAPTER ONE

"I'M PLEASED WE'RE now business partners. I think this venture will be a success."

Blake Knight laughed as he shook hands with Rafe Palazzo, gratified that the man had finally come to visit from San Francisco. Though Blake had known Rafe for many years, this was the first project the two of them had paired up on. The contracts were signed, and the deal would put a few more hundreds of millions into both of their already fat wallets.

"I don't think there's a venture out there with your name on it that isn't a success, Rafe."

"Ah, my friend, the same can be said about what you and your brothers do," Rafe replied without missing a beat.

"We're just that damn good, I guess," Blake said.

Though at first glance the two of them might come off as smug and self-satisfied, and they might look at multimillion-dollar investments the same way an average person looked at depositing twenty dollars into their savings account, the men were shrewd and their self-assessments were based on solid fact, not ego. They knew how to make money, and they knew they'd always keep making more.

Only a select few ruled the world, and when Blake Knight was a young boy and his parents' lives ended right before his very eyes, he'd decided right then that he would never be vulnerable again. He would never be one of the weak, never be easy prey to a world packed with predators. No one would sneak up on him and catch him unaware.

"Let's have a drink, and you can fill me in on what you've been doing for the past year," Rafe told Blake. "Too much time has gone by since our last visit."

The two of them moved toward the conference room doors at Knight Construction.

"You're the one who sold your soul to a woman and disappeared," Blake reminded his friend.

"Don't knock it, Blake. Ari has changed my life and made me a better man."

"Oh, please, *please*, for the love of all that's holy, do not continue," Blake said, horrified to hear these words coming from a man who was once one of the most ruthless bachelors he'd ever met. "I remember the days when you thought no woman was true, no woman could ever be trusted. Marriage — your second marriage — has ruined you. There's a term for it, you know…"

"There was a time, Blake, when I would have thrown you up against a wall for just thinking me the slightest bit weak."

"Ha! You would have tried," Blake said.

Neither of them was remotely upset by the exchange, of course. It was all friendly banter.

Rafe smiled and spoke reflectively. "I came to realize that the anger I'd held onto for too long was pointless. I also realized that having one woman to love didn't end my life or my freedom. It made everything better. Ari is full of surprises and delights that I'll never get tired of exploring. I know you'll scoff at such talk, but what she does for me is indescribable."

"Yeah, whatever, Rafe — and thanks for not describing it. I happen to be a big fan of variety. After a few weeks, anything gets old, and women are no exception. I always grow bored with them — always! Besides, though I know it's not politically correct to say this, face it: women are weak, pathetic creatures, and they always have an agenda. Once I've broken their spirit, there's no more fun to be had with the relationship."

Rafe knew the horror that Blake and his brothers had suffered together when their mother's little game hadn't ended the way she'd wanted it to end. The woman had hardened his friend's heart, and though Blake was letting his resentment toward one woman carry over to all of them, it was somewhat understandable, if not right or rational. Hell, Rafe had done the same thing after his first wife's betrayal. So he knew there was hope. Time would eventually change Blake because he was fundamentally a good man.

"Not every woman is like your mother, Blake. You'll see that someday." Before Blake could say anything, Rafe went off on a slight tangent. "Who are you seeing now?"

The two men had made it to the lobby of the building and were stepping out onto a busy Seattle sidewalk. They were heading toward a favorite bar of Blake's.

"No one at the moment. I just haven't had time — all of these deals to be closed. You know the drill. I've had to do a lot of the work here on my own with my brother Byron being off in Greece for the past year, and my other brother, Tyler, gone two years. Now that they are home, I may take some vacation time."

"Now that's a joke. Men like us don't do vacations," Rafe said. "Why were both your brothers away?"

"Byron was working on his own project in Greece. He was working with me on deals for the home front," Blake replied.

"It's good to branch out on your own sometimes, Blake. I would like to hear more about this from him. I personally love spending time in Greece. It's a beautiful country."

"Yeah, and Tyler was just gone for two years—we don't know where, and we didn't hear from him. I was about to send out the marines, but he finally came home."

"Now that sounds like a story," Rafe said.

Before Blake was able to give Rafe any details, the two men were interrupted.

"Rafe. Blake. How are you?"

Blake turned to look at Mathew Greenfield, a man who'd helped him through more than one bad time in his life. He was a business partner, but more than that, he'd been there when Blake had needed to choose which road he was going to take in life.

Luckily, Blake had taken a more positive path than the one he'd originally thought he would. Mathew had given him the support and praise he needed to change his life for the better — no easy feat, under the circumstances.

Mathew also knew all of Blake's dark secrets, and he was still someone Blake could not only count on, but trust fully, too.

"It's good to see you, my friend," Blake said.

"It's been a long time," Rafe told Mathew.

"Too long," Mathew replied.

"Join us for a drink," Blake said. "We're celebrating a new business venture." He knew Rafe wouldn't mind.

Mathew threw him a smile. "I have a few minutes. Why don't you tell me about it?"

The three men walked into the bar and proceeded to the back, where Blake had a table on standby at this same time every day in case he needed to conduct business away from the offices. A waitress quietly set down menus and disappeared.

Once the topic of business was out of the way, the conversation turned back to Blake's lack of a love life. That didn't make him a happy camper, especially since the last people on earth he'd want to discuss this with were teaming up on him.

"We all need to take time to have our itches scratched," Mathew said with a knowing look. "Have you heard of Relinquish Control?"

"What in the hell is that?" Blake asked with disdain.

"It's a place where you can get your needs met — discreetly," Mathew replied.

Rafe looked skeptical. "I haven't heard of it, and I'm not sure I want to."

"That's because you're a very happily married man who doesn't need a specialty escort service. It's only a couple of years old now, but there hasn't been a single complaint from any of the clients."

"I've never had trouble getting my needs met, and anyway…," Blake said just before the waitress dropped off their appetizers and new drinks.

"Yeah, but sometimes a man is just too damn busy. Relinquish might still be fairly new, but it's run by a very good friend of mine, and I promise you, you won't regret checking it out."

"Sorry, but there's no way in hell I'm going to a place like that."

"Well, here's their card in case you change your mind."

Mathew held out a nondescript white business card, and for some odd reason, Blake not only accepted it, but also found himself slipping it into his pocket. He told himself it was so he wouldn't offend a good friend and colleague. But as soon as he got home, he'd chuck the card into the trash. That was for damn sure.

"Why would you need to use an escort service, Mathew?" Blake asked.

"After my last divorce I decided I wouldn't marry again. And yes, Rafe, I understand that some people have great marriages, but I've been married four times now, and all I got out of each of those marriages was a lighter bank account and some gray hairs — hell, not even a T-shirt.

A monumental waste in time and money. My great friend McKenzie Beaumont opened the place, and it's perfect for people who need 'companionship' but don't want anything to do with love."

"Blake, ignore this crap," Rafe said. "We've both been assholes for long enough."

"Believe me, I'm not interested." Blake picked up his drink and took a long swallow.

Mathew wasn't a bit annoyed at their reaction. "Fine. Fine. But I know you, Blake. You'll think about it."

The subject changed, and no further mention was made of needs being met. Still, though the night finished on a good note, Blake found himself feeling restless by the time he arrived home.

For some odd reason, he pulled the card out of his pocket and placed it on his desk rather than into the wastebasket. There was no chance in hell he'd call. No need. No interest, even. But out of respect for Mathew, he kept the card. It would soon get lost in the shuffle.

Two weeks later, Blake found himself staring at the simple black writing on the stark white card. He wanted to punch his respected friend in the face for even suggesting an *escort service*. It just wasn't his thing. And yet, somehow, some perverse impulse led him to pick up his phone and dial before he knew what he was doing.

It wasn't that he couldn't get a date. That was never the problem! This was about having his needs met, his need for control, his need — he had to admit it — for corruption. Relinquish Control's website promised through veiled hints that a man could get any kind of woman he needed.

And right now Blake needed a woman to dominate.

CHAPTER TWO

"I'M SORRY, MS. Weston, but you haven't shown the courts anything we've asked for."

Jewell felt her legs wobble as she stood before the judge in her thrift-store suit, trying to tune out the sound of her little brother sobbing while his child advocate held him back.

"I understand that I don't have a full-time job yet," Jewel said, unable to keep from glancing nervously at little Justin, "but I was working part time until last week, and the temp agency promised more work, so within two months I'm certain I'll have enough saved to put down a deposit on an apartment. I already spoke to the manager of a complex over on West Street, and he guaranteed me a place."

"And where would you and your brother stay until then?" the judge asked in a level voice.

"I'm staying at a shelter." She knew she couldn't lie if she had any chance of getting her brother back. When Justin was little, their father had run off with another woman, and then, only four short months ago, he'd lost his mother. At the tender age of ten! In addition to all that, he'd been ripped from his childhood home right afterward and thrust into the unpredictable world of foster care.

"I am truly sorry, Ms. Weston. I want to reunite you with your brother. I even think the two of you need each other," Judge Malone said. "Which is why I won't close this case, and why I won't release him for adoption."

Jewell felt a spark of hope begin to well up inside.

But the judge spoke again, and his next words weren't quite as encouraging. "However, if your circumstances haven't changed by your next hearing, which comes in two months, I will be left with no other choice but to provide a more stable environment for your brother. He's been through enough, and the longer he's in the system, the less likely it is that he will return to you. He deserves to have a home, one where he can find comfort in routine, safety, and stability."

"I can take care of him. My mother wanted that for him — for us. She wanted us to stay together. The cancer was sudden, unexpected, and we lost everything, absolutely everything, but I can take care of my brother, I swear. Please, just let us be together while we work to put the pieces back together." Jewell hated that she had to beg.

The sad expression on the judge's face told her before his words did that she wouldn't be walking from the courtroom with Justin — not today, at least.

"This case will be adjourned for two months." With that, Judge Malone hit his gavel and rose before the bailiff could say a word. However the judge didn't leave the room immediately. He first turned toward Jewell with concern in his eyes. "I know you love Justin — I have no doubt of that," he said, and he sighed. "Sometimes, the best thing we can do for someone we love so much is to let them go so they can have a better life than one we might be able to give them."

He left Jewell shaking so badly that she was barely able to remain on her feet. But she looked resolutely into the sweet blue eyes of her brother and prayed she could keep her composure long enough to reassure him that they would indeed be together again. She went through agony each time she had to let him go.

"Jewell? Can we go back home now?"

Oh, how his innocent words ripped through her very soul.

"Ah, Bubby, soon. I have to do a few more things to prove to the judge that I can take care of you," she replied, disappointment thick in her voice as she walked right up to him and bent down to be at eye level. The advocate let him go and he fell into her arms.

"But why can't we go home? I miss you every day. Ms. Penny doesn't read to me like you do, and she makes me eat peas. I hate peas. You promised we'd be back together." His tears soaked through her thin suit jacket, and his small frame shook with each heartbroken sob.

"Oh, Justin, I promise that I *will* get you back. I'll do anything and everything for us to be together again. I love you more than the moon and the stars. I love you more than any other person on this planet."

"I love you too, Sissy. Please don't make me go back to that house."

"Ah, baby, it won't be much longer, and I'll come see you every single Saturday, okay? And then after eight Saturdays we won't have to be apart anymore."

"Eight Saturdays?" His eyes widened with hope.

Thank goodness he didn't understand that meant two months.

"Yes, only eight more Saturdays. And after that last Saturday, I will pick you up and you'll never have to go back to another strange house again." She would keep this promise no matter what it took.

"You swear?"

She was heartbroken at his question. How could any boy be so distrustful at such a young age? Her brother should be playing with action figures and Legos, not worrying about where he would sleep each night, or whether he would be with a mean foster parent or a nice one, or if his sister loved him.

"I swear." Or I'll die trying, she added silently.

"I love you, Sissy," he sobbed as the advocate shifted on her feet, letting them both know that their time was up.

"I love you, too, Justin."

His sobs grew into screams as the advocate removed him from Jewell's arms and pulled him from the courtroom. As soon as the doors shut, Jewell's mask of strength came crashing down and she collapsed into the closest chair.

When the court security officer told her she had to leave the room, Jewell stood and walked zombie-like into the cold white marble hallways of the courthouse. After making her way slowly to the restroom, she splashed her face with water and didn't even recognize the eyes of her reflection.

When her mother died, Jewell hadn't had time to grieve, because from the day of the funeral she'd been fighting to get her brother back from the state and the people who had taken him away. She and her little brother had lost everything in the last few months of their mother's life. But they couldn't lose each other.

Once she left the courthouse, Jewell wandered the streets of Seattle until it turned dark, and she slumped against a dirty brick wall, too tired to go on even a single step farther. So much anguish filled her every single day. Her mother had been her best friend, her rescuer, her only person to lean on and love in a world full of people who didn't care about her.

Closing her eyes, she thought of that phone call, her mother's strong voice, for once, sounding defeated.

"I need you to come home and take care of Justin. I have cancer, and I only have two months left."

The pain of those words still sat heavy in Jewell's chest. Of course, she'd come home immediately, and she would never regret her decision. The bills had piled up, the money had run out, and she and Justin had lost it all. Their home. Their security. Their mother. And now, each other. She wanted to give up, and if she were the only one she had to think about, she was afraid that she would.

She just didn't have the energy left inside her to go on. Wanting to stop feeling for at least a few hours, she waited and hoped for sleep to rescue her. For a few short hours she could dream, and with luck her dreams would be filled with images far more pleasant than the reality her life had now become.

How could dreams possibly be worse than what she was living through? They couldn't.

The Bound ebook is currently
available for FREE at all major online retailers

CPSIA information can be obtained at www.ICGtesting.com
Printed in the USA
LVOW11s2102150915

454271LV00001B/33/P